BOTTLENECK

Ed James

To Ian, the noisiest person I was ever in a band with.

OTHER BOOKS BY ED JAMES

Thursday
28th March 2013

1

Alistair Cameron pushed the body of his guitar against its amplifier sending squalls of feedback coruscating through the room. His free hand reached down and adjusted the controls, making the noise swell. He looked over at Roddie pounding the drum kit and realised the song wasn't going to end any time soon.

Grinning, he unstrapped the guitar and propped it against the amp before setting to work on his pedal board, fifteen Boss and Fender units interconnected in an array he'd taken months to perfect. He applied a layer of delay before gradually increasing the reverb. On a beat, his right hand slammed down on an overdrive pedal then a distortion two bars later, while his left mimicked a foot and added a wave of wah wah.

Through the noise, he could just about pick up Roddie's clattering drum pattern signalling the end. He looked over at Gary, head down and noodling away on his bass, keeping some semblance of song together. Their eyes locked. Alistair nodded at Gary then over at Roddie who swept into a long snare roll stretching over four bars. Alistair gradually switched off pedal after pedal before carefully retrieving his guitar just in time to crash in on the final chord.

The sound stopped dead, echoes of the cymbals dying away.

"If there was an audience," said Gary, "they'd be

going *mental* just now."

Alistair nodded as he looked around the practice room, four whitewashed walls and a bare ceiling above a concrete floor, the equipment of two bands rammed into the tiny space. "Not long till we have a proper crowd. And more than just my mates from Uni."

Roddie grinned. "You almost didn't make the last chord there. One pedal too many."

Alistair shrugged, trying to affect the cool the singer of a band should have. "I was tempted to put another one on." He sat down on his amp and flicked it to standby. "Reckon that's us for tonight?"

"Think so," said Roddie, before reaching round and tossing a can of beer over to Alistair.

"Cheers." He inspected it, a cheap supermarket brand. He wasn't one to turn down free beer, so tentatively opened it, careful not to catch the gush of foam on his clothes, shoes, guitar or pedals. The floor got it instead, another sticky patch that would take weeks to clear.

"That was a good practice," said Gary.

"Damn right." Roddie avoided the spray as he opened his can.

"Nice to kick back and relax now," said Alistair, feeling genuinely spent from the exertions of running through their twenty-five minute set four times, almost eradicating errors.

"Not quite," said Gary, taking a sip of vodka straight from the bottle.

"Eh?" said Alistair.

"Tonight's the night," said Gary, mouth twisting into an evil grin.

Alistair rolled his eyes. "You still on about that?" he

said, trying to sound tired.

"Aye, and I won't stop until you finally do it." Gary picked up a copy of *The List*, the Glasgow and Edinburgh what's-on guide, and showed it to Alistair. "The deal was, I arrange the gig and you go for a wander down there."

Alistair shook his head. "You're such a bloody child." He looked around, desperate for an excuse. "I need a torch."

Gary grinned again as he took one out of his hoodie pocket. "Here you go. No more excuses."

"You *really* want me to do this?" said Alistair, trying to sound grown up, challenging Gary to see the error of his childish ways.

It didn't work. Gary prodded him in the chest. "A deal's a deal," he said, punctuating each word with a poke.

Alistair's eyes pleaded with Roddie.

"Don't look at me," said the drummer. "This is between you pair." He cracked open another beer before belching.

"Fine," said Alistair, feeling his blood rise.

Gary turned to a dog-eared page. "Here."

It was an interview with Expect Delays, the local band made good. Alistair was obsessed with them, almost as much as Gary. Top five singles, a number one album and supporting U2 at Hampden next week. Miles better than playing to the proverbial 'three blokes and a murderer' at Bannerman's, like they would on Sunday.

"What am I supposed to be looking for here?" said Alistair.

Gary's fat finger pointed to a chunk of interview text. "This bit."

Alistair read the interview with Neeraj Patel, Expect Delays' guitarist, talking about the practice room they used as an unsigned band in Edinburgh.

"I know they practised here," said Alistair. "That's why we got the room."

"That's not it," said Gary. "Read on."

"Right, so they went for a wander along an old street under the Old Town? Big deal."

"Says you can walk for miles under here," said Gary. "Can't believe they did that, man. It's fate. If we do it, maybe we'll get signed, too."

"I don't think it works like that," said Alistair, sweating despite the cold.

"You're not going back on our deal, are you?" said Gary.

Alistair tried again with the maturity act, this time folding his arms. He got nowhere. "Right, fuck it," he said, getting to his feet and snatching the torch from Gary.

"Good man," said Gary.

Alistair stormed out of the room, swinging the torch by its cord. They were on the second level down and the entrance was on the next, the lowest. He waited with Gary while Roddie locked the door then headed down the stone stairs.

He heard the sound of at least one other band bleeding through the walls. He checked his watch - still another fifty minutes till they had to lock up.

Alistair stopped by the heavy door and turned round. "You coming with me?"

Gary rubbed his hands together. "Of course."

"Wouldn't miss this for the world," said Roddie.

Alistair grimaced before marching on. The lack of

whitewash was the only difference between the rehearsal space and the old street.

An old paraffin lantern hanging from a wall reminded him of Mary King's Close, the sanitised tourist attraction he'd visited with school.

This was different - an ancient road that led off Niddry Street before the buildings of South Bridge sprang up in the nineteenth century. The smell of damp - always present in their room - worsened as they progressed deeper.

They came to a crossroads that opened out slightly. Alistair quickly ascertained two of the paths were bricked up, leaving right as the only option. He shone the torch into the gloom, the beam dying long before it reached a distant wall. The hair on his arms pricked up. He marched on, trying to recall the exact terms of the deal - he reckoned another hundred footsteps ought to do it, but he didn't know whether Gary would see it that way.

"What was that?" said Roddie.

"Your burp," said Alistair, briefly turning round.

"No, I swear I heard something."

Alistair gritted his teeth and strode on, determined to get it over with. After another fifty or so paces, the path curved hard to the left. He was aware of their breath behind him, loud in the darkness. "This'll do."

"Nowhere near enough, mate," said Gary. "Keep going."

"Come on, man," said Alistair.

"Don't 'come on, man' me." Gary stabbed a finger at his chest. "*I* say when it's over, not you."

Alistair pushed on. After another twenty seconds, he stopped dead and turned to face the others. "I swear I heard something."

Gary scowled. "Quit it. Roddie's trick didn't work on you, so you're trying it on me now?"

Alistair swivelled back round, the torch dancing on the stone walls. The light bounced off something metallic. "What's that?"

"Enough," said Gary.

"I mean it," said Alistair, pointing down with the torch. "Look. Something's glinting."

"Might be some old money or something," said Roddie. He laughed and spoke in a stupid voice. "Maybe it's gold. Maybe a treasure chest."

"I doubt it," said Gary.

Alistair inched forward, flicking the torch across the ground. As they approached, he saw something long and thin. He stopped and looked closer. A screwdriver. He crept on, training the torch ahead. The light shone on something and he let out a gasp.

A body was propped against the wall.

2

Scott Cullen unlocked the main door and started climbing the steps to his flat.

He turned the key in the door, thinking a hard day was now behind him, most of it spent dealing with the fallout from a domestic in Pilton. A couple in their forties had knocked lumps out of each other all morning before a neighbour called it in, fed up with the screaming and shouting.

Both needed hospital treatment, meaning a simple case was complicated and extended by a series of forms seeking approval to access medical records. The husband had come off much worse and they were both determined to press charges.

He closed the door behind him, safe in the knowledge the case was out of his hands and over the line to the Procurator Fiscal's office.

At his feet, an overweight ginger cat looked up, yellow eyes trained on him. Kneeling down, he tried to stroke the animal. "Hiya, Fluffy." The cat took a step back and started miaowing.

"That you?"

"Honey, I'm home," said Cullen. "Any danger you could get your feral cat out of my way?"

"He's not feral, he's just misunderstood," said DS Sharon McNeill.

Cullen hung up his woolly coat and suit jacket and

headed through, carrying his mobile. The cat led the way, as if to keep himself between Cullen and Sharon.

The living room was the largest in the oddly-defined dwelling, effectively comprising the seating area, dining space and kitchen. The lighting was low and ambient, a world away from the all-lights-blazing approach Cullen preferred.

Sharon sat at the dining table intently focused on her laptop, U2 playing on the stereo. Cullen wandered over to his amp and turned the volume down to barely audible.

Sharon looked up. "How's my favourite Acting DS?"

Cullen shrugged as he took off his tie and hung it over the door. "It's just temporary. I'm looking forward to having a weekend off together, even if it's at my parents'."

"You're really lucky having parents like them," said Sharon.

"I suppose so," said Cullen, "but I'll have two days of interrogation from Mum about whether I've got in touch with my sister yet." He sat down beside her, putting his phone on the table. "What are you looking at?"

"Just houses."

"Right."

They'd been over this many times - Sharon wanted a house, Cullen wanted a two-bed flat somewhere in Edinburgh. Even that would be a push financially. Besides, he quite liked staying at Sharon's place in World's End Close. Being just off the Royal Mile was convenient for work and an easy stagger home from pubs, plus there were loads of decent shops nearby.

"There's a couple of nice ones," said Sharon. "A new build in Ravencraig and an old cottage in Garleton."

"I'm *not* moving to Ravencraig," said Cullen.

Sharon pointed at the laptop screen. "Four bedrooms for one eighty."

"There's a reason for that," said Cullen. "It's in Ravencraig. Besides, we don't need four bedrooms unless you're planning on starting a family."

"Very funny," said Sharon. She shut the laptop, reached over and kissed him. "Sorry, I should have shut that when you got back."

"Don't worry about it," said Cullen, kissing her on the neck. "I'll be arsing about on my phone before long, so we'll call it a draw then, right?"

Sharon play-punched him on the shoulder.

Cullen glanced at the table to see a copy of *The List*, half of Expect Delays looking moody on the cover. He picked it up and pointed to the singer. "Is his hair combed forward?"

"Are you jealous?"

"Seriously, is it?" said Cullen. He looked at the magazine - the singer, Mike Roberts, definitely appeared to have grown the hair out at the back and tugged it into a fringe to cover his baldness.

"You're the only one I find sexy," said Sharon, fingers caressing the back of Cullen's neck.

Cullen nodded down at the cat. "What about him?"

Fluffy was sitting to attention, staring up at them.

Sharon reached down to stroke him. "He's just a pussycat."

"Very good," said Cullen. "I'll tell you that next time he scratches me."

"It'll only be because you deserved it."

"They're playing next Wednesday, right?" said Cullen, tapping the magazine.

11

"Yeah. I'm excited about it."

"I've got bad memories of Hampden from the football. And from that distance, I won't even be able to work out if it's a comb-forward or not."

"I appreciate you coming with me," said Sharon, "and just be thankful you've got a full head of hair." She grinned. "For now."

Cullen's phone started dancing wildly on the table. "Here we go," he said, answering it.

"ADS Cullen, it's DI Methven. I need you to come to Niddry Street. Immediately."

"Can't it wait?" said Cullen. He was knackered and going back out was the last thing he wanted. There was ice cream in the freezer and football on the telly.

"Absolutely not," said Methven. "I need my team out on this, pronto."

"Be there in about five minutes, sir," said Cullen, before hanging up. He tossed his phone on the table.

"Duty calls?" said Sharon.

"Yeah," said Cullen, getting to his feet. "Typical Crystal. He called me ADS Cullen, but referred to himself as DI Methven. No mention of the fact he's Acting as well."

"He's a pompous arse," said Sharon.

"Yeah, but he's my pompous arse," said Cullen. His stomach rumbled. "Got any food before I go out?"

"With my cooking?" said Sharon.

"Good point," said Cullen.

He decided on a samosa from the shop on the corner.

3

Cullen walked up the High Street, a term he still struggled with - it would always be Royal Mile to him. The wind battered him and he pulled his coat tight. It might be late March, but this year had been unforgiving so far. At least the unseasonal snow had just about gone. Edinburgh was usually moderately temperate, but this spring made it truly feel like it was on the same latitude as Moscow.

He headed down Niddry Street and spotted a couple of squad cars alongside a police van halfway down the hill. A police cordon was set up around a nondescript entrance, guarded by Acting DC Simon Buxton. "Morning, Sarge," he said, his London accent out of place.

"Very funny," said Cullen. He nodded at Buxton's hair, freshly cut into the fashionable style David Beckham had been recently sporting - shaved at the back and sides with longer hair gelled and flicked out. Other footballers were copying and now it was percolating down to the plebs. "Just had that done?"

"Aye," said Buxton. "Needed a change, didn't I?"

Cullen nodded in agreement - his previous cut was the Britpop long fringe and side-lappers combination popular for about three weeks in the mid-nineties. "Definitely needed cut. Not sure about that style, though."

"For someone who's obsessed with other people's hair," said Buxton, "yours is pretty shit, mate."

"Aye, very good," said Cullen. "Anyway, you're keen tonight."

"Was just getting my coat after my haircut when Crystal Methven grabbed me," said Buxton. "Been in since six this morning, as well." He checked his watch. "Fourteen and a half hours. The OT would be good, but he'll no doubt mug me off on it, like always." He sniffed. "Besides, Chantal Jain is supposed to be taking over. Just on her way down now. Crystal didn't want an *Acting* DC manning this post for too long."

Cullen grimaced. "Where is he?"

Buxton handed him the clipboard. "He's downstairs, but you need to sign in."

"Fine," said Cullen, filling out the form. "What is this place?"

"Band rehearsal room," said Buxton. "Usually people pay by the hour, but you can rent these ones by the month. Huge waiting list, mate."

Cullen had never been one for guitar music, but knew Buxton had been in bands before joining the police. "Catch you later."

"That's for sure," said Buxton. "Crystal mentioned you're getting this case."

Cullen wasn't overly disappointed at the prospect of something interesting for a change. "Could do with something to get my teeth stuck into."

As he descended the steps, careful not to catch his coat on the whitewashed walls, Cullen was beginning to feel overworked. Aside from the domestic in Pilton, he had sixteen cases at various stages of completion. They weren't the sort that got the synapses firing, either, just required catching subhuman idiots through one of their many stupid mistakes.

At the foot of the stone steps, three flights down, Cullen put on a scene of crime overall and signed into the inner locus. There was an overpowering sense of damp, thick in the air. Cables ran down the stairs from the top to a series of arc lights just through the door at the bottom.

Cullen stepped into a long tunnel that seemed to stretch into infinity. It was regularly spaced with lanterns, which lit up the mould on the grey stone walls. Occasionally he passed bricked up entrances, which he figured were houses once.

Acting DI Colin Methven stood halfway round a slight kink in the path and nodded recognition.

"Good evening, sir," said Cullen, conscious the superior officer liked to be treated as such, even if his tenure was only Acting like Cullen's. Both of them were filling gaps until a formal Police Scotland structure was announced the following week. "What's happened?"

"There's a set of band rehearsal rooms just back there," said Methven. "Hired out by the ghost tour operator just down Niddry Street. One of the bands decided to go for a little wander under the city. Some sort of sodding dare." He rubbed at the stubble on his chin. "They found a body."

"Shite," said Cullen.

"Quite," said Methven. "They ran up to street level, dialled 999 and I got the call out. Sodding nightmare, Cullen. I can see this eating up the weekend and I'm doing a triathlon at Pitlochry on Saturday, plus I've got a dinner party."

"You'd better show me, then," said Cullen.

Methven led along the corridor. "This place would have been bustling about a hundred and fifty years ago. It was open to the sky before they built on top of it."

Cullen nodded slowly - he'd heard of the many abandoned streets under the Old Town, just didn't know it was so easy to get in without paying a tenner for the privilege. "Quite the history buff?" he said, thinking he'd stepped onto the set of *Time Team*.

"Man's got to have a passion," said Methven. "We're not sure, but we think these run for miles under here."

"Where to?"

"Probably a good way down the Royal Mile," said Methven. "Past the High Street, down the Canongate. But they'd go either side, as well. There are probably pub cellars abutting this path. It might even join up with Mary King's Close."

Jimmy Deeley, the city's pathologist, headed their way.

"Good evening, young Skywalker," said Deeley, stopping just shy of the body.

"No new names, please," said Cullen.

"Have it your way," said Deeley, a cheeky glint in his eye.

Cullen could see James Anderson, the usual SOCO he had to contend with, on his hands and knees examining the crime scene. He moved aside, giving Cullen a view of the corpse. It was just a skeleton propped up against the wall, pieces of flesh hanging off the skull. From the clothes, it looked like a man - jeans, t-shirt and big work boots.

Cullen was reminded of another case he'd worked where a body had been stashed in a barrel of whisky - this was worse. There was nothing left.

Cullen noticed Buxton appear behind Methven,

conspicuously avoiding eye contact.

"Any idea who it is?" said Cullen.

"Nope," said Deeley.

"His wallet and phone are gone," said Methven.

Cullen stroked his chin. "Given we think he had a phone, he can't have been down here that long, right? Must have been years to get like that, mind."

"He's wearing a Jeff Buckley t-shirt," said Methven, "so it's not like he's from the Victorian era."

"How long, then?" said Cullen.

"Eighteen months by my reckoning," said Deeley.

Cullen couldn't believe it - there was barely any flesh left. "Is that all? It's a skeleton."

Deeley nodded. "It's very moist down here. A body would just rot, much quicker than being in a coffin, that's for certain." He grinned. "I've declared death, obviously, but anything else will have to wait until I get the body back to my lair."

"When will that be?" said Methven.

Deeley gave a chuckle and winked at Cullen. "At least I could ignore Colin's predecessor. This boy is dangerously competent."

"Quit with the charm offensive," said Methven. "When do we get answers?"

Deeley raised his eyebrows. "I'm afraid you're more likely to get more questions. I've got so little to be going on with. Still, at least we know how he died."

Cullen frowned. "How?"

Anderson got up and handed Cullen a bag containing a screwdriver. "This. Still got blood on it, though it's very dry and in danger of flaking off. Doubt I'll find any fingerprints."

Methven turned to Cullen. "Sergeant, I want someone

on this immediately. I want a list of all screwdrivers sold in the Central Belt meeting that description."

Cullen nodded, looking at Buxton. "I'll get DC Jain on it," he said, though it had 'wild goose chase' written all over it.

"That's a blessed relief," said Buxton.

Methven wagged a finger at Cullen. "No favouritism here, Sergeant."

"Hardly," said Cullen, irritated by Methven. "Chantal's just a much better cop, that's all."

"Piss off," said Buxton, laughing.

Cullen grinned and turned back to Methven. "Who found the body?"

Methven jerked his thumb back in the direction they had come. "Bunch of students. Three boys, a band calling themselves Public Right of Way."

Cullen shook his head. "What a shite name."

"I've been in worse," said Buxton.

Cullen looked at Methven. "Are they still around?"

Methven nodded.

"I want to speak to them," said Cullen.

4

Cullen relieved DC Chantal Jain from her crime scene management duties at the front door, ensuring another competent officer took over.

"Great," said Chantal, as they walked down the first flight of steps, "I get to work for you again."

"It's as weird for me as it is you."

"You only got that job because your old boss was kicked off the force."

"That's not the only reason."

"Scott, you're just like all the rest as soon as you get a bit of power."

Cullen stopped outside the room, his blood burning. "I am not."

"Prove it," said Chantal, as she entered the band's room.

Two thirds of Public Right of Way sat around, posing like they were in a jeans advert. The third member leaned against the wall, appearing to be at least ten years older than the others who were clearly students. They all looked stunned.

The walls were the same whitewash as the corridor. Though it was only four metres by five, it was filled with equipment - Cullen figured there was barely enough room for the pretty boys to make rock star shapes with their instruments.

They got to their feet. "Is there any news?" said the

first, dyed blonde hair in a long fringe tugged backwards.

Cullen held his hands up. "There's nothing yet," he said, immediately deciding he was going to be bad cop. "Can I get some names?"

Fringe spoke first. "Alistair Cameron."

"And what do you play, Alistair?" said Chantal, eyes looking him up and down.

Cullen struggled to keep his eyebrows down - she was flirting with him.

"Guitar and lead vocals," said Alistair.

"The talent, then?" said Chantal.

"I write all the songs," said the drummer, a heavy-set lad who was holding out a hand. "Roddie."

"Do you have a surname, Roddie?" said Cullen.

"Roddie Brown."

"Thank you," said Cullen. He turned his gaze towards the third member, the bassist, a blur of spiky dark hair and angular jawline. "And you?"

"Gary Moncrieff."

"Okay," said Cullen. He sat on a guitar amp and got his notebook out, making a point to click the pen slowly and precisely. "Now, you." He pointed at Alistair. "You found the body, right?"

"Aye," said Alistair, nervously tugging his fringe.

"What were you doing down there?" said Cullen.

They looked at each other nervously for a few seconds, before Alistair held up a copy of *The List*, the same issue Sharon had in the flat. "The boys dared me."

"Would you walk off the Forth Road Bridge if they dared you?" said Cullen.

Alistair shrugged. "Don't be daft. We had a bet on who would get us our first gig. Gary blagged us one in Bannerman's." He tugged the fringe behind his left ear and grinned at Chantal. "We're playing there at the weekend."

"And the dare was to go for a wander down the streets under the Old Town?" said Cullen, determined to keep Chantal from flirting.

"That's right," said Alistair.

"We had torches here from the last time there was a power cut," said Gary.

"Your guitars wouldn't work in a power cut," said Cullen.

"They were to get out," said Alistair, his face curled into a smug grin.

"Right," said Cullen, reddening slightly. "Go on."

"I don't know what else there is to say, really. We walked down the, I don't know what it is, street? We walked down that for a bit then we came across the screwdriver and then the body." Alistair shrugged. "That's pretty much it."

"Do you know who the body is?" said Cullen.

They all shook their heads, looking genuinely mystified.

Cullen nodded slowly. "Right. You can all head home tonight, but I want you to report to DC Jain at Leith Walk police station first thing tomorrow."

"But I've got work," said the drummer.

"I'm sure they'll understand," said Cullen. "You're helping the police with their inquiries. It's standard practice."

"Should be fine," said Roddie, looking like he had a difficult conversation with an unsympathetic boss ahead of him.

"And you two?" said Cullen, eyes all over them.

"Not a problem," said Alistair.

"Aye," said Gary.

"Right, off you go," said Cullen.

He turned and left them. Cullen checked the room across the corridor was empty, before heading inside with Chantal.

"They're like a walking Gap advert," said Cullen.

"I'm sure the blonde one works in Hollister on George Street."

"I wouldn't know," said Cullen.

"You've got some nice supermarket jumpers," said Chantal.

Cullen tried not to grin. "Were you flirting with them?"

"Are you jealous?" said Chantal, arching a pencilled eyebrow.

Cullen laughed. "Hardly."

"Anyway, you proved my point," said Chantal.

"How?"

"Power trip," said Chantal. "Typical."

"Whatever," said Cullen.

"What now, boss man?"

"Best find out where Crystal has got to."

5

Methven was down at the bottom of the stairs, keeping Anderson from heading off somewhere else. Cullen's presence meant Methven relinquished his grip on the goateed SOCO, letting him trudge off upstairs.

Methven looked over. "Now what can I do for you, Sergeant?" he said, his eyes closed for a few seconds in the way that so irked Cullen.

"We've spoken to that band," said Cullen. "I reckon none of them have anything to do with it."

"Really?" said Methven, his eyes on Chantal.

"I'd concur, sir," she said. "We've got them coming in tomorrow to give detailed statements. I'll do a background check, but I doubt they have anything to do with what's happened here."

"Fine," said Methven. "Dismissed." He grabbed Cullen's arm. "Not you, Sergeant."

Cullen watched Chantal ascend, a grin no doubt plastered on her face at him being stuck there.

"Are you keeping her in check?" said Methven.

"Do I need to?" said Cullen. "She's one of the best officers we've got."

"Is that so?" said Methven. "Nothing to do with how she looks? I know your reputation."

"Not my type," said Cullen, "besides I'm taken and she's best mates with my other half."

"Right," said Methven. "We're going to be working

very closely on this, I suspect, so I'd appreciate if you kept your cowboy antics to an absolute minimum."

"Fine," said Cullen. "Wasn't aware I'd been naughty again."

Methven pointed a finger at him. "Watch your sodding lip. There's a big change coming next week, just you remember that."

"What are you saying, sir?" said Cullen.

"The restructure isn't a hundred per cent cast in stone yet," said Methven. "There are a few malleable parts."

The pending changes had played on Cullen's mind for the last few months. As of Monday, Lothian & Borders would disappear, along with all its siblings, to be replaced by Police Scotland, a national police force. The rumour mill in the station had predictably run riot, but nothing concrete had emerged, at least not that Cullen had heard.

"I'll bear that in mind, sir," said Cullen.

"Remember your position is only Acting," said Methven.

"So is yours," said Cullen.

Methven slowly shook his head. "Right. I'm afraid all leave is cancelled until we've got a result on this case."

"Fine," said Cullen. "I've none planned until May."

"I include weekends in that," said Methven.

Cullen swore under his breath. "I've got a weekend away booked, sir."

"Well, you'll just have to cancel it," said Methven.

He started up the stone steps to Niddry Street, leaving Cullen to fume in the harsh glow of the arc lights.

6

Cullen wandered slowly uphill to the top of Niddry Street before turning right down the Royal Mile, his mind lost in thoughts of how many streets lay underneath the city, maybe even below their flat.

Sharon was going to kill him. They'd not had a day off together for months, one or both of them being dragged into work on a Saturday or Sunday for one reason or another. This was sacrosanct, everyone knew it, and Methven had pissed all over it.

Inside, Sharon was sitting on the sofa, flicking through the channels. "The wanderer returns."

"Wish I'd been wandering," said Cullen, as he slumped down alongside her. "Instead I've been stuck under the city with Methven."

He gave her a blow-by-blow account of his evening, stopping short of telling her about the cancellation of the weekend.

"You're as good as him, you know," said Sharon. "You'll show him."

Cullen shrugged. "Yeah. Thing is, he's cancelled my weekend unless we get a result."

"He's *what?*" she said, mouth hanging open.

"He didn't give me a choice," said Cullen. "He implied my position after the restructure might be impacted by it."

"Wanker," said Sharon, clenching her fists.

"Me or Methven?" said Cullen.

"I'll let you decide.

Eventually, she smiled. "Him, of course." She sighed. "I suppose I'll have to see what Chantal is up to this weekend."

"Bad news," said Cullen. "She and Buxton are working for me."

Sharon shook her head. "He's only Acting. The power has gone to his head."

"Do you think it's because you're both going for that DI position?" said Cullen.

"Has to be. He's been trying to get at me for months, chipping away. If it was up to Cargill he'd have got it months ago. Fortunately, it's up to Turnbull."

"Here's hoping," said Cullen. He checked his watch. It was just after midnight. "I need to get to bed."

"Do you want me in it?" said Sharon, gently stroking his arm.

"Unless you've already had your little ginger lover in there."

Sharon laughed. "He's asleep on the radiator bed. The coast is clear."

They fell about laughing as they tiptoed to the bedroom.

Friday
29th March 2013

7

Cullen's eyes were open before the alarm went off.

He turned on his bedside light. A pair of yellow eyes looked up at him from the bottom of the bed, surrounded by a mass of ginger fur.

He shut his eyes, hoping it was a dream and he still had hours of sleep left. A forlorn hope.

His mind tugged him back to the exchange with Methven. While he finally had the position he'd long since coveted - even if only as Acting DS - he was on shaky ground. It could be taken away at any point.

Was Methven alluding to him being busted back to DC? Were that to happen, he tried to console himself with the notion he would surely have been briefed by now.

There was other pressure. He needed to bring in more money so they could buy a bigger house. Sharon was behind that and he couldn't begrudge her it. She'd lived in this flat for eight years, while he'd been here closer to eight weeks. The novelty of living on the Royal Mile had long disappeared for her.

He looked at her, surprised that turning the light on hadn't made her grumble in complaint. Her side of the bed was empty.

He looked back at the cat. "Are you man marking me, boy?"

The cat didn't answer, for once.

Cullen realised how deeply in love he was with Sharon since they had split up for a few days in October. He'd been an idiot over certain things back then, but she'd forgiven him and they'd worked on rebuilding trust, culminating in him moving into her flat. *Their* flat.

It surprised him how well he was adjusting to it. There had been incidents with dirty pants on the bathroom floor and the toilet lid being left up, but she wasn't a saint either - he saw to the fridge, washing and cooking when he had time.

Cullen got out of bed and started twenty press-ups. He was increasingly conscious of his growing belly thanks to years of strong lager and takeaways. He'd started running again and exercising properly. He didn't want to resort to fad dieting like his old man.

He strode into the kitchen, feeling his shoulders tighten, determined to have a proper breakfast for once rather than a bacon roll with Buxton in the canteen.

Sharon was perched on a stool at the breakfast bar, absent-mindedly stirring a mug of tea, the radio playing at low volume.

Cullen leaned over and kissed her on the cheek. "Morning."

She looked back, her eyes bloodshot. "Morning."

Cullen felt a jolt of worry. "You okay?" he said, resting a caring hand on her arm.

"I'm not well. A stinking cold." She sniffed.

"We were supposed to be driving up to my parents' tonight," said Cullen.

"Yeah, typical," said Sharon. "First hint at some time off and my body shuts down."

Cullen put bread in the toaster, adjusting the dial up from Sharon's usual setting, which required two goes before it even slightly browned.

"Methven is trying to rattle me," said Sharon.

"This again." Cullen glanced at the kettle, but decided coffee at the station would be preferable, or maybe he could pick something up en route. "I know he's a dick, but are you sure he's playing you?"

Sharon nodded and took a big glug of tea. "I think so. It's the sort of thing he would do."

Cullen sat down on the stool next to her, continually glancing over to watch for the slow slide of the toast as it finished. "He never strikes me as being that conniving."

"That's the sort you've got to watch," said Sharon. "He's on a power trip just now and he doesn't want anybody to steal his glory."

Cullen spotted the machine pop up. He got a plate out of the dishwasher, checking it was clean, and shovelled crunchy peanut butter on the toast. He took a bite, causing Sharon to turn up her nose.

"I hate that stuff," she said.

"It's good for you. Lots of protein."

"It's not good in the quantity you eat it." Sharon took another sip of tea. "All that stuff last night. Cancelling your leave. That's just to get at me."

"I'll do some digging about Methven today. See if there's anything in it."

"Okay." Sharon stared blankly at the counter.

Cullen took his plate and sat down next to her. "Hey. This isn't the Sharon I know and love."

She snuggled in close. "I don't feel like that Sharon."

Cullen kissed the top of her head and stroked her back. "You'll be fine."

"What if I'm not?" she said, her voice muffled.

"There are plenty of other things going on just now,"

said Cullen. "There are task forces being set up. It might do you good to get some other experience. You've been in CID for ages, maybe you need to reconnect with other areas of the force."

"True," she said, before sitting upright and draining her mug.

The radio changed track, the DJ's mid-Atlantic drawl announcing Expect Delays' new single *Bottleneck*, which he pronounced *Boddleneck*.

"That's all I need," said Cullen, as the song kicked in, half-spoken lyrics confusing the neck of a bottle with a girl's neck and a bottleneck guitar. "It's so contrived."

"You'd much rather listen to techno, I suppose."

"You don't have to say it like that. And yes, I would."

Sharon pushed her teacup away. "How are you finding having Chantal working for you?"

"About as much fun as Caldwell. She reckons I'm on a power trip."

"And are you?"

"Hardly."

"Wonder how Caldwell's doing," said Sharon, absently.

Cullen finished his toast and headed for the shower, wondering whether to do more press-ups.

8

DI Alison Cargill led the briefing in Leith Walk station's CID suite, fifteen officers sitting around in various stages of interest and wakefulness.

"So, in conclusion," said Cullen, "I've packaged up the domestic from yesterday and handed it to the Procurator Fiscal's office."

"Good work, Sergeant," said Cargill, smiling but with no discernible warmth. "Do you want to update us on the Niddry Street body?"

She was looking at Methven. He shrugged then gestured to Cullen. "Sergeant Cullen is probably best placed."

"There are music rehearsal rooms on Niddry Street," said Cullen. "One of the bands found a passageway that leads onto an old street, which has been built over. They had a dare going on, one of them took a torch and went for a wander. They found a body propped against a wall. This band is not under suspicion at present."

He glanced at Methven - his eyes were closed and he nodded along.

"There has only been a somewhat limited investigation so far," said Cullen. "We had no ID by the time I left the crime scene last night."

Methven picked up the thread. "We still have no confirmed ID. That's true. In fact, we have no potential leads either. The only options we've got are to wait for the post mortem to come through and for ADS Cullen's team to do some good, old-fashioned legwork."

He folded his arms. "Dr Deeley has given us an estimated date of death of approximately eighteen months ago, based on the state of decay and the conditions. There may be something in the Missing Persons reports around that time."

"And there might not," said Cargill, "but it's a good avenue to investigate. I'd still like to see if this is connected to the band who found the body."

Cullen nodded. "Will do. We've got them reporting to the station this morning to give statements. We don't believe there's anything on them."

"Certainly not the younger two," said Chantal. "The drummer is a fair amount older."

"Keep us updated," said Cargill.

"In terms of team," said Cullen, "I believe I've been allocated DC Jain and ADC Buxton, is that correct?"

"For now," said Cargill.

Cullen nodded. "Thanks."

"Good work," said Cargill. Her eyes swept around the room. "Is there anything else?" Nothing. "Dismissed." She collected her notepad and hurried out of the room, checking her watch.

Cullen tried to corner Chantal and Buxton before they left, but Methven intercepted him. "Is DS McNeill not in today?"

"It's her day off," said Cullen. "If you recall, I was supposed to be getting away early today as well, but you cancelled it."

"Operational matters take precedence, Sergeant," said Methven, before marching off in Cargill's slipstream.

Cullen looked around the room. Chantal and Buxton

had both escaped. "Bloody hell," he said, slumping on a desk chair.

It was going to be a long day.

9

Buxton stood up and stretched. "You fuck off, eh?"

Cullen looked over. "It doesn't work with your accent. But yes, I'll have a coffee." He got his wallet out of his coat pocket. "Where's Chantal?"

Buxton shrugged as he looked around the office. "No idea."

They walked to the canteen in silence. They'd been hard at it for over three hours since Cullen had eventually found them. He held the door open for Buxton and they joined the end of the queue, which snaked back almost to the door.

"They really need to fix this," said Cullen. "Takes forever to get served."

"Still, it means I can give you an update," said Buxton. "Never know when Crystal might pounce."

Cullen laughed. "I can't believe how many unresolved Missing Persons we've got."

"Tell me about it," said Buxton. "The stuff I've been through, most of them seem to be kids reported missing by their parents, but they turn up and nobody bothers to tell us. I've closed six cases already this morning."

Cullen nodded. "That still leaves, what, thirty?"

"Give or take," said Buxton. "I'm still not convinced there aren't more in the four hundred odd we've put to one side."

"We'll see if this gives us anything," said Cullen. He

frowned - he could hear a baby screaming. He looked but couldn't see anything. "I bloody hate people bringing their kids in."

Buxton laughed. "You're a ray of sunshine today."

Cullen almost smiled. "You used to be in a band, right?"

Buxton nodded. "I did, yeah. Six years ago now. Had one of them rooms on Niddry Street, too. They were like gold dust but somehow we spawned it. We were there four times a week at the start but then things fell apart and we gave it all up. In the end, it was just a storage space for our amps and drum kit."

"I heard that Expect Delays single on the radio this morning," said Cullen.

"Oh aye," said Buxton. "I supported them once, back in the day. Bunch of wankers."

"They were wankers before they were famous?" said Cullen.

Buxton snorted. "Complete pricks. We played with them just before they released their first single. The way they were talking, it was like the Beatles releasing *Abbey Road* or something."

They reached the front of the queue and ordered.

"No roll this morning?" said Barbara, Cullen's favourite canteen worker.

"Trying to be a bit healthier," said Cullen.

"What's wrong with my food?"

"Nothing," said Cullen, "just trying to avoid bacon and mayonnaise."

Barbara shook her head. "That'll not do."

Cullen thought she didn't seem herself. "You okay?"

"It's these cuts. I'm worried I'm going to lose my job. There was a bit in the paper this morning about getting rid of non-police resources. That means me."

Cullen smiled, trying to raise her spirits. "You're hardly going to be replaced, are you?" He thumbed at Buxton. "Can't see Simon here making such good coffee."

Buxton snorted. "I worked as a barista, you cheeky fucker."

Barbara pointed at him. "I've warned you lot before about your language."

"Sorry," said Buxton, head bowed.

Barbara scowled. "At least the worst of your lot has gone. Mouth like a toilet, that one."

"I'm sure you'll be fine," said Cullen.

"I heard someone say they're thinking of shutting this place down," said Barbara. "They've got to save millions in Edinburgh."

"You'll be okay," said Cullen.

"It's my girls I worry about," said Barbara, as she handed them their coffees.

They scanned the room, looking for a table.

"Now I see why there's always a massive queue," said Buxton, "she just will not shut up."

"Just because she told you off for your potty mouth," said Cullen, as they sat down. "You okay about all the restructuring stuff?"

Buxton avoided Cullen's gaze. "Yeah, I'm fine."

"You sure?"

"Not really, no. I think I've got the record for the longest Acting DC tenure in Lothian & Borders' history. At least you know you're in SCD."

Police Scotland would be separated into East, West and North, but CID resource would be split into local response teams and the new Specialised Crime Division.

Most likely, Cullen would fall into the Edinburgh Major Investigation Team.

Cullen sat back and blew on his coffee. "I don't know what grade I'll be."

"You know you'll be there, though," said Buxton. "That's something I don't have."

"Do you want me to speak to Cargill or Turnbull?" said Cullen.

"I don't know," said Buxton. His eyes darted up just as a strong hand grabbed Cullen's shoulder.

"Sergeant."

Cullen spun around. He smiled when he saw who it was. DS Bill Lamb. Cullen worked with him on a couple of cases out in East Lothian.

"How you doing?" said Cullen, getting up to shake hands.

"I'm well," said Lamb. "Very well."

Cullen reached over to stroke Lamb's top lip. "What's happened to the moustache?"

Lamb flinched. "I'd grown out of it."

"It wasn't at the other half's insistence?" said Cullen.

"Might have a bit to do with it."

Cullen gestured at Buxton. "Have you guys met?"

"Not had the pleasure," said Lamb, offering his hand. "Bill Lamb."

"No, we have," said Buxton. "The Mandy Gibson case last year."

Lamb nodded slowly. "That's right. You're a detective now, though. You were in uniform then, right?"

"Acting DC," said Buxton.

"You'll get there eventually, son," said Lamb.

Buxton didn't seem to take any consolation from it.

"So, what brings you here, Bill?" said Cullen.

"I had a meeting with Jim Turnbull."

Cullen's interest was piqued. "Oh aye, what about?"

"Nothing to do with you," said Lamb, tapping his nose. "Angela came in with me. She was showing young Jamie off."

Cullen looked around but couldn't see her. DC Angela Caldwell had worked both with and for him as the squad's Acting DC before Buxton. She'd just had a baby - the pregnancy a surprise as she put her missed periods down to stress from a painful divorce.

"Right," said Cullen. "That'll be where Chantal got to." He finally spotted them, sitting in bollocking corner. "How's fatherhood?"

"Good," said Lamb, exhaling deeply. "We've been lucky with wee Jamie. He sleeps like a log and not one with a chainsaw in it, either."

"I seem to recall having conversations with both of you about you never having kids," said Cullen.

Lamb shrugged. "Times change, I suppose."

"Going to make an honest woman of Angela?" said Cullen.

Lamb laughed. "That's the other thing she's showing off. A giant rock of an engagement ring. We're getting hitched next summer, make sure the wee man is a bit more settled by then."

"And her divorce is sorted, I suppose?" said Cullen.

"Finally came through," said Lamb. "No point in changing her name now."

"She's going to take your name, then?" said Cullen.

"Aye," said Lamb. "How's your other half doing? We'll need to get the pair of you to the wedding, of course."

"If she'll want me there," said Cullen, recalling how frosty things had grown between them.

"Water under the bridge now," said Lamb. "Anyway, how's it going with Sharon?"

"Good," said Cullen. "We moved in together in January. Looking at buying a place."

"No marriage plans yourself?" said Lamb.

"She doesn't want it," said Cullen.

"And you?"

"No comment," said Cullen. "Other than that, she's fine. Stressed about this promotion she's going for."

"Isn't everyone?" said Lamb. "Big changes afoot."

"Tell me about it," said Cullen.

"Grab your coffees, come over and see my wee boy," said Lamb.

Cullen replaced the lid on his cup and followed Lamb and Buxton.

Caldwell got to her feet, grabbing Cullen in a bear hug.

Lamb took her seat while Buxton hovered uncomfortably not far from Chantal, who was holding up the baby and blowing on him, making him gurgle.

"You're looking well, Scott," said Caldwell.

Cullen shrugged. "I don't feel it."

"Six months as an Acting DS is good," said Caldwell. "Maybe you'll stop moaning about not getting promotions."

"We'll see if they let me keep it," said Cullen.

"The glass is always half empty with you," said Caldwell.

"Never mind that," said Cullen. "How's the baby?"

"Good," said Caldwell. "I love him to tiny wee bits. When I found out I was pregnant I doubted I'd ever be maternal. Now, I just can't stop thinking about him. It's crazy."

"You are coming back, right?" said Cullen.

"Aye, of course," said Caldwell. "Couldn't afford to be a lady of leisure, much as I'd like to be." She looked at the baby. "I'm sure Sharon will be the same."

"Mm," said Cullen.

"Have I touched a nerve?" said Caldwell.

"Don't worry about it," said Cullen, avoiding eye contact.

Caldwell looked around. "Haven't seen her. Thought she'd be here."

"She's at home," said Cullen. "Got a stinking cold. Besides, it was supposed to be her day off. You could head up to the flat if you wanted?"

"Maybe," said Caldwell. "Do you want to hold him?"

"I'm not a big fan of kids," said Cullen.

"Really?"

"Really," said Cullen. "I don't want to be a dad."

"No need to be a dick about it," said Chantal, handing the baby to Buxton.

"I'm not being a dick," said Cullen, "I just don't want them thrust in my face, that's all."

"You're being a dick, Scott," said Chantal.

"Right, that's it. Back to work." Cullen smiled at Caldwell. "Nice seeing you." He nodded at Lamb. "Catch you later, Bill."

Lamb gave a mock salute and took the now screaming baby from Buxton.

10

An hour later, they had exhausted the likely victims in the MisPer file. They sat at their desks, with Cullen leading a progress update.

"Well, I've got two possibles," said Cullen. "Both are the right approximate age and IC1 males. Chantal?"

"Nothing," she said. "I only had three files to go through, though. I've typed up the interview notes from that band."

"Good," said Cullen. "Simon?"

"Got a promising one," said Buxton. "Vaguely recognise the name from my music days. White IC1 male again. Guy called James Strang. If I remember rightly, he used to go by the name of Jimi Danger."

Cullen rolled his eyes. "Jimi Danger?"

Buxton nodded. "I'm being serious. Spelled like Jimi Hendrix. He was in a good band, too. What were they called?" He clicked his fingers a few times. "That's it. *The Invisibles.*"

Cullen vaguely recalled the name, though not from music. He knew it would irritate him until he remembered.

"They were good," said Buxton. "Like the Stooges or MC5. Proper rockers."

"If he was a musician," said Cullen, "it's possible he used those practice rooms." He scribbled the name down in his notebook. "Who called in the disappearance?"

Buxton shuffled through the file and found the initial report. "Some boy called Alex Hughes." He checked his notebook. "I've tried calling him, but no answer on the number given. Then again, it's nineteen months since Strang went missing, so anything could have happened."

"Was he from Edinburgh?" said Chantal.

Buxton shook his head. "Never heard of the place he comes from. Dalhousie?"

Cullen's eyes bulged. "That's my home town."

Buxton grinned. "Maybe I'll start asking you some difficult questions, then."

"Never heard of the boy," said Cullen.

"So what do you want us to do?" said Chantal.

Cullen thought it through for a few seconds. "Simon, let's you and I go and visit the guys who lease the rooms out to the bands. They might be able to confirm whether this Strang boy did."

"And me?" said Chantal.

"See if we can get a DNA trace done," said Cullen. "We might have him on file."

"You've got an Acting DC for that sort of shite," said Chantal.

"I resent that," said Buxton.

"I'm serious," said Chantal.

"I want a detailed background on this band," said Cullen. "I'm not yet convinced they don't know anything. Find out a bit more about them."

"Fine," said Chantal.

"And Methven was wanting to know about the screwdriver," said Cullen.

"This isn't punishment for me saying how pretty the singer was, is it?" said Chantal.

"Would I be so petty?" said Cullen.

"I'll not answer that."

11

The Ghost Tours office was a few doors down Niddry Street, past a new pub Cullen had never heard of, but not as far as Bannerman's at the bottom. They found a parking space on the Cowgate and walked up.

Buxton thumbed at Bannerman's. "Used to play gigs in there."

Cullen had been in once, on a pub crawl as a student, and could barely remember it. "Did you do a lot of gigs?"

"Played anything we could," said Buxton. "Weddings, christenings, bar mitzvahs." He laughed. "Best gig we did was the G2 in Glasgow. That was mental. They reckon there were about a thousand people there."

"What happened to the band?" said Cullen.

Buxton shrugged. "Take your pick. Apathy, lack of success, the singer getting knocked up by the guitarist while she was going out with me."

"Nightmare," said Cullen. "That's not quite how you told it to me last time."

"You surprised?" said Buxton. "It's belittling, mate."

"Tell me about it," said Cullen, as they entered the Ghost Tours office.

A skinny man sat at the desk clad in a black suit with matching black shirt and tie, bony fingers tapping on a laptop. He looked up, his expression as severe as his haircut - a close skinhead. "How can I help, officers?"

"Is it that obvious?" said Cullen, showing his warrant card.

"I've got a knack," said the man, reaching out a hand. "Paul Temple."

Cullen introduced them.

Temple frowned at Buxton. "Do I know you?"

Buxton nodded. "Used to rent a room here."

"That'll be it," said Temple.

"Have you owned this place long?" said Cullen.

"A few years," said Temple. "Can I ask what this is about?"

"The body found near the practice rooms," said Cullen.

"I've already spoken to DI Methven," said Temple. "That's your boss, I take it?"

"It is," said Cullen. "We don't have identification of the body yet but we have a potential lead. A James Strang, AKA Jimi Danger."

Temple turned back to his laptop. "In *The Invisibles*, right?"

"We believe so," said Buxton. "What can you tell us about him?"

"I've got names, addresses and phone numbers for the whole band," said Temple. "I trust you've got a warrant?"

"Could easily get one," said Cullen. "Alternatively, I could make it difficult for you to cash in on the find."

"How do you mean?" said Temple.

"Don't tell me it's not crossed your mind to run ghost tours down there," said Cullen.

Temple sniffed. "It might have done, aye."

"Well, I could keep that place closed off for a very long time," said Cullen, "or I could have a word with the city council to keep it shut permanently."

"Right." Temple slouched back, before clicking the mouse. A large laser printer behind him whirred to life and he swung round to collect a sheet of paper. "Here you go."

Cullen checked the sheet before pocketing it. "Why do you keep these?"

"We want to know who's renting from us in case we need to reclaim cash," said Temple. "You wouldn't believe how often people don't pay, deposit or no, even with a room full of vintage guitars, valve amps, PAs and drum kits."

"Did you know Mr Strang?" said Buxton.

Temple shook his head slowly. "Can't say I did. Get a lot of bands through here every year."

Cullen thanked him then led outside into the cold air. "What do you reckon?"

"Dodgy as fuck," said Buxton. "Still, as long as you got the list of names out of him we're doing okay."

Cullen took the list out again and scanned it. "Looks like this Alex Hughes who reported it was in the band."

"What do you want to do?"

"I'll start calling through the list."

"Sure thing."

"I better head home to see how Sharon is."

"Give her my regards." Buxton unlocked the car. "See you back at the ranch, Sundance."

Cullen scowled at him. "Less of that."

48

12

As Cullen hurried up the hill, he dialled the names on the list.

Beth Williamson's phone seemed to be disconnected.

The number for Alex Hughes was the one Buxton had already tried and still wasn't answered.

He tried David Johnson. The call went to voicemail. As he left his number, he wondered when it would feel natural to say he was calling on behalf of Police Scotland. He hoped Johnson returned the call as he didn't fancy trying to trace the band members, especially when it wasn't definite the body was Strang.

He turned into World's End Close and climbed the stairs to the flat. Sharon was sprawled on the settee, the cat lying trustfully at her feet while he turned a mass of used hankies into a nest. Her eyes flickered open and she groaned.

"How are you doing?" he said.

"Been sick all day," said Sharon.

"Sick?"

"Ill, unwell."

"Right," said Cullen. "I better not catch it."

"Always thinking about yourself," said Sharon.

"Who'll look after you if I'm ill?" said Cullen.

"It's the other way around, Scott."

"Okay, Grumpy-drawers," said Cullen. "Do you need anything?"

"Angela came round with the baby," said Sharon. "She got me some soup, so I'm fine."

"I bumped into her at the station," said Cullen.

"She said."

"Oh."

"You need to talk about your attitude to kids," said Sharon.

Cullen's phone rang. "Saved by the bell," he said, holding it up before answering, not recognising the number.

"Is that Detective Sergeant Scott Cullen?" The voice was English.

"It is," said Cullen. "Who am I speaking to?"

"To *whom*."

Cullen scowled - who was this?

"Sorry, force of habit. It's David Johnson. Just returning your call."

Cullen struggled to recall the name before it clicked. He pulled out the list of names. "Thanks for calling me back, Mr Johnson."

"I wondered when someone was going to ring about Jimi," said Johnson.

"Jimi?"

"Yes, James Strang," said Johnson. "I take it his body has turned up?"

"We're not sure," said Cullen.

"I'll take a wild guess and say it was wearing a Jeff Buckley t-shirt."

13

Cullen stopped for a sandwich on the way, eating as he hurried to Leith Walk station. He was slightly out of breath by the time he found the interview room Buxton had secured, one of the more presentable in the public section of the station, usually reserved for grieving family members.

Cullen pointed to the door. "Is he in there?"

"He is, yeah," said Buxton. "And he reckons it's this Strang geezer?"

Cullen nodded, gulping down air. "Said he was wearing a Jeff Buckley t-shirt. Don't know why that wasn't in the MisPer report."

Buxton shrugged. "You saw how many of them there were. Hard to get too excited about them, I suppose."

"I hope it's not you who did the report back in the day," said Cullen. "It was your patch, right?"

"It wasn't me. Trust me, mate. I'd remember." Buxton pointed at the door. "How do you want to run this?"

Cullen thought it over for a few seconds. "Let's just play it by ear. I don't think he's done anything dodgy, yet. He was a bit of a pedantic arse on the phone, though. Pulled me up for not saying 'to whom'."

"Schoolboy error," said Buxton.

"Aye," said Cullen. "Public schoolboy error."

"Good one," said Buxton.

"They didn't teach grammar at Dalhousie High," said

Cullen, opening the door. "Come on."

He sat at the table before starting the interview, introducing himself and Buxton. A uniformed officer stood by the door, looking bored.

"Do I need a lawyer?" said Johnson. He was tall and athletic, much like Methven, though he looked a lot younger despite moderate hair loss.

"We're interviewing you to confirm it's Mr Strang we've found," said Cullen. "If at any point we deem you to be a suspect, we will pause the interview to allow you to consult a lawyer. For the record, Mr Johnson, you're not a suspect at this moment in time."

Johnson looked more nervous than he had sounded on the phone. "Okay."

"Can you recount the information you gave me earlier, please?" said Cullen.

Johnson cleared his throat. "Certainly," he said, a croak still present. "When you called me I instinctively knew it would be about Jimi."

"And, again, for the record," said Cullen, "Jimi would be James Strang?"

"Correct," said Johnson. "Everybody knew him as Jimi, though, like Jimi Hendrix. Of course, he got his stage name from *Gimme Danger* by The Stooges." He coughed. "I'm rambling, apologies."

"You don't appear the sort of person to be in a band influenced by Iggy Pop," said Buxton.

Johnson shrugged. "I love loud music. It's always the quiet ones you've got to watch out for, isn't that right?" He laughed, before tugging at the collar of his shirt, perhaps realising he shouldn't be joking. "Jimi asked me to play bass guitar in The Invisibles."

"Why you?" said Cullen. "You don't seem like a rock

'n' roller."

Johnson touched the tips of his fingers together. "Jimi was obsessed with image. Apparently, I fit the bill. We're all the same height. I think there was a quote attributed to Morrissey regarding Franz Ferdinand all being the same height, which made them look like a gang on stage. That's something Jimi clung to."

He smiled. "I'm a classically-trained pianist, though I'd given that up by university. I picked the bass up quickly, of course. There's also the fact I was studying English Literature and could help Jimi with some of his lyrics. He was very talented, both in terms of music and words - such *incredible* imagery - but he would sometimes struggle with the precise vocabulary. I suppose, in that sense, I added a fair amount to the band."

Cullen was sorry he asked. "Can you give us your account of what happened the night Jimi disappeared?"

"Well, we didn't know at the time it was the night he disappeared," said Johnson. "Nobody knew what happened to him, but it was certainly the last night we saw him."

"Had he gone off before?" said Cullen.

Johnson frowned. "Not as such. Jimi was someone who lived day to day, shall we say?"

Cullen knew he'd have to keep him on topic. "You had a gig?"

"Correct," said Johnson. "We were practising a lot. Jimi was really pushing us hard. We were building a following and things were starting to happen. We'd even been in the press. He was a driven man."

"So you'd rule suicide out?" said Cullen.

"Not for me to say," said Johnson, shrugging his shoulders.

"And this gig?" said Cullen.

Johnson nodded. "We had a concert booked in Glasgow, supporting Biffy Clyro. They were a big deal at the time. Still are, of course. We'd been in our practice room since six o'clock and finished up at nine."

He blinked away a tear. "That was the last practice before the concert. I think Jimi stayed behind to fix the intonation on his guitar. It sounded fine to me."

"That's making sure the guitar is in tune with itself," said Buxton, reading Cullen's blank expression.

"Right," said Cullen. "And that's the last time you saw him?"

"It is," said Johnson.

"What was he wearing?" said Cullen.

"Those preposterous big boots he always wore," said Johnson. "He used to say it was so if he bumped into racists or homophobes he could 'kick them in,' as he put it. I think that was for show. Jimi wasn't much of a hard man, despite his talk."

He took a sip from the plastic cup of water in front of him. "He was wearing jeans and his Jeff Buckley t-shirt. I gave it to him for Christmas one year."

"And this was when?" said Cullen.

"I think it was the third of September, two thousand and eleven," said Johnson.

Cullen looked over at Buxton, who gave the slightest of nods. "Was there something going on between you?"

"The t-shirt?" said Johnson, frowning. "Heavens, no. We all exchanged gifts. It was a band tradition. We'd play a Christmas show in the middle of the month, swap gifts and then pack up till early January. We all went back to our home towns for Christmas. It is merely coincidence Jimi was wearing that t-shirt, I assure you."

"And what was Jeff Buckley doing on this t-shirt?" said Cullen. He was vaguely aware of him - Sharon might have a couple of his albums.

"It was the cover of *Grace*," said Johnson, "his only true album."

"That's the t-shirt we found," said Buxton.

"Looks like he's our man," said Cullen, nodding. "We will, of course, be conducting DNA analysis to confirm it, if possible."

"Could I have a look at him?" said Johnson.

"I'm afraid not," said Cullen. "There's not much left to see."

Johnson nodded, looking disappointed.

"Tell us about the band, then," said Buxton.

Cullen hoped this was connected to the case and not just idle curiosity.

"We split up after Jimi went missing," said Johnson. "Of course, we didn't play the concert in Glasgow. Nobody knew what happened to him. I had to phone the promoter myself to cancel. The band just fell apart. Jimi was the driving force behind it."

"Tell us the whole story," said Buxton. "Everything. Something quite trivial might turn out to be important. Right from the start."

"Certainly," said Johnson, composing himself. "Jimi and Alex Hughes, the guitarist, got together in two thousand and five I think. We were all students at the time. They spent a few months writing songs, just the two of them. They wanted to be a three-piece and Jimi played bass as well as singing. It took them a while to find a drummer before they eventually got Beth."

"This would be Beth Williamson?" said Cullen.

Johnson nodded. "I've not seen her in a while. Beth

was very good, much better than Mo Tucker." He smiled at Cullen's expression. "Not a Velvet Underground fan, then?"

"Never heard of them," said Cullen. "Please, continue."

"The band did a few concerts and I went to see them as a friend," said Johnson. "They were clearly going places, but Jimi was struggling with singing and playing bass at the same time."

"And that's when they got you in?" said Buxton.

Johnson nodded. "Indeed. At first, I was just playing the parts Jimi taught me, but I soon settled into it and started making the bass lines my own, if you will."

"How did things go?" said Buxton.

"Really well," said Johnson. "We did a few tours, released a couple of singles and managed to get a reasonable amount of press."

"Were you ever close to getting signed?" said Buxton.

"A couple of times," said Johnson. "Jimi..."

He broke off, tears welling in his eyes. Until then, he had been ice and steel, stiff upper lip, but it seemed the realisation was settling in - Jimi wasn't coming back.

"Tell us about him," said Cullen.

Johnson composed himself and cleared his throat again. "He was incredibly talented, inspired by Jeff Buckley in a poetic way, but also by raucous bands like The Stooges, The MC5, New York Dolls, Velvet Underground and maybe a bit of Led Zeppelin."

"Was he that tortured artist type?" said Buxton.

Johnson nodded slowly. "That sort of thing," he said, rubbing his eyes. "He was gifted."

"Did he have a girlfriend?" said Cullen.

Johnson looked away. "Not that I knew of, I'm afraid."

"Any groupies?" said Cullen.

Johnson scowled at him. "We weren't that sort of band. We were *artists*."

Cullen didn't want to press the point just yet. "How was Jimi around the time he disappeared?"

Johnson stared at the ceiling for a moment. "On reflection, Jimi had been a bit distant, it's fair to say. The last rejection by a label hit him hard. Really hard. Jimi wanted success more than anything."

"I thought you were artists?" said Cullen, wound up.

Johnson threw up his hands. "Artists have to eat. We were all working in awful jobs. We just wanted to make our living from music. That's not too much to ask, is it?" He took another sip of water. "That band put my academic career on hold for years. Fortunately, I've been able to pick it up again without too much of a deleterious effect."

"Tell me about how the rejection was hitting him hard," said Cullen.

"Jimi didn't seem to enjoy the music much towards the end," said Johnson. "He still had the drive, of course, kept pushing us on, but he'd lost something on the way. I believe the phrase is 'phoning it in'."

Cullen leaned back. "Is there something you're not telling us?"

Johnson nibbled at his nails. "Jimi was obsessed with something," he said, eventually. "I don't know what. He didn't tell me."

"You have no idea?" said Cullen.

Johnson shook his head. "None, I'm afraid."

"But you thought he was obsessed," said Cullen, folding his arms. "How did this obsession manifest itself?"

Johnson rocked back and forth. "You could tell when Jimi was preoccupied. Usually, it was some part of a song that didn't work. He'd fret over it for days and then come up with something that just fixed it. We did a tour and he'd been all over it, irritating the tour manager of the band we supported until he relented."

He stopped moving. "He got this look in his eyes when something was going on in his head. It was like he wasn't all there."

"And he had this look in the days leading up to his disappearance?" said Cullen.

"I believe I told the investigating officer at the time I suspected Jimi had possibly run away," said Johnson.

"You thought his obsession was running away?" said Cullen.

Johnson nodded. "He'd often talk about New York. Of course, one would need a visa to settle there. To my knowledge, Jimi hadn't done any of that."

Cullen himself was prone to fits of single-mindedness, particularly when working hard on a case.

"What did you do after the band, then?" said Buxton.

"As I've alluded to," said Johnson, "I gave up music after what happened. I still play the piano occasionally, but nothing serious. I barely listen to anything with a guitar in it these days. I started my PhD, which I will hopefully finish next summer at my current rate of progress."

"What about the other band members?" said Buxton.

"Alex, the lead guitarist, is still performing in Glasgow," said Johnson. "I've met up with him a couple of times for dinner."

"And Beth Williamson?" said Buxton.

"Beth was like myself," said Johnson. "She got married

and gave up music. I don't really keep in touch with her, I'm afraid. Just the occasional text."

"We've been trying to get in contact with them," said Buxton. "Do you have numbers for either?"

Johnson nodded, fishing his mobile out. He took great pains to ensure Buxton copied the numbers down correctly.

"We need a bit more information about Mr Strang," said Cullen. "Where did he work?"

"In a record shop in Stockbridge," said Johnson. "It's closed down now. I think it became a Starbucks."

"He didn't work anywhere else?" said Cullen.

Johnson shook his head. "He was working there when I met him at university and he was still there by the time he vanished."

"What about friends?" said Cullen.

"He never had many close friends," said Johnson, "just lots of acquaintances."

"Anyone off the top of your head?" said Cullen.

"I'd have to come back to you on that, I'm afraid."

"What about people in other bands?" said Buxton.

"Other bands?" Johnson drummed his fingers on the desk for a few seconds. "There were a couple he was friendly with, but mainly to get gigs with them and so on." He frowned. "He was good friends with the singer and the bass player in Expect Delays."

Cullen scribbled it down.

"What about flatmates?" said Buxton.

"He lived in a shared flat," said Johnson, "but I don't think he mixed with his flatmates much. They were annoyed by how drunk he got and the noise he made recording demos on his four-track."

"Can you give us the address?" said Buxton.

"I'll try and recall it," said Johnson.

"Is there anyone who had a grudge against him?" said Cullen. "Someone he'd done over or let down?"

Johnson shrugged his shoulders. "Not that I can think, sorry."

Cullen thanked him and got to his feet. "We'll likely be in touch again, Mr Johnson."

"What about his family?" said Buxton.

Cullen cringed as he sat down. Schoolboy error.

"He was from a small town called Dalhousie, I believe," said Johnson, "but he didn't talk about it much. I know both of his parents were alive and well back in two thousand and eleven, but other than that, I'm afraid I can't help."

"Okay, you're free to go," said Buxton, ending the interview.

Johnson got up and hurried out of the room, led away by the uniform.

"I hope they kept his mouth shut in press interviews," said Buxton.

14

After a few minutes of searching, Cullen rounded up Methven and Chantal and took them into a vacant meeting room. He spent ten minutes recounting edited highlights of the interview with Johnson, stopping occasionally for Methven's questions.

"So, in summary," said Methven, eyelids closing, "we have a positive ID on the victim, then?"

"We obviously need to confirm it by formal means," said Cullen. He looked at Chantal. "Can you make sure Deeley and Anderson know about James Strang and check for DNA, dental records and so on?"

"Already on it, sir." The *sir* snapped out of her mouth.

"And this band you were speaking to," said Methven, "the ones who found the body in the first place?"

"Nothing suspicious, sir," said Chantal. "They check out. It looks like none of them knew him. Two were still at school at the time. One was in St Andrews and the other Inverness. The drummer is proving a bit trickier. He's a good ten years older."

"Keep on it," said Methven.

"There's something else, sir," said Chantal. "The singer is the one from St Andrews. His brother was studying in Edinburgh at the time and he visited him on a few occasions."

"Any suspicion?" said Methven.

She shook her head. "Got alibis. Just waiting for

61

confirmation, but it looks like Alistair Cameron was in St Andrews that weekend getting so drunk he had his stomach pumped. His brother was visiting his girlfriend in Glasgow."

"Excellent work, Constable," said Methven. "I want this investigation *tight.*" His gaze shifted to Cullen. "Plan of attack, Sergeant?"

"ADC Buxton and I will speak to the band while DC Jain carries out those additional checks on the drummer." Cullen looked at Chantal. "Can you dig into his workmates? It'll be difficult, the shop shut last year."

"Will do," said Chantal, noting it down. "I could do with some help here."

"I'll see what I can do," said Methven. "There may be a few hours of spare manpower somewhere we can rustle up for you." He looked at Cullen again. "And then?"

"ADC Buxton and I will speak to his parents," said Cullen.

Methven folded his arms. "You say he's from the same town as you?"

Cullen nodded. "That's right, sir."

"We need to be careful here," said Methven. "If there's a link to you at any point, we'll have to review the situation."

"I doubt there will be, sir," said Cullen. "Strang was a good few years younger than me and I don't recognise the name. Other than waiting on any other leads to jump out of the blue, we've still got the post mortem and forensics to come."

"Should get something back this afternoon," said Methven.

"The only other live leads we've got," said Cullen, "are the drummer, Beth Williamson and-"

Methven interrupted. "Can women play the drums?"

Chantal rolled her eyes. "They have to wear trousers, sir."

Methven blushed. "Well, of course."

"We've managed to get an address for her," said Cullen, trying to keep himself calm despite the constant interruptions. "We'll go there just now. Hopefully, we can confirm the identity before we head to Dalhousie."

"And the other live lead, Sergeant?" said Methven.

"We can't get hold of the guitarist," said Cullen. "A guy called Alex Hughes."

"Leave it with me," said Chantal.

15

Buxton rang the buzzer and they waited outside Beth Williamson's house in Dalkeith, a sprawling dormitory town just south of Edinburgh gobbling up its neighbours.

Cullen's phone buzzed. A text from Chantal. "She's still struggling to get hold of this Alex Hughes character."

The door opened. Beth Williamson didn't fit Cullen's picture of a female drummer. She was medium height, slight build, attractive and heavily pregnant. She'd be more at home in a washing powder advert than the main stage at T in the Park.

Cullen showed his warrant card and introduced them. "Ms Williamson, we spoke on the phone earlier?"

Beth swallowed. "About Jimi. You'd better come in."

She led them to a dining room overlooking a small patch of lawn and a square of patio, fruit trees dotted around the perimeter. She sat at the end of the long dining table forcing Cullen and Buxton to sit on either side.

"How far along are you?" said Buxton.

"Just over eight months," said Beth. "I'll be glad when he's out, I'll be honest. At least I don't have to go to work anymore."

"We'd like to ask you about James Strang," said Cullen.

"Certainly," said Beth. "Hopefully I can help."

Cullen asked the same questions they'd put to

Johnson, getting roughly the same answers albeit in less flowery terms. The only difference concerned Jimi's prowess with the ladies.

"Jimi was always with a groupie after a gig," said Beth.

"David Johnson said you weren't that sort of band," said Cullen.

"*We* might not have been," said Beth, "but Jimi was that sort of guy."

"Did you ever have a liaison with him?" said Cullen.

"Jimi tried it on once. Early on. We agreed it's best not to shit on your own doorstep."

Cullen raised an eyebrow at the slip of the yummy mummy exterior revealing the rock 'n' roll drummer underneath. "Do you know the names of any women Jimi was involved with?"

Beth shook her head. "David or Alex might, but I wasn't in the habit of tracking Jimi's bed hopping."

"So, what happened after the band?" said Buxton.

Beth looked out across the garden. "I gave up music. I'd had enough by then, to be honest. I liked writing new songs, but I wasn't enjoying performing, certainly nothing like the other three."

She fiddled with her wedding ring. "I worked in a record shop at the time and they made me store manager. It closed down last year. My husband works at Alba Bank and he got me a job there, so it's all worked out okay in the end I suppose."

"Was this the same record shop Mr Strang worked at?" said Cullen.

"He worked there, yes," said Beth. "That's how we met. I remember him putting up an advert looking for a drummer, years ago. Two thousand and six, I think. I used to play drums at school and it turned out I wasn't

65

too rusty."

"Would you have a list of employees from the time?" said Cullen.

"I might have something somewhere," said Beth, exhaling. "The assets were liquidated and I took some of the paperwork. I'll have a look and see what I can dig out."

"That would be excellent," said Buxton.

"One thing you could also help us with," said Cullen, "is we're struggling to get hold of Alex Hughes."

Beth gave a slight grimace. "He can be evasive at the best of times. Nothing malicious, of course, just never the most reliable. He's a very good guitarist, but incredibly flaky. That was how Jimi described him."

"Do you have a number for him?" said Buxton.

"I do," said Beth, before fiddling with the giant Samsung in front of her. She read out a number.

Buxton grimaced. "That's the one we've got."

"Well, if I hear anything from him," said Beth, "I'll let you know."

16

Cullen pulled into Broughty Terrace, one of Dalhousie's better streets, and turned off the engine. His parents lived two blocks over and he could still remember running down the pavement as a small boy, then using it as a shortcut home from high school as a teenager.

The Strang house was an old cottage three quarters of the way along, set back from the road. Much of the front garden was tarmaced over and turned into a drive, with a silver Ford Focus on the left, the right reserved for another car.

"You know these people?" said Buxton.

Cullen shook his head. "No. It's a big place. Second biggest town in Angus after Arbroath."

Buxton laughed. "That's a fantastic accolade. Doesn't seem too bad, though."

Cullen nodded. "Most professionals in Dundee will live here, Perth, Broughty Ferry or Carnoustie. This is furthest away, but that tends to bring different people. You can get into Dundee in forty minutes."

"Not bad," said Buxton.

"This isn't London, though," said Cullen. "Most people can afford to live round the corner from their office. That's a long commute in these parts."

A car parked behind them.

Cullen turned around. "That'll be the Family Liaison Officer."

"We're going to look a right bunch of muppets getting an FLO in if it's not definitely him," said Buxton.

"It is him," said Cullen. "I know it."

"Feel it in your water, can you?" said Buxton.

Cullen laughed. "You okay to lead? Good experience and all that."

"Trust me," said Buxton, "I've had more than my fair share of going into people's houses and telling them their son's dead."

They waited outside the car for the FLO, before getting the introductions out of the way quickly. PC Iain Taggart spoke with a broad Dundonian accent, all eh's and ken's. Cullen avoided joking about his surname, but he suspected not many of his colleagues would.

Taggart led them up the drive before knocking on the front door, a uPVC replacement matching the windows. He took off his hat and clutched it to his chest.

A woman in her early fifties answered, frowning. Taggart held up his warrant card. "Norma Strang?"

She nodded, her brow furrowing further. "Yes. Can I help?"

"My name is PC Iain Taggart. This is DC Simon Buxton and DS Scott Cullen. We'd like to speak to you about your son."

"I see," said Norma, running a hand through her greying hair. "You'd better come in."

They went inside leaving Buxton and Cullen to fight over who entered first, with Buxton just managing to sneak ahead. They were led into a room at the back, the bulk of one wall given over to a monstrous conservatory half filling the back garden.

"I would take you into the orangery," said Norma, "but it's far too cold at this time of year."

Cullen and Buxton sat on the settee, while Norma settled on an armchair opposite. Taggart opted to stand, leaning against the fireplace.

"How can I help?" said Norma.

Taggart seized the initiative. "Is your husband around?"

"George is at work," said Norma. "He should be back in the next hour or so, depending on how many meetings he had today."

"We're afraid we believe we have found the body of your son, James," said Taggart.

"I see," said Norma, flinching slightly. "Can I ask where?"

Taggart gestured for Cullen or Buxton to continue.

Buxton cleared his throat. "We found him in Edinburgh. Near the rehearsal rooms his band used to practise in."

"And you're sure it's him?" said Norma.

Buxton nodded. "The body matches the description of your son on the night he was last seen. We are in the process of performing secondary checks, but we have a high degree of certainty."

Tears filled Norma's eyes as she bit her lip. "I knew this day would eventually come. I kept telling George he wasn't alive, but he wouldn't listen."

She took a paper tissue from the sleeve of her cardigan and dabbed her eyes, the emotion passing. "How did he die?"

Cullen nodded. "We believe he was murdered."

"Oh, sweet Jesus," said Norma. "How?"

"A screwdriver was found with the body," said Cullen. "Tests will prove whether or not it was used to kill James."

"Can I see him?"

"I'm afraid that's not to be advised," said Cullen. "The body is in an advanced state of decomposition."

"Oh dear God," said Norma, running her hand through her hair again, leaving strands sticking up. "I won't even be able to have an open casket funeral."

"This is a murder inquiry until proved otherwise," said Buxton. "We have to investigate all potential leads or suspects."

Norma nodded slowly. "I see. I want to help."

"Can you think of anyone at all who may have wished to harm James?" said Buxton.

Norma shook her head. "We went through this with the police before. James was a lovely laddie. Very warm, very popular, lots of friends. He just lived for his music."

"Please, tell us about it," said Buxton.

"He was always playing that guitar," said Norma. "He did it at the school and we got him his first proper guitar at thirteen. He would spend hours at it. It used to be a right bugger to get him to do his homework. In the end, he did well enough to get into Edinburgh. That was James all right, capable of focusing at just the right time."

"What did he study there?" said Buxton.

"Chemical Engineering," said Norma.

"What about friends?" said Buxton.

"He was always with his band," said Norma. "Not too many people left in the town that he was friends with. He cut himself off from them over time. They all just drifted apart."

"Why was that?" said Cullen.

"You should know," said Norma. "You're the same."

"I'm sorry?"

"You're a Dalhousie laddie, aren't you?" said Norma. "I very much doubt you've looked back since you moved away."

Cullen couldn't remember the woman. "I suppose not. Was there any specific reason he left?"

Norma seemed to think it through, then slowly shook her head. "Just liked his Edinburgh life more. He was much more at home there."

"Was there anyone your son fell out with in Dalhousie?" said Buxton.

"James was bullied at school a bit," said Norma. "He was a very sensitive flower, just liked his books and playing his guitar. He was never one for sport. He really came into his own when he moved through to Edinburgh."

"Can I ask what you thought happened to James?" said Buxton.

"As I said, he was very good at cutting himself off from people if he'd had enough of them," said Norma. "He hadn't been home in months when he was reported missing. We'd not had a row as such, but we hadn't spoken to him on the phone for a couple of weeks."

"He was reported missing by Alex Hughes, who we understand was in his band," said Cullen.

Norma smiled. "Ah, Alex. He's a lovely laddie. He was very pally with James. He was sure something had happened to him. He used to call me up and talk about my boy."

"We're struggling to get hold of Alex," said Cullen. "Do you have any contact details for him?"

Norma gave them a mobile number.

"Can I ask what happened to James's possessions?" said Cullen. "Guitars, CDs, computers, that sort of

71

thing?"

"Most of his stuff was in Edinburgh," she said. "The police went through it all at the time. They gave it back after a couple of weeks."

"Do you still have it?" said Cullen.

Norma nodded. "I'm afraid I've turned his old bedroom into a bit of a shrine. It's exactly the same as when he left."

Cullen heard the front door open. A male voice called from the other side of the house. "I'm home!"

Norma looked concerned. "That's my George."

Taggart sprang into action. "Mrs Strang, if I may suggest you and I help your husband come to terms with the news, while my colleagues take a look at your son's bedroom?"

"That's a good idea." Norma looked Cullen up and down. "I know precisely everything that's in there. It's the first left at the top of the stairs."

Cullen and Buxton entered the hall and started climbing the steps, watching Norma and Taggart head off her husband.

"Has something happened?" said George Strang.

Cullen's heart sank when he watched the man's face lose all colour, his eyes darting to Taggart and both of them on the staircase.

17

James Strang's bedroom was like most teenagers of a certain era, even though he was twenty-six when he died. The walls were covered in music posters - Jeff Buckley, The Stooges, Muse and the classic, doe-eyed, black-and-white Kurt Cobain shot. He noticed a strange one by the window, some guy wearing a t-shirt that said *'Who the fuck is Mick Jagger?'*.

Beside the single bed was a large Marshall stack, mostly black with gold controls, a blue Fender guitar sitting on a stand in front of it.

"I always wanted a Telecaster," said Buxton. "That is a beautiful guitar."

"Thought you played bass?" said Cullen.

Buxton shrugged. "I can play guitar as well."

"Were you like this when you were a rock star?" said Cullen.

"All the posters and stuff?" said Buxton.

"Aye."

Buxton shook his head. "Lived with my bird, didn't I? We had a few pictures from IKEA and Habitat, that was it."

Opposite the amp stood a large CD rack, a stack of LPs resting on top. Cullen looked through, surprised someone younger than him wasn't purely into iPods and MP3s. The records were similar to the posters on the wall, plus a few others Cullen knew better - Massive

Attack, Portishead, Underworld - as well as some he couldn't stand or didn't know - Joni Mitchell, Bob Dylan, The Beatles, Scott Walker, Neil Young.

"This boy must have been gay," said Buxton.

"How do you mean?" said Cullen.

"The posters are all blokes," said Buxton. "He was in his twenties, prime of his life and he didn't have a single picture of a bird up."

"He wasn't."

They looked over at the door - Norma Strang stood there, hands on hips.

Cullen shot a look at Buxton. "I'm sorry. DC Buxton shouldn't have said that."

"It's fine," said Norma.

"How is your husband?" said Cullen.

"Your colleague is helping him. I was just getting in the way." She sat on the bed and inspected her nails. "I often wondered the same thing about my son, of course, but he had a couple of girlfriends I knew about."

"Were any serious?" said Cullen.

"Nobody serious enough to bring home and introduce to us."

"What about not serious?" said Cullen.

Norma smiled. "There was someone he was interested in. I think her name was Jane or Jan or something."

Cullen noted it down before taking a good look at the room. "Are these all the possessions he had with him in Edinburgh?"

"Yes," said Norma. "There were a few things he'd left here, some of his more embarrassing CDs I think. They're up in the loft."

Cullen nodded, surprised how calm the woman was, but then again she was an Angus wifie. They built them differently up here - his own mother would be the same if anything happened to him or Michelle. "Did James keep a journal?"

"Not that I know of," said Norma, shaking her head. "The police weren't able to get much off his laptop."

Cullen noticed the machine on the desk, quite a dated model, blacks and reds compared with the silver sheen of the one Sharon had just bought.

"I'd like to take this in as evidence," said Cullen, knowing it would mean a trip to Charlie Kidd, their Forensic IT Analyst.

"That's fine," said Norma. "If it will help you."

As Cullen hefted the laptop - heavier than he first thought - he noticed a cache of unmarked CDs at the back of the desk. He put the laptop down and inspected them - they appeared to be The Invisibles CDs. He realised they knew next to nothing about the band, what they sounded like, other than what David Johnson and Beth Williamson had told them. "Can I take a copy of the CDs?"

"Take those," said Norma. "George put them on his computer a long time ago."

"I think that's probably all from us just now," said Cullen, handing her a card. "In case there's anything else, please give me a call in the first instance."

"I will do," said Norma.

"We'll leave you in the capable hands of PC Taggart," said Cullen.

They crept down the stairs, leaving Norma Strang in her son's bedroom staring into space.

Out on the street, Cullen dialled the new Alex Hughes number. It rang for a while, not even going to voicemail. He pocketed his phone.

"Sorry for getting caught talking about her son like that," said Buxton.

"She didn't seem to mind," said Cullen. "I wouldn't make a habit of it, though."

"I'm not a homophobe, mate. It was a genuine question."

"Okay." Cullen pointed back at the house. "What do you think of him?"

"Seen his type a lot in the music scene," said Buxton. "Introverted guy, plays his guitar, listens to loud music, then becomes a rock star when he's pissed on stage."

"Guess so," said Cullen, leaning back against his car. "We've got no suspects and we still can't get hold of Alex Hughes."

"Reckon he's one?" said Buxton.

"Why call it in if you'd killed someone?" said Cullen.

Buxton shrugged. "Good point. What are we doing now?"

Cullen thought it through for a few seconds. "You're going to the local station to ask around, see if he's got himself into mischief and been run out of town or anything."

"You hooking up with an old flame or something, Shagger?" said Buxton, a leery look in his eye.

"Worse," said Cullen. "I'm taking my parents out for dinner."

18

"He does know me and Sharon were supposed to be coming up tonight, right?" said Cullen.

"You know your father, Scott," said Cullen's mother. "In fact, he's very much like his son." She took a sip of wine. "They're very busy just now and they've got a lot of deals going on. He's called a way a lot." She reached over the table and prodded him in the chest. "Anyway, the first I knew you weren't coming to stay was when you turned up on my doorstep an hour ago. I've lots of food in for the weekend. You'll have to take it home with you."

"Fine," said Cullen. "Suits me."

"A weekend with the pair of you would have been nice. How is Sharon?"

"She's got a stinker of a cold," said Cullen. "Doesn't look like we'd have been able to come up anyway. As it is, I'm going to be stuck in this case for the whole weekend."

"I worry about you, son. There's too much pressure on you."

"Aye, well," said Cullen, "I'm an Acting DS now and I'm not letting it go without a fight. Besides Sharon wants a new house. I've got a lot of responsibility, people reporting to me."

"That's good."

The waiter brought their food - pizza for his mother and a salad for Cullen, though it looked like the less healthy option with the amount of olive oil, cheese and pesto drizzled all over it.

His mother daintily cut into her pizza. "Have you spoken to your sister recently?"

"I knew this was coming," said Cullen, rolling his eyes.

"Well, have you?"

"It's up to Michelle to get in touch with me," said Cullen. "I've tried loads of times."

"Scott, your sister lived in Edinburgh for a whole year and you didn't meet up with her once. It's not like you live out in the countryside, you're on the Royal Mile. Now she's working in Glasgow, I don't see how you'll ever do it."

Cullen ate a forkful of tuna and lettuce leaves. "She's ignoring me. She even unfriended me on Schoolbook. That's just petty."

"Will you at least try again for me? I think she's hurt."

"She shouldn't be so bloody precious," said Cullen, shaking his head, feeling the anger surge. "I didn't do anything wrong, nothing Dad wouldn't have said."

"That's a bit of an exaggeration, Scott."

"How is the old bugger?" said Cullen, desperate to change the subject.

"You know your father," she said, "he won't stop playing his games, he's always up to something. And I'm not talking about computer games, though he's finally stopped playing that infernal Xbox so often."

"That'll be where I get it from," said Cullen.

"Well, it's certainly not from me," said his mother, eyes wide.

"Do you know a James Strang?" said Cullen.

"I know his parents. He disappeared, didn't he? They were devastated by it."

"You knew?" said Cullen.

"Is that why you're here?"

Cullen nodded. "Found his body in Edinburgh. Shouldn't really talk about it." He took a drink of lemonade. "Do they have any ideas what happened to him?"

His mum smiled. "Am I a witness in this case?"

"At the moment, I could do with anything," said Cullen. "The guy was three years younger than me, I don't remember him. He'd still have been a wee laddie when I left Dalhousie."

"I'll see what I can dig up on the grapevine."

Cullen's phone started buzzing - a text from Buxton, chasing him up. "I'll have to go back to Edinburgh just after this," he said, finishing his salad, a puddle of green goop at the bottom.

"No time for a coffee?"

"Wish I did," said Cullen.

"Well, this has been nice," she said. "Thanks for seeing me. It's a shame you can't come through, but I understand. You're forgiven for that time you were in Carnoustie and didn't call."

"I hope I don't get a bollocking for this," said Cullen, putting a twenty on the table.

His mother smacked his hand. "You put that away, Scott Cullen. This is my treat."

Cullen smiled. He leaned down and kissed her on the cheek. "I promise we'll be through soon."

"You make sure you fulfil that promise."

Cullen left the restaurant, feeling a tight knot in his stomach. Walking towards the car, he thought back to how much simpler life was when he was younger, part of him wishing he could go back.

The old town looked exactly as he remembered it, the

same shops, same restaurants and people. One of the things he loved about Edinburgh was how much change there was. Dalhousie, despite his old man's best efforts, was stuck in a rut, at least in the town centre.

"Scott Cullen?"

Across the road, a plump woman in her early thirties was pointing at him. She came towards him, finger stabbing the air, a car swerving out of her way.

"You fucking arsehole!"

"I'm sorry?" said Cullen.

"You fucking arsehole!"

She tried to slap him but he grabbed her hand.

"You fuck off away from me, Scott Cullen!"

Cullen got his warrant card out. "I'm a police officer. Unless you clear off, I'll arrest you."

She took a long look at Cullen then marched off in the direction she'd come from.

Cullen had absolutely no idea who she was.

19

Back at Leith Walk station, Methven had been busy. He'd acquired an Incident Room and, though it was the smallest of the three, all four walls were covered in whiteboard paint.

They'd put several photos of Strang on the wall though no connecting arrows had yet been drawn. Cullen inspected the pictures - they were taken over the course of two years, but Strang had aged, lines appearing on his otherwise fresh face and hair greying at the sides.

He was good looking, in a fey way. His face was long and thin and seemed to be symmetrical. His brown hair was spiked up in most of the pictures, the sides shaved ever closer as more grey appeared.

Buxton and Chantal stood around while Methven doodled on one of the walls. Cullen joined them.

"So, who have we got?" said Methven. "James Strang. AKA Jimi Danger."

"That's just been confirmed," said Chantal. "Anderson finished his DNA test. Strang was done for a breach of the peace in his student days. The DNA was on file."

"That's a result," said Buxton.

"Would have been nice to know when we spoke to his parents, though," said Cullen.

Chantal waved the paper in front of Cullen's face. "It's only just come through. Besides, you and Simon barrelled in oblivious to anything else."

Cullen tried to decide whether to make something of it.

Methven made the decision for him. "The post mortem is back. There is sufficient evidence to confirm the screwdriver is the murder weapon. The blood on the handle matches the DNA on file and the flecks of blood on the t-shirt."

He rubbed his stomach through his pristine white shirt. "The state of decay meant there was very little to perform an autopsy on. That said, the initial forensics report is of some interest."

He pointed to a photo of a pair of jeans, blown up to twice life size and occupying almost a whole wall. Cullen thought that sort of expense would soon be killed off by the new Chief Constable of Police Scotland, a notorious penny-pincher from his days in Strathclyde.

Methven indicated dark marks at the bottom of the jeans with his pen, an expensive-looking ballpoint. "There are traces that show the body was dragged from somewhere. These are wholly inconsistent with usual wear patterns and there is sufficient blood mixed in to confirm our suspicions."

Cullen was irritated that Methven was taking over his investigation. "Which are?"

"It looks like he wasn't killed where the body was found," said Chantal.

Cullen frowned. "The steps are stone. Somebody should have seen something, the trail would have been visible."

"That's a good point," said Methven. "Our killer was lucky here. Nobody was looking at the steps or the passageway that far down. We visited the room Strang's band used. It was the only one on the bottom level so it's possible nobody else would have been down. We should check with the band who shared their room. Chantal?"

She nodded.

"Didn't the original investigating team look into this?" said Cullen.

Methven gave a shrug. "We'd need to ask them, but I very much doubt it. The time allocation for a MisPer is very different to a murder investigation. They wouldn't have had access to detectives, let alone forensics."

"Besides, they thought he ran away," said Chantal. "They wouldn't have searched these band rooms."

"I want to speak to the investigating officers," said Cullen.

"Fine," said Methven. "Just don't labour it too much."

"As if I would," said Cullen, with a wry grin.

Methven grunted. "We currently have no suspects."

"I'd agree with that," said Cullen.

"What about that guy in the band with him, Johnson?" said Buxton. "The stuff about the t-shirt weirded me out."

Cullen looked at Chantal and Methven then tapped a photo of the remains. "What Simon is alluding to, is the Jeff Buckley t-shirt was a gift from David Johnson, the bass player."

"Come on, Constable," said Methven, "that's hardly enough to suspect someone of murder?"

Buxton shrugged. "It's just odd."

"Let's move on," said Methven, turning back to his mind map. "We've only got five direct connections. His parents are two and the three bandmates."

"There's another," said Cullen. "His parents mentioned a girl called Jane. We don't know anything else about her."

Methven wrote it down. "Right. Hold that thought for now." He looked at the whiteboard. "We've spoken to two of the band already, is that correct?"

Cullen nodded. "David Johnson and Beth Williamson. We need to get Beth in to give a formal statement. The Johnson interview transcript should be with us tomorrow."

"I expect you two to close that out," said Methven.

"Will do," said Cullen. "The only blocker we've now got is we can't get hold of Alex Hughes."

"Is that suspicious?" said Methven.

"Could be," said Cullen. "Might be he's on holiday or has a new phone number."

"That's two phones we've tried, though," said Buxton. "I called Tommy Smith in the Phone Squad on the way back." He held his own mobile up. "He's got nowhere in tracking either phone down."

"What do you think, Sergeant?" said Methven, losing patience.

"I don't think he's a suspect," said Cullen. "Yet. Nobody has mentioned any antagonism between Hughes and Strang. Quite the opposite, in fact. He's been speaking to Strang's mother about her son."

"I want that on the top of your radar tomorrow," said Methven.

"The top of my what?" said Cullen.

Methven snorted. "Just get it done." He looked back at the board. "You've interviewed the parents?"

Cullen nodded. "Other than the Jane potential lead, we've got nothing. Some interesting background for a biography on him, but that's it."

Methven's gaze turned to Chantal "And the work

colleagues?"

"Strang worked in a record shop, which Beth Williamson eventually went on to manage. He was casual labour with no formal employment contract. We've got the previous manager coming in tomorrow to give a statement, but he didn't remember much about Strang when I spoke to him on the phone. The one thing he did say was Strang was always in early every day, half an hour before his shift, so he could listen to the new music and talk to people, usually about his band."

Methven scribbled a link to the manager, prompting Chantal for the name. "Any other colleagues we should be bringing in?"

"Not spoken to anyone yet," said Chantal. "Still waiting on the list from Beth Williamson." She pulled a hand through her hair and refastened her scrunchy. "If that doesn't appear, God knows what we're going to do."

"Did they have a manager or an agent?" said Methven.

"Johnson told us Strang did all that," said Cullen. "He was a bit of an obsessive."

"Next," said Methven. "Flatmates."

"We've not progressed that yet," said Cullen. "From the discussions with Williamson and Johnson, it looks like it won't come to anything. He just had a room in a flat, didn't seem to interact with his flatmates."

"They might know something," said Methven.

"They might not," said Cullen, before looking at Buxton. "One for you, Simon."

Buxton grimaced. "Got a call back from Johnson earlier. The flat was on Marchmont Road. He also gave me a list of friends I should speak to."

Methven let out a deep sigh. "Okay, so we've got

sodding nothing to show for a day's work."

"That's a bit harsh," said Cullen. "We know the victim."

"We need to do better," said Methven. "Hopefully tomorrow will be a bit more productive. You can all head home for the night."

20

Cullen got to the flat at the back of ten, dumping his stuff on the sofa and getting a glass of milk from the fridge, downing it in one. He spotted a note on the breakfast bar saying Sharon had gone to bed.

The cat bleated at him again, baring the large fangs in his pink mouth. Cullen reached down and picked him up. He weighed an absolute ton. He started tickling him under the chin, eventually making him purr.

"See, I'm not so bad," said Cullen.

He put the cat down, then retrieved Strang's stack of CDs. After a few minutes, he found his DJ headphones and plugged them into his stereo, the set of separates that had superseded Sharon's mini system, which Cullen couldn't stand the sound of.

He sat listening to the music for half an hour or so. He didn't know what to make of the band. It wasn't Cullen's cup of tea, squalling guitars and pounding drums, but they were offset against strange vocals, oscillating between screaming and shouting to the sweetest singing he'd ever heard. He struggled to find the talent and genius Johnson's hyperbole had attributed to his bandmate.

As he let the music wash over him, he wrote up an action list for the following day, his tired eyes drying from his contact lenses. It felt too short and they didn't have anywhere near enough to go on.

He couldn't quite fathom out the strange t-shirt arrangement with Johnson. Was there anything there? He'd had a similar thing at school with his two best mates, both called Richard, where they'd buy each other CDs every Christmas. Eventually it became a joke, with Cullen stopping after he received *Never Mind the Bollocks* by the Sex Pistols, his old man's number one record.

Beth Williamson had gone from being a muscular drummer to a housewife in eighteen months, quite a rapid change. She looked like she was in a settled relationship and had been for quite some time.

Just like Buxton, Johnson and Williamson gave up on a music career without a second thought. The dream turned sour.

Alex Hughes was a mystery, still plugging away at music. Tomorrow's main action was to find him, most likely rooting around Glasgow.

He picked up the magazine by the sofa, half of Expect Delays staring out at him. They were still trapped in the belly of the beast, living the dream. He didn't know if they'd made enough to never work again. Maybe they'd have to retrain in a more useful vocation when it all fell apart, or exploit the next generation of musicians as managers.

He put the CDs back in a pile and went to bed.

As ever, Sharon was partly over his half. He spooned into her.

"Don't get any ideas."

*Saturday
30th March 2013*

21

Cullen got into the station at six that morning, trying to cobble together ideas to expand his sketchy action plan, determined to show Methven up. He kept coming up blank.

At the back of eight, he grabbed Buxton and they drove to Queen Charlotte Street station in Leith.

"It's your old mate Willie McAllister, isn't it?" said Buxton as he parked.

Cullen nodded. "His legend prevails."

"He worked for you on a case a couple of years back, right?"

"Aye. I had to move him on pretty quickly."

"What's he doing investigating uptown if he's based down here?"

"He was working at St Leonard's when Hughes called it in," said Cullen. "Another week and he'd have been back down here and I wouldn't have to deal with him again."

They entered the building and went through to the station's meagre canteen.

"Here's Robocop," said McAllister, not getting up. "Heard they made you a sergeant, that right?"

"Acting," said Buxton, sitting next to McAllister.

Cullen glared at him before taking the third chair, only discovering it had a wonky leg when he sat. The veteran cop looked worse than ever. "Only a couple of months to go, is that right?"

"Due my date from Personnel any day soon, son," said McAllister. "Not long now."

Cullen couldn't wait. "We just need to ask you a few questions about the disappearance of James Strang."

"Fire away."

"We believe it was reported by one Alex Hughes," said Cullen.

McAllister retrieved a battered notebook. He put on a pair of reading glasses, looking over the rims at Cullen, but still had to hold it at arm's length. "This Hughes boy called up to report his mate missing. I was covering a maternity at St Leonard's. Luckily, I got posted back down here not long after, which suits me fine as I live just up the road in Lochend."

"How much investigating did you do?" said Cullen.

McAllister looked thoughtful for a moment, then flicked through a few pages. "We spoke to some people who knew the laddie."

"Who?"

"Hughes," said McAllister. "Some lassie called Beth or Bess or something. We went up to sheep-shagger land to speak to the boy's family."

"They were all you spoke to?" said Cullen.

McAllister shrugged. "Standard practice, son. You'd know if you'd done proper policing recently. Shouldn't even have gone up to Dalrymple or whatever the place is called."

"Dalhousie," said Cullen, grinding his teeth. "Are there any open leads you didn't close down?"

"What are you saying?" said McAllister.

"Nothing," said Cullen, losing patience with him. "We're wondering if there was anything you couldn't investigate at the time. It's a murder investigation now. We've got more resources than you had back then."

"Nothing springs to mind," said McAllister.

Cullen nodded down at the now-closed notebook. "And in there?"

McAllister shook his head. "Afraid not."

Cullen got to his feet. "Thanks for your help. I'll keep you posted as to how it goes. I know how you old-timers dislike your loose ends as you head to retirement."

"Aye, fine," said McAllister.

Cullen marched off to the front entrance, through the security doors and out into the cold air.

"You need to start a fan club," said Buxton. "Do you think McAllister might start one for you when he retires?"

"Very good," said Cullen.

"Not in the mood?"

Cullen slumped back against the car and folded his arms. "This is a joke. We're getting nowhere with this."

"Come on, mate," said Buxton, "it's not like your career is resting on it."

"I thought you'd stopped trying to be funny?" said Cullen.

Buxton held his hands up. "Calm down. Whatever happens on Monday, happens."

Cullen could see the sense in what he said. "Right. We need to speak to the band again. I don't like not being able to get hold of Alex Hughes."

"What tack do you want to take?" said Buxton.

"I don't care," said Cullen. "Finding him seems to be our only hope. If we don't get anything from the pair of them, we'll need to get a search done in Glasgow."

"Where to next, boss?" said Buxton.

"Let's get Beth and Johnson in again," said Cullen. "See if they can point us towards Hughes."

22

Cullen and Buxton waited in the deserted canteen, eating bowls of lumpy porridge made by one of Barbara's stroppier girls, before Buxton got a call informing them Johnson and Beth had finally arrived. They raced down to the interview room.

Beth handed Buxton a sheet of paper as he sat down. "That's the list of employees from the record shop."

"Cheers."

"At present," said Cullen, eyes flitting between the two, "the only active lead we have is Alex Hughes. We've so far struggled to get hold of him." He held their gaze for a few seconds each. "One of you knows something about this and I would like to get it out of you."

Beth screwed her eyes up. "I'm *pregnant*. You can't do this to me."

"Do what?" said Cullen.

"Interrogate me like this."

"I'm investigating the murder of a former associate of yours," said Cullen. "Nobody is being interrogated here."

Beth folded her arms. "It feels very much like it."

Cullen smiled. "I can charge the pair of you with obstruction and get your lawyers in if you'd rather."

Johnson turned round to face her. "Beth, the officer is trying to do his best. I think we should assist him."

"Fine," said Beth, waving her hand in the air and looking away.

"What can you tell us about Mr Hughes?" said Cullen.

Johnson started. "Alex was a bit of a drifter, always doing casual jobs, never settling into anything long term. Technically, he was a fantastic musician in some ways, capable of creating the most wonderful textures with his guitar, but he could be so unfocused. He had an unfortunate tendency to forget where different sections of the songs started, that sort of thing."

"Jimi would shout and scream at him," said Beth.

Cullen's interest was piqued. "Tell me more about that."

"Nothing to tell, really," said Beth. "He just used to get angry with him." She shrugged. "Have you heard our music?"

Cullen nodded. "I received a CD from Mr Strang's parents."

Beth leaned forward, placing her hands on the tabletop. "Well, you'll know our sound was quite dynamic. We could make a racket, don't get me wrong, but we had some very pretty bits in our songs. The structure was very complex."

"So what you're saying is Mr Hughes would play a loud bit over a quiet bit?" said Buxton.

Beth shrugged. "That's about the size of it."

"Put it this way," said Johnson, "Jimi found it hard to sing a sweet song with a Marshall turned up to eleven screaming behind him with God knows how many pedals on."

Cullen nodded as he thought it through. Something tugged at the back of his mind. "Did this ever happen on stage?"

"A couple of times," said Beth, nodding slowly.

"Early on, mainly," said Johnson.

"But it still happened?" said Cullen.

Johnson nodded his head. "It did."

"Did Mr Strang ever blame Mr Hughes for your lack of success?" said Cullen.

"We *were* successful," said Beth, arms folded again, lips pouting.

"But you weren't signed," said Buxton. "I think that's what my colleague is getting at."

Beth stabbed a finger in the air, her accent getting coarser. "Jimi and Alex were the best of friends. Jimi disappearing like that really cut him up."

"I can imagine," said Cullen. "Which is why we need to speak to him. Is there anything you can think of?"

Beth and Johnson shared a look before she broke off.

"Alex did have a girlfriend," said Johnson, biting his lip. "I don't know if they kept in touch or not. She might be worth a shot."

"What was her name?" said Cullen.

"Marta Hunter," said Beth. "I think she lived in Niddrie."

"I think so, too," said Johnson.

Cullen ended the interview, satisfied they were finally a step forward.

23

It took them a while to find Marta Hunter. At some point in the last nineteen months, she'd changed her name to Phillips by marriage. But they did find her.

She lived on one of the new streets created in the ongoing urban renewal of Niddrie, in the top floor of a white house adorned with bright blue panelling.

As agreed on the way, Buxton would lead. He tried the door intercom and they waited a few seconds before pressing it again.

"Hello?" The female voice was frail and uneven.

"Marta Phillips?" said Buxton. "This is the police. We need to ask you a few questions."

"Just a minute."

It felt like five. They climbed the stairs to her flat and stood by the door.

Marta led them into the living room. It was bedlam - three young kids running around, all under five with the youngest just over a year old in Cullen's estimation.

He decided to stand and Buxton followed suit.

Marta sat in an armchair, the type Cullen had seen in many cheap furniture shops in Easter Road and Abbeyhill. She pulled her cardigan close and shivered, though the room was baking. She looked like she was on drugs, Cullen reckoning heroin was most likely from her sunken cheeks.

"It's not Phillips anymore, by the way," said Marta.

She had a vaguely Slavic look but spoke in a broad Edinburgh accent. "Got divorced. Went back to my maiden name."

Cullen frowned - that was a quick turnaround. Not the quickest he'd ever heard of - one of Sharon's friends from university had managed to go from meeting a man to divorce in ten months. They'd just had invites for her next wedding.

"I'm sorry to hear that," said Buxton.

Marta sniffed. "Shug was a wanker. No skin off my beak."

"We believe you were acquainted with an Alex Hughes?" said Buxton.

"Aye, Alex." Marta rubbed at her eye. "He was the love of my life, that boy. Can't believe he left me."

"Why did he?" said Buxton.

Marta looked away. "I don't know."

"Nothing to do with your kids?" said Buxton.

She shook her head. "No."

"Would it be the drugs?" said Cullen.

"Drugs?" said Marta, avoiding eye contact.

"I know heroin when I see it," said Cullen.

Marta slumped back in the chair. "Aye, it was the drugs. I'm a recovering smack head. You lot probably prefer to call me a recovering heroin addict."

Cullen was only slightly pleased his suspicion had proved true. His main thoughts were for her children.

"I'm on methadone. Just trying to wean us off the skag." She looked over at her kids. "Last chance saloon for me with my boys."

"Was Alex into drugs?" said Cullen.

"Just a bit of blow," said Marta. "He smoked the H a couple of times but he wasn't into it. He kept on at me to give it up."

"And that's why he split up with you?" said Cullen.

"Aye."

Cullen inspected her afresh. She was thin, but not as skinny as the stereotypical heroin addict, and her personal hygiene didn't seem to be too bad. That said, he struggled to see what Alex Hughes saw in her - she didn't seem particularly warm, intelligent, funny or good-looking.

"Are the kids his?" said Cullen.

"Before and after." Marta laughed and pointed at the children, now playing a game on the TV. "Wee Xander there, my middle one, he was born when I first met Alex."

"Did Alex ever want to become their father?" said Cullen.

Marta nodded. "He did, aye. In the end, though, he couldn't deal with me being the way I am."

Cullen decided he'd had enough of this - he knew her plight would haunt his dreams. "We need to speak to him."

"He lives in Glasgow now," said Marta. "Still doing the music."

"Do you have an address?" said Cullen.

Marta nodded. "He sent me a letter once." She got up, patting one of her sons on the head as she went, and rummaged around in a set of drawers at the other end of the room. She came back and handed a sheet to Cullen. "Here."

Cullen read the letter. It was impersonal and focused on his music. There was nothing to suggest the two had ever met, let alone been an item. He looked back at Marta, staring intently at her kids, a tear in her eye.

"Mind if I take this?"

She shook her head. "Go for it."

Cullen knew the street on the top left of the page. It wasn't far from Glasgow University.

24

Cullen and Buxton entered the Incident Room, finding Methven wearing jeans, shirt and jumper.

Methven looked them up and down. "You look like a sodding pair of police officers. Nobody has worn a suit at the sodding weekend since nineteen fifty-eight."

"What about at a wedding?" said Buxton.

"Are you planning on going to one, Constable?" said Methven.

"I've got one tomorrow, sir," said Buxton.

"You'd better clear that with me," said Methven.

Cullen ground his teeth. "I don't usually work on a Saturday, sir."

Methven shook his head slowly and folded his arms. "Do you have good news for me to take upstairs?"

"Maybe," said Cullen. "Got an address for Alex Hughes."

Methven frowned. "DC Jain couldn't find one for him."

"We managed to get it off an ex-girlfriend," said Cullen.

"Hughes is the member of the public who reported Strang missing, right?" said Methven.

"He is," said Cullen.

"And?"

"Well, can we go and see him?" said Cullen.

"Are you asking permission?" said Methven.

Cullen shrugged. "Yes. I thought you'd want to do this by the book, what with all the restructuring."

"Just sodding go through there," said Methven. "I don't have time for this."

"Shouldn't we speak to Strathclyde CID?" said Cullen.

"Is Hughes under suspicion of murder or other serious offences?" said Methven.

"Well," said Cullen.

"Spit it out, Sergeant."

"We believe Hughes and Strang had some bust-ups," said Cullen.

"Hughes was a bit unfocused," said Buxton. "He struggled with some of the dynamics in their songs."

"Dynamics?" said Methven.

"The difference between the loud bits and the quiet bits," said Buxton.

"Right, go on," said Methven, hands jingling change in his pockets.

"He'd make mistakes," said Buxton. "He played loud in a quiet bit, that sort of thing. Strang didn't like it."

"Enough to kill him?" said Methven.

"It's a possibility," said Cullen. "We've got nothing to support it, though."

"Is he likely to be under surveillance by Strathclyde?" said Methven.

"No," said Cullen.

"Well, don't bloody bother asking them," said Methven. "Christ."

Cullen shared a look with Buxton. He didn't know what had got into Methven, but whatever it was, he wanted to be miles away from him. Glasgow seemed quite tempting for once.

Chantal entered the room. "What's going on here?"

"I've got to sign sodding permission forms for the children's school trip to Glasgow," said Methven.

The corner of Chantal's lip turned up. "DI Cargill caught up with you, then?"

"Yes, she sodding did," said Methven.

Chantal looked at Cullen. "I much prefer DIs who fucking swear fucking properly."

Methven reddened. "I want a status update from you. *Now.*"

"Fine," said Chantal, flicking through her notebook. "Turns out the screwdriver is a local brand made by a small company out Dunbar way. According to the owner, that model was only on sale between February and August two thousand and eleven before the company went bust."

"How many stockists were there?" said Methven.

"Just sold direct from his house," said Chantal.

"I assume we can get a list of customers?" said Methven.

"I'm trying," said Chantal. "He's having problems with his computer, though. The old one broke and he didn't repair it when he got a new one."

"Get Charlie Kidd on it," said Methven. "Did you speak to the other band?"

Chantal nodded. "Tracked them down. They still use the room. Bunch of stoners, never saw anything."

"Buggery." Methven looked over at Cullen. "As for you pair, I want this Hughes character brought in for questioning by the time I have to clear off to my dinner party tonight. Clear?"

Crystal, thought Cullen, but he nodded instead.

"Missed my sodding triathlon," said Methven, "and I've got to bloody deal with this nonsense."

Cullen walked out of the Incident Room, heading for his car.

Buxton jogged to catch up. "The *fuck* is up with him?"

"No idea," said Cullen. "I'm keeping well out of his way."

25

"This looks like it," said Buxton.

Cullen slowed his Golf to a crawl as they drove down Loudon Terrace, trying to find the street Alex Hughes lived on. He inspected the numbers, quickly finding twenty-seven but no spaces.

"Better watch where you park," said Buxton. "Don't want some museum trying to claim your car."

"Very funny," said Cullen.

"Close to becoming a classic this," said Buxton. "Shame it drives like a bloody tank."

"It drives fine," said Cullen. "Might be a bit exciting for an amateur passenger like yourself."

Buxton laughed. "You never think of getting a decent motor?"

Cullen shrugged. "To be honest, I'm not really much of a car man," he said, mindful of Buxton being prone to lengthy anecdotes about his brother's collection of drag-racing cars. "We're supposed to be saving for a house, though I think I'd prefer a bigger flat. Not ready to move out to the country."

"Big step," said Buxton.

"Sorry, don't mean to rub it in," said Cullen, conscious that Buxton was a frustrated singleton.

Buxton just nodded.

Cullen drove on, through the west end of Glasgow, rows of red sandstone tenements on wide streets. He doubled back onto Byres Road.

"Used to live round here for a bit when I was in that band," said Buxton.

"Thought you were in Edinburgh?" said Cullen.

"Yeah well, we moved here at the end," said Buxton. "It was much better for music and we used to come here at the weekends to play gigs and go to record shops and so on. Moving was the last throw of the dice."

Cullen grabbed a space the second time round on Loudon Terrace. "This'll do."

They got out of the car and started walking.

"This it here?" said Buxton, outside the flat door.

"Think so," said Cullen, before consulting his notebook and confirming they were after twenty-seven. "Aye, it is. Flat six."

The stairwell was open to the street, the door intercom smashed in. Cullen started up the stairs, the lights flickering. He knocked on Hughes' door and waited.

Something hit him from behind.

He stumbled to his knees.

His shoulder was grabbed and his arm locked behind his back. He was pushed face down.

Across the red ceramic tiles, he could see Buxton in a similar position.

"You are under arrest!"

26

"We're police," said Cullen.

"Are you fuck," said the voice above, male with a harsh Glasgow accent.

"I'm DS Scott Cullen. My warrant card is in my coat pocket."

"Fucking likely tale. Returning to the scene of the crime, are you?"

"What the fuck are you talking about?" said Buxton. "We're Lothian & Borders."

"Fucking English one as well, Davie."

"Chuck him in the fucking Clyde, Damo. Best place for them."

Cullen struggled against the hold. "We're Lothian & Borders CID. I can get my Chief Constable to have a word with yours if that makes any difference."

There was a pause. Eventually, Cullen felt the grip slacken.

"Show us your credentials, then."

Cullen was released. He struggled to see the figures in the glow from the failing strip light. He righted himself, then reached into his jacket pocket for his warrant card. He held it up, before calloused fingers snatched it away.

"Fuck's sake."

Cullen's card was tossed on the floor in front of him.

"You should have told us you were coming."

Cullen dusted himself off and stood up, Buxton doing

the same. They got a good look at their assailants.

The one nearest Cullen was an overweight man in his late thirties, his head bald. He offered a hand. "DS Damian McCrea." He nodded at his colleague, younger and thinner. "DC Davie Lucas."

Cullen shook the offered hand. "DS Scott Cullen. And this is DC Simon Buxton."

"I'll ask you again," said McCrea. "What the fuck are you doing on our patch?"

"We're working a murder case," said Cullen. "We're looking for an Alex Hughes."

McCrea rubbed at his forehead. "For fuck's sake. Why?"

"He reported our victim missing nineteen months ago," said Cullen. "We've tried getting in touch with him, but no joy."

"Right." McCrea took a deep intake of breath. "You pair need to come back to the station and have a word with my DI. This is a fucking disaster." He shook his head. "Follow us."

They accompanied Cullen and Buxton back to the car. Cullen tried to figure out what the hell was happening. Where was Hughes? Why were Strathclyde at his flat?

An old Ford Escort drove past, Lucas leaning out of the passenger-side window and waving them to follow.

"When did they even stop making Escorts?" said Cullen.

"I'm struggling to think, mate," said Buxton. "Early nineties is my best guess." He grinned. "Bet you're glad someone's got a worse car than you."

"My shoulder is bloody killing me," said Cullen, "and I've no idea what's going on here."

"Cagey geezer, isn't he?" said Buxton.

McCrea led them to the M8, heading south before its meander out towards Greenock and Paisley. Their station was in Govan, just off the motorway, and Cullen managed to squeeze into a space next to McCrea, already out and locking his car.

As they walked to the station, Cullen pointed towards the floodlights above Ibrox stadium, home of Rangers. "That'll be convenient for you lot."

"With a name like mine," said McCrea, "would you be surprised to know I worship at a church that's not in the third division?"

Cullen held the door open for Buxton and Lucas behind them. "Celtic fan?"

"Aye," said McCrea, before signing them through security, the waiting room full of the bruised and damaged. "You?"

"Aberdeen," said Cullen.

McCrea laughed at him. "We're supposed to be moving to Gartcosh next summer."

"Being stuck with the Scottish FBI will be fun," said Cullen.

McCrea raised his eyebrows. "Tell me about it." He pointed to a vacant interview room. "Wait in there, if you don't mind."

"And if I do?" said Cullen, trying to keep his face straight.

"Look, do you need a towel for any cuts and bruises or anything?" said McCrea.

"No."

"Right, well, wait here and I'll be back soon," said McCrea.

They went inside the room. Cullen felt too edgy to sit

down, instead leaning against the wall, arms folded, foot tapping, eyes continually flicking to the door.

Buxton sat, resting his head in his hands. "I'd like to know what the fuck is going on here."

"You and me both," said Cullen. "Let's just wait and see what happens."

The door to the next room opened and two men left in a hurry. Cullen frowned - he would recognise the comb-forward anywhere.

Buxton leaned over. "That's Mike Roberts. Expect Delays."

"What's he doing here?" said Cullen.

"He's helping us with our inquiries," said McCrea, entering the room. "The gaffer will be along soon."

Cullen sat down, his back to the door. "Why are you speaking to Roberts?"

McCrea sat opposite. "He was supposed to meet up with Alex Hughes. Hughes never turned up."

"I'm still not quite sure what the hell is going on here," said Cullen.

"They used to know each other from the music scene in Edinburgh, I believe," said McCrea. "Mr Roberts was helping out with some contacts, maybe getting him a job in a studio." He pointed a finger at Cullen. "I better not see anything about this on Twitter. Be bad if him being in a police station leaked out."

"Hardly." Cullen pointed a finger back at McCrea. "You really need to tell me what's going on here."

The door slammed shut behind them.

"Well, if it isn't the fuckin' Sundance kid."

27

Cullen stumbled to his feet, his heart racing. He took a step back, away from the desk.

DI Brian Bain marched forward and sat down alongside McCrea. "Fuck me, Sundance. I wish I had that effect on half the boys I have in here under arrest."

Cullen hadn't expected *this*.

"Bit weird seeing your old boss, Sundance?"

"I look back fondly on those eighteen months of misery, belittlement and swearing."

"Thought you'd have heard I was back in Strathclyde?"

"Working for an old croney, no doubt." Cullen straightened his tie and sat down, aware he was in danger of looking like a prize idiot. "You seem a lot more relaxed than when I last saw you."

"I'm away from that wanker Turnbull and his little pit bull," said Bain, rubbing at his top lip, now bereft of his trademark moustache. "Besides, I'm getting married again, got a wee Thai lassie."

Cullen couldn't believe it. "Mail order?"

"Don't be so crass, Sundance," said Bain. "It's love."

"I bet," said Cullen. "You don't know the meaning of the word."

Bain sniffed. "I'm not quite the swordsman you are. Is your better half still into other birds?"

"Shut up," said Cullen, fingernails digging into the

palms of his hands.

"I went to see Alan Irvine in Bar-L a few weeks ago," said Bain. "He told me to congratulate you on getting your stripes."

Cullen was Acting in Irvine's old role. "He should feel guilty."

"Don't talk about that case," said Bain, his smile disappearing.

"Is it a bit too close to home?"

Bain's nostrils flared. "What the fuck are you pair doing through here?"

"We found a body down an old close under the Royal Mile," said Cullen. "A rock star in the making. Got no leads other than Alex Hughes, who reported him missing nineteen months ago."

A flicker of amusement danced across Bain's face. "Hughes?"

Cullen hit his hand off the desk, much harder and louder than intended. "Can one of you tell us what's going on here?"

Bain and McCrea exchanged a look, grinning.

Bain folded his arms. "Now you know what it feels like to be kept in the dark, Sundance. I lost count of the number of times you went off on your lonesome and pulled a rabbit out of a fuckin' hat."

"Hughes," said Cullen. "Tell me now, or we're leaving and I'm getting DCI Turnbull involved."

Bain leaned back in the chair and started laughing. "I'm in charge of his murder investigation."

Cullen's mouth felt dry. "Hughes has been *murdered*?"

"Aye," said Bain, pulling a wad of paper out of his file. "Here you go, Sherlock."

Cullen flicked through the pages. It was true. "What

happened?"

Bain rubbed his top lip. "Couple of uniform got called to his flat in the wee small hours of the morning. They had to break the door down. They found Hughes dead. A stabbing."

"Ours was stabbed, too," said Cullen.

Bain leaned forward. "Are you trying to steal my case here? Bit of a coincidence your body is found the same week his mate gets stabbed."

"Nothing of the sort," said Cullen. "I think we should keep the cases independent."

Bain sniffed. "Not sure. It all sounds a bit suspicious, if you ask me. I might need to co-opt your investigation into mine. Need to make sure we leverage all opportunities here."

"You sound like Turnbull," said Cullen.

"You should have checked with us before you came through," said McCrea. "Just as well me and Davie were interviewing his upstairs neighbours when you blundered in."

"Whatever," said Cullen.

Bain got to his feet. "I'll get the paperwork going on taking over your case. If I were you, I'd be here tomorrow morning for my seven am briefing."

"I need to speak to Cargill and Methven about this," said Cullen.

Bain waved from the door. "Say a big hello to them from me."

28

Cullen and Buxton got back to Leith Walk station just over an hour later. They finally found Cargill at her desk near Turnbull's office, poring over a spreadsheet on a laptop. Methven was nowhere to be seen.

Cullen cleared his throat.

Cargill waved him off, still staring at the screen.

"Ma'am."

She looked up and slowly closed the screen. "Can this wait?"

"Afraid not," said Cullen, wheeling a desk chair over. "I don't know how to say this, so I'll just come out with it. You know the case I'm working?"

"The Strang case," said Cargill, nodding. "Stabbing. Tunnels under the Old Town. Correct?"

"Right," said Cullen. "I'm afraid it's just taken a turn for the worse."

Cargill rubbed her forehead. "I have a feeling I'm not going to like this."

"It's linked to a case on Strathclyde's books," said Cullen.

"Strathclyde?" said Cargill. "It'll all be water under the bridge soon."

"That's the thing," said Cullen. "The case is run by DI Bain."

"Now I see."

"There are slight similarities," said Cullen. "The

person who reported our guy missing is their victim. He was found dead in Glasgow on Thursday morning."

"Could just be a coincidence," said Cargill.

"I don't believe in coincidences."

"So what was our esteemed former colleague saying, then?"

"He's trying to take over our case. He told me to attend his seven am briefing tomorrow."

"I'm not having that," said Cargill, shaking her head. "I'll speak to Jim and we'll get something sorted out."

"Thanks," said Cullen.

"You know DI Bain has a particular axe to grind with a few of us through here. Try not to be deflected from your own investigation. Just get on with it and treat it as a separate case until I tell you otherwise, okay?"

"Will do," said Cullen.

Experience told him not to believe her. His gut ached with the dread of getting stuck back in Bain's vortex of chaos.

29

Cullen sent Buxton and Chantal to speak to Strang's colleagues at the record shop, chase up his friends and try to find his flatmates. Hopefully, that would give him peace and quiet to get stuck into something that progressed the case.

"Are you going to be here long, Sergeant?"

Cullen looked up at Methven putting his leather jacket on. "Probably, sir."

"Remember the Clear Desk Policy."

Cullen looked down at his desk, now covered with photocopies of the case files for Strang's murder and his disappearance in 2011. "I'll clear up before I leave tonight."

Methven checked his watch. "I'll hopefully get to Mellis's before they shut. Got a sodding dinner party I'd much rather not be attending."

"Wife's friends?"

Methven scowled. "Worse, her work colleagues."

"You could have us all round."

"I don't want to get divorced." Methven put a stack of coins in his trouser pocket. "I'll maybe call later."

Cullen watched him stroll off, relieved to be on his own. He jolted upright, determined to get stuck into work.

Caffeine drove him on as much as the determination to keep the case separate from Bain's. The new Chief

Constable of Police Scotland was the current head of Strathclyde - unless they got a result by Sunday night, Cullen feared his influence would push the cases into a merger.

He took a swig from the bottle of water he'd bought with lunch and looked around the almost-empty office.

Cullen turned to his computer and logged onto the newspaper archives, focusing on the six months leading up to Strang's disappearance. There was the occasional feature about the band. As Johnson and Williamson said, they were getting some semblance of a profile.

The biggest was a review of the last Invisibles gig in the *Argus* by someone called Sonny Bangs. Cullen had a vague recollection of the name Lester Bangs from his old man's punk obsession. He hadn't thought it was a real name.

The review covered a whole page of the broadsheet, which Cullen thought was unusual for an unsigned band. He carefully read it, full of gushing praise, touting the band as the next big thing, *'sure to eclipse Expect Delays'.* The picture alongside showed Strang in full-on Iggy Pop mode, cutting open his chest onstage with a broken beer bottle. It was so busy people were standing on tables to see the band.

A second inset picture showed him smashing a guitar like the cover of The Clash's *London Calling.* Cullen frowned, recalling the expensive Fender Buxton had drooled over in Strang's bedroom. The guitar in the photo was red. He googled it and found a musicians' forum recommending switching to a cheap guitar for the last song as an economical way of looking like The Who in the sixties.

The band played four songs in twelve minutes and

Bangs cited the Jesus and Mary Chain, referencing a notorious series of short and angry gigs in London during the mid-eighties, at least one of which led to a riot. Cullen googled again and found he knew a couple of their songs from the film *Lost in Translation*.

According to the review, the last song of the concert - the last song James Strang ever performed - was a wall of feedback. Strang was shouting 'they took all the money and all the fame', turning it into a mantra and inciting the crowd to sing along. He smashed the guitar halfway through and walked off through the crowd, blood dripping from his torso.

According to the article, there was some trouble after the gig. Cullen took it to be more hyperbole. He checked through police reports of the night, finding a couple of arrests on the Cowgate as a result of crowd violence, unclear whether it was from the gig or the football.

He dug into Lester Bangs - he was a punk rock journalist, helping fuel the American punk movement in the mid-seventies before covering the rise of the Sex Pistols, The Clash and countless others in the UK a few years later. Sonny Bangs was definitely a made-up name, someone trying to set themselves up as some sort of local punk rock figurehead. Maybe he was associated with the band.

Cullen needed to speak to Sonny Bangs about James Strang.

30

Cullen parked his car on Holyrood Road and walked to the *Argus*'s offices, just across from *The Scotsman* and Dynamic Earth. It was round the corner from the municipal swimming pool that passed for the Scottish Parliament building.

He shivered as he marched on down the road, the early evening wind cutting through him, the sun close to setting.

He entered the concrete, chrome and glass construction. The building teemed with activity through the floor-to-ceiling windows, the Sunday edition just about ready for the press, last minute football stories no doubt throwing the sport section into disarray.

Manning the reception desk was a young Asian man, wearing a sharp suit and a beard that would take a good twenty minutes of chiselling every morning.

Cullen smiled as he produced his warrant card and introduced himself. "I'm looking for a Sonny Bangs. He works on your features desk."

"One moment." He checked on his computer. "There's nobody of that name here."

Cullen pulled out a print of the article. "This was written in August two thousand and eleven."

"There's nobody on the system."

"Can you try-"

"We got a problem here?"

A grey-haired man in his late forties was frowning at Cullen.

"Sorry, who are you?" said Cullen.

The man pulled an ID badge out of his pocket. "The name is Alexander Spence. I'm the Editor."

"I need to speak to Sonny Bangs as part of a murder inquiry."

"He doesn't work here any more," said Spence. "We let him go in the last round of cuts."

Cullen knew exactly what he meant. Newspaper circulation in Scotland was in free fall, continual rounds of redundancies the only weapon the owners seemed to have in their armoury. He could see a time when there was just one Scottish national paper rather than the current three.

"Can you give me a phone number?" said Cullen.

"Have you got a warrant?"

Cullen ground his teeth. "I'll get one."

"You do that," said Spence. "Now kindly clear off will you? I've got all seven days under my belt now and a Sunday edition to put to bed."

Cullen stared him down for a few seconds then decided it was best to leave it. Decimated readership figures or not, the press still had power. He nodded slowly, before leaving the building.

Cullen's Plan B was his ex-flatmate, Richard McAlpine, who worked for the paper. He got out his phone and called as he walked.

No answer.

31

Cullen buzzed the door and waited. At least they'd got the intercom fixed. He felt a slight pang of guilt, realising he hadn't been back since moving out, only seeing Tom and Rich once each since.

"Yo."

"Hi Tom, it's Scott."

"Who?"

"Very funny."

"Up you come, mate."

Cullen trudged up the stairs, getting flashbacks of every time he'd climbed them, drunk and sober.

Tom stood in the doorway.

Cullen was shocked by how much weight he'd lost. "I'm looking for Tom."

"Aye, very funny," said Tom, tapping his receding belly. "5:2 fasting, mate. It bloody works."

"I can see that," said Cullen. "My old boy has been doing it. You look knackered, though."

"Cheers," said Tom as he let Cullen in. "Been working in London a lot. Big project down there in Corporate."

"Are Alba Bank branching out?" said Cullen.

Tom shrugged. "We've always had a presence down there, nothing like RBS or Lloyds have, but let's just say it needs some TLC. Bit of a fucking disaster, to be honest with you."

Cullen knew too much about Tom's employers, one of

the three big banks in Edinburgh, from years of living together.

"How's my room?" said Cullen.

Tom spoke in a whisper. "The guy who rents it now is a bit of a weirdo. Don't think I'll renew his lease."

Cullen handed him a pile of CDs. "Cheers for these. Some good stuff there."

"You still love a freebie, Skinky."

Cullen laughed. "Remember when you did music? Did you ever come across a guy called Jimi Danger?"

Tom shrugged. "Is he a DJ?"

Cullen shook his head. "Sang in a band."

"Well, it's not likely a techno DJ would meet a singer from a band, is it?" said Tom.

"I guess not." Cullen shrugged. "Does the name The Invisibles mean anything to you?"

Tom frowned. "It's a comic. Grant Morrison did it. One of my very favourites."

Cullen clicked his fingers. "I knew it. It's been bugging me all day."

"I'd lend you it," said Tom, "but it's a bit advanced for you. Very metaphysical."

"Very good."

"So, what brings you back?"

"I need to speak to Rich," said Cullen.

"What's he done this time? Lost his phone again? Had to scarper from some bloke's flat after his boyfriend found them *in flagrante delicto*?"

"Nothing like that," said Cullen, laughing. "You two getting on okay?"

"Yeah, fine," said Tom, looking the opposite, but as though he couldn't be arsed talking about it. "Not seen him, but I think he's in. I've been working all afternoon."

"Cheers." Cullen walked to Rich's door and knocked, knowing from bitter experience never to barge in without an invite.

"Come in," said Rich.

"Are you alone?" said Cullen, as he entered.

Rich was sitting at his desk, laptop open. His eyes widened and he slammed it shut.

"That a porn site you're on?" said Cullen.

Rich rubbed his chin. "It's a detective book I'm writing."

"Interesting."

"Aye," said Rich. "It's harder than I thought it would be. Writing about the real world is much easier than writing fiction, that's for sure. The stuff I've seen would seem over the top in a book."

"Try living the life of a detective," said Cullen. "Feels like everybody makes money out of policing except for the police."

"Well, I'll give you some kickbacks if I ever get published," said Rich.

"How you doing?" said Cullen.

"I'm okay," said Rich, grinning, "but I know that expression. This isn't a social call, is it?"

Cullen nodded. "Perceptive as ever. I was just at your work."

Rich's eyes shot to the ceiling. "Tell me you didn't mention me."

"Relax," said Cullen. "I can do discrete. Is Alexander Spence your boss?"

Rich grimaced. "He's kind of the boss's boss, but aye."

"He's a piece of work," said Cullen, retrieving the article from his jacket pocket and handing it to Rich. "I need to speak to this journalist."

Rich looked at it. "Sonny Bangs?"

"I'm investigating the death of James Strang," said Cullen.

Rich frowned. "That's the boy who disappeared a few years ago, right?"

"It is," said Cullen. "Do you know anything about it?"

Rich shook his head. "Don't look at me, mate. I was in London at the time."

"Okay," said Cullen, laughing. "Sonny Bangs, then. He seems to know a fair amount about him. Might even be a mate. Spence told me he was let go in the cuts. Is that right?"

Rich nodded. "Alan Stephens is his real name. Think he lives in Midlothian somewhere."

"Thanks."

"I'll text you his mobile number," said Rich.

"Cheers," said Cullen. "I still can't understand why you moved back from London. That place seems decimated."

"It is. I wanted to get away from London and focus on writing books. There was stuff happening at the paper, so I took the easy money. It's much cheaper to live up here, especially on London money."

"It's hard enough living here on Edinburgh money."

32

Cullen knocked on the door of the modern bungalow in Penicuik and waited, encouraged by the lights and noise from inside.

Alan Stephens answered it, layers of stubble piling up on his face. Cullen's warrant card solicited a surprised look and entrance to the house.

Stephens showed him to the living room. "Sorry about the mess," he said, sitting down on an armchair. "My wife left me three weeks ago."

Cullen figured it was once a family room, but was now descending into bachelor squalor.

"I gather you were let go from the *Argus*. Is that right?"

Stephens nodded. "I've not worked since I was made redundant. I managed to pick up some agency work, but that dried up quickly."

Unlike him, thought Cullen - there were many half-empty bottles of spirits dotted around the place. "That must be difficult."

"Aye," said Stephens. "The cuts have been bad. Even the few lucky ones left will have to work twice as hard for the same money." He stroked his stubble. "The house is on the market. Doubt we'll get what it's worth. My savings are all gone. It's a bloody mess."

Cullen nodded as he took out The Invisibles concert review. "I'm looking for information about one James Strang. You probably knew him as Jimi Danger."

Stephens' eyes narrowed, lost on the page, finding focus for the first time since Cullen had arrived. "Jimi?"

"His body has been found," said Cullen.

Stephens swallowed. Cullen thought he might have sobered up in that instant, a spike of adrenalin purging his system of the alcohol. "I knew the lad had disappeared. He's dead?"

Cullen nodded. "I gather you knew him reasonably well?"

Stephens pinched the bridge of his nose. "I sort of knew him. He used to pester me for gig reviews and features. He had a lot of front, I'll give him that. He was living the life of a rock 'n' roll star, or at least trying to. In my business, it's quite important to build up a legend around the person. Jimi had that already."

"Tell me about that concert," said Cullen.

Stephens shrugged. "You've read my piece. What more do you want to know?"

"It was only a week or so before Mr Strang went missing," said Cullen. "We now believe he was killed at that time."

Stephens stared back at the review clipping. "Jimi looked like he hadn't slept in days. The boy was totally crazed, eyes all over the place. When he went onstage that night, he was drunk out of his head." He pointed at the photo of the singer. "He had a bottle of Jack Daniels on stage with him. Tanned half of it in ten minutes."

"Had you seen them live before?"

"Loads of times," said Stephens. "I used to go to gigs most nights, sometimes in Edinburgh but mostly in Glasgow. I didn't get to see a lot of stuff I liked, but I loved what that band did. My sort of music."

"How did Mr Strang seem over the few months

leading up to his disappearance?" said Cullen.

"I saw them about six or seven times in that last year," said Stephens, "and I'd say he got progressively worse over the last few months."

"Worse in what way?"

"One of the things I heard Jimi talking about was a record deal," said Stephens. "I think it fell through and he struggled to cope with it."

"Can you elaborate?" said Cullen.

"He reckoned they were offered a contract," said Stephens. "They'd taken it through lawyers and so on and they were close to signing. Something happened. I don't know what. It was pulled. No idea why. Jimi just sort of imploded after that."

Cullen felt a flare of irritation. Why hadn't this come from the band?

He needed to speak to them again.

33

Back at Leith Walk station, Buxton was working at a laptop in the Incident Room.

"Have you seen Chantal?" said Cullen.

Buxton looked up. "Think she headed off to see a mate."

Anger started to well up in Cullen before he remembered the number of times he'd left early while a major investigation was underway. "I wanted an update from her. Crystal will be chewing my balls about it, no doubt."

"Sorry, mate," said Buxton. "Anything I can help with?"

"Doubt it," said Cullen. "How'd you get on with the workmates?"

"Needle in a bloody haystack," said Buxton. "Even figuring out who was working there at the time is next to impossible. They were all casual labour. The level of documentation is light, shall we say."

Cullen sighed - it was another Methven red herring. "Are you in tomorrow?"

"I can't, mate," said Buxton. "As I told Crystal earlier, I've got to go to a wedding. In Fife of all places. Arse end of Dunfermline. You?"

"No choice," said Cullen, feeling the entire case on his shoulders. "I've got a mountain of stuff to get through. Aside from this one, I need to get on top of just about every other case I've had in the last month. They all seem to be heading to court at the same time."

Buxton got to his feet and stretched. "I'll be thinking of you when I'm drinking Stella tomorrow."

"Yeah, in Dunfermline," said Cullen.

Buxton laughed. "You know, that paperwork sounds more appealing by the minute." He flicked his hair back again. "We got nowhere with the friends Johnson and Williamson gave us. Me and Chantal spoke to every single one of them. Nothing."

"What about the flatmates?" said Cullen.

"Nothing so far," said Buxton. "Only managed to track half of them."

Cullen furrowed his brow. "Remember his mother said something about a girl, Jane maybe? Did anyone mention it?"

Buxton flicked through his notebook. "Don't think so, mate." He tapped on a page. "Oh, Crystal got Charlie Kidd to go through his Facebook, Myspace, Google+ and Schoolbook accounts."

"No Twitter?" said Cullen.

"Not that we could find, but I wouldn't put it past him." Buxton shrugged. "Anyway, Charlie found nothing. Strang just spammed people about gigs and CDs. Not so much as a personal message in there."

"Worth a shot, I suppose," said Cullen, irritated by Methven going over his head.

"Need anything else from me?" said Buxton.

Cullen shook his head. "That's probably it. Have fun tomorrow."

Buxton sloped off, leaving Cullen alone in the Incident Room. He sat down at his laptop and starting sifting through the last few days' emails, which only added to his action list. He completed a few of the more important items, the tasks most likely to incur a bollocking if not completed.

He took a break after half an hour, deciding music would help. He opened the YouTube app on his phone and found a video for The Invisibles' only proper single - *Goneaway* - in amongst a load of concert footage taken on smartphones.

As he worked, typing up sections of his notebook, he listened to the video on a loop. He found himself singing another tune, eventually working out it was an Expect Delays song, an older one that irritated him as much as their new single.

The music cut off - he had an incoming call from Methven.

"Good evening, Sergeant."

"Evening, sir," said Cullen. "I tried looking for you, but couldn't see you anywhere?"

Methven groaned down the line. "Got a dinner party tonight. I'm on dessert duties. Had to get a selection of cheese in and now I'm making baked Alaska. The whole thing is costing me an arm and a leg."

"Your wife earns a fair wedge, though," said Cullen. He didn't know how much he wanted to push it - Methven was easy to get a rise out of, but he was certainly one to lash out quickly.

"Give me an update," said Methven, sounding in no mood for banter.

Cullen briefed him - other than discovering Alex Hughes' death, the only real progress he'd made that day was with Stephens.

"And Bain is running the Hughes investigation," said Cullen, closing off.

"DI Bain?" said Methven. "Sodding hell. I'll need to strategise with Alison on this."

"You got off lightly," said Cullen. "You didn't have to speak to him."

"Going back to this band, then," said Methven, "they were offered a record deal and it was subsequently rescinded. Is that correct?"

"That seems to be the size of it," said Cullen.

"And you got nothing of this from the other members of the band?" said Methven.

"Not even a sniff."

"Interesting," said Methven. "You mentioned Strang felt under a lot of pressure. Could it be suicide?"

"You were at the post mortem," said Cullen. "I wasn't. What did Deeley reckon?"

"It was Sweeney, not Deeley," said Methven. "He just attended."

Cullen rolled his eyes. "What did *she* reckon, then?"

"That suicide was highly unlikely," said Methven. "Given the forensic evidence we subsequently obtained, it was upgraded to impossible."

Cullen was glad Methven couldn't see him making faces. "We could use it to our advantage with Bain. Suggesting it's not a murder would clearly separate the cases."

"No games here," said Methven. "We do things by the book."

"Bain will play games," said Cullen. "You know he'll ride roughshod over this, try to find some easy suspect and we'll have to stop him from getting up to God knows what."

"You're probably right," said Methven, "but I don't like to play that way. What other leads do we have?"

Cullen looked at his notebook. "I need to speak to the other two about this record deal. Having access to the Strathclyde files on this Hughes guy might be a good idea as well. Other than that, Strang comes from Dalhousie, which is where I'm from. I could do some more digging up there."

"It's an option," said Methven.

Cullen didn't know where else he could steer the conversation. "I'm going to write up where we've got to, then I'm going to head. Is that okay with you?"

"I'll let you decide, Sergeant."

"What's that supposed to mean?" said Cullen.

"You're a DS now, Cullen, I expect you to exert the judgment of one."

34

In the end Cullen decided to finish typing up his notes before going home, figuring any evidence Methven had of him falling behind wouldn't be in his favour. He left the station just before ten, leaving his car in the garage.

He walked onto Leith Street, passing the Saturday night crowds leaving the Playhouse or piling into the club in the Omni centre. He didn't know the name of it - he'd only been to the cinema with Sharon a few times. He crossed Waterloo Place onto North Bridge, the bitter wind slicing through him.

He passed the smokers outside the Royal Mile pubs and wondered where his life had got to. Usually, he'd just be starting to get into his Saturday night stride, already mentally navigating the optimal route between bars and clubs, but instead he'd worked until ten. All because of the restructure and the dangled carrot of promotion.

Monday was the big day of reckoning, when the force would change for good. At the back of his mind was the fact he'd heard nothing. Aside from Methven's innuendo and pep talks, nobody had formally briefed him. He hoped no news was good news.

At the entrance to the close, he spotted a teenager pissing against the bins just behind the stair door.

Cullen called after him, making the ned hurriedly tuck himself in before running off. He shook his head as he unlocked the main door, counting the number of times he'd done something similar.

As he hung up his coat, Fluffy started bleating again. Cullen knelt down. "Are you a guard dog trapped in the body of a fat cat?"

The cat reared up and rubbed his chin against Cullen's finger.

"He's sensitive about his weight," said Sharon from the bedroom.

Cullen walked through. He kissed her on the forehead then sat on the edge of the bed.

"No kiss on the lips?" she said.

"I don't want to catch your germs," said Cullen.

Sharon smiled. "Believe me, *I* don't want you to catch it."

"How are you doing?"

She groaned. Her hair was lank and greasy and her eyes puffy. "I've been in bed all day, choked with this bloody bug. I feel terrible. I'm shivering. That's not good, is it?"

"Could be flu," said Cullen.

"I told you I've got the flu."

"Not what most people call a cold," said Cullen. "*Actual* flu, as in influenza."

"Pedant," said Sharon, smiling. "I'm supposed to be back in on Monday but I don't know if I'll make it." She grimaced. "This is the worst possible time to be sick."

"Take it easy," said Cullen. "The most important thing is to get well. People die of flu."

"Thanks. That's really cheered me up."

"Have you had your ginger bed friend while I've been away?" said Cullen.

Sharon grinned mischievously. "I've substituted one ginger for another."

"I'm hardly ginger," said Cullen. "Fuck's sake."

She held his hand. "I'm just joking. You're clearly dark blonde."

"My hair is *brown*," said Cullen. "My stubble might be ginger, but I'm never doing Movember. Happy to pay for the privilege, mind, but nobody wants to see my moustache."

"I forgot you were so sensitive about your colouring," she said, smiling.

"What have you been up to today?" said Cullen.

"Just reading. Chantal came round for a bit."

"Right, so you're the friend she was going to see," said Cullen, looking away.

"You don't need to keep an eye on her all the time," said Sharon. "You can trust her."

"I know," said Cullen, "but I needed to get an update from her in case Crystal wanted one from me."

"The joys of management," said Sharon. "I remember the time you used to report to me. Bain was a nightmare for knowing exactly what everyone was up to, especially you."

Cullen winced at the mention of the name.

"What's the matter?" said Sharon.

"You'll never guess who I bumped into today," said Cullen.

"Oh no," said Sharon, shutting her eyes. "Bain?"

"Got it in one," said Cullen. "He's working in Glasgow. Turns out he's heading up the Strathclyde murder squad. One of my leads lives through there, so me and Budgie went to his flat. He was murdered last week."

"That's just what you need," said Sharon.

"Tell me about it," said Cullen. "He's up to his old tricks again. It's like nothing happened." He laughed.

"Oh, he's got a mail order Thai Bride now."

Sharon held her hand up to her mouth. "Oh my God."

"I hope laugher is the best medicine," said Cullen, "but I doubt it. I'm absolutely starving, can I get you anything?"

"I'm fine, thanks," said Sharon, settling back down against the pile of pillows behind her.

"Lemsip? Hot water bottle?"

"I'm fine, really," she said. "Just sort yourself out."

Sunday
31st March 2013

35

Despite his exhaustion, Cullen had a poor night's sleep thanks to Marta Hunter, her kids and her drugs. He hadn't been able to stop thinking about them.

As he sat in Cargill's nine am briefing, he was already on his second strong Americano of the day. There were very few in, just Cargill, Methven and Chantal, though the rest of the station was busy with uniformed officers.

Methven finished his update and Cargill's gaze shifted to Chantal, skipping Cullen. "DC Jain, can you give us your update, please?"

Chantal nodded. "Certainly, ma'am. I've got a few leads under active investigation. First, there's the screwdriver. I'm getting nowhere but I'll chase the vendor again if I have another day like yesterday."

She ticked something off on her pad. "Next, ADS Cullen asked me to look into Strang's workmates at the record shop. It's proving difficult as they were all casual labour." She gestured at the mind map on the wall. "I'm having to rely on whatever Beth Williamson tells me, which isn't ideal."

She turned to a new page in her notebook. "Next, I'm going to continue working through the flatmates."

"Fine," said Cargill. Her eyes locked on Cullen. "Sergeant, I need you to go through to Glasgow."

Cullen struggled to show anything other than abject disappointment. "Shouldn't I focus on Edinburgh?"

"DC Jain can cover," said Cargill.

"You know it's only a matter of time before Bain sees me as his resource, right?" said Cullen.

"I just want you to investigate from the Lothian & Borders perspective," said Cargill. "See if there is a connection or not. Alex Hughes is our only lead here. We need to find out if he knew anything about our guy."

"That'll be difficult without getting dragged into their case," said Cullen.

"Regardless, we do need a presence through there and I'm seconding you to the investigation."

Cullen looked out of the window. "Yes, ma'am."

"Dismissed," said Cargill.

Cullen stood there, stunned. *Glasgow.* He wouldn't be able to manage Chantal and Buxton from forty-odd miles down the M8. With Methven and Cargill taking a more active role, he was surplus to requirements.

He felt a hand on his shoulder.

"A word, Sergeant," said Methven, tugging him by the arm and leading him over to a corner of the emptying Incident Room. "I'm a bit disappointed with your attitude there."

"You know what Bain is like," said Cullen. "If it's just a case of me going through there and maybe finding some leads, then fine. You know what his agenda will be, though."

"Just go through their files," said Methven.

"It won't work like that," said Cullen. "DI Cargill has seconded me. That's it."

"Keep Bain at arm's reach," said Methven.

"Like you did?" said Cullen. He'd never seen Methven even attempt to keep Bain's excesses in check.

"You've been given a clear direction," said Methven.

"Arm's reach."

"I thought I was supposed to be acting like a DS?" said Cullen. "I need to manage DC Jain."

"She's an adult and she can look after herself while you're gone."

"What did you mean about me acting like a DS, then?" said Cullen.

"You need to grow up."

36

Cullen pulled into the Govan station car park, a familiar purple Mondeo following him in, parking a couple of spaces away.

Bain got out, beaming at Cullen as he walked over carrying a tray of coffees. "Nice to see you pitch up, Sundance. Didn't expect you'd actually show your face. We've been here for hours."

"Just following orders," said Cullen.

"Did you get any donuts for us from that new place?" said Bain.

Cullen shook his head. "It was queued right out to the M8. Besides, I'm not sure you deserve it."

Bain looked at Cullen's bottle green Golf, seventeen years old. "I would have thought someone who earned a DS's wedge would get a proper motor."

Cullen ignored the bait. "I need to review your case files for any correlation with ours."

"No, you don't," said Bain. "A little birdie called me and told me you're seconded to my investigation."

"That's not what I was told," said Cullen, avoiding eye contact as he lied.

"I don't care, Sundance," said Bain. "You're shadowing McCrea while you're through here."

"We keep going back to this," said Cullen. "I'm not under your control."

"You are an ADS, Sundance," said Bain. "I'm a DI,

you're seconded to me. You're doing what I tell you."

"Just let me see the case files," said Cullen, fed up with him.

"You're shadowing McCrea."

"How about I get familiar with the case files while you have a word with Methven and conclude whatever 'pissing up the wall' contest you're playing?" said Cullen.

Bain looked Cullen up and down, grinning. "I always liked the way you do absolutely fuckin' anything to avoid taking orders."

Cullen bit his tongue, conscious of the stream of expletives that might flow out.

37

By eleven, Cullen had taken pages of notes on the case. In the busy Incident Room, he'd put his earphones in and gone through the forensic report and post mortem before attacking the master case file.

The body was found by a police officer responding to complaints of noise raised by a neighbour. Alex Hughes was stabbed in the kitchen of his flat and left to bleed out, the kitchen knife found at his feet subsequently confirmed as the murder weapon.

Cullen looked at the summary notes he'd made of the post mortem. The coroner had ruled out suicide.

A suicide would show telltale signs - a particular angle of entry, markers such as wrist cuts from previous attempts and the likelihood of Hughes lifting up his clothes rather than stabbing through his t-shirt and cardigan.

The fresh wounds Hughes had were almost certainly defensive wounds, implying he was attacked.

The other angle was drugs. The blood toxicology report, open on Cullen's desk, noted traces of cannabis and opiates in Hughes' bloodstream. Cullen struggled to reconcile it with Marta Hunter's account - Hughes had ended their relationship because of her addiction. Yet, Hughes had traces of a similar drug in his system. Marta mentioned something about Hughes smoking heroin - it must have escalated.

Nagging in Cullen's mind was how Hughes managed to live in a one bedroom flat in an upmarket area of Glasgow, full of students and young professionals.

McCrea swung by, carrying two mugs of black coffee. He handed one to Cullen. "The gaffer said you were a fiend for the coffee."

Cullen took a sip. It tasted burnt with at least four spoonfuls of sugar. He couldn't work out if it was Bain or McCrea playing a joke. "Thanks." He pushed it to the side, determined not to touch it again. He tapped at the blood toxicology report. "Says there were opiates in Hughes' bloodstream. Is it heroin?"

McCrea nodded. "We think so."

"Injecting or smoking?"

"We think he mostly smoked the heroin rather than injected it," said McCrea, perched on the edge of the desk, pretending to inject into his arm. "That said, we found his works. Hypodermic needle, strap, spoon, lighter, the whole shooting match. Didn't find any gear, though."

"What about the knife?" said Cullen.

"We found a knife at his feet," said McCrea. "Part of a set he had in the kitchen. John Lewis's finest from about two thousand and four, came with the flat." He took a slurp of coffee. "They didn't find any fingerprints or DNA except the victim's."

"That's far from ideal," said Cullen.

McCrea shrugged. "It is and it isn't. It could be a professional job. We just don't know."

"What leads do we have?" said Cullen, immediately regretting the use of 'we'.

McCrea put his empty mug down. "Not a lot. It's nowhere near as bad as your case, mind."

"Any suspects?" said Cullen, almost grinding his teeth.

"None yet. Got a few irons in the fire. Nothing to trouble you with but we're not doing too badly."

"How could he afford a one bedroom flat in the West End?" said Cullen.

"Ooh, get you," said McCrea, grinning. "You know about the West End. The posh bit."

"I know Glasgow fairly well," said Cullen. "Plus, the knife is 'John Lewis's finest' as you said. That's not a cheap flat. Have you thought about it or not?"

McCrea smiled. "Aye, we have. It's nothing to write home about."

Cullen nodded slowly, disbelieving him. "I'm just about finished here. Can we go and have a look round the flat?"

McCrea tilted his head. "Don't see why not. The Scene of Crime boys have been through it a couple of times now and given us the nod."

"I hope your lot are as much fun as ours," said Cullen.

"Don't worry, they'll be a combined nuisance soon."

38

Cullen was relieved to get inside Hughes' flat without being assaulted.

It was a lot smaller than Cullen had imagined, taking up a thin sliver of the building. There were only two rooms - a combined living room and kitchen with a separate bathroom overlooking the communal drying green at the back.

"We found him in the kitchenette there," said McCrea.

Cullen felt a pang - his gran used to call her kitchen that. She passed away in January and the wound still felt raw.

"Time was they all would have been a wee bedsit like this," said McCrea. "The rest of this block has been bought up and turned into bigger flats. Get a fair bit more money for it these days, especially round here. No idea why this is still a bedsit." He kicked a sofa bed, still unfolded. "Bloody SOCOs were supposed to pack that away when they finished."

An expensive-looking guitar and a small practice amp sat alongside. There was no TV or stereo, just a netbook on the desk.

McCrea pointed to the rolls of tinfoil in the kitchen area, supermarket own brand. "That's why we think he was a smoker."

"You're an absolute genius," said Cullen.

"Less of that," said McCrea. "The gaffer said you

149

could be a bit of a cock. Normally, I'd be tempted not to believe him but I'll start siding with him if you keep that up."

"Thought you'd found his works?" said Cullen.

"We did, aye."

"And yet you think he chased the dragon rather than mainlining," said Cullen.

"Listen to you. Sounds like you've just read *Trainspotting* while listening to Spacemen 3." McCrea tapped his forearm. "There were very few track marks on the boy's arms. But there is a shitload of tinfoil. I'll let you work it out."

Cullen tried to avoid shaking his head. McCrea was starting to come close to Bain in Cullen's ranking of least favourite officers. Instead, he had a look around the room. There were stacks of books on the floor, mostly fiction, but a few piles seemed to be rock biographies. Julian Cope, Joe Strummer, Morrissey, David Bowie, John Lennon.

"You got anything off the computer?" said Cullen.

"Like what?"

"Tell me you've had it looked at?"

"Why would we?" said McCrea. "Bit of a kibosh on spending on that sort of thing, big man. We live in a time of austerity. Might not seem like that in Edinburgh but it's certainly like that through here. We got his mobile."

One of the first things Cullen would have done was have a Forensic IT Analyst pore through files and emails. He looked around the room, fists clenched. Beside Hughes' computer was a stack of flyers. He went over and picked one up.

He showed it to McCrea. "Some band called The Ferocious Butterfly are playing at Stereo at two pm today. Do you reckon he could be involved?"

"Must be," said McCrea. "Look at the number of posters on the wall."

Cullen looked up. They were mostly gig posters for The Ferocious Butterfly with the occasional one for The Invisibles. "It's this afternoon. Do you fancy going?"

"Why not?"

39

As McCrea drove them through the Glasgow lunchtime traffic, all Cullen could think about was that the flats looked just like parts of Edinburgh. It felt like he was being driven through his own city in some mad dream, the streets configured slightly differently.

"Never been to a lunchtime gig before," said McCrea.

"I didn't know you got them," said Cullen. "In my experience they're usually in dark rooms at eight o'clock, with bouncers trying to rush things through before they chuck everyone out before the club night."

McCrea chuckled. "That's about the size of it. Glasgow's a funny city, though. I think it's something to do with how big the place is but, as well as your neds and gangs and that, you've got this amazing music scene. It's full of scenesters and schmoozers and all that, but it's amazing how many big bands have come out of Glasgow."

"You sound like you're talking from experience."

"My wee brother was in a band that did quite well," said McCrea. "Played T in the Park a few times. Gigs in London and Manchester. Works in a bank now."

McCrea pulled them into a parking bay on Argyle Street and led them to a bohemian-looking pub next door to a more earthy boozer. Cullen resented the five quid on the door, but didn't want to resort to privileges of his job to get in.

The long, thin room seemed busy for a Sunday lunchtime and was full of skinny boys and girls with hipster t-shirts and trendy haircuts. Cullen felt out of place in his suit and shirt.

They headed for the bar and were quickly served by a man with dyed blonde hair.

"I'm a police officer," said Cullen. "I'm not going to cause any trouble, I'm just looking for The Ferocious Butterfly."

"Well, they're playing two sets today and they're between them just now. You'll need to wait until the end if you want to speak to them."

Cullen's stomach reminded him he hadn't eaten much all day. "Can I get a bacon roll?"

The barman folded his arms. "You know this place is vegan, right?"

"What does that mean?" said Cullen.

"No meat or animal products."

"So, what have you got?" said Cullen.

McCrea barged in. "Get us two burgers. Chips with both."

The barman passed the order through to the kitchen. "Can I get you boys something to drink?"

Cullen was sorely tempted by the impressive selection of bottled lagers - Czech and German - and a fair amount of British and American craft beer, but ordered a cola in the end.

The band returned to the small stage. They were a three-piece and didn't look like they belonged in the same city as each other, let alone the same band. The singer was skinny, the acoustic guitar strapped to his body looking like it would topple him over. The drummer had an undercut, his hair tied back in a ponytail and shaved around the sides. The female keyboard player looked like she was trying to hide behind her instrument.

Cullen and McCrea stood with their pints of organic cola and took in the show. It was far from being Cullen's thing, but McCrea seemed to be getting into it. Virtually all of their songs stemmed from Belle and Sebastian, one of the bigger Glasgow bands. Cullen wasn't a fan - an ex-girlfriend had been obsessed with their early output and he'd heard more than enough to last a lifetime.

The Ferocious Butterfly singer had an irritating habit of introducing his songs with lengthy descriptions along the lines of "This song is called *The girl in Morrisons didn't give me cashback*, it's about a girl in Morrisons not giving me cashback" and then singing "The girl in Morrisons didn't give me cashback."

"We should have waited outside," said Cullen, halfway through the show.

The barman handed over their food. Cullen lifted the lid on the roll and inspected the burger - it looked healthy, perfect for his new regime. He spooned relish on and devoured it. The chips were covered in Cajun spices and hit the spot.

Cullen pushed his plate away as the band finished, applause and whistles filling the room. Thankfully, they didn't indulge in an encore. Cullen walked towards them as they packed their gear up.

McCrea grabbed his wrist. "Give them five minutes."

"They'll get away," said Cullen.

McCrea shook his head. "No, they won't. They've got a load of people to speak to. Five minutes won't hurt."

40

Cullen secured a back room, which stank of stale beer. It was filled with crates and barrels and was quite possibly the least glamorous place Cullen had ever been in.

"Alex couldn't bother himself to turn up to our last two practices," said James Preston, The Ferocious Butterfly's singer, his nostrils flaring. "Had to spend three hours last night sorting out our songs so they can be done without lead guitar. Fuck it, man, they're better for it." He shook his head. "He's dead to me."

"He's dead full stop," said Cullen.

Preston frowned. "I'm sorry?"

"Mr Hughes' body was found on Wednesday night," said McCrea. "He was stabbed. We believe it was murder."

Preston sat down heavily on a beer barrel, looking at the other two members. "Did either of you know?"

They both shook their heads.

"You didn't know he was dead, then?" said McCrea.

Preston glared at him. "Would we have played a gig if we'd known? Why the fuck has it taken so long for you guys to find us and tell us? We were his *friends*."

"Less of the language, please sir," said McCrea. "I get enough of that at the station."

Cullen picked up the thread. "We would appreciate any assistance you can give us. What can you tell us about Mr Hughes?"

"He was a good lad, you know?" said the drummer, playing with his ponytail. "He was a bit older than the rest of us. His last band had done well, so he could help us work out our shit. He found some labels who were interested in us."

"Really?" said McCrea. "Was there anything in the offing?"

Preston shook his head. "Nothing concrete. Someone in London sounded like she wanted to put our record out."

"Knowing the singer in Expect Delays can't exactly harm things," said Cullen.

"Eh?" said Preston.

"Hughes was friends with Mike Roberts."

"I don't believe you," said Preston.

"You didn't know?" said McCrea.

"No," said Preston, emphatically.

"Was Mr Hughes unreliable?" said Cullen.

Preston nodded slowly. "Not turning up wasn't an isolated incident. Happened a few times."

"Did Mr Hughes talk much about his Edinburgh days?" said Cullen.

Preston shook his head slowly. "Not really, no. Talked about tours and gigs and stuff. His last band fell apart when he split up with his girlfriend."

"Is that what he told you?" said Cullen.

"Isn't it true?" said Preston.

Cullen held up a copy of the morning's *Sunday Mail*, a photo of James Strang inset at the top right. "The singer disappeared. This guy."

"Jesus," said Preston.

"We believe Mr Hughes might have been a drug user," said McCrea.

Preston shrugged. "He didn't really mention it."

"Didn't really?" said McCrea. "Or did?"

"No comment," said Preston.

"I know this isn't a particularly comfy place," said McCrea, "but we can do this down the station instead if you'd rather. It's just down the road."

Preston rocked back on the barrel. "He liked to smoke, aye."

"Cannabis? Heroin? Crack?"

"Fuck's sake, man," said Preston. "Cannabis."

"You're sure?" said McCrea.

"I wouldn't be in a band with a smack head," said Preston.

"He had traces of heroin in his bloodstream," said McCrea.

"What?"

"He used to smoke heroin," said McCrea. "Are you trying to tell me you didn't know?"

"Alex would get us a half Q of resin every so often, that's all," said Preston. "That's not dealing, is it?"

"Sounds a lot like it," said McCrea. "And he sold the drugs to you?"

Preston looked away. "Aye. Look, I just like to have a smoke to help me sleep, man. That's it."

"Where did he work?" said Cullen.

Preston sniffed. "He didn't."

Cullen nodded - Hughes was looking more like a dealer. "Did he have any friends?"

"Kept himself to himself," said the keyboard player, looking deep in shock.

"Maybe a girlfriend?" said Cullen.

"There was a lassie, aye," said Preston, looking up at Cullen. "Lived in Pollockshaws, I think."

"Got an address?" said McCrea.

"Afraid not," said Preston. "You'll need to work your police ju-ju, won't you?"

"A name would be helpful," said McCrea.

"Rowan or something like that," said Preston.

41

McCrea pulled up outside the flat, the street filled with rows of three-storey buildings, no doubt a mixture of flats and maisonettes, surrounded by multi-storey towers.

"How did you find her?" said Cullen.

"Magic," said McCrea, tapping his nose. "Police ju-ju."

"Quit it, Harry Potter," said Cullen. "You had a name and an area, and you managed to come up with Rowan Taylor and an address. How?"

"Connections," said McCrea.

"Come on."

"Okay," said McCrea. "You *are* a persistent bugger."

"It's one of my more endearing attributes," said Cullen. "Spill."

"I had a word with a couple of boys I know in the Serious and Organised Crime Agency," said McCrea, taking great pleasure in using the full name of SOCA. "They've got a drugs database that covers all their leads and sources and God knows what else. Rowan plus Pollockshaws gave us this."

"Assuming it's her," said Cullen.

"Of course."

"So, if it is her, she's known to SOCA?" said Cullen. "I don't like this. We spoke to Hughes' ex in Edinburgh the other day. She was smacked out of her head, with a troupe of kids she's lucky to still have."

"Were they his?"

"No," said Cullen. "Looks like she had a couple before they went out, then one since."

"Sure the one since isn't his?"

Cullen shook his head. "She said it wasn't. We checked it out and the timelines don't match."

"Right," said McCrea. "Wouldn't catch me getting anyone up the stick."

Cullen shook his head but he agreed with the sentiment, no matter how crassly it was put. "I'm surprised Strathclyde's crack murder squad didn't track down the fact he had a girlfriend."

McCrea stared at him for a good few seconds before nodding at the flats. "Shall we?"

They traipsed through the rough patch of grass at the front. One of the buzzers listed Taylor. McCrea got them let in.

Rowan Taylor stood in her doorway looking a total mess, eyes struggling to focus. She was thin and her head was shaved. She wore skinny black jeans and a baggy grey jumper. Cullen had to double-check she was a she.

McCrea held his warrant card up. "DS Damian McCrea of Strathclyde Police and DS Scott Cullen of Lothian & Borders. We need to speak to you about Alex Hughes."

Rowan scowled at them. "I've nothing to say to him."

"That's just as well," said McCrea. "He's dead."

Her eyes bulged. She stood shivering by the door, tears rolling down her cheeks. "What?" she said, her voice shrivelled up.

"I said Mr Hughes is dead," said McCrea. "We're investigating his murder. We'd like to come inside, if that's okay."

Rowan nodded slowly and led them inside the flat, showing them into the living room while she went to the toilet. Cullen kept an eye on the bathroom door in case she made a run for it. The place had the same number of rooms as Hughes' flat and was virtually empty, just a mattress in the middle of the living room.

"I keep expecting Sick Boy or Spud to show up," said Cullen.

"You know *Trainpotting* was filmed in Glasgow, right?" said McCrea.

"Is that because Glasgow is still as much of a dump as Leith was in the eighties?"

McCrea winced. "Hardly. I was in Leith last year. Still a dump."

Rowan returned, her eyes red. "What do you want from me?"

"Your boyfriend, Alex Hughes," said McCrea.

"He's not really my boyfriend," said Rowan. "Just a fuck buddy. Helps us get my gear. That's it."

"So, you let him have sex with you in exchange for drugs?" said Cullen.

"It's nothing like that," said Rowan.

"Does money change hands?" said McCrea.

"I'm not telling you boys nothing," said Rowan.

"So you're telling us something?" said McCrea.

"Eh?"

McCrea shook his head. "There are programmes you can go on to get off the drugs, you know?"

"I'm fine as it is," said Rowan. "Thanks for asking, though."

McCrea moved away from the window and approached her. "Rowan, someone stabbed him at his flat on Wednesday night."

"Stabbed?" She crumpled down to the mattress, hugging her knees close to her.

"Would you know anyone who would want to stab your fuck buddy?" said McCrea.

Rowan shot a look up at him. "No."

"Is that true?" said McCrea. "He didn't owe anyone any money or anything like that?"

"Not that I know of," said Rowan.

"Did Alex smoke heroin?" said Cullen.

Rowan looked over at him, eyes rolling in their sockets. "A bit."

"What about injecting?" said Cullen.

"Not so much," said Rowan, hugging herself tighter. "Can't believe he's gone."

Cullen kneeled down in front of her. "If you want to help us find his killer, tell us where he gets his drugs from."

"Do you think I'm stupid?" said Rowan, sneering. "He's not really dead, is he? You're just playing me."

McCrea shook his head. "He is dead, Rowan. An autopsy has been performed. His body's in the morgue. My boss has been speaking to his mother. She really wants to bury her son but she can't until we close this case."

Rowan looked away and wiped a tear from her cheek. "I don't know anything."

"That *really* true?" said McCrea.

"Aye," said Rowan. "He'd just get me my drugs, that's it."

McCrea had an evil grin on his face. "In exchange for sex. Is that right?"

"Not quite," said Rowan.

"But it's mostly right?" said McCrea.

Rowan shrugged. "I suppose."

"Did Mr Hughes ever make you have sex with any other men in exchange for drugs?" said McCrea.

Rowan threw her hands up in the air. "It was *nothing* like that. He was a good man."

"Then who did he get them from?" said McCrea.

Rowan looked away again. "I don't know."

Cullen caught a wink from McCrea. He could tell what he was thinking - she definitely knew. They just needed leverage.

"I'll tell you a wee story, Rowan," said McCrea. "We went to see this band at lunchtime up in town. They were good, you know? Well, I enjoyed them, my colleague here didn't. Anyway, we spoke to them and they told us something we didn't know. We found out Mr Hughes had a girlfriend."

Rowan looked up at McCrea but said nothing.

"All they gave us was a first name and a district of this fair city," said McCrea. "The area was Pollockshaws. The name?"

"Rowan," she said, her voice almost a whisper.

"That's right," said McCrea. "We managed to find you based on a name and an area." He kneeled down in front of her. "You're known to the authorities, Rowan. Luckily for you, you're just a peripheral figure in a cavernous drugs organisation." He grinned. "Now, if I was to go back to my pals who provided me with your name and address, I suspect we could add a few more sections to your file. Seems like prostitution would be the start of it."

"I'm not a whore," said Rowan.

"Really?"

"I'm *not*."

McCrea nodded. "I'm willing to believe you." He turned away from her and winked at Cullen. "Do you believe her, Sergeant?"

Cullen folded his arms - he didn't know whether to play good cop or bad. "I'm not sure I do, Sergeant."

McCrea glared at him. He turned back to Rowan, a smile returned to his face. "See, my colleague is from Edinburgh. He doesn't know how we operate through here. He'd be perfectly happy to drop you with the boys in SOCA. It's a national squad, you know? They'll listen to an eastie beastie as much as they will me. I can protect you."

Rowan mouthed something Cullen couldn't pick up.

"What was that?" said McCrea.

"Shug McArthur," said Rowan.

McCrea beamed. "Big Shug?"

"That's who he told me he got his gear off," said Rowan.

McCrea patted her on the arm. "Do yourself a favour and get off the drugs, okay?"

"Right."

McCrea nodded at Cullen. "Come on, Sergeant. I think we're done here."

He led Cullen back to the car with renewed vigour, striding across the grass and getting in his Escort.

"Eastie beastie?" said Cullen, once inside.

McCrea shrugged. "I had to improvise. You weren't supposed to go all bad cop on me."

"You need a signal," said Cullen, thinking back to the elaborate system of tie pulls and adjustments they'd developed back in Edinburgh. "What do you reckon?"

McCrea sat in silence for a few seconds, fingers drumming the steering wheel. "I'm pretty sure this is drug related. Silly bastard probably took on a debt too many, used it to get his end away with her upstairs, but forgot to pay for the gear."

"It would need to be a fairly big debt," said Cullen.

"Or he really pissed off someone big."

Cullen looked back at the block of flats. "I could buy that. What about the lack of forensics on the knife or the crime scene?"

"I told you," said McCrea. "It's a pro job. Wipe everything clean, leave no loose ends."

"Wouldn't a pro make it look like suicide or someone else?" said Cullen. "Maybe make it point to Rowan?"

"Or just leave it closed," said McCrea. "No leads, no investigation. They know how we work."

Cullen could see the logic. "Off to see this Shug, then?"

McCrea laughed. "Aye, very funny. You don't do intelligence through east, do you?"

Cullen reddened. "Okay, so what are you suggesting we do?"

"Shug is the big player through here," said McCrea. "We can't just pitch up and speak to him about some dead junkie."

"Right, so it's over to Bain's legendary decision making, then?" said Cullen.

"I'm growing to quite like you," said McCrea, as he gunned the engine.

42

Cullen left Glasgow at four, as Bain and McCrea went into a meeting with their superior officer, making it back to Edinburgh in reasonable time.

He sat with Methven and Chantal in their Incident Room, updating them on the latest thinking from the other end of the M8.

"So, in summary," said Cullen, "Strathclyde are suggesting the deaths of Strang and Hughes *are* just coincidence. They're going with Alex Hughes being killed over drug money."

"How much evidence do they have?" said Methven.

Cullen shrugged. "Nothing concrete as yet. They do know he was a heroin user."

"Define 'user'," said Methven.

"Mainly smoking, but also injecting. He sourced his drugs from Hugh McArthur, or Big Shug as he's known through there. According to DS McCrea, he's one of the biggest players just now."

A frown briefly flickered onto Methven's forehead. "Do you agree?"

Cullen weighed it up for a moment or two. He was stuck halfway between raising serious concerns with the theory and not wanting to return to Glasgow. Keeping his mouth shut would ensure the latter, but it wasn't his style. "I remain to be convinced."

Methven nodded. "You've done your best, I suppose."

"You suppose?" said Cullen.

"As well as can be done with that maniac in charge through there," said Methven.

"Don't I know it," said Cullen. "I don't know if I believe it or not. I've seen Bain go for an easy collar a few times, as you well know. He'll have the whole squad trying to connect Hughes and this Big Shug character."

"Leave it with me," said Methven.

"Leave what?" said Cullen, unsure whether there was anything to be left.

"What to do next."

Cullen opened his notebook. "What's been going on here?"

"I spoke to David Johnson and Beth Williamson again about the record deal," said Chantal. "They said Strang was losing it towards the end."

"What was the reason?" said Cullen.

Chantal dismissed it with a flick of her wrist. "The record deal stuff. They said he was into some band called the Stooges. Never heard of them myself, but they said he started copying what the singer did."

"Iggy Pop was the lead vocalist," said Methven.

"Isn't he the guy off that insurance advert?" said Chantal.

Methven grinned. "The man is a rock 'n' roll legend. Used to smash glasses and cut himself on stage."

Chantal scowled. "And that's what it takes to be a legend, is it?"

Cullen knew Strang was doing that on stage, but wondered if he'd been self-harming. "Was he cutting himself?"

"As far as they knew it was just at their gigs," said Chantal. "He used to take his top off on stage, but he started cutting his chest open at the last few gigs. Even smashed his guitar a couple of times."

"Shame there's no forensics to back it up," said Cullen. "What else?"

"Strang was seeing a psychoanalyst," said Chantal. "I've got an appointment with him tomorrow. Don't fancy our chances of getting anything, mind."

Methven got to his feet and clapped his hands together. "Thanks for your efforts, everyone. I appreciate you've all been putting the hours in, so go home, spend some time with your loved ones and get some shut-eye. Big day tomorrow."

Chantal left, but Cullen wanted to file his paperwork.

Methven got his feet and started jangling the change in his pocket. "I don't like coincidences, Cullen. These two deaths are so intricately linked. I just can't let it go."

"I don't like them either, but I've been through the reports." Cullen held up one of his wads of paper. "I've got a copy of the files as of eleven this morning and I don't see any other possibilities. Do you really want Bain taking over a joint murder inquiry?"

"Don't remind me," said Methven. "I've had enough of that man's poison to last a lifetime, I can tell you."

"Be thankful you've managed to keep yourself away from him," said Cullen.

"I'm *not* avoiding DI Bain," said Methven, eyes closed in the usual way. "I've got four DSs to supervise, Cullen, not just you."

"Really," said Cullen, his tone level enough to be ambiguous. He checked his watch. "Do you mind if I go home now?"

"Fine," said Methven. "Big day tomorrow."

"Don't keep reminding me," said Cullen. "I wouldn't

mind some sleep."

"Are you confident?"

Cullen looked up at the ceiling. "No."

Methven smiled. "Good, it looks like you've learnt something then."

"What am I supposed to have learnt?" said Cullen.

Methven closed his eyes again. "Not to take things for granted. It's an important lesson."

"Doesn't feel like it," said Cullen.

"Maybe one day you'll appreciate all of this."

43

Cullen hurried home, desperate to wrench something from his lost weekend and spend some time with Sharon. At the door, he received the customary greeting from Fluffy. He picked him up and carried him through to the living room. Sharon sat at the breakfast bar in her dressing gown, eating ice cream straight from the tub.

Cullen put the cat on the counter. "That better not be the Phish Food."

"Relax," said Sharon, "it's Caramel Choc Chew."

"That's a relief." Cullen leaned forward to kiss her, only getting her cheek.

"Sorry I didn't kiss you. I just feel bleurgh."

She gave him a mouthful of ice cream as compensation.

"Don't worry, I'll have caught the germs from the spoon," said Cullen.

Sharon laughed. "How are you?"

"Bit of a nightmare today," said Cullen. "Back through in Glasgow doing Methven's dirty washing."

"Bain?"

"Bain," said Cullen. "Tried to avoid him and largely succeeded. Got stuck with his new gorilla, though. Didn't end up that much further forward. They reckon it's drug related."

"Dope?"

"Heroin," said Cullen. "Their guy smoked it and

might have injected, too." He scowled. "There was no forensic evidence at the crime scene at all."

"I know that look," said Sharon. "Suspicious?"

"Could be," said Cullen. "Or the killer was just lucky. Makes us think it was a professional drug hit."

"Us?"

Cullen scowled.

Sharon tapped the spoon in Cullen's general direction. "You're not sure."

"I've worked for Bain too long to just settle on something. There's got to be some evidence pointing one way or another. If it's drugs then fine, let's get hunting down who killed him."

Sharon arched an eyebrow. "Otherwise?"

"Otherwise, our cases might be related and we've got a bloody turf war on with Bain and his cronies."

"What are you going to do, then?" said Sharon.

"I'm going to assume it is drug related," said Cullen. "Ours clearly isn't, which helps us. Until Bain or his boys dig something up, I'm keeping well away from him and that bloody city."

Fluffy started bleating at Cullen again.

"He's been doing this a lot. Is he annoyed with me, or something?"

Sharon shrugged. "It's just his way of showing affection."

Fluffy reared up to be stroked.

"That looks much more like affection to me" Cullen sat next to her. "Eating ice cream in your dressing gown isn't a good sign."

"It isn't. I've still got that cold. I've needed today to get over it." She chucked the spoon in the sink. "It's the big day tomorrow."

171

"Only if you're feeling better."

Sharon saluted. "Yes, nurse."

Cullen laughed. "What have you been up to today?"

"Do you want a cup of tea?" she said.

"That would be good."

She got up and filled the kettle.

"You can't have just cuddled the cat all day."

"He would let me." Sharon reached down to stroke Fluffy. "Chantal came round for a bit at lunchtime. While you've been annoying Bain in Glasgow, she's been at the mercy of Methven."

"I see," said Cullen, feeling some sympathy for her.

"I think she's missed me at work."

"Okay, so I've worked out an hour of what you were doing. What else?"

Sharon put the ice cream in the freezer. "Chantal's talking of joining a dating website."

"Her?"

Sharon looked down her nose at Cullen. "What do you mean 'her'? Do you think she's pretty?"

"Not my type, but I'm surprised she's still single. Didn't she get off with Budgie at that night out?"

"One night thing," said Sharon.

"Other than idle gossip, what have you been doing?" said Cullen, irritated by her evasion.

The kettle reached boiling point and Sharon poured water into the teapot. She sat down on the stool, letting the tea brew.

"Scott, I think I'm pregnant."

44

"You can't be pregnant," said Cullen.

"Well, I can and I am."

Cullen's brain broke down. He couldn't process it.

How could she be pregnant?

There was no way on earth he was going to become a dad. It just wasn't possible. He swallowed hard, hoping he was asleep and it was just a nightmare.

"Scott, we need to discuss this."

"How?"

"You talk to me and I listen," said Sharon. "I talk to you and you listen. That sort of thing."

"No, how can you be pregnant?" said Cullen. "We're normally so careful."

"It must have been that night," said Sharon. "Budgie's birthday."

"But we-"

"Did we? We were both so pissed."

"Shit," said Cullen. "Shit, shit, shit." He rubbed furiously at his hair. "I can't fucking remember."

Sharon went back to the teapot and poured out two mugs before putting the milk back in the fridge. He focused on her belly and what was growing in there. His seed, his child, his stupidity.

Sharon handed him the mug. "What are you thinking?"

"I thought you were avoiding something when I came

home," said Cullen.

Sharon nodded slowly. "I've felt so crap over the last few days."

"Is it a cold?"

"No, it's not," said Sharon. "Well, not entirely. It's morning sickness and a cold and God knows what else."

"How do you know?" said Cullen.

Sharon blew on her tea. "Chantal brought a few tester kits round. Tried different brands and everything. They should have them on multi-buy."

"Stop joking about it," said Cullen. "Are you definitely pregnant?"

"I need to get it confirmed by a doctor, but three brands of pregnancy kit all agree."

"Shite."

Sharon took a big drink of tea. "You'd make a good dad."

"When I'm ready, *maybe*," said Cullen. "Not now."

"Really?" said Sharon, a frown flickering across her forehead.

"I don't know," said Cullen. "I just don't know."

"It's a huge thing. You need time to get used to it."

Cullen watched the cat as he poked his head out of the covered litter tray. "Did you do this on purpose?"

"Of course I fucking didn't." She slammed the mug down on the counter. "Christ, Scott, do you honestly think I could even consider doing that?"

Cullen looked away. "No. I don't know why I said it. Sorry."

Sharon's eyes were wide with anger. "Are you?"

"Yes," said Cullen. "I'm genuinely sorry."

Sharon shook her head, rage still etched on her face. "Never accuse me of anything like that again."

"Then don't get pregnant again." Cullen held his hands up immediately. "That was a joke. Instinct. I'm sorry." He rubbed at his face. "I'm really sorry. I'm not taking this at all well. I just don't know what the fuck to think."

Sharon nodded, looking slightly less angry but just as disappointed. "What do you want to do?"

"I have absolutely no idea."

Sharon looked down, finger circling the rim of the mug. "We don't have to keep it."

"There's no way your mother is going to be all right about you having an abortion," said Cullen.

Sharon said nothing.

"Is there?"

"I spoke to her and she was okay about it," said Sharon.

Cullen felt anger surge. "Am I the last to know about this?"

"I swear you're not. Christ, Scott, this isn't just about you, you know? Your body isn't going to get massive and your boobs aren't going to swell up."

"I thought mine already were," said Cullen, grabbing his man boobs. "It's called lager."

Sharon laughed hard. "Enough joking about, Scott. I'm scared. I don't know what to do."

"That's probably the first time ever," said Cullen. "How pregnant are you?"

"I'm one hundred per cent pregnant, Scott."

"I meant the amount of time," said Cullen.

"Six weeks, I reckon," said Sharon. "The doctor should confirm it."

"Okay, so we've still got plenty of time to decide."

"I guess so." Sharon got up and poured another cup

of tea, looking out of the window.

Having children was a huge step. It needed to be planned, not something that just happened to you. Too many people ended up in the situation and just weren't ready for kids, tearing their relationship apart.

Cullen was lucky to have parents who still loved each other, warts and all. Many of his friends' parents were divorced and he saw the toll it could take. Then again, it was worse to stay together for the sake of the kids, heaping misery, resentment and guilt on them.

Sharon sat down with her fresh cup. "I think I might like to keep it."

"I need to think this through," said Cullen.

"We need to *talk* it through," said Sharon. "*Together*."

"I need space to think," said Cullen. "I need to go to my cave like in that book you made me read."

Sharon slouched back. "That's the only thing you took from it, isn't it?"

Cullen shrugged. "It's useful. I need space and time to think. I'm going to have something to eat and then watch some mindless foreign football."

Sharon screwed her face up. "And that's it?"

"Sharon, you've just told me I'm going to be a father," said Cullen. "That's fucking *huge*. I need to focus on it. My head is full of shit right now. I'm a DS, I'm working with Bain again and I'm leading a murder case. I'm all over the place. I need some perspective."

"Well, *I* need to talk about it," said Sharon.

"So talk," said Cullen. "I need to cook. You've got a captive audience."

He marched to the sink and refilled the kettle. He took ingredients from the cupboard - onion, garlic, passata and pasta shells - and started chopping.

"Pasta again?" said Sharon.

"You're eating for two and all that," said Cullen.

She folded her arms. "Can you be serious about this for once?"

"I'm trying," said Cullen. He put the knife down, returning to her side and held her tight. "Look it's okay. We need to think this through, then we'll know what we're doing, okay?"

"Okay." Sharon kissed him. "I love you, Scott."

"I love you," said Cullen. "I'd rather go through this with you than anyone else."

The cat bleated again, his yellow eyes staring at Cullen. They both laughed.

"I'm serious," said Cullen, "we need to work out if we're keeping this thing or not. And I'm not talking about the cat."

"He's staying."

Monday
1st April 2013

45

Cullen woke up early next morning, his mind twisting over all the shit in his brain. He'd watched the football while Sharon read, not discussing the baby at all until his eyes closed and then it was all he could think about.

During brief snatches of sleep, Marta Hunter haunted his dreams, her army of children looking more like wild cats than humans. It didn't take a great intellect to connect it to the little thing growing inside Sharon, determined to one day ruin Cullen's life.

Could it save his life? Would it force him to grow up, settle down and take on responsibility?

He just didn't know.

In the harsh cold of the early morning, he knew he should have talked to Sharon rather than retreating to the cave, which hadn't helped in any way.

He got up, dressed and showered, then drove the short distance to the station, leaving Sharon snoring. He was so tired, he probably should have walked, but he didn't know which city he'd be in that day. A coffee would take the edge off.

In the car park, Cullen spotted Buxton by the panda cars. He did a double-take as he approached - Buxton was peeling stickers off the cars, removing *Lothian & Borders* and leaving only *Police*. Rumours had circulated of beat cops having to unstitch the lettering from their clothes to save money, but this beggared belief.

181

"What are you doing?" said Cullen.

"Order from the top," said Buxton. "Can't outsource it or it'll cost a packet so anyone of constable grade is being press-ganged."

Cullen shook his head in disbelief. Surely there were crimes deserving more attention than *stickers*.

As he neared, Cullen was almost blown away by the stink of booze. "Watch for any stray fags from the smoking area."

"Eh?"

"The fumes coming off you are likely to catch light," said Cullen.

Buxton reached into his pocket for some mints. "Heavy session yesterday afternoon."

"Smells like a heavy night as well."

"Got home just after eight," said Buxton. "I'll be the first to admit I wasn't exactly sober."

"Or this morning I bet," said Cullen.

"There's that too."

"Best stick to the mints," said Cullen.

Buxton crunched away. "Heard any gossip from the announcement?"

"Nothing," said Cullen. For once, when he got up that morning there were no waiting text messages. "The jungle drums are dead. How long have you been in?"

"Got in at half five," said Buxton. "Seen a few other DCs but no juice yet." He pulled the last sticker off the car, dropping it in the bucket at his feet. "Be interesting to see what transpires, shall we say. What'll happen to you, do you reckon?"

"Hopefully, I'll get made a full DS," said Cullen, not exactly feeling or sounding confident. "God knows they need more."

"Good luck with that," said Buxton. "I'd heard whispers to that effect."

Cullen's heart beat faster. "Who from?"

"Methven was blabbering away on his mobile as he came in," said Buxton. "Don't think he saw me."

"Yeah, he does that," said Cullen. "Did he say anything else?"

"He asked someone what the date was," said Buxton.

Cullen frowned. "First of April."

Buxton laughed. "April Fool, mate."

Cullen clenched his fists. "You twat."

"At least you know you'll still be in SCD," said Buxton.

"Yeah, whatever," said Cullen. "You must be pissed off still being an ADC."

"Better than being on the beat, mate."

Cullen headed up to the canteen, worrying about what the day would hold.

46

DCI Turnbull's staff briefing was held at seven, before the bulk of the operational briefings.

Cullen sat in the third row, clutching his second coffee of the morning, the first not having quite hit the mark. Looking around, he noticed a few faces from his stint at St Leonard's lurking at the back of the room.

Turnbull cleared his throat and brought them to order. "Briefings such as these are happening, right now, all over Scotland. This is an exciting dawn, the first steps in a brave new direction."

The current Lothian & Borders logo filled the screen behind him. Turnbull clicked a button on the small device he held, making the logo shrink down and move to the top.

Buxton leaned towards Cullen and whispered in his ear. "Death by bloody PowerPoint, mate."

"Tell me about it."

"Brave steps my arse," said Buxton. "It's a load of bollocks. My mate in the Met reckons Turnbull is getting a DCS gig down there."

"He's just a DCI, though," said Cullen.

"Just passing on what I hear."

Cullen didn't know whether to believe it or not.

Turnbull was having difficulty with his clicker. Eventually, two boxes filled the bottom of the screen with arrows splitting out from *Lothian & Borders*.

"The first big change is that Edinburgh City is now a key division in the Police Scotland East structure, discrete from Lothians & Scottish Borders, now a separate regional division."

He talked for a few minutes about how the move would give more local accountability and national consistency before clicking again. The presentation switched to a busy slide entitled *The future of CID...*, filled with text in such a small font that Cullen couldn't quite read it.

"The next big change will impact most people in the room," said Turnbull. "CID will be radically overhauled. This is not just a fresh lick of paint, either. There will be those who remain in the first-response CID units in the Divisional areas, but most officers will move into the central Major Investigation Team structure in SCD."

The slides switched and showed a blank page, with *Edinburgh MIT Structure* appearing at the top. Turnbull clicked and his name flew in from the left, sitting top middle.

Cullen had to read it twice.

Detective Superintendent Jim Turnbull.

Cullen's stomach fluttered again - if Turnbull could be promoted, then surely he could?

"As of this morning, I will be heading up the Edinburgh MIT," said Turnbull. "I will report into DCS Carolyn Soutar, head of the MITs nationwide. The bulk of officers from the Torphichen Street, St Leonard's and Leith Walk CID units will be merging under my command and will be based here in Leith Walk."

Turnbull clicked again. "My number two will be DCI Alison Cargill."

Another promotion.

The next click brought in a row of three names. "DCI Pieters now takes the grade of DI in the new structure alongside DI Alistair Davenport from St Leonard's and Colin Methven from Leith Walk, now a full DI."

Sharon swore under her breath, loud enough for Cullen to hear.

"There is, of course, a vacancy for a fourth DI," said Turnbull.

Cullen turned to face Sharon again - she raised her eyebrows.

Turnbull clicked and names appeared one by one. "At the DS level, we have Bryan Holdsworth in the Admin Officer role, then Sharon McNeill and Catriona Rarity, both from Leith Walk, and Brian McMann from DI Davenport's team. DS McKern will be taking early retirement and-"

Turnbull clicked but nothing happened.

The butterflies in Cullen's stomach were doing somersaults.

Click.

"Finally, DS Bill Lamb from East Lothian will be the fourth DS."

Cullen couldn't believe it.

"Moving on," said Turnbull, "we have the DCs."

The screen changed, now showing a hierarchy of DCs reporting to DSs. Cullen, Chantal and Buxton worked for Rarity now.

Cullen stared open-mouthed at the screen. His extra stripe had gone. No-one had the courtesy to brief him in advance.

Idiot.

He barely took in the rest of the structure. Stuart Murray from Lamb's team was in, alongside another face from Cullen's past, Eva Law.

Turnbull's next slide covered the officers moving to the local CID and was just noise to Cullen. He was publicly humiliated. He looked around the room, trying to see who was pointing at him and laughing.

Idiot.

Why did he think his tenure was going to be made permanent? All the chat with Buxton, how assured he was. He thought he'd arrived.

Naïve.

Turnbull looked around the room, but Cullen felt he received more focus than others.

So much for being a *rising star*.

"I appreciate this will be disappointing for some of you," said Turnbull, "but all I ask is you behave in a professional manner. These are straitened times and, while you might not get the stripes just now, you will get experience that will help in future." His eyes settled on Cullen. "Dismissed."

Cullen got up, ready to head God knows where. Anywhere to hide his shame.

Sharon grabbed his arm. "Breakfast?"

Cullen nodded, realising how desperately he needed to talk.

47

"Reckon you'll get the DI vacancy?" said Chantal.

Sharon shrugged. "I doubt it. Might be someone from another force."

Cullen was sitting in silence while they prattled, still reeling from shock. There was so much he needed to get out of his head. When Sharon asked if he wanted breakfast, he thought it would be just the pair of them, but then she'd invited Buxton and Chantal along.

Why had no one told him? Was he just a name on a spreadsheet?

Methven must have known beforehand. He'd had at least two opportunities in the previous forty-eight hours to let Cullen know and he'd dodged it.

This was his reward for all the hours he'd put in over the years, letting others take the credit for his results. The only *possible* explanation was they'd had their hands full with the enforced retirements and making sure the St Leonard's officers were properly briefed, so they avoided formal grievances with HR.

As he watched Sharon talk to Chantal, he just wanted to speak to her. He deeply regretted the way he'd reacted the previous night, clamming up like that.

The baby.

Fuck.

If Cullen believed in a higher power, then this would be a test. He'd changed so much in the two years he'd been a full DC, but in some ways he'd changed so little. His ego pushed him several steps ahead of where his more rational head told him he should be.

He caught himself. He was in his thirties - he needed to act like a grown-up. Forget the promotion until it was formal. Look on the bright side - almost six months as Acting DS would look good on his record, like detachments to murder cases had helped him become a detective.

There might be a trickle-down from the vacant DI position.

"Why have they not put an Acting DI in there?" said Chantal.

"I've no idea," said Sharon.

"Well, I reckon you'll get it," said Chantal.

"I doubt it," said Sharon. "It's got Bill Lamb's name written all over it."

"Crystal Methven did well out of the restructure," said Chantal.

"Of course he did," said Buxton. "He's a sneaky two eight six eight."

"A what?" said Chantal.

Buxton snorted, eyes full of amusement. "Type it on your phone. Like an old Nokia or something."

Chantal fiddled with her fingers. "Aunt?" Something twigged and she burst into laughter. "Oh, that's good."

Cullen folded his arms, making eye contact with Sharon before looking away.

"It's weird seeing Bill Lamb again," said Chantal.

"Was he there?" said Buxton.

Chantal nodded. "Yeah, stood at the back, him and Stuart Murray." She wolf-whistled. "The things I'd let Murray do to me..." She bit her lip and flicked up an eyebrow.

"And then you'd blank him, right?" said Buxton.

Chantal studied her coffee cup, pulling an uncomfortable silence around the table.

"Scott, are you okay?" said Sharon.

Cullen shrugged. "I'll be fine."

"You don't seem it," said Sharon.

"I should have expected it, really. Bill Lamb got my job."

"But it's not your job, though, is it?" said Chantal. "You were just keeping the bench warm."

"Whatever," said Cullen, "I'm just pissed off nobody had the decency to take me aside and brief me beforehand. Don't you think they owe me that?"

"At least you've got a tenure, mate," said Buxton. "Just found mine's up in two months. No chance it'll be renewed."

"You'll be fine," said Cullen.

Buxton sighed. "I doubt it."

Cullen looked over at Sharon, receiving a slight smile. "Sharon, can we-"

"DS McNeill, I need to brief you."

Cullen twisted around. Turnbull towered over them. Lamb stood just behind, rubbing at the back of his neck.

Sharon got up and mouthed "Sorry" at Cullen.

Turnbull disappeared as quickly as he came, the two DSs following him. He didn't even acknowledge Cullen.

Cullen really needed to clear all the shit out of his head.

48

DS Catriona Rarity was now in charge of the Strang case.

She congregated them in the small Incident Room for a handover from the team. She'd earmarked an hour of Cullen's time afterwards to get a full debrief from him before he reverted to his new demoted role.

Rarity wasn't an officer Cullen knew particularly well. She'd only joined the team in the last six months and hadn't set the world alight as Cullen saw it. Then again, nobody got burnt in the process unlike when he worked his magic. In Cullen's eyes, she was all process and procedure with very little inspiration or leadership. He suspected she was seen as a safe pair of hands.

"We need to speak to everyone Strang knew," said Rarity.

"We've done that," said Cullen.

"What about his parents?"

"Done that, too."

"What about the people he was in a band with?" said Rarity.

"Done that," said Cullen. "We've spoken to two of them, the third one is dead. Strathclyde are investigating his murder. I suppose it'll be the Glasgow South MIT now, but you know what I mean."

Rarity looked like she was finding Cullen's responses difficult. "So, we've hit a wall, is that it?"

"I'm not the DS here," said Cullen. "You tell us."

He immediately regretted it.

Rarity tipped her head up, shaking her shoulder-length hair out. She politely smiled at Chantal and Buxton. "Can I ask you both to leave us for a moment?" she said, a false smile plastered on her face.

They couldn't get out of there quickly enough.

Once they were alone, Rarity fixed her eyes on Cullen. "I thought we got on well. Do you have a problem with me?"

"I was just stating a fact," said Cullen. "I'm sorry if it seemed a bit snippy. You're in charge of this investigation. As of this morning, I'm back on the bottom rung of the ladder. You're now the one who takes vague instructions from DI Methven and then gives me actions to make a mess of. Am I right?"

Rarity hit her hand on the table. "Your attitude *stinks*."

"*My* attitude stinks?" said Cullen, eyes wide. "One minute, I'm an Acting DS and then I get demoted."

Rarity sat there for a few seconds, staring at him. "Well, I have to say I'm surprised you had the chance to be an ADS."

"I got it because I get results," said Cullen. "I'm good at what I do."

"We do have a problem, then," said Rarity.

"I'm sorry," said Cullen. "I'll probably take a while to adjust to this. I'm sorry if I'm acting like an arse, but I'm irritated and that's putting it mildly."

Rarity eyed Cullen nervously. "I can understand your frustration, Scott. Surely you'll have had the chance to air your disappointment with Alison?"

"I would if she'd spoken to me," said Cullen.

"I'm sorry?"

"The first I heard I was no longer a sergeant was in that room this morning," said Cullen.

"Oh."

"Oh, indeed," said Cullen.

"In that case, I can only offer my sympathies, Scott. That shouldn't have happened. It's clearly unacceptable. I'll discuss the matter with Alison and Colin and see what reparations we can make."

"Getting my tenure back would help," said Cullen.

"That's not going to happen in the short term," said Rarity. "Any outbursts similar to the one you just gave me are going to undermine any support you might otherwise have in this station."

"Look, I'm sorry," said Cullen. "I don't have any issues working with you. I'm just frustrated I'm not doing your job and with finding out in a conference room."

"I've had very little information from DS Methven on this case, so I'm going to need your help."

"I'm more than committed to solving the case," said Cullen. "I'll try not to let my disappointment get in the way."

"From what I can tell, the only real lead we've got is in the mortuary in Glasgow," said Rarity. "Correct?"

"That's about the size of it," said Cullen. "Do you want me to go to Glasgow again?"

"The instruction I received from Alison and Colin is that, as your role has changed, the secondment is no longer valid."

"It's hardly a secondment if it's just a day," said Cullen.

Rarity shrugged. "I'm not party to the conversations." She sat and thought for a few seconds. "Strang is from your home town. Is that right?"

"Correct," said Cullen. "He was."

"I see," said Rarity. "Can you go and investigate in Dalhousie, please?"

Cullen struggled to think how he could spend any amount of time in the place. "And do what?"

"What you apparently do best," said Rarity. "Get a result."

Cullen frowned. "Am I being pushed out of the way here?"

"Quite the opposite," said Rarity. "I think we might only have skirted the surface of the investigation in the town."

"That's probably a fair assessment," said Cullen. "I was stuck in Glasgow yesterday."

Rarity nodded. "I'm as uncomfortable as you are about the political games being played here. I can speak to Alison and Colin about the situation."

Cullen was relieved he didn't have to go back to Glasgow and Bain. "Fine."

"DC Jain and I can close off the Edinburgh side of things," said Rarity. "I want you to see what you can dig up. Spend a few hours there, maybe a couple of days."

"It's not the sort of place you can spend even an hour in," said Cullen, smiling.

"Just see what you can do," said Rarity. "It might help you adjust to the new status quo."

49

Cullen finally managed to find Sharon in the general office area.

"You okay?" she said.

Cullen shook his head, nervously looking around. "I need to talk."

"Finally," said Sharon. She tugged his arm and they went back to the canteen, sitting in the seclusion of bollocking corner.

"Rarity has sent me to Dalhousie," said Cullen. "Feels like a wild goose chase to me."

"How are you feeling?"

Cullen frowned. "I'm not happy. I can't believe I've been demoted but it's something I'm going to have to take on the chin, I suppose."

Sharon nodded. "Try and remember you were never actually promoted, all right? I kept on telling you that."

"Yeah, I know," said Cullen. "I wouldn't listen, would I?" He laughed. "Besides, you got promoted without ever being an ADS."

"I was just lucky," said Sharon.

"And better than me?"

"Did I say that?" said Sharon. "I was just in the right place at the right time. It's a different place now. We're taking an absolute hammering - pensions are being eroded and overtime is much harder to come by. Half of Jim's time will be spent trimming his budget whereas before it was about getting results."

Cullen nodded, seeing the truth in what she said. "I need to play a long game here."

"You do," said Sharon. "I've told you that."

"It took me so long to get out of uniform and my pay didn't change much when I became a DC. It's tough."

"I know, Scott. You need to learn to be a bit more patient, that's all."

Cullen nodded. "What did Turnbull have to say?"

"Are you changing the subject?" said Sharon.

"It's what I do."

Sharon leaned back in the chair. "It's between me and him."

Cullen frowned. "You won't tell me?"

Sharon laughed as she grabbed his hand across the table. "No, you idiot. The vacant DI position is between me and Bill Lamb."

"With you now. Sorry, I'm tired."

"Bill's got four years experience on me as a sergeant, plus he was an Acting DI about three years ago."

"When do you find out?" said Cullen.

"We've got to go through an assessment centre in the next week. Both of us. Then we'll see."

"I take it you didn't tell Jim, then?" said Cullen.

Sharon looked away. "It's nowhere near twelve weeks. Anything could happen."

"So, other than Chantal, who else knows?" said Cullen.

"My mum. That's it."

Cullen smiled. "Right, so your dad, my parents, your sister and half of Edinburgh?"

"She *can* keep a secret," said Sharon. "It has been known to happen."

"Believe it when I see it," said Cullen.

"We do need to talk about it, Scott."

"I know. I've been thinking about it a lot."

"And?"

"And I just don't know what to think."

"I can have an abortion," said Sharon.

Cullen looked away. "I can't believe we've been so careless."

"You think I've been careless, don't you?" said Sharon.

Cullen reached out across the table and grabbed her hand. "It's not your fault. If anything it's mine. When the dick is hard, the mind is soft and all that."

"If you think it's a fault, then you don't want it, am I right?"

"Look, pregnancy is an STD to me. It terrifies me. Now it's real and in my life, I just don't fucking know what to think."

Sharon glared at him. "I think you should maybe spend the night at your parents."

"If you're chucking me out," said Cullen, "then I'll go cap in hand to Tom, begging for my old room back. He's fed up with the guy who's renting it now, anyway."

Sharon grabbed Cullen's hands. "I'm *not* chucking you out, Scott." Her eyes intently focused on him. "My flat is *our* home. Both of us. And Fluffy. And this *thing* I've got in my body." She rubbed her belly. "What I mean is you should speak to your mum about it. You know how good you thought the counselling was, right? Well, maybe talking to your mum would help?"

Cullen had always been able to share problems with his mother and she was a good listener. After all the shit he'd got up to as a teenager, she was forgiving and hadn't judged him for any of it. "You're probably right. Tom and Rich aren't exactly great listeners."

"I love you, Scott. If I'm going to have kids, it's going to be with you."

"Same here," said Cullen. "I just don't know if I'm ready, that's all."

"Nobody's ever ready at this stage," said Sharon. "They've got seven and a half months to get ready."

50

Cullen returned to the flat to start packing. He sat on the edge of the bed and yawned.

He'd got into work for six that morning, like an absolute idiot, desperate to solve the Strang case. All those hours of unclaimed overtime he'd worked for free when they could really do with the money.

No matter how many results he managed to get, he was still nowhere near where he wanted to be. Maybe policing wasn't for him any more.

He caught himself and tried to snap out of it, struggling to remember why he'd joined the police in the first place.

When he'd worked in Financial Services, an industry drowning in cash, ambition and promotion, he quickly learnt he wasn't motivated by money. He'd given all that up to do something worthwhile with his life, rather than answering phones or managing people answering phones.

Tom was getting fat and stressed for a job he hated, chasing the money but adding nothing to society. Cullen had taken murderers off the street. That was giving something back.

The baby, if they had it, was going to eat up their time and expendable income. They couldn't bring a child up in a one bedroom flat in the city centre. They'd need to move to the suburbs or into the country and that cost money. He felt ever more pressure pile up on his shoulders.

Working for Rarity was going to be yet another challenge he needed to overcome. She was, at best, a peer. He'd have to work with her and bide his time, making his case for promotion another way.

Fluffy stretched out on the carpet in front of him then climbed up on the bed. He started rearing up and rubbing against Cullen's chin.

"At least someone will miss me."

51

Cullen parked outside Dalhousie police station, The Invisibles playing on the stereo. He'd driven all that way and he still had no idea what he was going to do there, his mind on other things entirely.

The heater in his car was broken, a repair he couldn't afford. He knew he had to replace the Golf at some point, but all the overtime in the world wouldn't pay for anything barely adequate.

He got his brand new Police Scotland warrant card ready for heading inside. Seeing Detective Constable Scott Cullen again in black and white brought it home. He'd got used to being DS Scott Cullen, the silent A for Acting.

He decided to rise above it all, knowing he could be his own worst enemy. He had enough fire in his belly to prove them all wrong. If either Sharon or Lamb got the final DI position then there would likely be another Acting DS tenure.

Cullen needed to get momentum back in the case - getting stuck in Glasgow had killed it. He got out of the car and walked to the station.

When he was still in uniform, he'd visited the older building before they moved to the outskirts, nearer the rougher housing estates. The shopping centre and supermarket around the new station were fields when he was growing up.

He waved his warrant card at the desk sergeant and signed in, learning there was a DC in the station who could help him. He headed to the office space at the back, past the holding cells. It didn't strike Cullen as being a particularly sensitive design, but making interviewees walk past them might encourage honesty.

He saw a familiar face perched on the corner of a desk, chatting to a female officer. Richard Guthrie.

"Scott Cullen," said Guthrie, walking over and holding his hand out. "I did not expect to see you here today."

Cullen shook hands, unable to avoid grinning. "How you doing?"

Guthrie was an old school friend, though they'd drifted apart at university and beyond. Unbeknownst to each other, they had joined the police at around the same time and rekindled their friendship at Tulliallan police college.

"I'm good," said Guthrie, looking Cullen up and down. "You look tired, Skinky."

"Been busy, mate. Eighth day in a row. Running a murder case."

Guthrie frowned. "Running it?"

Cullen shrugged. "I was."

"Just got back from my briefing in Dundee," said Guthrie. "Big changes."

"How did the restructure affect you?" said Cullen. "I would've thought you'd be in Dundee MIT?"

"MIT North didn't want me," said Guthrie, failing to mask his disappointment. "I was based in Dundee but I'm now North Division local CID for the rest of my life." He coughed. "What about you?"

"Edinburgh MIT," said Cullen.

"Good for you, mate," said Guthrie. "What brings you

back here?"

"James Strang," said Cullen.

"I know the name," said Guthrie, frowning. "Folks still live here?"

"Aye."

"Right," said Guthrie. "I'll ask again, because I always need to with you, what are you doing here?"

"Digging up Strang's life," said Cullen. "He lived in Edinburgh but we've come to a dead end there. There might be something here that kick starts us again."

"Let me know if you need any help," said Guthrie.

"I could do with an extra pair of hands, especially someone who hasn't forced everything about this town out of their head," said Cullen.

"Shouldn't be any problems getting approval," said Guthrie, smiling. "We're all part of one big family now."

"Aren't you busy?" said Cullen.

"Wish I was. It's slim pickings here. I'm the only DC in Dal. My DS is in Dundee and I hardly ever see her. I'm bloody quiet. I keep praying for a murder."

"Don't say that," said Cullen, laughing hard.

"Yeah, you're right," said Guthrie. He rubbed his hands together. "Come on, then."

He led him back to his desk, covered in boxes of files, an Aberdeen mug, some empty burger wrappers, three half-empty Coke bottles and a neglected-looking computer.

"Bring me up to speed on this case, then," said Guthrie.

Cullen pulled over a seat and took Guthrie through the case so far, his earlier enthusiasm diminishing as he went.

"It's not a lot to go on, is it?" said Guthrie.

"No," said Cullen. "I'm kind of at a loss as to what to do. The only thing I can think is to speak to his parents and see if we get any leads there."

Guthrie nodded again. "How long you here for?"

"I don't know," said Cullen. "Might be a couple of days, might not."

"Staying with the olds?"

"I hate that," said Cullen. "You sound like someone off *Neighbours*."

Guthrie laughed.

"I'll be back at chateau Cullen. They don't know it, yet. My room is always made up and they're not away on holiday for once."

"I'll need to clear the decks this afternoon," said Guthrie. "Got a court appearance in Arbroath in an hour then a load of admin to catch up on."

"Tomorrow, then?"

"Aye," said Guthrie. "If you're still around."

Cullen looked around the deserted office. "Any danger I could get a desk?"

"I'll have to speak to the sergeant," said Guthrie, his face stern.

Rage built up in Cullen's gut. "But there's nobody here."

Guthrie laughed. "Should see your face, Skinky."

Cullen's anger dissipated. "Right," he said, shaking his head. "You bastard."

"Fancy a pint tonight?" said Guthrie.

Cullen nodded, but knew he'd eventually regret it.

52

Cullen pulled up outside the Strang's house, spotting the same car in the drive.

He sat behind the wheel for a bit, thinking through his plan of attack. There must be nuggets that didn't seem obvious when Strang disappeared but which meant something in the context of a murder.

He was back in the world of shoe leather, a doer rather than a leader. It was for him to chase down every single lead, rather than the officers working for him. Having help from Guthrie would be useful, adding a bit of local knowledge to the investigation.

He walked up the drive and knocked on the front door. Eventually, it opened.

Norma Strang screwed her eyes up at him. "Have you found my son's killer?"

Cullen shook his head. "Not yet, I'm afraid."

"Oh."

"I need to ask some further questions about your son," said Cullen.

"Well, you'd better come in then, Sergeant."

Cullen didn't correct her.

She led him into the living room. The mantelpiece was now filled with cards, a perverse inversion of Christmas.

"My husband is sorting out the arrangements at the funeral director's office," said Norma.

"I'm sorry to miss him."

"Have you got anything to report?"

"Nothing much, I'm afraid," said Cullen. "It would be very useful if you could provide us with any other people we could speak to about your son."

"People who could have caused James harm?" said Norma. "I told you already."

"No," said Cullen, "people who can give us some background."

She looked hurt. "We've not given you enough already?"

"We can't overlook any avenue in a case like this," said Cullen. "Did James have any brothers or sisters?"

"He's got a sister, Audrey," said Norma. "You're from Dalhousie, aren't you?"

"Yes."

"What year did you finish school?" said Norma.

"Two thousand and one."

"Did you do sixth year?" said Norma.

Cullen nodded. "I did."

Norma did some mental arithmetic. "You'll have been in the same year as my Audrey."

Despite how antiquated the name now seemed, there were a couple in his year alone. He couldn't remember Audrey Strang. "Can I have her address and phone number?"

"Certainly."

Cullen scribbled the mobile number down. "What about any friends?"

"There's Paul McKay," said Norma. "That's all I can think."

Cullen didn't recognise the name. "Anyone else?"

Norma stared into space, drumming her fingers on the

edge of the sofa. "There was another laddie. What was his name?"

Cullen gave her time.

She clicked her fingers. "That's it. Mark Andrews."

Cullen wrote it down. "No more?"

Norma shook her head. "I'm afraid not. I know both those laddies' parents, just enough to speak to in the Tesco. I think they both work in Dundee."

Cullen was relieved he didn't have to go to London or similar.

53

Cullen drove to Dundee and now sat on a designer chair in the reception of Indignity Design, the video game company Mark Andrews worked at. Cullen thought working in computer games must beat the shit out of the police. The place had the feel of money, glass and chrome everywhere and a healthy buzz among the staff.

He'd returned to Dalhousie police station first, to search for McKay and Andrews. He quickly discovered rural stations in Angus didn't quite have the level of IT systems he was used to. He eventually got current phone numbers and addresses for both, though he'd only managed to get hold of Andrews, leaving a few missed calls and voicemails for McKay.

Cullen had never been one for computer games aside from his annual addiction to *Football Manager*, a game he deemed career threatening in its addictiveness. He could lose himself in it for days at a time. One of the best things about moving out of Tom's flat was getting away from the cycle of 'just one more game' at three in the morning. Sharon wouldn't tolerate it and last year's edition was still in its shrink-wrap.

Cullen recognised some Indignity games from posters on the wall, mainly from adverts on Sky Sports. *Dawn of Heroes* was a role-playing game, the sort of thing played by the kids at school Cullen took the piss out of. *War Games* was one of those shooting games that seemed popular these days - killing people with guns, killing buildings with tanks. *Indignity* itself was their biggest, which involved playing as a gangster, killing people, stealing cars, selling drugs and doing God knows what else, all from the comfort of your own sofa.

A man approached Cullen, wearing a t-shirt, jeans and big NHS glasses, his hair gelled back like a gangster in a Scorsese film. He walked in a strange manner, his skinny shoulders raised up and his body practically immobile apart from the long legs. Despite the hairstyle, all Cullen could think was *dweeb*.

"DC Cullen?"

Cullen got to his feet and offered a hand, limply accepted. "Mr Andrews?"

Andrews nodded. "Come through to my pod."

If it involved *pods,* Cullen thought working in the company wouldn't be much fun after all.

Andrews' pod turned out to be his office, a circular room etched in glass. The single wall was occupied with stills from films such as *Pulp Fiction, Goodfellas, The Lord of the Rings* and *Die Hard*.

Cullen sat on a bar stool while Andrews kneeled on a strange seat behind a glass desk, a custom-built PC with a monstrous monitor occupying most of the space.

Andrews folded his arms, his leg jigging up and down. "Speaking to a real life police officer is very exciting."

Cullen took an immediate dislike to him. Whatever he thought about computer games, he couldn't approve of glorifying the sort of shit he dealt with on a daily basis. "I believe you were acquainted with one James Strang from Dalhousie."

"Jimi." Andrews shook his head slightly and smiled. "I don't know him that well any more, I'm afraid."

"What happened?"

"We were good friends at school but you know how it is," said Andrews. "We just drifted apart during uni. We saw each other a fair amount in the first couple of years but it became more sporadic after that. I haven't seen him in a long while, come to think of it. We mostly just emailed each other."

Cullen nodded. "He's been murdered."

Andrews' eyes bulged, his childlike excitement disappearing. "My god. When?"

"We think it was approximately nineteen months ago," said Cullen. "The body was only recently discovered in Edinburgh. Have you any idea what could have happened to him?"

"No idea at all," said Andrews. "As I said, I haven't seen him in years."

"Did the police speak to you at the time of his disappearance?"

"No," said Andrews. "This is genuinely the first I heard of him being missing. I honestly thought he'd just stopped emailing."

"It was in the press, I believe," said Cullen. "Mr Strang featured in a national campaign."

Andrews shrugged. "I don't read the papers unless one of our games is featured."

"When was the last time you had contact with him?" said Cullen.

"I had a flurry of emails from him about a year and a half ago," said Andrews.

"How would you describe them?" said Cullen.

"Odd," said Andrews. "The last few emails were a bit cryptic. Before that, it had all been about his band and the music. He used to spam me a lot about gigs and what have you but I never had the time to go. I told him to stop sending me that shit and he took it a bit personally. There was radio silence for a few months, then he started up again with some bizarre stuff."

"When was this?" said Cullen.

Andrews swallowed, his large Adam's apple bobbing up and down. "About nineteen months ago."

"I see," said Cullen. "These emails, what do you mean by cryptic?"

Andrews screwed his face up. "Just *bizarre*." He picked up a foam stress ball from his desk and start squeezing it. "It was like he was writing sort of poetry, you know?"

"Do you still have the emails?"

"Let me check," said Andrews, before tapping on his computer. "Here we go. I'll just print it for you."

He left Cullen alone for a minute or so while he walked through the office. Cullen took in the open-plan space outside the *pod*. Andrews was clearly a big shot here - four people approached him on his way to the printer, apparently looking for approval for something or other.

Andrews returned and handed the pages over. "Printer was out of paper. Sorry."

"Don't worry about it," said Cullen, focusing on the emails, eighteen or so lengthy messages over several pages.

"I'd asked him how the record deal was going," said Andrews. "He'd mentioned it in one of the previous emails, but it all went quiet."

Cullen found the paragraph, two months before the disappearance. Strang was telling a tale of how he was going to become a big shot. "Do you know anything else about the record deal?"

Andrews shook his head. "Afraid not. What Jimi sent back was a bit weird, though."

Cullen glanced through the last email. "Did you reply to this?"

Andrews shook his head.

Cullen read the email.

I could have paid it forward, but instead I'll pay it back
I could have moved forward, but instead I'll paint it black

Matte Black walls
Black Matt steals time
Time will get us all
When is our time up?
When is up down and down up?
When do I go under the waves?

Under the water
Let me drown
I'm not waving
I'm going down

I failed, but to succeed is to fail fully.
In failing, I failed to fail.

In the end, I was reduced to it.
Stealing what wasn't mine, taking what didn't belong to me, coveting my neighbour's wife.

Betrayal is the hardest part.
Dishonesty, theft, hiding.

Cullen tossed the sheets down on the desk. It was

clearly the work of someone with a broken mind or who'd had a lot to drink. "What the hell does it mean?"

"I've no idea," said Andrews.

"Is there anything in there you can make head or tail of?" said Cullen.

Andrews shook his head. "I tried but I just gave up."

Cullen could picture the hours he'd lose to looking through the passage, trying to decrypt and decipher it. It would be like being back at university.

"When is the funeral?" said Andrews.

"You'll need to discuss that matter with Mr Strang's mother," said Cullen. "Is there anyone else I should speak to?"

"You'll have met the guys in his band, right?" said Andrews.

Cullen nodded.

"Other than that, no," said Andrews. "Sorry."

"What about Paul McKay?"

Andrews' eyes widened. "Well, you can certainly try. Jimi and Paul hadn't spoken since school."

Cullen collected the sheets and got to his feet. "Thanks for your time, Mr Andrews. That's been very helpful."

"Best get back to it," said Andrews. "This company won't run itself."

Cullen frowned. "Do you own this place?"

Andrews smiled. "I do."

Cullen got to his feet, trying not to feel insignificant compared to his success.

54

Cullen finally got hold of Paul McKay and met him at his work, a nondescript office in the city centre. As Andrews had alluded to, McKay and Strang hadn't spoken since school and there was no string of emails to decipher, no hidden leads.

He drove back to Dalhousie, parking outside his parents' house. They weren't in. He toyed with whether to call Rarity and give her an update but, in the end, he decided to let her do the calling.

He had The Invisibles playing, trying to get inside Jimi's head and failing. All he was achieving was reasserting his hatred of guitar music. He reached over and put on some Ólafur Arnalds. Tom had lent him it a few months ago, heartbreakingly beautiful Icelandic piano music.

His tastes were moving away from techno a little, but maybe not too far - the music was minimal and sparse in the same vein as most of the other tunes he would listen to, just lacking the solid four-to-the-floor bass drum and off-beat hi-hat.

The rush of emotion he felt in his stomach, the piano chords and melodies intersecting with the caffeine in his veins, made him think of Sharon.

The baby.

Her promotion.

She hadn't called him, but then he hadn't called her.

He hoped she was okay.

He realised he'd managed to distract himself from wallowing in his situation, wrapping himself in a cloak of work. It had been good for him - maybe Rarity was wiser than he gave credit for.

Rather than check if his old key still worked, he picked the stack of papers off the passenger seat. He flicked the light on then looked through the emails between Strang and Andrews.

The bulk of the older mails were full of the usual banality - weddings, bragging about successes, gossip about school friends and Strang talking about himself a lot. Cullen found it interesting that Andrews, the bona fide success of the two, barely mentioned anything about the fact he owned one of the most successful computer games companies in the world, let alone the UK.

Cullen finally gave in, focusing on *the poem*.

I could have paid it forward, but instead I'll pay it back

What was he paying back? There was that saying about 'paying your dues' in music. Was it that?

Paying it forward was an American concept Cullen remembered from sitting through a film with Sharon. The idea was about passing on good things to people rather than waiting for it to come to you, a modern twist on instant karma.

Strang was saying he hadn't paid anything forward. He was going to pay something back. Or pay someone back.

I could have moved forward, but instead I'll paint it black
* * *

Paint It Black was one of the few Rolling Stones songs Cullen's dad would allow in the house. He remembered his sister going through a Stones phase, mainly aimed at annoying their father, and he had a vivid memory of *19th Nervous Breakdown* filling the house from her giant stereo.

Was Strang into the Stones? Cullen didn't know. The only thing he could remember was the poster on his wall, *'Who the fuck is Mick Jagger?'* A quick search on his phone revealed it was Keith Richards, the Stones guitarist.

Either way, Cullen didn't know if it meant anything or not.

A quick search on Wikipedia told him the song was about a girl's funeral. He could spend hours decoding some hidden meaning but it was most likely just used to rhyme and fit the meter.

Matte Black walls
Black Matt steals time
Time will get us all
When is our time up?
When is up down and down up?
When do I go under the waves?

Who or what was Black Matt?

There were lots of nautical references. Sharon loved Jeff Buckley, the subject of one of Strang's posters in his room and the t-shirt he'd been wearing when his body was found. Cullen did a search and found he died of drowning. Was it a reference to that? Was there anything to it or just hero worship?

* * *

Under the water
Let me drown
I'm not waving
I'm going down

More water.

What was he on about? It just didn't make any sense to Cullen. His degree had attempted to train him in analysing imagery and so on, but it just left him cold and confused.

In the end, I was reduced to it.
Stealing what wasn't mine, taking what didn't belong to me,
coveting my neighbour's wife.

The only thing Cullen thought was it could be a reference to having an affair with someone but who?

Beth Williamson immediately sprung to mind. She was attractive and in the same band. She'd told them Jimi tried it on with her but he got the feeling nothing happened there.

With David Johnson, all Cullen could determine was he had been single for years, suspecting he was probably gay. It was maybe worth another look if they got even more desperate.

Strang's mother had mentioned a girl, Jane or something, but they'd failed to find her or anyone who could validate it.

The only other possibility was Marta, Alex's girlfriend.

She was a heroin addict with children. She wasn't bad looking, Cullen figured, and maybe Strang was bewitched by that rock 'n' roll thing. The allure of heroin captivated the whole seventies scene, giving the stupidity a hint of danger and a sense of rebellion.

Live fast, die young, leave a good-looking corpse. Strang's own corpse certainly didn't qualify.

Could Strang have slept with Marta? Could Hughes have killed Strang in revenge? Stabbing someone with a screwdriver seemed desperate, a real crime of passion. An accident?

I failed, but to succeed is to fail fully.
In failing, I failed to fail.

It was just mumbo jumbo. What a fucking mess.

Cullen looked up. The light in his parents' house was now on. He chucked the paper on the passenger seat and got out, collecting his overnight bag and walking over, his heartbeat quickening with each step. Curtains twitched next door as he walked up the drive and rang the bell.

"Are you getting that?"

Looked like both were in.

Cullen's mother opened the door, still dressed for work. She looked him up and down. "Scott, what are you doing here?"

"Got a room for the night?"

55

Dinner was ready by seven, giving Cullen time to talk football with his old man and how broken the Scottish form was these days. They ate in the dining room, as they did when he was growing up, the four of them round the table until Michelle went to university. Cullen's dad's two greyhounds sat on their sofa in the living room, intently watching for any scraps from the table.

Cullen had two helpings of lamb stew, rich and tender. He'd enjoyed talking to them, helping him forget all the shit of the last twenty-four hours. He struggled to recall the last time he'd just let that happen. Everything felt so hard these days.

At the back of his mind lurked all the demons that stopped him sleeping, stuff he needed to get out of his head and deal with.

"I got demoted back to DC," said Cullen.

"It's hard making it in the world, my boy," said Cullen's dad. "Remember that old saying though. 'That which doesn't destroy us can only serve to make us stronger'."

"I'll try and remember that, Dad."

His dad checked his watch. "Is that the time? The football's just about to start. Will you come and watch it with me?"

"Maybe later," said Cullen, remembering he was meeting Guthrie.

His old man got up and stretched his back. "Well, I'll leave you pair to it," he said, before waddling through to his reclining chair.

His mother poured another glass of wine for Cullen.

"Thanks." Cullen stared at the glass, thinking that one day soon he too would be a dad, leaving his son or daughter to talk to Sharon while he limped through to the living room.

"I know that look," said his mother.

Cullen looked up. "What look?"

"Your father gets it. Something's up, isn't it?"

Cullen rubbed his ear. "I'm fine."

"I know when you're lying to me, Scott James Cullen."

All three names never meant anything good. "Sharon's pregnant."

"That's wonderful news."

"Really?"

"Another grandchild," said his mother. "You always said you weren't going to have children."

"Wasn't planning on it," said Cullen.

"Oh, Scott, have you been a silly boy again?"

Cullen slammed his glass down. "What do you mean *again*? I've not got anyone else pregnant that I know of."

"You're usually to blame," she said, smiling.

"Thanks," said Cullen, shaking his head. "Why does everyone blame *me*?"

"You were always such a naughty boy, Scott. And it usually was your fault."

Cullen felt a tangle of emotion build up in the pit of his stomach.

"Do you want the baby?" she said.

Cullen sat quiet for a few seconds, mulling over just how much to tell his mother. The wine made the decision for him. "I just don't know. It's such a huge thing. Financially, I don't feel anywhere near ready to do it. I've got some money in the bank, but we need somewhere proper to live."

She looked disappointed. "I can see that."

"Do you think we should have it?" said Cullen.

"I don't know. I'm trying not to let my grandmotherly desire kick in." She took a sip of wine. "I don't think you're very mature, Scott. Remember what happened with you and Sharon last year?"

"How could I forget," said Cullen. "We've got over that, though."

"Have you? That was definitely your fault."

"The F-word again," said Cullen. "I was an idiot. Everyone knows that. I've admitted it to everyone. I've said sorry so many times."

"Do you love Sharon?"

"Yes," said Cullen. "Absolutely."

"Enough to say you'll commit to her for the rest of your life and give your child a secure home?"

Cullen looked away. "I'm not sure I'll ever be able to do that."

"With Sharon?"

"No," said Cullen, "but I'm an idiot, right?"

His mother laughed. "What do you want to do, Scott?"

Cullen drained his glass and got to his feet. "I want to get drunk and forget all about it."

56

Cullen was ten minutes early. He stood outside the Dal Ferry and watched the waves crash off the town's redundant harbour, lit up in the cold night air. Years ago, a ferry ran to Leith but it stopped with the coming of the trains, the pub keeping its name in tribute.

He got out his phone and called Sharon. "Evening," he said when she answered.

"You've been drinking, haven't you?" said Sharon.

"Just a glass of wine with dinner," said Cullen.

"You're outside a pub now, though."

Cullen laughed. "You'd make a good detective."

"Very funny. How are you?"

Cullen's reverie evaporated. "I've had better."

"Sorry for being a selfish bitch earlier."

"Don't worry," said Cullen. "I was a selfish prick last night."

"I understand about the cave," said Sharon.

"I wish it had done me some good," said Cullen. "We should have had that talk."

"I'll remind you next time."

"You better not plan on getting pregnant again."

"Scott..."

"Sorry. Coming up here was definitely the right thing to do, though. I had a good chat with my mum."

There was a long pause on the line. "And?"

"And that's all," said Cullen. "My head is still full of

shite, I just don't know what I think about it."

"I miss you," said Sharon.

"Yeah, me too. You know, this is the first night we've spent apart since I moved in."

"Really?"

"You've got a ready-made replacement, though," said Cullen.

"Fluffy isn't ginger enough."

"Very funny."

"So, what are you doing tonight?" said Sharon. "Watching the football with your dad?"

"I'm meeting up with Richard for a pint," said Cullen. "McAlpine?"

"No, he's still in Edinburgh," said Cullen. "Guthrie."

"As in DC Richard Guthrie?"

"Don't tell me you know him?"

"Not in a biblical sense," said Sharon. "I was on a course with him a few years ago. He's from Dundee, isn't he?"

"Yeah, he was based there but he got kicked out to Dalhousie," said Cullen. "I was at school with him."

"Spooky."

"It's weird that you know him," said Cullen. "Such a small world." He spotted Guthrie's approach. "I'll probably be back tomorrow to face the mighty Rarity. Better go. Love you."

"Love you, too."

Guthrie grinned as he saw Cullen. "Evening, Skinky."

Cullen smiled. "Evening, Goth."

"Fuck me, I've not heard that one in a long time," said Guthrie.

"You've grown out of all that Marilyn Manson shit, though, right?"

"Never."

Cullen could still picture him. "I take it your colleagues don't know about you wearing makeup?"

"No way." Guthrie led them inside, before ordering pints of Peroni.

Cullen found a table by the window overlooking the North Sea, the waves seeming larger this close.

The football was on the large screen - Liverpool dishing out a solid hammering to Newcastle. The place was dead, only a few middle-aged men too tight to pay for Sky nursing their solitary pint well into the second half.

Cullen raised his glass. "Cheers."

Guthrie reciprocated. He pointed at the football. "Can't believe how bad Aberdeen are doing."

Cullen nodded. "It's depressing, isn't it? I'm glad Brown is going. Derek McInnes should be good."

"Anyone other than Brown, right?"

"Definitely," said Cullen. "Good win against Hearts on Saturday, though."

"Aye, decent," said Guthrie.

"Do you still go?"

Guthrie nodded. "Still a season ticket holder for my sins. One of the best things about CID is that it's nine to five, give or take, so I get my weekends off for football."

"I'm supposed to be the same, but it never quite works out like that," said Cullen.

"You were always ambitious, though, Skinky."

Cullen shrugged. "I guess."

"You got a bird?" said Guthrie.

Cullen nodded. "Turns out you know her. Sharon McNeill."

Guthrie's eyes bulged. "Holy shit. Punching above

your weight there, mate."

Cullen laughed.

"How's she doing?" said Guthrie.

"Well," said Cullen. "She's in line for a DI position."

"How does that make you feel?"

"I've been an ADS," said Cullen, "so I'm not jealous or anything."

"I heard you got demoted."

Cullen almost spat beer on the table. "How the fuck did you find that out?"

"There was a national announcement came out on the email this afternoon. After our wee chat earlier, I had to look. If you'd been working instead of arsing about in Dundee, you might have seen it."

"Must have been busy," said Cullen.

"How do you feel?"

"Fucked off, to be brutally honest," said Cullen.

"What are you going to do?"

Cullen took his pint past the halfway mark. "The way I see it, I've got to stop giving a fuck. Sharon can earn the money. She's going to be a DI, I'm happy to bide my time, keep things steady."

Guthrie grinned. "Proper little house husband."

"Something like that," said Cullen. "Enough about me, though. How's your love life?"

"It's on a ventilator, put it that way," said Guthrie. "I can feel my virginity growing back."

"That's my line," said Cullen.

"It's not like you've copyrighted it, though, is it?" said Guthrie. "I don't mind being single. Saves on arguments and stuff. See enough of that in the job."

"And your job prospects?"

"I'm happy as a DC," said Guthrie. "I'm doing a

proper job, solving crimes, helping people. If I got promoted, I'd be managing half of Angus. I'd be like a supermarket area manager or something. I get paid the same as you and it's cheap as chips to live up here."

"Aye, Edinburgh's not cheap."

There was an explosion of sound from the football crowd as a penalty was awarded and a red card shown to the Newcastle goalkeeper.

"You still keep in touch with the other Richard?" said Guthrie.

"Mr McAlpine is very well. He moved back to Edinburgh last year. We were sharing a flat for a bit."

"Is he still doing all that gay shit?" said Guthrie.

"Fuck's sake, Goth, he's gay. Get over it."

"Hang on, you asked if I was still doing all that goth shit," said Guthrie. "That's a hate crime now."

"Fuck off it is," said Cullen.

Guthrie shook his head. "Still don't like it."

Cullen laughed. "I can see why you never left Dal."

"Why would you want to?" said Guthrie.

"Why indeed."

The front door opened and three men walked in. Cullen recognised them immediately, total wankers from their year at school. Matt MacLeod, Alan Thomson and Gregor Smith, all looking three sheets to the wind.

Guthrie looked round. "It's those arseholes."

"I've not seen them since I was at uni," said Cullen.

"They've got worse," said Guthrie. "MacLeod lives down your way now."

"Edinburgh?"

Guthrie nodded. "Still a wanker."

Even though there were plenty of empty tables, they sat down next to Cullen and Guthrie.

"Look who the cat dragged in," said MacLeod. "The big city boy is back in town."

"You live in Edinburgh, too," said Cullen.

"Aye, and I make a fucking load more cash than you do, you cunt," said MacLeod, stabbing a finger at Cullen. "You're a pig as well, aren't you, Skinky?"

"Whatever," said Cullen.

"Oink!"

Thomson and Smith started making pig noises.

Cullen got his warrant card out. "We can make this official."

MacLeod held his hands up like he was raising a handbag. "You not brought your boyfriend with you, Cullen?"

"What are you talking about?"

"Rich McAlpine," said MacLeod. "Someone told me you were living with him. Must be *nice*."

"I see you're still a total wanker, Matt."

"That the best you've got?" said MacLeod. He burped. "How's your sister, by the way?"

Cullen sunk the rest of his pint. "Come on, Goth, there are plenty of other pubs in this town."

57

"Still the best bag of chips in Scotland," said Cullen, munching noisily.

They were outside the chip shop on Church Street, leaning against the window as the staff closed up.

Guthrie tapped his belly. "That's why I'll never make a DS."

"One of many reasons."

"Ha ha," said Guthrie, his voice devoid of humour.

Cullen balled up his bag, feeling woozy from the beer and wine. "Can't believe we saw those pricks earlier."

"Thomson and Smith still live here," said Guthrie. "I've sorted them out a few times over the years, usually when the pool league gets a bit rowdy."

"What about MacLeod?"

"No idea," said Guthrie. "I've not seen him for years. Just knew he lived in Edinburgh. He did a bit of damage a few years back, walking on cars and shit, had to arrest and charge him. He dropped off the radar after that."

"Twat."

"Aye."

Cullen finished his bottle of Irn Bru then walked over to chuck it in the bin.

"Scott Cullen!"

Cullen turned around. The mad woman from the other night was pointing at him.

"You big fucking bully!"

Cullen's shoulders slumped. Here we go again.

She marched up to Cullen and started shouting at him again. "You bullied me!"

Guthrie got between them. "I'm warning you. Clear off or it's a night in the cells for you."

Her eyes danced between them, before she eventually walked off the way she'd come, glaring at Cullen as she went.

Cullen watched her enter a stairwell just down the road. "That's second time she's done that in the last week. I've no idea who she is or what I've done to her."

"She was in our year," said Guthrie.

"Still don't remember her."

"You sat next to her in French."

Cullen frowned, trying to mentally overlay the fat face of the adult onto the thinner one of the girl. "She's put on a lot of weight, then."

"Haven't we all?"

"What's all that bullying shit?" said Cullen.

"Beats me. You were a bit of a wanker at times."

"Why do I keep on bumping into her?" said Cullen. "Last time was just up the road at the Italian."

"She lives on this street," said Guthrie. "Maybe something to do with you investigating her brother's murder."

"What?"

Guthrie pointed a chip after her. "Audrey Strang."

"Of all the people to bloody bump into." Cullen started off after her.

Guthrie grabbed his shoulder, tugging him back. "What are you playing at, Skinky?"

"I need to speak to her."

"Not in this state."

"I'm not pissed."

"No, but you have had a fair few pints. Leave it till tomorrow."

Cullen looked down at the street, breathing hard. "Right, fine."

Guthrie balled up his own chip wrapper. "I need to get home. We'd best make an early start tomorrow. See you in the station first thing?"

"Aye."

Cullen was relieved there was no offer of a whisky in Guthrie's flat.

Tuesday
2nd April 2013

58

Cullen jolted awake. He had no idea where he was.

The dream of Marta Hunter again, her children's faces replaced by Matt MacLeod and his two accomplices.

He sat up and fumbled around on the bedside table, eventually touching a lamp. He had to run his fingers down the back of the unit to find the power button.

It took a few seconds for his eyes to adjust. He was back in his old room, heavily redecorated since he left twelve years ago.

His head stung slightly from the edges of a hangover, but he'd had the foresight to put a pint of water beside the bed. He drank it then checked his watch - it was just after eight.

He slumped back and rubbed his head. He'd needed the sleep but his body was telling him he could do with another few hours. He struggled out of bed and headed downstairs.

His parents were gone. Both would already be at work. There was a Post-It note on the kitchen table. *'Call your sister! Love, Mum.'* Michelle's mobile number was underneath.

Ignoring the note, he failed to find cartridges for their new espresso machine and settled for a mug of tea instead. He skipped breakfast, the chips still heavy in his stomach.

The dogs wandered through, looking for affection or leftover toast - Cullen didn't know which they'd prefer. He knelt down and patted them as one of them licked his face.

He sat at the table, reading the Angus edition of the Dundee *Courier* as he drank his tea. He kept seeing the Post-It, annoyed that it was him being told to call his sister.

Michelle had been an arse to him since she went to uni in Glasgow. Why should *he* bother? She was a year older. She was supposed to be the grown-up one.

Cullen shook his head and stabbed Michelle's number into his contacts, replacing the old one. It explained the lack of response the couple of times he had bothered to text.

He called Sharon.

"Did you have a good night?" she said.

"Sort of."

"I'm not even going to ask."

Cullen laughed. "It wasn't too heavy. Just a few pints, talking about football and putting the world to rights."

"I can well imagine."

"How are you doing?"

"Better," she said. "I'm over this bug, finally. I'm going to show Turnbull what's what."

"Remember not to push yourself too hard," said Cullen.

"Scott, I'm pregnant not disabled."

"I know," said Cullen. "I'm just saying. As it stands, I don't think either of us wants the decision taken out of our own hands, do we?"

"No," said Sharon, eventually. "When do you think you'll be back?"

"So, you actually missed me last night?"

"Of course," said Sharon, her voice sounding edgy.

Cullen knew not to push it. "I'll see how things are here. Got a lead or two, maybe, but nothing concrete. Should be back tonight hopefully."

"I'm looking forward to it."

"I meant what I said last night," said Cullen. "We do need to talk."

"I know we do."

"Can we do it somewhere other than the flat?" said Cullen. "I don't want you getting all territorial."

"I'm not territorial."

"You can be," said Cullen. "Look, let's go for dinner. Neutral venue and all that."

"Fine."

"I love you," said Cullen. "I'm looking forward to seeing you."

"Me too."

Cullen ended the call, still with no idea what to do about the baby.

59

Guthrie knocked on Audrey Patterson's door. No answer.

Cullen leaned against the tenement wall. "We should have spoken to her last night. She's not in now."

"We've got all day."

"You cleared to help me, then?"

"Aye. Got in at the back of seven and got through the last of the paperwork upstairs are chasing me for. Managed to palm last night's two burglaries off to uniform. By the looks of things, neither has anything to do with those fuckwits we bumped into last night."

"I'll believe it when you get a conviction," said Cullen, smiling.

"What's the plan of attack, then?"

Cullen thumbed at the door. "We need to speak to her. It's embarrassing how little we know about him."

"He was like that at school."

"I don't remember him."

"He was a pretentious little prick." Guthrie hammered the door again. "Even though he was three years younger than us he used to march around thinking he was so fucking cool."

"How come I've forgotten him?"

"You're just shit," said Guthrie. "It was the same with his sister and you sat next to her in French."

"Yeah." Cullen knocked on the door, his head throbbing from lack of coffee. "Open up, Ms Patterson."

"No!"

It was the first time she'd responded.

"Ms Patterson," said Cullen, "we need to speak to you about your brother."

"I know what you're trying to do!"

Cullen's already thin patience was stretched almost to breaking point. "What are we trying to do?"

"You want to rape me like my husband did!"

Cullen took a step back. "What the fuck is going on here?"

Guthrie rubbed his neck. "Long story. Remember Dean Patterson? He was in the year above us?"

Cullen pictured a neanderthal knuckle dragger in his sister's class. "I remember him."

"Well, he married her," said Guthrie. "We were out here all the bloody time, domestic after domestic. Anyway, push came to shove one night. He got drunk and raped her, said it was his marital right and all that shite. We put him away for it. Not much later, her brother went missing. She's not been the same since."

Cullen shook his head. "Christ."

Guthrie stepped forward and hammered the door again. "Come on, Audrey. This is about your brother. Don't make us get your parents involved again."

The door slowly opened. Audrey Patterson led them into the living room and sat on a futon. There was no other furniture, so they remained standing. The place was immaculately tidy. It was a different sparseness to the heroin addicts' flats, an active choice of minimalism rather than having sold everything to buy drugs.

Audrey looked up at Cullen. "Are you here to say sorry, then?"

Cullen took a long look at her, starting to recognise the

237

young girl from his French class. "What am I apologising for?"

"The way you treated me at school!"

Cullen was used to people shouting at him, but knowing there was something personal and longstanding behind the anger was a lot harder to deal with than some abstract hatred for authority. "How did I treat you?"

"You used to take the mick out of me," said Audrey. "You and your friends. Every day for *two years*. I had no self-esteem by the time I left school." A tear slid down her cheek. "That's why I married Dean, the first man to show me the time of day. I still shake when I hear your name, Scott Cullen. I couldn't believe I saw you on *my street*."

Cullen kept a distance "Audrey, I'm sorry. I didn't mean any harm."

"You said I smelled!"

Embarrassment burnt its way up Cullen's neck. "Come on, I was just being childish."

"You said it and it hurt. You used to chip away at me, you and Gareth and Linda and Melanie. Chipped away at me all the time. I felt so small and tiny."

"I'm truly sorry, Audrey. I shouldn't have done that. I'm a police officer now. I protect people. I should have protected you back then."

Audrey's eyes locked onto his for the first time since they'd arrived. "But you didn't."

Cullen still couldn't remember taking the piss out of her though he vaguely recalled the other names. "I'm sorry."

"Scott is working on your brother's murder, Audrey," said Guthrie.

Audrey's eyes lit up and danced between them. "Jimi?"

"Yes," said Guthrie. "The police in Edinburgh are investigating. Scott is one of the detectives."

"Mum told me he'd been found. How can I help you?"

Cullen decided to get straight in while the clarity and focus remained. "I want to know if there was anyone who was upset or angry with your brother at any point leading up to him going missing."

Audrey thought about it for a few seconds. "Not really. I don't think so. I've been over it so many times in my head, you know?"

Cullen could well imagine. "And there's nobody? What about at school?"

Audrey gritted her teeth. "Jimi was bullied a lot by some of the boys in our year. Alan Thomson, Gregor Smith, Matt MacLeod. Those bad boys."

Cullen exchanged a brief look with Guthrie, who merely shrugged. "What sort of thing?"

"You know how cruel kids can be," said Audrey. "They used to beat him up and tease him for being gay."

"Was he?"

Audrey laughed through the tears. "God, no. Jimi was one for the girls."

Cullen had to be careful not to inflict his own personal opinion on the case, but Matt MacLeod and those idiots he was drinking with were starting to look like a lead. "Anyone else?"

Audrey shook her head, her long hair dancing.

"You've been a great help, Audrey," said Cullen. "Thanks."

He locked eyes with her.

"And I really am sorry for any hurt I've caused you."

60

They sat in a cafe, Cullen's head finally starting to push into gear with his second Americano. They were squaring off their notebooks should push come to shove with anything from the interview with Audrey.

"So, what do you think about her?" said Guthrie.

"She could be on to something," said Cullen. "Matt MacLeod lives in Edinburgh, right?"

"Has done for years, I think."

"Right," said Cullen. "If he bullied the boy when they were younger, then Christ knows what could have happened in Edinburgh."

"Killing him and leaving him down a tunnel, though?" said Guthrie.

"I've seen some strange things in my time. I could see it. I really could."

"It's worth a shot."

Cullen took a sip of coffee. "I still can't remember her from school."

"You're losing your mind, Skinky. It's hardly my fault if you can't remember people you were at school with. Maybe you've got Alzheimers?"

"Very funny," said Cullen. "My gran had that, you know?"

"Maybe you should get checked out?"

"I'm just tired," said Cullen. "Not sleeping much and I'm putting myself under so much pressure just now."

"Did you mean it when you said sorry to her?"

Cullen rubbed his neck. "I think so. You said I was a wanker at school. I probably was. You know what that place was like, though. It was dog eat dog. If you didn't piss on the heads of the people below you then you'd get fucked over by Johnnie Gardner or Craig Wilkie or one of those guys."

Guthrie nodded. "True. I think it's got a lot better since they moved to the new school."

"Couldn't get any worse."

Guthrie seemed to want to say something, but he kept quiet.

Cullen looked across the quiet cafe, thinking they might be starting to get somewhere.

He'd been running on fumes for the last few weeks. He was pushing himself so hard he was starting to worry he'd do himself a mischief. He'd been struggling with words, failing to finish sentences. Not remembering people he was at school with wasn't a great sign. He needed a holiday.

After he got a conviction.

Matt MacLeod was somebody he did remember from school. The boy was a total wanker and it seemed like the man was even worse. MacLeod was never in with the hard kids - the ones who ended up in prison or the army or both - but he knew how to deflect bullying onto others and was capable of a lot of it himself, way worse than anything Cullen had done.

The email.

"Fucking Black Matt," said Cullen, reaching into his pocket for the print-out. "Matt fucking MacLeod." He read the lines. "*Matte Black walls. Black Matt steals time.*"

"What the fuck is that?" said Guthrie.

"We need to bring MacLeod in."

61

The MacLeods lived at the other end of the street from Cullen's parents. The houses shared a design though they'd diverged over the years in rear extensions, conservatories and loft conversions.

"This it?" said Cullen.

"Aye," said Guthrie.

A man in his mid-sixties marched past them on the pavement, carrying his *Courier* and a bag of morning rolls, the lightweight packets of air and flour Cullen despised.

"It's too quiet these days," said Cullen. "I remember playing football on the street when we were kids."

"Might have been playing with MacLeod," said Guthrie, whose parents still lived at the other end of town, albeit in separate houses with new partners.

"The street is still full of people our parents' age growing old together, kids all left home," said Cullen.

"You're in a cheery mood, Skinky."

"Yeah, sorry," said Cullen. "Force of habit."

"MacLeod should be in," said Guthrie.

They marched past the collection of ceramic frogs on the tarmac and Cullen knocked on the door, warrant card ready.

MacLeod answered, wearing a dressing gown and looking like death. "Sorry, my parents are both at work." He started shutting the door.

Cullen's foot blocked it. "Mr MacLeod, we need to ask you a few questions in relation to the disappearance and murder of James Strang."

"Piss off," said MacLeod.

"I'm sorry?" said Cullen, as he pocketed his warrant card.

"You pair have a cheek after the state I saw you in last night," said MacLeod.

"This isn't something you have a choice in," said Cullen, "other than doing it here or down the station."

MacLeod pushed the door shut, knocking Cullen's foot back out, his toes sending waves of pain to his brain. The key turned in the lock.

Cullen looked down - MacLeod had torn a chunk out of his new shoes. "This isn't happening." He looked at Guthrie. "Wait here."

He jogged round the side of the house, getting his suit jacket caught on brambles in the back garden.

The back door was wide open.

Cullen ran for it.

The door slammed shut just before he got there, MacLeod's face grinning through the distorted glass.

Cullen tugged the handle, managing to push the door open again.

"Get to fuck," said MacLeod.

Cullen tried to keep his grip tight but eventually had to let go. The door slammed shut and MacLeod locked it.

Cullen swore. He lost sight of MacLeod in the kitchen and ran back to the front of the house.

"What's going on?" said Guthrie.

"He's locked both fucking doors."

Cullen knelt down and shouted through the letterbox.

"Mr MacLeod, I can call your parents if you prefer. I'm sure our dads play golf together."

"I've not done anything," said MacLeod.

"Then let's talk about this down the station," said Cullen. "I don't want to have to charge you with obstruction or resisting arrest."

"Not done nothing."

"Come on down the station, then," said Cullen. "Prove your innocence."

No answer.

"Mr MacLeod," said Guthrie. "We can charge you with obstruction. You'll get a fairly sizeable fine."

The door finally opened.

62

MacLeod's solicitor turned up promptly, responding to the phone call Cullen allowed him before they left his street. He looked like a friendly PE teacher, wholly dissimilar to the usual lawyers Cullen dealt with in Edinburgh.

"Mr MacLeod," said Cullen, "did you know one James Strang?"

MacLeod glanced at his lawyer, who returned the briefest of nods. "Yes. I did."

"We have reason to believe you bullied him at school," said Cullen. "Is that correct?"

"Have you got anything official from the school or other appropriate education authorities to that effect?" said the solicitor.

"We have witness statements," said Cullen.

"You've got nothing," said MacLeod.

"What we've got, Mr MacLeod," said Cullen, "is someone you bullied at school being found dead in Edinburgh, the city you've lived in for the last twelve years. Is that a coincidence?"

"Of course it is," said MacLeod.

"I hate coincidences," said Cullen.

"Me too," said Guthrie. "Usually they're not coincidences."

"I knew Jimi lived through in Edinburgh," said MacLeod. "I bumped into the wee guy in HMV once and in a pub another time. We got on well, I think."

"Did you bully him?" said Cullen.

"Are you whiter than white?" said MacLeod. "I heard some stories about you and his sister, Audrey. Remember her?" He grinned. "Shouldn't you be under investigation?"

"Answer the question," said Cullen, not rising to the bait.

MacLeod threw his hands up in the air and laughed. "There's nothing to answer. Unless you've got something on me, pal, you're wasting my time."

"It's funny finding you back in your home town after James Strang was found dead," said Cullen. "You've not gone to ground or anything, have you, Mr MacLeod?"

"Mr Cullen," said the lawyer, "are you implying something about my client here?"

"There's no implying anything," said Cullen. "I'm investigating an avenue of inquiry."

"The reason I'm here is I've got a few things going on in my private life." MacLeod fiddled with his watch strap. "My girlfriend left me and I'm between jobs. I've kicked my tenants out of my flat and I'm just about ready to get back in there. I'm just staying with my folks while things sort themselves out in Edinburgh."

"And you are definitely not lying low?" said Cullen.

"Would I admit it if I was?" said MacLeod. "Would I go out on the lash in the town on a Monday night if I was lying low?"

"You are under police interview here," said Cullen. "This is on the record."

"Whatever," said MacLeod, waving his hands away.

"Did you know James Strang?" said Cullen.

"We've been over this," said MacLeod. "Yes, I knew

him. A bit. If you're going to ask me what happened, I've told you. Any more of that and I'll stop co-operating until you charge me. I know my rights, Skinky."

"Don't call me that," said Cullen.

MacLeod smirked. "Have I touched a nerve?"

"Does *Black Matt* mean anything to you?" said Cullen.

MacLeod frowned. "Should it?"

"See, there's another coincidence," said Cullen. "Mr Strang sent an email which included the term *Black Matt*. You think that's merely a coincidence?"

"I'm not black, am I?" said MacLeod. "I'm as white as you pair. I know the police don't like a person of colour, do you?"

The lawyer's eyes bulged. He leaned over and whispered in MacLeod's ear.

"Do you wish to retract that comment?" said Guthrie.

"Aye," said MacLeod. "I didn't mean anything by it. Sorry."

"So, just for the record," said Cullen, "the phrase *Black Matt* means nothing to you?"

MacLeod leaned forward. "This has got nothing to do with your sister, has it?"

Cullen scowled. "Why would it?"

MacLeod looked at Guthrie. "I slipped his sister a length back in the day. Don't think Mr Cullen got over that. Maybe he fancied a go up her."

Cullen gave him his business card, still on Lothian & Borders stationery, his hand shaking. "If you think of anything then please don't hesitate to call," he said, through gritted teeth.

"Of course I won't," said MacLeod, getting to his feet, grinning wide.

Guthrie arranged for a uniform to show them out then

closed the door.

"I never liked that fucker," said Cullen.

"Tell me this has nothing to do with him going out with your sister?" said Guthrie.

"Nothing," said Cullen. "I'd totally forgotten about it."

"Really?" said Guthrie. "You've been forgetting a lot recently."

Cullen shrugged. "I told you, I'm stressed and tired. Got a lot going on in my private and professional lives."

"The way you were going at him there, I almost started to feel sorry for him."

"That would take a lot," said Cullen.

"You're telling me," said Guthrie. "So, what do you reckon, then?"

"I need to get approval to investigate him," said Cullen. "Maybe put a tail on him."

"You think he's a suspect?"

"I do. He's got a clear motive and potential opportunity in Edinburgh."

"I still don't get how they could have had a fight beneath Edinburgh and Strang ended up dead," said Guthrie. "Why there?"

"Good place to hide a body," said Cullen. "He'd never have been found if those kids hadn't read *The List*." He tried to think it through logically. "They could have met in a pub and then MacLeod found out about the practice rooms. He went there and they got into a fight. Who knows?"

"This is your case," said Guthrie, raising an eyebrow.

"I'm going to get approval for surveillance on MacLeod," said Cullen.

Guthrie looked at the ceiling. "You mean me, don't you?"

Cullen nodded. "Of course."

"Remind me never to hit on your sister."

63

Cullen got back to Leith Walk just after one, heading straight for the Incident Room. It was empty.

His stomach rumbled, the booze and chips calories having been spent. He headed to the canteen for lunch, opting for macaroni cheese and more chips.

He spotted Buxton and Rarity and joined them.

"Welcome back, Constable," said Rarity. "I trust your head is sufficiently clear?"

Cullen snorted. "Something like that." He eyed the industrial-strength coffee on his tray.

Between mouthfuls, he gave her an update on the slight progress he'd made in Dalhousie - the emails, Strang's sister and Matt MacLeod.

"That's something, I suppose," said Rarity. "Nothing else?"

"Think it's dried up," said Cullen. "And how's it going here?"

"We're progressing," said Rarity. "That's about all I can say."

"How far?" said Cullen. He doubted they were any further forward.

Rarity ran her hand through her hair. "Have you any avenues you wish to progress?"

"I want surveillance put on MacLeod," said Cullen.

"That's quite an expense," said Rarity.

"Look, I've brought you a clear suspect," said Cullen,

"all I need is two bodies to tail him for a few days to see if he does anything dodgy."

"We're talking twelve hour shifts," said Rarity. "The cost will soon build up. I'm not sure I can sanction that. It seems a bit far-fetched and I'm not sure it isn't a personal vendetta."

"Excuse me?"

"You head home for a couple of days and then come back with someone you were at school with as a suspect."

"He's got means and opportunity," said Cullen.

"And no evidence," said Rarity.

Cullen was close to losing his cool. "That's why I want him tailed."

Buxton frowned. "Why do you think it's him?"

"He's got previous," said Cullen. "He bullied Strang at school. He lives through here, said he met Strang a couple of times."

"Why would he kill him, though?" said Buxton. "Seems extreme."

"This isn't one of the good guys," said Cullen. "He's a nasty piece of work. I suspect he's lying low, waiting for the coast to clear here. The discovery of the body was in the press, right?"

Rarity nodded.

"Well, then," said Cullen.

"We'll need to get Superintendent Turnbull to approve the budget." She prodded a finger at Cullen. "You're lucky. Before yesterday, it would have been cross-division, but the MIT's remit is national. You went on the training so you know where I'm coming from with this."

Cullen looked away. "Can we go and see Turnbull, please?"

"Fine," said Rarity.

64

Turnbull ushered them into his office. He had five minutes between meetings about the new structure. Cullen thought there seemed to be a continual review in place, the old command and control model transitioning perfectly to the new world.

"Now, how can I help you?" said Turnbull.

Rarity laid out the case, slightly more succinctly than Cullen had put it. Coming from her it sounded simple and rational, rather than confused and insane like his summary.

"And this is all entirely on the level?" said Turnbull, looking at Cullen.

Cullen nodded. "This is based on intel I pick up in Dalhousie, sir. I was doing some background checks into Strang. It initially came from his sister."

"I see," said Turnbull. "I do feel we might need to round-table this. Has DCI Cargill been briefed?"

"Not yet," said Rarity.

Turnbull frowned. "So, you've gone over her head?"

"We couldn't find her," said Rarity, "and this is, of course, a pressing operational matter."

"I see." Turnbull swivelled his chair round to look out of the window onto Leith Walk. "I have to admit I am more than moderately concerned about the potential reputational ramifications of this surveillance."

"How so?" said Cullen.

"This is my call and mine alone," said Turnbull. "There's a somewhat unhealthy blame culture forming in the early days of the new structure, I'm afraid. You say MacLeod is based in Dalhousie?"

"Correct," said Rarity.

"Well, this will add non-Edinburgh resource to my budget," said Turnbull. "I cannot have this looking like a land grab."

"Sir, the suspect is normally based in Edinburgh," said Cullen. "Unless we bring him in, we might lose him."

"He might slip off the radar, is that it?" said Turnbull.

"Precisely," said Cullen. "As it stands, we have him in Dalhousie at his parents' house. We don't know how long he'll stay there."

"And this is genuinely your only suspect?" said Turnbull.

"Correct," said Rarity.

Turnbull looked at Cullen. "Constable, you'll know how I feel about vendettas. You're from Dalhousie, aren't you?"

Cullen shrugged. "That's got nothing to do with it."

Turnbull got to his feet and paced over to the window. "What are you expecting this surveillance to bring to the fore?"

"We'll know he's guilty if he makes a run for it," said Cullen. "Plus, we'll know where he is."

"Fine," said Turnbull. "It's approved, but I'm not particularly comfortable about this course of action."

"Thanks," said Rarity. "And noted."

"I want a full investigation into this MacLeod character," said Turnbull, "and I want you to dive down every avenue that presents itself. Am I clear?"

Cullen had no idea how one was supposed to dive

down an avenue, but he nodded. "Absolutely, sir."

Rarity held the door open for him as Cullen followed her out to the stairwell. "I want to make it clear I've backed you up here."

"I appreciate it," said Cullen.

"Just so as you know," said Rarity, "if it subsequently transpires you're messing about with this, I will not hesitate in having you put on a disciplinary."

Cullen shook his head and walked past her.

65

Back at his desk, Cullen immediately called Guthrie. "It's approved."

"I'd say good," said Guthrie, "but this is going to be a nightmare."

"It's a chance to do some proper detective work," said Cullen, "rather than trying to find out who did a jobbie in the eighteenth hole of the Championship course or however else you fill your days."

Guthrie laughed. "I'll see what I can do."

"My DS is just phoning yours," said Cullen. "Wait until you're formally notified but I'd personally find someone who isn't too irritating to sit in a car with for a few days. Let me know if anything comes up."

"You'll be the first to know," said Guthrie.

Cullen ended the call and logged it in his notebook.

Chantal huffily sat down next to him.

"You're in a good mood," said Cullen.

"I forgot just how shit this job could be," said Chantal.

"I'm continually reminded."

She laughed. "Good to see you back. Nice holiday?"

"Hardly a holiday."

"You've got that hungover look," said Chantal.

Cullen ignored her. "What have you been up to?"

"You're not my boss any more," said Chantal.

"I'm just asking."

Chantal looked him up and down for few seconds

then slumped back in her chair. "Been on the phone with a lead from Strang's work. It turns out Strang was sleeping with the girlfriend of someone in the band."

This was news to Cullen. Another line from the poem jumped out at him.

Stealing what wasn't mine, taking what didn't belong to me, coveting my neighbour's wife.

"Any idea who it was?" said Cullen.

Chantal shook her head. "The boy said Strang was a shagger on the Russell Brand scale. I've got him coming in to give a proper statement this afternoon."

"Who do we think it is?"

"I think we can rule Beth out," said Chantal. "Pregnant woman with wedding ring and all that."

"This is nineteen months ago," said Cullen.

"Don't think it was her," said Chantal. "Beth worked at the shop, remember? They would surely have said he was getting it on with her, wouldn't they? Plus, she told us it wasn't her."

"I see your point," said Cullen. "It's definitely a girlfriend of someone in the band?"

"Definitely," said Chantal. "Which leaves David Johnson or Alex Hughes."

"Hughes," said Cullen. "I would put money on Johnson being gay."

"Is it the posh boy thing?"

Cullen shrugged. "I'm not being homophobic, I just think he could be, that's all."

"Those posh boys love to lull us girls into a false sense of security," said Chantal. "We think they're our mates, come shopping with us and then, all of a sudden, they're sticking the tongue in."

"Sorry I even mentioned it," said Cullen. "Right, so he

was cheating with either Johnson's or Hughes' girlfriends. Which one?"

"We need to speak to Johnson and Marta Hunter," said Chantal.

"Did you get round to catching up with his psychoanalyst?" said Cullen.

Chantal patted her hair. "We spoke to him, but he pleaded patient confidentiality."

"Is it worth pushing him?" said Cullen.

"Not yet."

Cullen nodded. "Great. Come on, let's go and see Marta Hunter."

"Don't you want to run it past Rarity?" said Chantal.

"Not really."

"Your funeral."

66

Cullen knocked hard on Marta Hunter's door. After a while, the door pulled back on the chain, her sunken cheeks peering round the edge.

"Can we speak to you?" said Cullen.

Marta let them in. "Come on through." She staggered to the living room.

"No kids today?" said Cullen.

"They're with my mother," said Marta. "Had Glasgow police here earlier."

Cullen leaned against the window frame and frowned. Bain's squad should have cleared it with Methven as the Senior Investigating Officer on the Strang case. "What were they wanting?"

"It was just stuff about Alex," said Marta.

"What sort of thing?"

Marta shrugged. "Can't remember." She clearly found it amusing.

Chantal cut straight to the chase. "How well did you get on with James Strang?"

"Jimi?" Marta seemed thrown. "He was okay. Nice enough. Only used to see him when the band played."

"You never went to the pub or to the same parties, nothing like that?" said Chantal.

"Afraid not," said Marta. "I wasn't much for going out." She looked at her feet. "Would much rather stay in."

"You'd rather take drugs, is that it?" said Cullen.

"I'm not answering that," said Marta.

"Did Alex take heroin as well?" said Cullen.

"I'm not answering that either," said Marta. "Those Glasgow policemen were asking about it and they got nothing."

Chantal glared at Cullen before smiling at Marta. "We have reason to believe that James slept with a girlfriend of someone in the band. Obviously that removes Beth, but includes David Johnson and Alex Hughes. You were Alex's girlfriend at the time, Marta, weren't you?"

Marta nodded. "I was."

"Did you sleep with James Strang?"

Marta looked away. "I'm not answering that one without a lawyer."

Chantal knelt in front of her and spoke in a low voice. "Well, you'd better arrange one. You'll need some childcare while we take you in. I'd imagine it'll take more than a few hours to find a lawyer and that's before we start asking questions."

Marta scratched her wrist and stared into space. "Fine." She bit a nail. "I never had sex with Jimi but he tried it on with me once. Must have thought I'd be an easy junkie or something. I knocked him back."

Chantal got to her feet, taking a few steps away. "When was this?"

"It'll be about two weeks before he went missing, I think," said Marta. "I'm not too good with keeping track of time. Alex was in Glasgow with one of his pals so Jimi knew I'd be alone in the flat, just me and the kids. His hands were everywhere as soon as he was through the door. I had to tell him to fu- to get away from me."

"How did Mr Strang respond?" said Chantal.

"He just started shouting, didn't he?" said Marta. "Screaming about how I'd led him on and let him down, that sort of thing."

"Had you led him on?" said Cullen.

A tear streaked down Marta's cheek. "No. My bairns were here. It wasn't right."

"I think we've heard enough," said Chantal. "We'll need an additional statement from you. We'll send some uniformed officers around to collect it later."

Marta nodded but didn't look up as they let themselves out.

Outside, Cullen had to shout at some kids by his car to get them to clear off. Luckily they hadn't keyed it.

Cullen buckled his seatbelt. "Can't believe Glasgow South have been speaking to her. We should have been told about it."

"What would they have been after?" said Chantal.

"Proof of the drugs motive."

"You going to do anything about it?"

"It's for Rarity or Methven to progress."

She flipped the sun visor back, checking her make-up in the mirror. "What do you want to do now?"

Cullen put the car in gear and pulled off. "Let's go and see Johnson."

67

David Johnson's office at the university was a pigsty. A box of Lego Technic lay open on a side desk and Johnson was halfway through building some sort of tractor. The rest of the small room was filled with papers and books. A blackboard sat across from the main desk, covered in scribbles.

"Mr Johnson, we understand your band was offered a record deal, is that correct?" said Cullen.

Johnson nodded.

"Why aren't you driving Rolls Royces into swimming pools, then?" said Cullen.

Johnson stared at the blackboard for a few seconds. "We were just about to sign the papers when the deal disappeared from under our feet, just like that." He clicked his fingers.

"That seems a bit strange," said Cullen. "Any idea why that happened?"

"None at all," said Johnson.

"How did it make you feel?" said Cullen.

Johnson's eyes darted between Cullen and Chantal. "Listen, am I a suspect here?"

"I don't know, are you?" said Cullen, his expression set.

Johnson's hands twitched. "Shouldn't we be doing this at the station with lawyers present?"

"There are two officers here," said Cullen. "This will

stand up in court if needs be. Are you trying to tell us you were involved in Mr Strang's death?"

Johnson shook his head. "No."

Chantal cleared her throat. "Mr Johnson, did you have a girlfriend at the time?"

Johnson looked away. "Yes, I did. Ailsa."

Cullen raised an eyebrow. His tenner would have been wasted.

"Did she have a relationship with Mr Strang?" said Chantal.

"I'm not prepared to comment on that, I'm afraid," said Johnson.

Chantal did the flirty head tilt Cullen had seen so many times. "Can I ask why?"

"It's nothing to do with this murder," said Johnson.

"So, something did happen?" said Chantal.

Johnson rubbed at his neck, struggling to keep his hands in one place. "No comment."

"We have reason to believe Mr Strang slept with the girlfriend of someone in the band," said Chantal. "Was that your girlfriend?"

"No comment."

"What was her name?" said Cullen.

Johnson stayed quiet.

"You already said Ailsa," said Cullen. "That's just a couple of phone calls."

Johnson gave the briefest of nods. "Ailsa McHardy."

"Do you still keep in touch?" said Cullen.

"Occasionally," said Johnson. "She lives in Falkirk now."

"Did she sleep with Mr Strang?" said Cullen.

"No comment."

Cullen smiled and put his notebook and pen away.

"We need you to report to the police station to give a statement."

"Certainly."

Cullen got to his feet and towered over the man. "No later than tomorrow."

They walked back to Cullen's car, double-parked on Buccleuch Place with a sign reading *On Police Business*. Neither spoke until they were inside.

Cullen pulled onto Buccleuch Street, turning left towards the most direct route back to the station. "What do you think of Johnson, then?"

"There's something there," said Chantal. "He was so evasive."

"Is there enough, though?"

"I don't know," said Chantal. "I really don't know."

"I think we need to go to Methven about this," said Cullen.

"What about Rarity?"

"She can come with us," said Cullen.

"Remember you're not an ADS any more," said Chantal.

"Doesn't stop me being a leader."

68

Cullen and Chantal briefed Methven, Rarity and Buxton in the Incident Room. She hadn't said anything, but Cullen just knew Rarity was annoyed with him going over her head to Methven earlier.

"This has been a slog," said Cullen, "but we've got three clear suspects. Matt MacLeod for one, and Alex Hughes and David Johnson, the other two men in The Invisibles."

Methven's eyes were flickering. "What's your thinking, Constable?"

"First," said Cullen, "we know MacLeod bullied Strang at school and they both lived in Edinburgh."

Methven frowned. "There better be more."

"You should meet the guy," said Cullen.

"Just because we sodding dislike someone," said Methven, "doesn't mean we go around arresting them."

"They clearly didn't like each other," said Cullen. "Maybe Strang attacked MacLeod, it got out of hand and Strang was killed."

"Not sure," said Methven.

"I've got surveillance on MacLeod," said Cullen. "He's still in Dalhousie."

"You've got sodding surveillance on this guy?" said Methven.

"Cargill and Turnbull have both approved it," said Rarity.

"Why the sodding hell have I not been informed?" said Methven.

"You were busy, sir," said Rarity.

Methven shook his head, arms folded and leaning back in his seat. "Go on, Constable."

"The other two suspects, Alex Hughes and David Johnson," said Cullen. "From a source of Chantal's, we believe Strang may have had an affair with one of their girlfriends. At the moment, it looks like it could be either of them."

"Is this plausible?" said Methven.

"We believe Strang might have been losing it towards the end, sir," said Chantal. "Their record deal fell through. I'm sure Scott's told you a lot of the stuff he's found."

"How are we progressing with these?" said Methven.

"We interviewed Alex Hughes' ex-girlfriend," said Cullen. "We will get a formal statement from her today but she confirmed Strang tried it on with her."

"Is she a suspect?" said Methven.

"I doubt it," said Cullen. "For Johnson, we need approval to bring him in for a formal interview. He was evasive when we spoke to him."

"Consider approval given," said Methven. "Is there any forensic evidence here?"

"Not that I know of," said Cullen.

"We've got nothing to link Strang to a suspect," said Chantal.

Methven glared at Cullen. "You had my hopes up for a minute there."

"I've been going through a list of people who bought screwdrivers," said Chantal. "James Strang was one."

Methven screwed his face up. "What the sodding hell

would he have been doing with one?"

"They were using tube amps," said Buxton. "Lost count of the number of times I had to go in the back of my old Ampeg to fiddle with it when it broke."

"So, you're saying there would be a valid need for a guitarist to have a screwdriver around?" said Methven.

"Definitely," said Buxton. "The whole reason for those practice rooms was to leave your gear there." He looked around the room. "These are serious musicians, so they'd spend half their money on guitars and amps and pedals and stuff. You're quids in if you can fix your own gear."

Metvhen looked bored. "Okay, we know it's his screwdriver, so what happened? How did he die?"

"There might have been some sort of struggle in Jimi's practice room," said Cullen. "Somebody attacks him with a screwdriver, kills him and drags him down the corridor to bleed out and die."

"I think you're probably right," said Methven. "We're dealing with a psychopath here."

Cargill entered the room and stood at the back. "Don't mind me."

"I think that's us anyway," said Methven. "It feels like we're finally starting to get somewhere with this case." He looked at the other three officers. "You're all free to go. We just need a word with DC Cullen."

Cullen's stomach squirmed.

"Fine," said Chantal. "I'm heading out to Falkirk to meet Johnson's ex-girlfriend. I'll take ADC Buxton with me."

They left Methven, Cargill, Cullen and every single butterfly in his stomach.

"How are you doing?" said Methven.

"I'm fine," said Cullen. "Might have a cold on the

way."

"I meant about being a DC again," said Methven. "I didn't get the chance to speak to you yesterday, what with all the chaos and everything. I looked around for you but you'd gone home to your parents, I believe?"

"I was working," said Cullen. "DS Rarity instructed me to do some further investigation in Dalhousie, which so happens to be my home town as you know."

Methven frowned at him, his giant eyebrows arched.

"I'm telling the truth here," said Cullen. "I was working with DC Richard Guthrie, based in Dalhousie nick."

Methven briefly closed his eyes. "I see."

"I'm the one who's got us these leads," said Cullen.

"Okay," said Methven. "How are you doing with what happened?"

Cullen paused, taking time to consider his response. "I'm fine. This is something I need to go through, I suppose."

Cargill smiled. "That's a very mature attitude."

Cullen shrugged. "I need to take the rough with the smooth if I want to achieve my goals. I've been a bit too quick to anger before."

"I think that will go some way to reassuring us of your maturity," said Methven.

"I'm disappointed that I wasn't briefed," said Cullen. "I was an Acting DS and I think briefing me was the least you could have done."

Methven and Cargill shared a look.

"I'd like it noted that I could have made a stink about this," said Cullen. "I haven't. I understand there's a lot going on just now and you might not have had the time."

"I appreciate your honesty," said Cargill.

"We apologise for the oversight," said Methven. "It shouldn't have happened."

Cargill cleared her throat. "We need you to go back to Glasgow tomorrow."

Cullen felt disappointment seep through his lungs, sucking the air out. "I thought we were through all of this."

"Politics, I'm afraid," said Methven. "DI Bain has escalated it up the chain of command."

Cargill shot him a look before smiling at Cullen. "We need you to make sure a proper job is being done over there. Jim was personally asked by the Chief Constable to ensure we have eyes and ears on the ground. These are early days for Police Scotland. Nobody wants a mess."

"I'm not known to tread lightly on eggshells," said Cullen. "You both know that."

"That's why we thought of you," said Cargill.

"Do DC Jain and ADC Buxton have enough to be getting on with?" said Methven.

"They're not my resource anymore," said Cullen. "Ask DS Rarity."

Methven nodded. "But as far as you're aware?"

Cullen shrugged. "I think so."

"And your tasks, are they complete for the day?" said Methven.

"Just about," said Cullen.

Methven smiled. "Go and get yourself home. You look atrocious."

69

Cullen found Sharon in a crowded Incident Room before he left. "I'm heading home."

She looked up from her desk. "You look tired."

"I feel it," said Cullen. "Will I wait for you?"

"I don't know when I'll be done," said Sharon.

Cullen felt any remaining air deflate from him. "I thought we were supposed to be going for a meal to talk about-" He leaned in close and whispered. "-the baby?"

Sharon looked around the busy room. "I'll get away when I can."

Cullen pecked her on the cheek and left her to it.

He walked back to the flat, his mind consumed with thoughts of the beast growing in her stomach. Just after six, he slumped on the sofa and got stuck into the last of the ice cream. The cat snuggled up to him, chin on Cullen's thigh and permitting to be stroked for once.

As Cullen ate, unpicking a rich seam of marshmallow, he tried to face up to returning to Glasgow to babysit Bain and McCrea. He wasn't a political animal, never had been and doubted he ever would be. He'd much rather get on with stopping criminals than jockeying for position across the expanded force. The thing he'd hated most about his brief elevation was the murkier political side of the job, getting involved in playground spats and having to take sides.

Despite his frequent moaning, he never managed to

find the time to prepare his own case for promotion.

If he was being honest with himself, he found it difficult to sing his own praises in a formal manner. Off the record, he let everyone know how much better he was than them but he lost his edge in front of a blank form in Word.

He reached the point in the tub where the top half of the ice cream was still frozen, but the bottom was melted. He flipped it over, spooning up the liquid chocolate and ignoring how many calories he was ingesting. He stopped himself finishing it off, replacing the lid and putting it back in the freezer compartment.

He went to the toilet. As he sat fiddling with his phone, he noticed a yellow puddle in the bath. Fluffy appeared in the doorway and bleated at him. "Is that why you were being so friendly to me?"

He finished up on the toilet and set about inspecting the litter tray. Urine in the bath was a sure fire sign of two overly busy people not finding time to change the poor cat's litter. Sure enough, it stank. Cullen guiltily emptied the tray and half-filled a bin bag, before putting fresh litter in. Before the lid was on, Fluffy got straight in and started pissing.

Cullen laughed at the cat and took the bin bag downstairs to the communal bin.

"My God, are you being useful for once?"

Sharon stood in the close.

"Trying to do my bit," said Cullen. "Don't want to get kicked out. Besides, I remember Caldwell saying pregnant woman aren't supposed to change cat litter."

Sharon kissed him on the lips. "I'm sure Fluffy will appreciate it."

"And you don't?"

She laughed. "I could grow to like it. How are you doing?"

Cullen shrugged. "Tired. Coping, just about. You?"

"I'm shattered," said Sharon. "I never knew pregnancy was going to be this tough."

"I'm not going to say you're glowing or anything."

Sharon led them back upstairs. "The last thing I feel is glowing. How was your night at your parents?"

"Good," said Cullen. "Went out with Richard for a few pints, which was good fun."

"How do you manage to get pissed so often?" said Sharon.

"Skill?"

"It's not funny."

"I wasn't really pissed," said Cullen. "Besides, I'm not as bad as I used to be."

"Not sure."

"I managed to find a suspect," said Cullen, evading the subject of his piss artistry. "A guy I was at school with."

Sharon shook her head as she opened the flat door. "Just don't let any shit that happened at school cloud your judgment."

"I'm not Bain," said Cullen, before going into the bathroom to wash his hands. "Crystal sent me home early. I've got to head back through to Glasgow tomorrow morning."

"Tough luck." Sharon started tugging her shoes off. "Did you put any thought into what the fuck we are going to do?"

Cullen sat alongside her and started massaging her feet. "I don't know what to do. I'm scared. I still feel like a wee boy inside my head."

"If it's any consolation, you act like one."

"Thanks," said Cullen. "I'm trying to be honest here. I just don't know how the hell I feel. I've no idea what to do. What do you think?"

"It's such a shitty time. I'm still trying to work out when it happened. I'm not sure it was Budgie's birthday."

"Does it matter?" said Cullen. "We'll just end up getting into a fight about it. It's both of our responsibility. I know you'll suffer more for it."

"Are you saying you expect me to be a housewife?"

"I meant you having an abortion," said Cullen.

"Oh." Sharon looked away. "So that's what you've decided, is it?"

"All I've decided is to talk it through with you," said Cullen. "Having a kid frightens the living shit out of me, especially in this fucking city. I'm barely capable of looking after the cat let alone a child. He's pissed in the bath again."

"It's both of our job to change his litter."

"You need to stop doing it."

She nodded. "What do you want to do tonight?"

"Let's go and get something to eat, like we agreed, then let's watch some telly and see how we feel about it all."

"Deal."

70

Cullen was a man of few favourite restaurants, much preferring drinking in a pub and picking up some food from a shop or takeaway. Viva Mexico on Cockburn Street was one of those very few, the others being a couple of curry houses, a Thai on Thistle Street and a burrito place on Lothian Road that did haggis.

His burrito was stuffed with steak, beans and rice and it was *hot*, probably something to do with all the sauce he'd poured over it. He kept having to wash his mouth out with lager to keep the heat down.

"You should be drinking milk," said Sharon.

"Milk?"

"To kill the chilli. I think it's the lactose in it."

"I know that," said Cullen. "I can't order a pint of milk, though."

"Let your pride get in the way of a burning mouth, why don't you."

"Why do they serve beer with curry, then?" said Cullen.

Sharon shrugged. "To get drunken rugby players through the door?"

"It's not just rugby players."

She held up her hands. "Please spare me your rant."

"Fine," said Cullen.

He finished his burrito and set his cutlery down, letting the fire in his mouth abate. The endorphins were kicking in and he started to feel okay again.

Sharon daintily ate her huge bowl of chilli con carne. She looked at him, arching an eyebrow. "So?"

Cullen held her gaze for a few seconds. He felt a surge of love, his stomach doing cartwheels. He'd never admit it to anyone except Sharon, but the way he felt about her made him crazy. He simply didn't know how to act. "So? It's a good burrito. Nine out of ten."

She dropped her fork to the plate. "About the baby, Scott? The reason we're here?"

"Right. Look, I know one thing, okay? I never want to be apart from you. All that shit we went through in October, which I've apologised for so many times, I never want that to happen again. Whether we have kids or not, I want to be with you. I wouldn't have kids with anyone else."

"You mean that?"

"Honestly," said Cullen.

"So, what are we going to do?" said Sharon.

"Thinking about it is the only thing I can think of doing," said Cullen. "We've still got time. We need to talk and consider all options."

"How do we make a decision?" Sharon put her plate to the side, three-quarters empty.

Cullen was tempted to finish it off, but resisted. "Whatever feels right."

"What, though?"

Cullen smiled. "You're panicking, aren't you?"

She hit the table. "Of course I am. I've got something growing inside me that I don't know if I even fucking want. Every hour we don't make a decision is an hour closer to not being able to get out of this situation." She took a drink. "On top of that, I've got all this shit about my promotion. I don't need this now."

He reached across and took her hand, stroking it. "Please don't push yourself too hard. If we decide to keep it, I don't want it fucked up because you're stressing yourself out about this. Even if we get rid of it, I don't want you stressed like you have been."

Sharon scowled. "Do you want to carry it?"

Cullen pulled his hand back. "I'm just saying, that's all."

"If I get a DI post then we could get a house outside the city," said Sharon. "There's a nice development going up in Garleton."

"I've told you I'd rather not live there," said Cullen. "Too many bad memories."

"It'd be near my sister."

"You're really selling it to me." Cullen took another drink.

She paused for a few seconds. "Suppose I get an abortion."

"How would your parents react to that?" said Cullen.

"Because they're Catholics?"

Cullen shrugged. "Aye."

"They're not hard line. Mum said they'd be fine with it. They'd much rather I was happy."

"That's a relief." Cullen played with his ear. "Wouldn't want you to have to choose one way or another."

"I would never have to, you idiot," said Sharon. "I'd always choose you over them. Look, we should think about it but we need to make a decision at the weekend. This isn't the sort of thing I want hanging over our heads. Let's go out for dinner on Saturday - *my* choice - and then make the decision. If we choose to get rid of it, you're coming with me to the clinic and holding my hand."

Cullen felt relief that progress was being made. "Wouldn't have it any other way."

71

They got back to the flat in time for the second half of the football, Sharon snuggling up to Cullen and falling asleep by the time the second Arsenal goal went in. She stumbled to bed not long after the Bayern Munich equaliser, leaving Cullen to watch the London side limp out of the Champions League once again. The pundits in the TV studio were stuck in a heated debate about a meaningless penalty so Cullen switched it off.

He picked up *The List* from the table by the sofa, drawn in by the cover - two members of Expect Delays respectively looking moody and jokey. That bloody article was the start of this whole case, he thought - if those Gap kids hadn't read it, they'd never have been inspired to head down into the catacombs and find Strang's body. Who knew how long it could have sat there, waiting to be discovered?

He started reading the interview, five pages focusing on the local boys done good and their U2 support slot at Hampden. He quickly skimmed to the relevant section, the reporter having mostly got responses from Neeraj Patel about how it felt to tour with U2, a band Cullen didn't care for much.

List: You're an Edinburgh band originally. Tell us a story about Glasgow or Edinburgh that nobody has heard before.

NP: I've got one. We used to have a practice room in Niddry Street, just between the Cowgate and the High Street.

MR: Oh, not this one. Please, don't print this!

NP: This is a good story, man.

MR: I'll let your readers be the judge of that...

NP: Ignore him. It's a good story. Anyway, we used to rehearse in there. To be honest, we wrote most of our first two albums in this room. We moved to Glasgow when we signed to Indigo and we've got a huge rehearsal space through there now. At the time, though, having our own room was great and it made us feel like a real band.

MR: We always were a real band, Neej.

NP: Anyway, this particular tale would be about the time we wrote 'Where has he gone?'. *We were into dares and betting and Mike here was bet he couldn't go down to the hidden street.*

MR: You'd better explain what the hidden street is.

List: The Hidden Street was the title to your second album, right?

NP: Aye, but this is where we got it from. Where we used to rehearse in Niddry Street, there was a staircase that led down to this door. Through the door was an old close, like Mary King's Close, but it went right under the Old Town. You could walk for miles, man.

MR: The streets were covered over in the nineteenth century when they rebuilt the place.

NP: Right, aye. Anyway, Mikey was dared to go down the street.

MR: (Laughs) And I did.

NP: He totally shat it, though. Came screaming out of there like there was something after him.

MR: That was just to frighten you, you tube!

* * *

279

List: How far did you go?

MR: I don't want to encourage anyone to go down there. It was stupid and dangerous. Kids, if you're reading this, don't go down there.

NP: I don't think that'll stop them.

MR: (Laughs) Kids, go down there, it's ace.

List: The second edition of The Hidden Street featured your hit single 'Where Has He Gone?' which many people have attributed to saving your career. It's very evocative and mysterious with the meaning being somewhat opaque. What was it about?

NP: He just makes up any old nonsense, you know? It's not about anything.

MR: Shut up! I don't do that.

NP: Alright, what's it about, then?

MR: It's about that kid at school, the one who's destined for greatness when you're fifteen, who just never makes it. I think I got it from this guy I was at school with. He was going to be an artist and everyone knew it. He was the best in school, best in the whole district. Years later, I bumped into him one day and he had just been let out of prison. He'd got into drugs. It's about that sort of thing, the boy who had so much promise, what happened to him?

NP: I've honestly never heard that story before. Wow.

The piece started to indulge the band even more, so Cullen tossed the magazine aside. It was an interesting story and he could see why Public Right of Way would want to copy them.

He had a thought - could Roberts be lying and the song was actually about Strang? He fiddled on his phone. The song came out three months before Strang's death.

His mind sparked to Audrey Patterson. She blamed Cullen for ruining her life. He could barely remember the girl, let alone bullying her and making her into the mess he'd seen in Dalhousie. Gradually, he managed to piece together an image of her, younger and thinner. He honestly didn't think he'd bullied her, but it was all about perspective - if she thought she was being bullied, maybe she was.

If anything, he might have been slightly attracted to her. The cockiness he grew into hadn't yet blossomed at school. He'd been overweight and shy, a year or so before he'd started running and getting into shape, transforming his growing body into a weapon to use against impressionable girls.

There must have been something in it - the people he sat with were notorious for bullying. He could only think some of his banter, as he saw it, was taken as serious insult.

He got up, stretched and went to bed.

Sharon turned over. "Remember we've got that gig tomorrow night."

"I'll see if I can get away," said Cullen.

He wasn't relishing the prospect of standing in a football stadium with a pregnant girlfriend, watching Expect Delays and U2, two bands he hated.

Wednesday
3rd April 2013

72

Cullen drove through the outskirts of Glasgow, inching ahead of the tidal wave of traffic, waves of high-rise buildings on either side.

He stopped at a garage with an M&S and got a coffee. He needed to kick into gear after a broken night of sleep, constantly waking up and thinking about the baby.

Mucus dripped from his nose as he paid. He reached for another hankie on his way back to the car and blew. He'd definitely caught Sharon's cold.

He drove to Govan and blagged the last free space. He walked across the car park in the twilight, before showing his warrant card to the security guard.

"Sorry, son, you'll need to be signed in."

Cullen wasn't in the mood for admin or process. "This is a Police Scotland warrant card."

"I don't care, son. You're through here, you're signed in by one of the locals."

Cullen rolled his eyes at him, before phoning McCrea.

"Sorry, I'm too busy."

"I've driven all this way," said Cullen.

"Aye, all right."

Eventually, McCrea appeared through the security barrier and signed Cullen in, making sure he was cleared for the rest of the week.

"Pleased to see you," said McCrea, looking anything but. "How has it been through there?"

"Getting nowhere then getting somewhere, then getting shoved back here."

"The gaffer will love to see you," said McCrea.

"Really?"

McCrea led them into the Incident Room, the idling Glasgow South MIT waiting for their morning battering from the DI.

Bain stood up at the front of the room and loudly cleared his throat. "Morning. First thing is the Hughes murder. As it stands, we've got very few suspects. Only lead we've got is his ex in Edinburgh."

He rubbed his top lip. "Someone in Edinburgh MIT has grassed to their Detective Superintendent. Apparently, we were naughty boys and girls when we spoke to Marta Hunter without their say-so, so we need to make sure we follow due process or we'll have a meeting in Tulliallan with the big knobs."

He looked around the room, clearly not believing his own words and giving Cullen absolutely no confidence his subordinates would take it on board.

"Anyway, we're no further forward with the case. There are no forensics that haven't already been pre-cleared as belonging to the deceased or to an officer on the case. As it stands, everyone we've interviewed is a likely suspect."

He smiled. "We've been tying a few things together with the drugs angle and we got a lead late last night which looks promising. Turns out he was definitely doing a bit of dealing. This ties in with him having two girlfriends who were known addicts, one in Pollockshaws and one in Edinburgh. We need to lock this down."

He gestured at Cullen, looking him up and down.

"We've got a special guest star here today to help out

with the Edinburgh angle." He grinned. "That, or he's babysitting us. As some of you will know, DC Cullen used to work for me. You all have actions, nothing new. Dismissed."

Cullen approached Bain. "Thanks for the intro."

Bain smiled, looking calm and relaxed. "Just know you're being watched here, Sundance."

Cullen's breath quickened as he realised he was already deep in one of Bain's games. "We don't have a drug angle in our case."

"As if they're the same case, Sundance," said Bain.

"You seem to think they are."

"If they are, I'm taking over," said Bain. "I'm like the mountains, Sundance, I've got a fuck of a long memory. That bitch took over my case six months ago, no danger it's happening again. I'll show her what's what. She's getting a taste of her own fuckin' medicine."

Cullen desperately wanted to avoid being a bit part in a Bain-Cargill standoff. "What do you want me to do?"

"Speak to McCrea, Constable," said Bain, relishing the use of Cullen's revised title. "I'm sure he'll find something for you. Just keep out of my fuckin' hair."

73

Cullen went through the case file again, spending an hour to little or no benefit. He'd been brushed off by McCrea, who muttered about giving him something to do before disappearing.

Cullen looked around the bustling Incident Room and let his shoulders sag. Officers milled around, no doubt with the same level of dedication he'd shown while working for Bain, lest they get their arses handed to them.

He didn't know where the nearest decent coffee shop was but there was nothing doing in the station. He found a drum of supermarket own-brand instant coffee and scooped in a few heaped teaspoons along with some hardened coffee whitener. His stomach was already starting to rumble.

He felt he was being taken for an idiot, having busted a gut to get there for the seven am briefing.

Cullen knew more than most how far the game between Cargill and Bain stretched back. Bain received his comeuppance in Lothian & Borders at the hands of Cargill. Now they were in Police Scotland, there were new rules. Bain was better connected in the new regime, his eleven years in Strathclyde giving him a clear advantage over Cargill's time in Lothian & Borders, Central and Grampian. The upper echelons in the new force were heavily weighted towards the west coast, which worked in Bain's favour.

He sat back down again and looked at his notes, figuring his morning was a complete waste of time. All they'd done in the last two days was perform a classic Bain sting, expending a lot of effort on tightening up notebooks and making sure everything was nailed down.

Big Shug was their main focus. They'd collated all available intelligence on the man from across Scotland. Cullen skimmed through a SOCA report but couldn't decide whether they were on the right track.

"You finding much in that?" said McCrea.

Cullen tossed the report to one side and looked up. "Not really. I'm still not convinced by this whole drugs angle."

"You mentioned that to the gaffer?"

Cullen shrugged. "As if he'd listen to me."

McCrea made a crybaby gesture. "Poor DC Cullen."

Cullen shook his head. "Mature."

McCrea sat on the edge of the desk. "You don't think we're capable of doing this right, do you?"

Cullen folded his arms. "I'll admit to a certain amount of scepticism."

"What are you going to do about it, then?" said McCrea.

"I'll just wait and see what happens."

"Just remember who's in charge of this police force now," said McCrea.

Cullen laughed. "Is that a threat?"

"Is what?" said McCrea.

"If I find anything dodgy, I'll go to Bain about it," said Cullen. "If he does nothing, then I'll have no choice but to go to my superiors in Edinburgh."

"I'd recommend you don't do that, Constable."

Cullen rubbed his forehead. "Is there a point to this?"

"I'm letting you know what's what," said McCrea. "That's all."

"Fine, you're the big boss man," said Cullen. "Are you going to give me something to do or are you just going to flirt with me?"

McCrea laughed. "That's good. I like that." He snorted. "No, for once I need your help."

"Oh?"

"We're raiding Hughes's dealer's house," said McCrea. "We need your presence there."

74

Cullen sat in the passenger seat of McCrea's Escort with another two male detectives in the back. Other than driving north, Cullen had no idea what they were trying to achieve.

"You need to get me up to speed on the plan for this drugs raid," said Cullen.

"You're a DC again," said McCrea, "so you do what I tell you."

Until then, Cullen had enjoyed sparring with McCrea. The DS was without any redeeming features. Bain seemed to attract that particular flavour of wanker - timeserving and arse covering.

"Fine," said Cullen. "I'm asking what we're doing here. That's all."

"We've got a few teams of uniform in place," said McCrea, "six detectives and an Armed Response Unit." He tossed a set of photographs over.

Cullen looked through them, A4 black-and-white shots of a shifty-looking man in a tracksuit. "Who's this?"

"Should have paid attention to the file on Big Shug," said McCrea, grinning.

Cullen heard a brace of sniggers from behind. He ground his teeth. "Is this Big Shug?"

McCrea shook his head. "Malky Nicholls. He's been fucking with us for years but he's always kept himself clean."

"I don't get it," said Cullen. "I thought you were after Big Shug."

"We're not going to get Shug," said McCrea, turning off the motorway onto a traffic-laden dual carriageway. "While you were playing with yourself through in Edinburgh, or whatever the fuck you've been doing, the actual proper coppers have been getting on with some solid graft."

"Could you introduce me to these proper coppers?" said Cullen.

"Shut your mouth," said McCrea.

Cullen looked out of the window, hiding his smile from McCrea, pleased with scoring some laughs from the back seat.

"How have you managed to get hold of Nicholls, then?" said Cullen.

McCrea pulled onto a road through a residential area filled with blocks of flats and two-storey houses. "We found out Hughes was getting his drugs straight from Nicholls. We managed to get it locked down yesterday when we spoke to Marta Hunter in Edinburgh. Got our search warrant approved first thing this morning. The gaffer wanted to get in there right about now, reckons it'll catch him off guard."

"You'd better hope Nicholls doesn't have any bent coppers in his pocket," said Cullen.

"We don't have them through here," said McCrea. "We keep a tight ship."

Cullen didn't want to get dragged into an east versus west spat. "Tell me about Nicholls."

"As I say, we've been after the boy for years," said McCrea, "but now he's fingered in a murder, he's fucked."

"How big a player is he?"

"See, that's the thing," said McCrea. "He's small scale but he's a fucking pest, gets kids their weed then eventually gives them a wee taste of heroin before he sells them onto another of Big Shug's network. Recently, he's been getting further up the supply chain and more into the wholesale market, as it were."

McCrea pulled into a rough council estate, shabby houses circled by six multi-storey tower blocks. Cullen didn't know where they were. He guessed it was somewhere on the way to Dumbarton and Loch Lomond.

McCrea parked then led them over to a meat wagon. They met up with eight officers who looked bored as they stood against the far wall.

"Right, gather round," said McCrea. "Malky Nicholls stays in the next street. You should all know what he looks like. We've got a boy dressed as a postman who'll mark his house out. I want two detectives with each group of four uniform."

He pointed at the four next to them. "Cullen and me are taking squad alpha."

He nodded at the two who had driven out with them. "Willie and Jim, you pair are squad beta.

"Alpha, we're entering the house. Beta, you lot are to establish a perimeter. It's like a jungle in there so be wily, all right?"

He looked around the group, arms waving as he tried to gee them up like a football manager.

"Alphas, we're waiting until the perimeter is established before we enter. Other than that, it's the usual protocol. You've got your Airwaves, listen to them." He clicked his fingers. "Move out."

Cullen's heart pounded as they left the police van and jogged down the street, heading through a narrow vennel before hitting a long road. It was lined with two opposing blocks of flats, six storeys high. Exterior corridors ran down the length of the buildings, the front doors facing onto the balconies. From the layout of the front doors, Cullen assessed they were maisonettes inside.

He spotted the fake postie on the third floor, twitchy eyes monitoring the street below. Two uniformed officers ran ahead of the pack, sprinting to the far end of the building, one entering slowly, the other standing guard outside.

Cullen followed McCrea up the nearest stairwell, six officers behind him, two waiting to cover the bottom of the stairs. They entered the open corridor and clocked the postie standing outside a door two-thirds of the way along.

McCrea hammered on the door as a burly officer hefted a battering ram. The door was a reinforced steel model, a sign a drug dealer lived there.

"Mr Nicholls," said McCrea. "It's the police. Please open the door."

"Fuck off!"

McCrea shook his head. "We have a search warrant, Mr Nicholls."

"He's not here, big man!"

McCrea stepped to the side. "Fuck this." He motioned to the officer with the battering ram. "Open it up."

It took three full swings before the door burst off its hinges.

Cullen was one of the first in. The flat was full of people spilling out of the living room. Cullen quickly recognised Nicholls as he made his way up the staircase.

"He's gone upstairs," said Cullen.

"Over here!" McCrea wielded his baton at three men in tracksuits who surrounded him. He overpowered one, forcing him to the ground.

Another brandished a flick knife. Cullen barrelled into his back, sending him flying. He got on top and hooked his arm around the thug's neck, pushing him slowly to the ground.

A uniformed officer took the third down.

"Are we clear?" said McCrea, passing control of his assailant to a uniform.

"Think so," said one of the others.

McCrea turned the guy with the knife over. "Where is he?"

"Who?"

"Nicholls," said McCrea.

"No idea, pal." He sniffed. A bulge was already appearing on his forehead from the tussle with Cullen.

"He went upstairs," said Cullen.

One of the uniforms relieved Cullen, putting cuffs on his ned.

McCrea stormed off towards the front door, grabbing the postie. "Has anyone come out of here?"

The postie shook his head. "Not in the last hour, sir."

"He can't have disappeared," said McCrea.

"Look, will you just listen to me?" said Cullen. "Nicholls was here. He went upstairs."

"Fine," said McCrea.

Cullen took over. He pointed at the uniforms. "Stay here and start ferrying those three out."

He led them upstairs, taking the steps slowly. He swung his baton through the air, the appearance of the knife making him wary of heading into danger too recklessly for once.

They scoured the floor, made up of three bedrooms and a bathroom. They checked the back bedroom last, finding nothing again.

"He can't have just disappeared," said McCrea, hands on hips, glaring at Cullen. "You *definitely* saw him?"

"Yes," said Cullen. "It was definitely him."

Cullen looked around the room. The doors to a built-in wardrobe in the corner were hanging open from McCrea's hasty check. He looked inside, screwing his eyes up and spotted something in the corner. He pointed at the top. "What's that?"

"It's a fucking hatch," said McCrea.

"You think he's up there?"

"He might be," said McCrea. "Was he armed?"

"I didn't see him that well."

McCrea went back into the corridor and shouted down. "I need two of you up here."

A pair of officers trudged up the stairs. McCrea pointed at the one who carried the battering ram. "You're going to lift Cullen up."

"I'm not going up there," said Cullen.

"I'm ordering you," said McCrea, tossing a torch at Cullen.

Cullen practically had to bite his tongue as he extended his baton again. He squatted to be lifted by the uniform, who swayed with the effort. He pushed the hatch and raised his head. He didn't need the torch.

Covering an entire floor of the building was a room that looked like some twisted snooker hall - beneath rows of strip lights sat crops of cannabis plants in wooden planters lined with tinfoil.

Cullen turned to take in the full picture.

Something flashed in the corner of his eye.

A boot smashed into his face.

He toppled down, sending his carrier sprawling inside the wardrobe. Cullen landed hard on the floor.

"He's up there," said Cullen, blood pouring out of his burst mouth.

"Is he armed?" said McCrea.

"I've no idea," said Cullen, dabbing at his lip. "You need to sort him out."

McCrea clenched his fists. "Get me that armed response squad."

75

Cullen and McCrea got back to the CID office in Govan station an hour later. Cullen still dabbing at his split lip.

Bain sat at his desk in the middle of the Incident Room, hammering on his laptop. He took one look at Cullen's lip and exploded with laughter. "What the fuck happened to you, Sundance?"

"I found out where your suspect was," said Cullen.

"Did you, really?" said Bain.

"Found a nice little hydroponics factory."

"We got hold of Nicholls," said McCrea. "Had to use the ARU."

Bain looked like he knew a bollocking was heading his way. "Was he armed?"

"We weren't sure." McCrea sniffed.

"Was he armed, Sergeant?" said Bain.

"No."

Cullen held up his hands. "This is nothing to do with me. I got lifted up to have a look. Nicholls kicked me rather than shooting me. Calling in the Armed Response Unit was entirely DS McCrea's call."

"I stand by my man," said Bain.

McCrea shrugged. "Either way. Nicholls is going down for this."

"Good work, Sergeant," said Bain.

"Are you sure he killed Hughes?" said Cullen.

"One hundred per cent."

"I've seen you like this before."

Bain stabbed a finger in the air. "I'd advise you to keep your fuckin' thoughts to yourself, Cullen."

"If you can't convince me this is your killer," said Cullen, "then I don't see you being able to convince the PF, let alone a jury."

"We know Nicholls was Hughes's dealer," said Bain. "Hughes owed him a large sum of money."

"And that's it?" said Cullen.

Bain shook his head, before turning his attentions to McCrea. "A word in private, Sergeant." He led McCrea out of the room.

Cullen slumped down in a chair and picked at the wood of the desk, fed up with whatever shite Bain was trying to pull here. They had very little evidence pointing to Nicholls being behind Hughes' murder.

Bain and McCrea came back in just as Cullen sneezed.

"You shouldn't be here if you've got a cold, Sundance," said Bain. "Don't want you spreading your fuckin' germs everywhere." He grinned. "Then again I know your sickness record has held you back a few times over the years."

Cullen stared at him for a few seconds then shook his head. He got up and left the room, marching to the front of the station.

Taking a deep breath of bitter April air, he let the dull grey morning envelope him and watched the meat wagon finally arrive, ferrying Nicholls and his acolytes in. If Bain was wrong, the conviction for the weed farm might get a bit sticky.

He reached into his pocket and got out his phone. Cargill, Methven or Turnbull? He picked one.

Cargill sounded harassed. "How can I help?"

"Have you got a couple of minutes?" said Cullen.

"Not really. Make it quick, please."

Cullen rapidly recounted what had happened with Nicholls, including his split lip and the possible abuse of an Armed Response Unit.

"It feels like I'm being used as Glasgow resource," he said. "I'm not progressing our case in any way, shape, manner or form."

Cargill was silent for a few seconds. "Right, get back through here. I'll get Jim Turnbull to deal with this."

"Thanks." Cullen ended the call.

He went back inside and found Bain alone in the Incident Room scribbling on a notepad. The room had emptied since Nicholls arrived, even the pair of DCs who normally sat in the far corner had gone. McCrea had disappeared as well.

Bain looked up as Cullen approached. "What is it now?"

"I'm heading back through to Edinburgh," said Cullen.

"No, you're not," said Bain. "You're my resource, Sundance."

"I'm not your resource. I'm with Edinburgh MIT. Speak to DCI Cargill."

"When the fuck did she become DCI?" said Bain.

"I suggest you keep on top of your briefings," said Cullen, thinking back to Guthrie's knowledge of his own demotion.

"I'm too busy doing actual fuckin' work." Bain looked at Cullen long and hard before he nodded slowly. "All right. I know what's happening here. Sundance, you've made your bed so I'll let you lie in the wet patch."

"Classy."

"You've not heard the fuckin' last of this," said Bain.

Cullen looked Bain up and down, before laughing. "Go fuck yourself. You're lucky to still have a job, you bullying wanker."

"Excuse me?"

"You heard," said Cullen. "I don't have to put up with you any longer."

"You can't speak to a superior officer like that," said Bain.

"Like what?" said McCrea, appearing from nowhere.

"He told me to go fuck myself," said Bain.

"Aye, he did," said McCrea.

Cullen leaned in close to Bain, his voice unsteady. "After the way you treat people, you honestly think you can make something of this?"

"Insubordination is written all over your record," said Bain. "Even I struggled to manage you. You were always trying to be the hero and heading off on some wild goose chase."

Cullen tried to hold the reptilian gaze but had to break off. "Just speak to Cargill."

"I will be escalating this," said Bain.

Cullen felt sweat trickle down his back as he left the room.

76

Half an hour later, Cullen sat in a cafe on St Vincent Street in Glasgow, his restless fingers folding and unfolding a Post-It as he waited. His car was just round the corner, abusing the *On Police Business* sign. His phone lay face down on the table, the ringer on mute.

Michelle Cullen walked in, looking harassed. She eventually spotted him and gave the briefest smile before coming over to his table, dumping her coat on the chair opposite.

"Thanks for seeing me at short notice," said Cullen.

Michelle's eyes were on the board behind the counter. "Thanks for getting in touch."

He pushed his empty mug to one side. "Can I get you a coffee?"

"I'll get them in, little brother," said Michelle. "You're just a police officer, after all."

"An Americano," said Cullen, through gritted teeth.

"Be right back."

He watched her go to the counter and order. "Just a police officer. Fuck's sake." She was *just* an IT worker.

She'd put on weight since he'd last seen her and her hair was dyed entirely the wrong colour for her skin. It struck him that she looked like a shorter version of him with long hair.

Michelle returned with two big mugs. "There you go. Loads of milk, just how you like it."

"Thanks." Cullen stirred his coffee. "How've you been?"

"Good," said Michelle. "Busy, but good. It's been full-on since we had Emily, though."

"In what way?"

"It's just hard having a small child, Scott." She poured a sachet of brown sugar onto her latte and stirred. "And I'm not talking about Jeremy."

Cullen laughed. He'd got on okay with Michelle's husband, an English guy she met when she worked in London, a man-child just like her brother. "How's he doing?"

"He thinks a screenplay is going to be his saviour now."

"Gave up on the books, then?" said Cullen.

"They gave up on him, more like."

"He's still not working?" said Cullen.

"No," said Michelle. "I'm the breadwinner. He does a good job around the house, to be honest. We're having so much work done and he's great at managing it."

"Finally found a use for him, then."

"He's really patient with Emily," said Michelle. "Much more than me." She stared into the middle distance. "I mean, I'm working through here and I don't usually get home till after seven so I barely see her."

"That must be tough."

Michelle shrugged. "Yeah." She took a drink of coffee. "How's your flat? Still living with Tom?"

"I moved in with Sharon," said Cullen. "We live just off the Royal Mile."

Michelle smiled. "How is she?"

"She's good, I suppose," said Cullen, looking away.

"What is it?"

Cullen stared into the swirling coffee in front of him. "She's pregnant."

Michelle's eyes bulged. "I didn't know you had it in you, little brother."

"Very funny," said Cullen. "I'm shitting myself."

"You'll make a good dad. You're a total idiot but I think you've got a good sense of what's right."

Cullen raised his eyebrows. "An idiot?"

"I mean it," said Michelle. "Not the idiot bit. I mean about you being a good dad."

"Aye, maybe when I'm ready."

"Scott, you're thirty-one next month," said Michelle. "When *are* you going to be ready?"

"Not now," said Cullen. "I earn fuck all and stuff is weird at work."

"What about Sharon?"

"I love her," said Cullen.

Michelle laughed. "No, I meant is she ready?"

"I don't think either of us are. We had all that shit last year as well."

"Mum told me," said Michelle. "She was pretty upset about it."

"Was she?" Cullen shook his head. "Sharon's pushing for a DI position. She's under a lot of stress. I don't think it's good for her in that condition."

"Look after her," said Michelle. "I liked her the one time you let us meet. She's a keeper."

"Let us meet?"

"You know what I mean," said Michelle. "You can be a bit of a stranger at the best of times."

"It's called being busy." Cullen took a drink of his coffee, gripping the handle tight. "It's good coffee. Better than the shit in the station."

Michelle ran a hand through her hair. "I really like it in here, which is why I suggested it."

"You guys live in Linlithgow now, right?" said Cullen.

"Lots of questions, Detective Sergeant Cullen."

He looked away. "It's Detective Constable again."

"Mum didn't say," said Michelle. "You really annoyed me, you know?"

"I'm sorry," said Cullen. "Really I am. You need to stop being so precious, though."

"It wasn't funny, Scott. Jeremy and I had a huge argument about the card you sent."

"*How?*"

Michelle screwed her face up. "*Congratulations, see you in eighteen years?*"

"And?"

"That's not very sensitive, is it?"

"I'm your brother. I was just taking the piss."

"I know you're just a year younger than me," said Michelle, "but you can be too close, you know?"

"I'm just having a laugh," said Cullen. "You should lighten up."

"You're one to talk."

Cullen took a deep breath. "Look, I'm sorry, okay? I didn't mean to upset you. I take it all back."

Michelle took a drink of latte and traced the lines of her eyebrows with her thumb and forefinger. "Apology accepted," she said eventually.

"Thanks."

"So, why are you so keen to see me?" said Michelle.

"Can't I just want to?"

"Not you, Scott. There's always an agenda with you."

Cullen tossed the Post-It on the table. "Mum gave me this."

Michelle picked it up and inspected it. She shook her head. "I still don't buy it."

Cullen laughed. "Fine. Matt MacLeod."

Michelle rolled her eyes. "That wanker."

"You went out with him, didn't you?"

"He was in *your* year at school," said Michelle, as if accusing him of ownership.

"I hated him," said Cullen. "I think that's why he went out with you."

"Nothing to do with how good my blow jobs were?"

Cullen came close to snorting coffee through his nose. "I forgot you're as depraved as me."

"Blame Dad," said Michelle. "So what's he done to you? Tell me you're not digging up old grievances."

Cullen rubbed his ear for a moment. "I probably shouldn't be telling you this but he's a suspect in a murder case."

Michelle covered her mouth. "*Matt* is?"

"Aye," said Cullen. "Do you remember James Strang?"

"I knew his sister," said Michelle. "She was a bit weird. She was in your year, wasn't she?"

"She was, aye." Cullen nodded. "Apparently I used to bully her but I've managed to totally forget it."

"You heartless bastard," said Michelle, grinning. "I don't think it was too bad. Some people just need to man up, you know? Or woman up."

"Well, it's obviously fucked her up. I feel guilty about it."

"Some people get fucked up going to the shops."

Cullen laughed. "So, Matt MacLeod. Did he have anything to do with the Strangs? Did he bully him?"

"Can't remember," said Michelle. "Matt was in a band, wasn't he? They were the big thing in your year.

Weren't they playing the school hall all the time? I think the one James Strang was in supported them at a school show or something."

"So they knew each other?"

"Aye," said Michelle.

"Why on earth would he kill him, though?" said Cullen.

"That's why you get paid the little bucks." She laughed at her joke. "If I remember correctly, you got angry with Matt for going out with me, didn't you?"

Cullen's face reddened. "Did I?"

"Yes," said Michelle. "You were always very protective of your big sister."

"I just knew he was a wanker. That's all."

"I found out quickly." She smiled and flicked her eyebrows up. "Of course, you've got a motive to kill him."

"To kill MacLeod." Cullen pointed a finger at her. "Not Strang." He took a drink of coffee. "Sadly, Matt MacLeod is still alive."

"Whatever." Michelle checked her watch. "I need to run, I'm afraid. This has been good. We should do it again soon."

"Agreed." Cullen drained his mug.

"Maybe next time you could just want to see me rather than need help with a case, though, right?" said Michelle.

"I'll try."

77

Cullen lurched back into Leith Walk station just after noon, heading straight to the canteen. He managed to avoid speaking to anyone while he devoured an unsatisfying chicken salad sandwich.

He returned to the Incident Room to catch up on progress. Only Chantal was there.

"How's it going?" said Cullen.

Chantal tugged at her sleeves. "Not great. Rarity has just had us tidying up paperwork."

"Exciting."

"Heard you had an eventful morning," said Chantal.

"The drugs raid?" said Cullen. "We got a good haul. Hope they get a conviction."

"I meant telling Bain to go fuck himself."

"Oh," said Cullen. "Never ceases to amaze me how fast bad news spreads. Combining the forces seems to have multiplied the bloody jungle drums."

Chantal laughed.

"How did you find out?" said Cullen.

"It won't surprise you to learn your former master has been on the phone to Cargill, Turnbull and anyone who'll listen to him. He wants you on a disciplinary."

Cullen rubbed his eyes. "Even if it was true, how could Bain have the balls to do someone over some pretty light swearing given the continual barrage of fucks coming from his mouth?"

"What about your lack of respect for authority?"

Cullen shrugged. "I'm not that bad, am I?"

"I'm surprised he's never hauled you over the coals before."

"There were no witnesses," said Cullen.

"So you did do it?"

"No."

Chantal raised an eyebrow. "Some DS through there is backing Bain up."

"McCrea." Cullen punched the back of the office chair he was leaning against. "He wasn't even *there*."

Chantal laughed. "You don't half make it difficult for yourself sometimes. Cargill has been trying to call you all morning."

"My phone ran out of battery."

"You'd better charge it, then," said Chantal.

Cullen followed through on his lie, finding a vacant desktop computer and plugging in his phone. "What did Ailsa McHardy have to say?"

"You're not running this case any longer, Cullen."

He clenched his fists. What was it with female DCs thinking he was either coming on to them or on some power trip? "Relax. I just want to know whether Strang was at it with Johnson's girlfriend."

"Do you need to know?"

"Yes!" He was close to losing it with her. "Look, what's your problem here?"

"Is there a problem?"

"You're giving me the same sort of attitude I got from Caldwell," said Cullen. "I've not done anything that bad, have I?"

Chantal evaded his look. "I suppose not."

"What did she say?"

"They slept together," said Chantal. "Just the once."

Cullen nodded slowly. "So, our single lead from the record shop has split in two. Strang tried it on with both Hughes' and Johnson's girlfriends?"

"Looks that way."

"When was this?" said Cullen.

"Two weeks before he disappeared," said Chantal. "She was totally torn up by it. Her guilt made her break up with Johnson."

"And well she might."

"What's that supposed to mean?" said Chantal.

"Never mind." Cullen thought of his own attitude to being cuckolded. He got up and headed for the stairs.

"Where are you going?" said Chantal.

"I'm going to see a man about a laptop," said Cullen. "While I still have a job."

78

The Forensic Investigation Unit seemed filled with hordes of the undead, their skin pallid from lack of natural sunlight. At one o'clock in the afternoon, every curtain was drawn.

Charlie Kidd's desk was about halfway down. He now faced towards the stairwell, better able to watch for the likes of Cullen marching over to chase him up. As he looked up, his breezy expression dipped.

"That's no way to greet an old friend," said Cullen.

Kidd nervously tossed his ponytail. "How can I help, officer?"

"I brought in a laptop from James Strang's parents' house," said Cullen. "Just wondering how the investigation is going?"

"Slowly." Kidd gritted his teeth. "Systems are being integrated across the force and it's going badly. I've been pulled into fixing it, despite the fact I'm supposed to be an investigative resource."

"That's not good," said Cullen. "Do you need me to escalate it?"

"Should be fine, Dad."

Cullen laughed. "Did you get a chance to look at the laptop?"

Kidd nodded. "Aye, I did. I found the email from Strang to Mark Andrews you were after. The boy sent a couple of others that day, all with similar wording." He handed Cullen a few sheets of print.

Cullen flicked through them, finding the same poem repeated. "Did you get anything else?"

"Not yet. Doubt I'll get much else out of it, to be honest."

Cullen got up and headed downstairs to look through the emails in more detail. The Incident Room was mercifully empty by the time he got there. He put his headphones on and listened to music as he read.

They were as Kidd said and broadly similar to the mail Strang sent to Andrews, though some paragraphs were rearranged and the wording slightly different. The second last contained a few typos and, curiously, many instances of the = symbol. The last one, sent an hour later, was much worse.

m=m=Mq=attt=e Bls=ack wq=alll=s
Black Mattt=t= = = == =str=eak=ls tu=to=ime

Cullen frowned - he'd seen that sort of thing before, but couldn't remember where.

He knew what it was *supposed* to be - *Matte Black walls, Black Matt steals time*.

Where had he seen writing like that? It dawned on him - in his dark days as a student, he went through a phase of going to the computer lab after he'd been out getting wrecked and sending emails only his drunk self could comprehend. They were filled with ='s.

The = key was next to the backspace on a computer keyboard. His alcoholically-impaired motor skills constantly hit the wrong keys.

Strang must have been drinking heavily when he'd sent the emails, starting out fairly coherent but ending up a trail of gibberish. Andrews was third on the list and received one of the more sober emails.

Black Matt steals time

Cullen hadn't received an update on Matt MacLeod, so he called Guthrie.

"How's it going?" said Guthrie.

"Good."

"Heard you've been a naughty boy in Glasgow."

"Fuck's sake," said Cullen. "How does everybody know about that?"

"It's amazing, isn't it?"

"Nothing happened," said Cullen. "I told my DCI to fix it, that's all."

"A likely tale, Skinky." Guthrie laughed. "Anyway, how can I help?"

"How's the MacLeod surveillance going?"

"Speak to your DS, Skinky."

"Come on, Goth."

"All right," said Guthrie. "We've had two skulls on him at all times. He stayed at his parents' house pretty much for the duration. Went to the Co-op a couple of times, once in his car, once on foot. His parents came back from work last night then he drove through to Edinburgh at the back of eight."

Cullen sat forward. "Last night?"

"I told your DS," said Guthrie. "Rarity, is it?"

"Why didn't you tell me?"

"I was knackered, mate," said Guthrie. "I was told to report to Rarity, she's the one who requisitioned it."

"I told you to call me."

"Yeah, sorry," said Guthrie. "You'll forgive me eventually."

"Cheers." Cullen stabbed his finger on the screen and

ended the call.

He got up and hunted down Rarity, finding her drinking a cup of tea in the canteen, staring into her phone.

"What's going on with the surveillance?" said Cullen.

Rarity looked him up and down. "Nice to see you, too, Constable. I'm on my break, can't it wait?"

"No. I need to get an update on the Matt MacLeod surveillance."

Rarity dropped her phone on the table. "He returned to Edinburgh last night. We've got two men outside an address in Gorgie."

"Why wasn't I told?"

"Did you need to be told?"

"You should keep me in the loop at least," said Cullen, "especially when I've been in Glasgow."

"Fine," said Rarity. "DCI Cargill has been looking for you, by the way."

"I spoke to her earlier. I just got back from Glasgow."

"I gather you've been up to your usual high jinks."

"What's that supposed to mean?"

"Never mind," she said. "Why the sudden interest in MacLeod?"

Cullen showed her the emails. "I think he might be our man."

"You've shown me these before," said Rarity. "This isn't evidence."

"He knew Strang a lot better than we thought," said Cullen. "At school, they both played in bands and Strang's supported MacLeod's once. They knew each other pretty well." He paused for breath. "I'd like to bring him in again."

"You've already spoken to him."

"I'd like another shot," said Cullen. "If he's done nothing, then he'll clear himself and we can let him go and stop the surveillance."

Rarity tapped her fingers for a few seconds. "Fine."

79

Cullen didn't know the two officers on surveillance duties, figuring they must have been St Leonard's or Torphichen Street boys. They sat in an unmarked Astra on a street just behind Tynecastle, the home of Hearts, who looked like they were going to follow Rangers down the toilet of liquidation.

He rapped on the window and got in the back seat.

"It's Cullen, isn't it?" said the first of the two. Ginger hair and stubble.

"It is."

"Heard you told Bain to go fuck himself," said the other, a dark-haired skinhead. "That true?"

"No comment," said Cullen.

"Good on you, mate," said the first one.

Ginger held out his hand. "DC Edwards, by the way."

"DC McKeown," said the skinhead.

Cullen reluctantly shook both hands, not liking how his reputation was preceding him. Previously, he wouldn't give a fuck about that sort of thing, but these days it was different. Aiming to be a DS, he needed to command a bit more respect. *Some* respect would be a start.

"Is MacLeod still inside?" said Cullen.

"He is," said McKeown. "We've been sat here since seven this morning. We relieved a couple of boys from Leith Walk who were here from ten last night." He checked his watch. "Should be knocking off in a few hours, but this is approved overtime so I'm not turning that down in a hurry."

"I want to bring him into the station," said Cullen.

McKeown looked disappointed. "So why is he under surveillance, then?"

"To make sure he didn't piss off," said Cullen. "I'm starting to get a better picture of how he fits into the case."

"Right."

"One of you stay outside," said Cullen, "one come up with me."

"Fine," said McKeown.

Cullen led them across the road, lined with tiny front gardens, at best a metre wide. The stair door was open, the intercom lying on the patch of weeds outside the ground floor flat.

Cullen nodded at Edwards. "You stay here."

They jogged up the stairs, heading to MacLeod's flat on the top floor. Cullen knocked on the door. "Mr MacLeod, it's the police."

MacLeod opened it. He stood in his dressing gown, looking tired. He blinked. "What the fuck are you doing here?"

"I need to ask you a few questions," said Cullen.

"You've had your go at me, Skinky. Try someone else from school."

McKeown frowned at Cullen.

Cullen struggled to keep it formal and professional. "We need to ask you some further questions, Mr MacLeod."

MacLeod stared at him for a few seconds. "In you come, then."

Cullen glared at him. "Down the station."

"Mind if I get dressed, then?"

"Be my guest."

MacLeod went inside.

"Charming," said McKeown.

"Tell me about it," said Cullen.

"You two got previous?"

"In a manner of speaking," said Cullen. "Can you and Edwards take him in your car? I'll meet you down at Leith Walk."

"Sure thing."

The door bundled open again. MacLeod wore jeans and a shirt, carrying a navy coat with him. He locked his flat door behind him.

"I'm ready for my interrogation, boys."

80

Cullen and Buxton sat in the interview room, the PCSO standing guard by the door. MacLeod had dragged things out, making them wait for his lawyer to turn up.

Cullen didn't particularly like MacLeod - quite the opposite in fact - but he was only under suspicion and not under arrest yet. The flicker of possibility of being a suspect meant everything had to be done by the book.

"Mr MacLeod," said Cullen, "can you confirm the reason you returned to Edinburgh last night?"

"My flat was ready for me to move back in. That's why."

"Nothing to do with the coast being clear?" said Cullen.

MacLeod sat back and folded his arms. "No comment."

"Can you confirm for the record you were acquainted with a James Strang?" said Buxton.

"No comment."

"Mr Strang went to school with you in Dalhousie," said Buxton.

"No comment."

"Mr Strang was three years below you."

"No comment."

That had become a common tactic in Scotland since a famous case made it mandatory for a lawyer to be in attendance. Gone were the days of getting the suspect alone to slip up on the record before legal counsel was involved.

Cullen lost his patience. "Mr MacLeod," he said, struggling to keep his voice level, "we have you on record in a previous interview discussing Mr Strang's whereabouts, so please cease the no comment."

MacLeod looked at his lawyer, who nodded. "Fine, I knew him."

"It would appear Mr Strang died in horrific circumstances," said Cullen. "We believe he was stabbed with a screwdriver and left to bleed out."

MacLeod's mouth hung open as he tried to keep his cool. "And what's changed since yesterday?"

"How well did you know Mr Strang?"

"As I told you," said MacLeod, "I knew him to speak to. If I saw him in the pub, he's the sort of guy I'd have a wee chat with. We weren't particularly close."

Cullen let the space grow, waiting for MacLeod to fill it.

"I'd spoken to him maybe twice since I moved to Edinburgh. Once in HMV, once in a pub. That was it."

"You know he was involved in the music scene, don't you?" said Cullen.

"So?"

"At school, his band supported yours once, correct?" said Cullen.

MacLeod laughed. "Man, you lot are desperate. Yes, I played bass in a band when I was seventeen. We were bloody awful. We played Oasis and Robbie Williams and Stereophonics songs really, really badly. I haven't touched a musical instrument since. I've barely listened to anything with a guitar. I'm mainly into dance music these days. Is that enough for you?"

"You knew nothing about Mr Strang's music career?" said Cullen.

"I think he spammed me when I saw him in the pub that one time," said MacLeod. "He gave me a flyer for a gig, tried to sell me a CD. As it happened, a mate's band was playing that night, so I ended up being there anyway."

Cullen perked up. "And yet you insist you only met him in Edinburgh on two occasions?"

MacLeod lost his cool. He looked at his lawyer, who barely seemed interested. "Look, I didn't speak to Strang at that gig. He was always surrounded by his groupies and hangers on."

"Would anyone be able to verify that?"

MacLeod tightened his arms around him. "Am I a suspect here?"

"We haven't cautioned you yet." Cullen flicked back a few pages in his notebook. "So, you didn't speak to Mr Strang at all that night?"

"Have you got a hearing problem?" said MacLeod. "I did *see* him a couple of other times, but I didn't speak to him on either occasion."

Cullen looked at Buxton. "Now we're getting somewhere." He looked back at MacLeod. "Can you expand on these sightings?"

MacLeod stared at the tabletop. "My mate's band was supporting Jimi's. I don't even know what they were called."

"The Invisibles," said Buxton.

"Right," said MacLeod. "The Invisibles. My mate used to be in that whole scene. They'd go to gigs and clubs and stuff. He dragged me along a few times." His eyes sparked and he sat forward, bouncing his clenched

321

fist off his lips then pointing at Cullen. "He was with that Mike Roberts both times."

Cullen scowled. "The singer in Expect Delays?"

"Aye," said MacLeod. "He's on the cover of *The List* this fortnight, right?"

Cullen's mouth was dry. "Did they know each other?"

MacLeod shrugged. "How on earth am I supposed to know that?" He shook his head. "I saw them in a club together a few times, that's it."

Cullen terminated the interview. "We'll be in touch."

"Am I in the clear here?" said MacLeod.

"Mr MacLeod, I don't particularly like you," said Cullen, "but I am not and have not been treating you as a suspect in this case. I am merely looking for leads."

"It feels very much like I'm being prosecuted," said MacLeod.

"Maybe you're guilty of something else."

MacLeod didn't reply.

Cullen left him and his lawyer in the room, instructing the PCSO to see them out.

In the corridor, Cullen paced ahead.

Buxton caught up with him. "What are you thinking?"

"Have you read *The List* this week?" said Cullen.

"No, why?"

"The interview with Expect Delays," said Cullen. "That's where that band got the notion to head down into the hidden street under the Old Town."

"*The Hidden Street* is an Expect Delays album," said Buxton.

"Exactly," said Cullen. "It's where the name comes from."

Buxton frowned. "Wait, are you saying Mike Roberts is a suspect?"

Cullen stood and thought it through, trying to tie the loose strands together.

Could he have killed Strang?

When Cullen first went through to Glasgow, Roberts was being interviewed. He was the last person due to see Hughes before he died.

"Either way," said Cullen, "we're heading back to Glasgow. I better tell Rarity."

He marched off in the direction of his superior officer.

81

Rarity wasn't comfortable making the decision herself, so it went through layers of management - Methven, Cargill, then finally Turnbull - with Cullen making his case each time and finally obtaining permission to interview Roberts, providing Bain approved it.

Cullen stormed into the Glasgow CID office, heading straight for Bain.

Bain looked up and grinned. "Sundance, now there's a fuckin' sight for sore eyes. I need my car washed."

"Very funny."

"Who's your boyfriend?" said Bain, scowling at Buxton.

"ADC Simon Buxton. I worked for you for six months. *Sir.*"

Bain raised his eyebrows then looked around the room to see who amongst his team had heard. Only McCrea. "This you apologising is it, Sundance?"

"What for?"

"You fuckin' know," said Bain. "Telling me to go fuck myself."

"I would apologise if I said it," said Cullen. "I didn't, so I won't."

Bain's fingers drummed on the desk. "Well, if that's how you want to play it."

"Spreading stories about me doesn't make it any more true," said Cullen.

"I heard you," said McCrea.

"You didn't," said Cullen, still not one hundred per cent sure.

Bain scowled. "What are you here for, Cullen?"

"I need to speak to you about Mike Roberts."

"Who?"

"You interviewed him a couple of days ago," said Cullen. "The singer in Expect Delays."

"Red fuckin' herring, Sundance," said Bain. "Forget it. We've moved on."

"When you had him in did you ask him about James Strang?"

"Why the fuck would I?" said Bain. "You hadn't told us about your case yet, had you?"

McCrea bellowed with laughter, overdoing it in Cullen's eyes.

"We need to speak to him," said Cullen.

"Our case is locked down," said Bain. "It was a drug money killing. As you well know, we've got a boy in downstairs who's away to confess. You'd know if you bothered attending any of my briefings since your ill-disciplined performance this morning."

"I've just spoken to our other suspect," said Cullen. "He's put us onto Mike Roberts."

"Here we fuckin' go." Bain put his head in his heads. "Another merry wee jig from Cullen."

"Roberts and Strang were friends," said Cullen, ignoring Bain. "There was an interview in *The List* with Roberts about the street where Strang's body was found."

"You're off on one again." Bain laughed. "Might set up a popcorn stand. Make a fuckin' killing."

"I'm serious," said Cullen. "There is a definite link between them. On my way here I was putting together a semblance of a motive."

"So, you're falling for this other suspect's stories, right?"

"He didn't give us the link," said Cullen. "It's called deduction, *sir*." His anger hadn't abated since their earlier altercation. "Look, after everything we've been through together, you should know by now to listen to me."

Bain rubbed his top lip for a few seconds. "Right, Sundance, you get your shot at him."

"Are you sure, gaffer?" said McCrea.

"Not really," said Bain, "but fuck it, it's Cullen's funeral."

"I'm not happy, sir," said McCrea. "We've got a dead-cert conviction with Nicholls downstairs. From what you've told me about Cullen, he'll do everything he can to stop it."

"I've got nothing to do with your case," said Cullen, "other than being told to be here because of some fucking politics." He turned to Bain. "I need to speak to Roberts. I've got approval from Turnbull to speak to him on my own. He wants to make sure we do things properly. He won't tolerate any obstruction."

Bain rubbed his top lip again then looked at McCrea. "What do you reckon?"

"Your call, gaffer. I've told you what I think."

Bain stared at the ceiling for a while. "Fine," he eventually said. "Just don't piss him or any lawyers off, cos I'll get the fuckin' blame."

"And that's not a wise move," said McCrea.

"Don't worry." Bain held his hand up. "I'll be in there with him to make sure there's no funny business."

"I know where the funny business will come from,"

said Cullen.

"I'm warning you, Sundance." Bain pointed his finger at him. "No fuckin' about here." He looked at McCrea. "Find something for Cullen's wee boyfriend to do, preferably something he can't fuck up. And get some gorillas in woolly suits to bring Roberts in."

McCrea slammed the door as he left the room.

"Do I not get to sit in on this?" said Buxton.

"No chance," said Bain.

"Great," said Buxton. "Nice wasted trip."

Bain pointed at Cullen. "Remember, Constable. No fuckin' about with this."

"None at all."

Bain shook his head then followed McCrea out of the room.

Buxton leaned in close. "If you fuck this up, you'll never be able to forget it."

"Don't I know it."

82

Cullen and Bain had come to a loose agreement while they waited for Roberts to be brought in. Just like MacLeod, he'd insisted on bringing his solicitor with him, the same pinstriped thirty-something Cullen had seen him with the other day. From his attire, he suspected Douglas McGuire specialised in the music industry rather than criminal law.

Roberts played with his hair, tugging it forward. "Can we make this quick?"

Cullen could see the lack of roots at the front - definitely a comb-forward. "I'm sorry?"

"You might have heard I'm playing a gig at Hampden Park tonight," said Roberts. "I'm supporting U2 in my home town, you know?"

"Thought you were from Edinburgh," said Cullen.

Roberts shrugged. "Whatever. Just need to get out of here, don't I?"

Cullen adjusted his collar. "This is a serious police matter. I'm sure you'll have sound checked already."

"Aye, don't worry about it," said Roberts. "It's not like it's the most important day of my life or anything."

McGuire perked up. "This had better lead to something critical for your investigation, otherwise my client will have grounds to lodge a complaint."

"On what basis?" said Bain.

"As stated, my client is preparing to play an important

concert tonight," said McGuire. "I would rather you didn't waste his precious and expensive time here with this charade."

"Who says we're wasting his time?" said Bain.

"I shall be the judge of that," said McGuire.

Bain held his gaze for a few seconds. "I don't want any disruption. Your client is here to assist us. I'd hope finding the killer of a mate is motivation enough for him."

"Very well," said McGuire.

Cullen cleared his throat. "Mr Roberts, do you know one James Strang, also known as Jimi Danger?"

Roberts snorted. "Sure, I knew Jimi."

"You do know he's dead, don't you?" said Cullen.

"Dead?" Roberts frowned. "I know he disappeared a few years back."

"We found his body last week," said Cullen. "In Edinburgh."

"Oh aye?" Roberts looked bored.

"It was close to somewhere you knew," said Cullen. "A set of medieval streets under the Old Town."

Roberts laughed. "Are you serious? I'm playing the biggest gig of my life tonight and you've got me in here to talk about some crap Neeraj said in a magazine?"

Bain sat back and folded his arms, a smirk flickering on his face.

"Is this correct?" said McGuire.

"We're investigating a likely connection in the case," said Cullen. "When was the last time you saw Mr Strang?"

Roberts threw his arms in the air. "I don't know, do I? That's ancient history, man."

"Can you try and think?" said Cullen.

"DI Bain," said McGuire. "My client is doing his utmost to assist here. He can't recollect so I'm asking you to desist."

"Please try," said Cullen.

"It was probably when he played that gig where he cut himself up," said Roberts. "That was extreme, you know? It wasn't a pretty sight."

"That was definitely the last time?" said Cullen.

"If that's what my client says, then it's what happened."

"I remain to be convinced," said Cullen. "We believe you were friends with Mr Strang. How did he seem around the time he disappeared?"

"I've no idea," said Roberts.

"Take some time," said Cullen. "Try and remember. It might be important."

Roberts leaned back in the chair and crossed his legs, staring into space for a few seconds. "I think he was fine."

"I gather you used to drink with Mr Strang?" said Cullen.

"For a bit, aye," said Roberts. "We used to go out clubbing together. Jimi was a good guy, could always attract the ladies, that's for sure."

"How was your friendship?" said Cullen.

"Fine, I think," said Roberts.

"He wasn't annoyed with you about anything?" said Cullen. "No fights?"

"No." Roberts tapped his watch.

"I believe you were due to meet with an Alex Hughes on the evening of Wednesday the twenty seventh of March," said Cullen.

"Woah woah woah." Roberts made 'time out' hand gestures.

"My client has already answered questions on that matter," said McGuire.

"Agreed," said Bain.

"I find it interesting you've got strong connections to victims in two murder cases," said Cullen.

Roberts started laughing. "I could name ten bands you could get in here. Aren't you going to bring Neeraj in given he started all this?"

McGuire got to his feet. "My client has to get to the stadium for his concert." He fastened his suit jacket. "Unless you have any concrete questions for him, I suggest you let him get back? I don't need to remind you precisely how much money is resting on this particular event, including public money for policing?"

"I think we've probably asked enough of Mr Roberts for one day," said Bain. "Do you have any other questions, Constable?"

Cullen didn't know what else he could do. "Fine. We'll be in touch."

83

Cullen had no idea where Buxton had got to - given what he'd caught him doing the other morning, Cullen wouldn't be at all surprised if he was actually washing Bain's car.

He found a laptop and started typing up the interview transcript, his fingers hammering so hard the E key bounced off. He spent a minute trying to put it back on.

He looked over to a thud from the adjacent desk.

Buxton glowered over a pile of filing. "This is the last time I come with you on one of these."

"One of what?"

"Your little runs," said Buxton. "I've been doing *filing*, mate."

"Sorry."

"I should have been in there with him," said Buxton. "I know the bloke."

"Sorry," said Cullen. "You heard Bain."

"What happened?"

"Nothing much," said Cullen. "I think I annoyed his lawyer."

"This isn't going to end well, is it?"

"I doubt it," said Cullen.

McCrea appeared beside them, grinning. "The gaffer wasn't impressed with that."

"Really?" Cullen looked up.

"Said he looks like a right idiot," said McCrea. "Not

happy at all."

"How?"

"For fuck's sake," said McCrea, "you brought in a pop star and you're trying to pin some load of bollocks on him."

"He's involved in this," said Cullen, avoiding eye contact. "He knows something. I'm sure of it."

"Feel it in your water, do you?" said McCrea.

Cullen just sighed.

"His concert tonight might be a bit more important, don't you think?" said McCrea.

"Are you seriously telling me a concert takes precedence over finding a killer?" said Cullen.

"It's ancient history," said McCrea. "Interesting how you get the cold cases whereas we get the live ones through here."

"It's hardly a cold case," said Cullen.

"You're lucky you've still got a job after what you said to the gaffer earlier," said McCrea.

"Right," said Cullen. "After the way he speaks to people?"

"It's the insubordination," said McCrea. "If you saw that, you might not still be a DC." He grinned. "And bringing up the Hughes case in that interview, big mistake. Thought you'd read through the case?"

Cullen nodded. "I had. In light of the recent evidence we obtained in Edinburgh, I thought it was pertinent, don't you?"

"Pertinent?" said McCrea. "Look who's swallowed a dictionary." He folded his arms. "Listen, these aren't the same case and you're barking up the wrong tree."

Cullen's phone rang. He checked the display - Cargill. "Got to take this." He held the phone up to McCrea, who merely shook his head and looked away.

Cullen went to the corridor to answer it.

"Glad you finally answered," said Cargill. "I've been looking for you all day."

"Sorry, I've been busy."

"I need you to head to Tulliallan," said Cargill.

Cullen shut his eyes. Tulliallan wasn't a good sign - the training college was now used as Police Scotland's headquarters until permanent offices were built. "What for?"

"A certain ex-superior officer of yours has decided to report your behaviour to our mutual DCS."

84

Cullen stood in the corridor in Tulliallan feeling like shite. The cold was definitely in the post.

He got his mobile out and called Sharon. "I doubt I'll get to this gig tonight."

"Did you not get my text?"

"I'm drowning in unread texts today." Cullen hadn't checked his phone all afternoon. "What did it say?"

"I gave the tickets to Chantal. I don't feel like going."

"Okay," said Cullen. "I think I've caught your cold."

"You have been pushing yourself a bit hard," said Sharon.

"Yeah, I know. And to what end?" He ducked into the stairwell as he saw Bain, McCrea and one of their superiors marching down the corridor. "How are you doing?"

"Shite," said Sharon. "You?"

"Had an eventful day. Told a DI to go fuck himself and now I'm going to get battered for it."

"Methven?"

"He's been fine for once," said Cullen. "Well, fine for him."

"Not Bain?"

"Aye."

"Jesus, Scott."

"I know," said Cullen. "I'm at Tulliallan just now. Turnbull and Cargill are meeting me here. I'm going in front of Soutar."

Sharon laughed. "Getting hauled in front of Turnbull's boss is certainly a way to make your name in the new regime."

"Bain is having a laugh," said Cullen. "I didn't do anything out of order. There were no witnesses and if he conjures one up then they're lying."

"Remind me why I go out with you again?" said Sharon.

"My natural poise and balance."

She snorted down the phone.

Turnbull came barrelling down the corridor, wearing full uniform, his face like thunder. Cargill and Methven followed.

"Better go," said Cullen. "We're going in. I'll call you later."

"Constable," said Turnbull, acknowledging Cullen. He pushed past him into the room, Cargill following.

Methven stopped.

"What's going on, sir?" said Cullen. "Is this about what I allegedly said to DI Bain?"

"I've no sodding idea," said Methven. "Alison and Jim have been on the phone to their opposite numbers in Glasgow all afternoon and neither spoke in the sodding car. It might be wider than that." He checked his watch. "We're late, so we'd better get in."

Entering the room, Cullen consoled himself with the idea that Turnbull was finally getting his round table.

DCS Carolyn Soutar sat at the end of the table and took a roll call.

Turnbull and Cargill were on one side, across from Bain, McCrea and Turnbull's opposite number, Detective Superintendent Keith Graham.

There were a couple of faces Cullen didn't recognise, presumably part of Soutar's central team.

As he sat in the chair next to Cargill, Cullen realised he knew very little about Soutar, but on first impressions she clearly had presence. Unfortunately, she had a voice like Margaret Thatcher.

"Thank you for gathering here." Soutar looked around the room and made eye contact with every officer present, before licking her lips. "We should *not* have to put up with this sort of thing so early in the new force. I expected a lot more." Her eyes settled on Cullen. "DC Cullen, I have heard your name a fair amount today. Why?"

"He's a smart little bastard is why," said Bain.

"Enough," said Soutar. "It would appear we have managed to get ourselves into a bit of a situation here. I don't know or care how we've got to this but I want to clearly state that, from this point on, both investigations are now formally under Glasgow South direction."

Turnbull started spluttering an objection but Soutar held up her hand to silence him.

"Any further incidents of this nature and I shall bring in some of my old colleagues in the Met. I don't have to remind you how bad that will look for the new Scottish police service as a whole, do I?"

"I don't think it would be prudent to merge the cases," said Turnbull.

"Please elaborate," said Soutar.

"While I'm happy to acknowledge there are certain connections," said Turnbull, "are we positive they are, genuinely, one and the same?"

"They're not," said Bain. "Our boy was killed for drugs. No idea why theirs was."

"What problem are we trying to solve here?" said Cargill. "It seems like DI Bain and his team are running a different case to us and we have co-operated fully."

"Go on," said Soutar.

Cargill cleared her throat. "They've been using one of our best resources, DC Cullen, to run errands in Glasgow when we could have otherwise used him in Edinburgh. Carolyn, you should be aware of DI Bain's reputation for man-management."

"Now wait a minute," said Bain. "What are you saying, sweetheart?"

"We've worked together." Cargill left it at that.

"Don't I know it," said Bain.

"Carolyn," said Cargill, "DI Bain had to go cap in hand to Strathclyde looking for a new role due to his particular management style."

Bain stabbed his finger in the air in Cargill's direction. "You watch what you're saying."

"We don't want to go into the other reason why you're no longer in Edinburgh, do we?" Cargill had a smirk on her face.

Bain looked away. "I was cleared of any wrongdoing."

"Assaulting a senior officer would have been a serious mistake," said Cargill.

"But I didn't actually assault one, did I?" said Bain.

"Well, you certainly came very close," said Cargill.

"Are you trying to make a point here, Alison?" said Soutar.

"DC Cullen's actions were entirely in keeping with a rational reaction to DI Bain's somewhat unorthodox investigation methods," said Cargill.

"Well, if a junior officer told him to 'go fuck himself', I wouldn't suggest the blame lay with DI Bain," said

Soutar.

"That word is a particular favourite with a certain officer," said Cargill.

Soutar pursed her lips. "Alison, this is a modern world. While I myself do not use such industrial language, DI Bain is perfectly within his rights to express himself in such a manner."

"I see." Cargill stared at the table.

"Regardless, it's not the words DC Cullen used," said Soutar, "but the attitude behind them. I will not tolerate insubordination."

"I wholeheartedly agree," said Turnbull. "That said, I have strong reservations about the veracity of the allegation."

"I've just had a phone call from the Chief Constable's office," said Soutar. "Some London lawyers have been making noises regarding one of your officers bringing in Michael Roberts, thereby putting at risk a concert at Hampden tonight."

"DC Cullen acted in good faith," said Cargill. "He had a lead. This is a murder case, after all."

"There is a time and place for everything," said Soutar.

"And we needed to move," said Cargill. "We had a lead and we acted on it."

Soutar looked at Cullen. "It's interesting how we have the same officer involved in an act of gross insubordination and with a formal complaint to the Chief's office."

"An *alleged* act of insubordination," said Turnbull.

Soutar narrowed her eyes. "What are you trying to say here?"

"I don't think the investigation should be placed under

DI Bain," said Turnbull.

"He is not fit for purpose," said Cargill.

"You better be careful what you're saying, princess," said Bain, "your new boss is listening in."

"In case you aren't aware," said Cargill, "I'm now a DCI and I'm not subordinate to you."

Turnbull banged his fist on the table. "I fundamentally disagree with this proposal, Carolyn."

Graham raised his eyebrows. "Afraid of seeing it done properly?"

"Hardly." Turnbull looked at Bain. "Brian, I think you're saying these are separate cases."

"I'm saying ours is a drug-related crime," said Bain. "The evidence I've seen from Sun-, sorry Cullen, has been sketchy at best. I'm not even sure you've got a case, big man."

"You've broken protocol," said Cullen. "You spoke to a suspect in Edinburgh without seeking our approval first."

Turnbull cut across him. "Carolyn," he said, his voice pleading, "I'm not sure what we could possibly gain from having these disparate cases under a single MIT."

"I'm sure you of all people can appreciate there are synergies we can leverage," said Soutar, smiling. "Lothian & Borders, God rest its soul, had some high profile cases over the last few years where investigations weren't particularly well focused."

"With all due respect," said Turnbull, "DI Bain was responsible for at least one of those cases."

"He was under your command at the time," said Soutar.

Turnbull glowered at her, disappointment etched all over his face.

"While it may be under Glasgow MIT supervision,

can I suggest the Edinburgh investigation is managed at arm's reach?" said Methven. "We're forty miles apart and I worry we'll lose agility if we have to seek approval from Detective Super Graham or DI Bain every time we want to speak to a suspect."

Soutar tapped her pen against her pad for a few seconds. "Very well. I want twice-daily conference calls as long as both are fully active investigations."

"Very well," said Turnbull.

Soutar stared at both Turnbull and Graham. "Gentlemen," she said, her voice deep and authoritative, "I expect this to work seamlessly and without further intervention on my part. I will hold both Detective Superintendents accountable if this is not a success."

Silence lingered in the room.

"You both know the consequences of another incident."

85

Turnbull led them in search of a meeting room, Cullen and Methven lagging behind.

"I thought that went better than expected," said Cullen, as he climbed the stairs.

"How can you say that?" said Methven. "We've lost control of the case."

"I thought I was going to lose my job."

"This isn't over yet."

Turnbull found a room, occupied by two uniformed Inspectors. He marched in. "I need to ask you to vacate this room."

"Excuse me?"

"I'm pulling rank." Turnbull pointed to the stripes on his sleeve. "Detective Superintendent James Turnbull."

They left the room looking irritated.

"That'll no doubt come back to bite me." Turnbull sat at the head of the table.

"How did we lose our case?" said Cargill.

"Bain and Carolyn go back a long way," said Turnbull. "They were both DCs at the same time."

"Glasgow, right?" said Cullen.

Turnbull nodded. "Strathclyde as was."

"Where does the accent come from?" said Cullen.

"Ten years in the Met," said Turnbull.

"So, we've lost out because of Bain's old pal's act?" said Cargill.

"I'm afraid so." Turnbull looked at Methven. "Good work, Colin. You did well there. Some potential leverage."

"Can we use it to our advantage?" said Cargill.

"I think so," said Turnbull. "Arm's reach never works. This gives us a certain amount of latitude."

"Cullen, you'll have to be our eyes and ears on the ground in Glasgow," said Methven.

Cullen looked up at the ceiling. "I knew that was coming."

"How's our case going?" said Turnbull.

"It's on a slight hiatus, sir," said Cargill. "DCs Jain and Buxton are looking into the few remaining options we have. We probably need to think about *Crimewatch*."

Turnbull nodded. "That will be good publicity for Police Scotland. We can put Graham and Bain in their boxes if we manage it appropriately."

"The only suspect we've got so far was under surveillance by Angus CID," said Cargill.

"Good Christ," said Turnbull, eyes wide. "I'm not still paying for that, am I?"

"Relax," said Cullen. "He returned to Edinburgh last night."

"So the surveillance is definitely cancelled?" said Turnbull.

"Yes," said Methven. "Stopped this afternoon when DC Cullen brought him in for interview."

"I'm not sure he's a suspect now," said Cullen. "I'd like another go at Roberts."

Turnbull hit the desk. "No. That's what's got us into this situation in the first place, Constable. The record label is putting severe pressure on us not to interfere. Apparently, supporting U2 will boost their sales figures and ability to turn a profit. We do not want to leave ourselves open to lawsuits. I want no further contact with Roberts without a formal sign-off from both myself and Detective Super Graham."

"Right," said Cullen.

"Am I making myself clear?" said Turnbull. "While I do have a lot of time for you, Constable, you have a tendency to get carried away with yourself."

Cullen clenched his fists under the table. "If anything comes up, sir, I will formally raise it with you through the appropriate channels."

"Good," said Turnbull. "I'm glad we're coming to an understanding here. We might make a senior officer out of you yet."

Cargill cleared her throat. "We will need you to resume your secondment to Glasgow South."

"So that's it," said Cullen, disappointment starting to bite. "I'm back in Glasgow?"

"That's right," said Cargill. "You'd better head through now. I expect a call from you first thing tomorrow updating me on progress."

"How is me being stuck through there going to help anything?" said Cullen.

"We need someone there who is more than aware of DI Bain's modus operandi," said Turnbull. "I need to be apprised of any funny business."

Cullen shook his head at the orders. "Fine."

"Is there something you wish to raise?" said Turnbull.

Cullen leaned back in the chair. He didn't want his balls chewed again, but he was feeling sick to the stomach of the games being played. "Earlier, you were talking about using the distance to our advantage. Two people are dead here. We shouldn't be thinking about politics and positioning, we should be finding out who killed them."

The reactions on their faces made him immediately regret it.

"It's not as simple as that," said Turnbull, his voice raised. "Please learn to look at the bigger picture if you want to become a leader, Constable."

"I think I am looking at it, sir," said Cullen. "Much as I hate DI Bain, we surely need to just get on with it."

"We must *manage* this," said Turnbull. "This is outwith our control and we have to wrestle it back." He had lost his tightly guarded temper. "DI Bain has an axe to grind and he's certainly sharpening it. There's no way to get him out of the picture. You saw how they were in there, any further complaints will just get their backs up."

"I agree," said Methven.

Turnbull pointed at Cullen. "You're known as someone who gets results but I will not have you up to your games, okay?"

Cullen bowed his head. "Sorry, sir."

"You must become more of a team player if you wish to advance," said Turnbull. "I asked DI Methven to brief you on that when your Acting DS tenure ended."

"I wasn't briefed," said Cullen.

Methven glared at him.

Turnbull frowned at Methven then Cargill. "We're done here." He got to his feet and led Cargill out of the room, leaving Cullen alone with Methven.

"I'd advise you to watch your mouth when speaking to Superintendent Turnbull," said Methven. "This isn't DI Bain you're dealing with, Constable."

"Noted," said Cullen, fire burning in his gut.

"I want you to inform me of your activities on an

hourly basis," said Methven.

"What about DS Rarity?"

"Come directly to me," said Methven.

"If I'm to head to Glasgow, someone has to take Buxton back to Edinburgh."

"Why is he here?"

"To speak to Roberts," said Cullen. "He knew him."

"And did he speak to him?"

"No," said Cullen. "Bain wouldn't let him."

"For the love of goodness," said Methven. "Right. I'll take him back. Any more of your sodding cowboy heroics, you clear it with me first, okay?"

86

Cullen trudged through the Govan station security and made his way to the Incident Room.

McCrea looked over, grinning. "We had a bet on. The gaffer reckoned it would be you who'd come. Never one to shy away from a high profile investigation."

"I'm here to help," said Cullen. "I think it's best if I look for connections to the Edinburgh case, don't you?"

"Won't get an argument from me," said McCrea. "Just keep yourself out of my hair." He pulled on his jacket and got to his feet. "You're welcome to my desk, by the way. I'm off to see U2."

He hurried out of the station and left Cullen in the bustle of the Incident Room. He sat down at his desk and stared at the laminated wood.

U2.

Of all the tedious, overblown, stadium...

Cullen hated U2. Despite his punk roots, Cullen's dad loved nothing better than blasting out *Sunday Bloody Sunday* on a Sunday morning.

In Cullen's eyes, they were music for people who hated music.

He was wasting his time in Glasgow, stuck between two warring factions of idiots, both as bad as each other. Bain was one of the worst human beings he'd ever encountered, but the politics and posturing on his own side sickened him. He didn't know which was in the right, if either.

All he could do was put his head down and get on with it. He pulled over the file and tried to make notes. He read for half an hour, only making a single scribble. He wished he was back in Edinburgh. He wished he wasn't working.

Near the back of the file he found a listing of Alex Hughes' calls leading up to his death. Two DCs sat at a desk just behind him. He craned round. "Has anyone been through these?"

They both looked blank. "Don't think so."

"Who would know?" said Cullen.

"Big Davie. Admin officer."

Cullen knew who Davie was, a bald officer in his early forties, lucky to have found his niche in admin. He found him after not too much searching.

"Cullen, isn't it?" said Davie.

"Aye. Has anyone looked through the phone records, do you know?"

Davie frowned. "Let me check." He picked up a ring binder, over-stuffed with paper. "Right. No, is the answer." He scratched his chin. "Should have been one of McCrea's lads."

"Cheers," said Cullen. "I'll do it."

"Lucky you," said Davie, scribbling on a form.

Cullen returned to his desk and sat down, relieved to have something to get on with. His nostril started twitching, a sure sign a cold was definitely on its way.

It took him a good forty minutes to build a decent cross-reference from the case file, ticking off the items on the list one by one, leaving just a single number he couldn't find. A ten-second phone call and a short wait later, his old mate Tommy Smith in Edinburgh Phone

Squad came up with the goods.
It was Audrey Strang's number.

87

Cullen managed to get a space just outside the close on the Royal Mile. He sat in his car at the back of nine, his head now thick with the cold. He slowly got out and climbed the stairs to the flat, still full of resentment at being sent back to Glasgow.

Eyes and ears.

Checks and balances.

It was all bollocks.

"Dinner's in the cat." Sharon's eyes were focused on a soppy romantic comedy starring some actors Cullen recognised but couldn't name.

"He needs to go on a diet," said Cullen.

"He's just cuddly."

"When you said I was cuddly, I went on a diet," said Cullen.

"How was your bollocking?"

"I've still got both. I think Cargill and Turnbull's are a bit sore."

She laughed. "Mind if I watch this?"

"It's fine," said Cullen. "I've eaten, by the way."

"Good." Sharon pressed play again.

As he sat there, he tried to summarise sufficiently to allow him to get some sleep. Driving back, aside from bemoaning his superiors, Cullen had tried to work out how Audrey Strang and Alex Hughes were connected, other than through her brother.

Why would Strang's sister be calling his ex-bandmate?

Cullen recalled Strang's mother saying she'd spoken to Hughes on the phone a number of times.

Maybe the cases *were* linked after all.

He threw a few ideas around in his head, but it simply came down to needing to speak to Audrey Strang again.

Sharon paused the film. "What's up?" She folded her arms.

"How do you know something's up?"

"You're twitching," she said. "It's distracting."

"Sorry."

"Well?"

Cullen sat up. "So, you know I've been sent back through to Glasgow, right?"

"Was this before or after you told Bain to go fuck himself?"

"Both," said Cullen. "I did some digging just before I left. I found a connection between their victim and our victim's sister. They were speaking to each other on the phone."

"You should tell them."

"I will."

"Scott..."

"I *will*," said Cullen. "Once I've investigated it myself."

"You need to watch what you're doing," said Sharon. "You've got away with your cowboy stuff in the past but it will catch up with you in the end. Besides, Bain will hang anyone out to dry to cover his own arse. With a high profile case like this, Cargill and Turnbull won't want any blame attached to themselves."

"I'll let them know." Cullen sat back on the sofa. "I met up with Michelle this morning."

"In Glasgow?"

"Aye," said Cullen. "It was weird. In some ways it was good, but it was tough. I forgot how much of a total ball buster she is."

"It's a bit out of character for you to do something your mum has moaned at you about for months," said Sharon.

"It was connected to the case," said Cullen. "She used to go out with a suspect."

Sharon laughed, shaking her head. "You are unbelievable, Scott. You really are."

"Well, I am glad I met up with her," said Cullen. "That's got to count for something."

"Only in your head, Scott."

She pressed play again.

Thursday
4th April 2013

88

Cullen found Bain's number and called him.

"The briefing's just about to start," said Bain. "Where the fuck are you?"

"I won't make it in," said Cullen.

"Sundance, you're fuckin' supposed to be through here," said Bain. "You're their ears on the ground though here. Fuck me, I shouldn't be the one telling you what games they're playing."

"Look, I don't think I'll make it to the briefing," said Cullen. "Might make it in later. I've got this stinking cold. Picked it up off Sharon."

"You did, did you?" said Bain. "Fuckin' convenient it came the day after you were told to report to me, isn't it?"

"You can think what you like," said Cullen. "I'm not well. I'm on maximum strength Lemsip just to stop my brain dribbling out of my ears."

"When the fuck do you reckon you'll be back, then?" said Bain.

"Might be later on today," said Cullen. "Will see how it goes."

"Fuck's sake, Cullen. Can't believe the first thing I've got to do with you again is fuckin' sickness admin."

"Sorry."

"Remember I know when you're shittin' me, you silly bastard," said Bain.

"I just need some sleep and I'll be fine."

"Give me a call at lunchtime, all right?" said Bain.

"Will do."

Cullen hung up. He pocketed his phone, glad that was out of the way.

He walked out of the Kinross service station, taking a sip of coffee and crossing the busy car park. He fished his mobile out of his pocket and called Guthrie.

"What time is it?" said Guthrie.

"Seven."

"I'm not even awake yet," said Guthrie. "What are you after?"

"Just checking in."

"I'm strictly nine-to-five," said Guthrie. "Just as well the surveillance is now handled by your lot in Edinburgh."

"It's finished," said Cullen. "I don't think MacLeod is our man."

"That's nothing to do with me any more, then."

"You can help me, Goth. I need to speak to Audrey Strang again."

"Here we go on the Cullen merry-go-round," said Guthrie.

"Just bear with me. I'll be there in about an hour." He ended the call.

Cullen put the cup in the door and turned the key, before taking the Golf onto the M90 and towards Dalhousie.

89

Cullen met Guthrie outside Audrey's flat in Dalhousie.

"How's it going?" said Cullen.

Guthrie yawned. "You need to work on your small talk, mate."

"I'm serious." Cullen shrugged. "How are you doing?"

"Just got told they've seconded me to the Glasgow South MIT for this case. Thanks for that."

"Sorry. I'll make it up to you. Promise."

"I thought you were supposed to be in Glasgow yourself?" said Guthrie.

Cullen rubbed his nose. "I'm not well."

"So, why are you here?" said Guthrie.

Cullen shrugged. "I'm being looked after by my mother."

Guthrie shook his head. "Always the games with you, Skinky."

They looked up at Audrey's flat on the second floor.

"So, what are we doing here?" said Guthrie.

"Looks like she's been on the phone to Alex Hughes a fair amount," said Cullen.

"That's the Glasgow murder, right?"

Cullen nodded. "Aye."

"What are they speaking about?"

"Let's find out." Cullen buzzed the intercom.

"Hello?"

"Audrey, it's the police," said Cullen.

The door clicked open and they walked up to her flat.

Audrey stood outside the door. "What do you want?"

"I believe you've been on the phone to Alex Hughes," said Cullen.

"Aye, I have," Her eyes danced around the corridor. "Come on inside."

They went into the living room, Audrey taking her place on the futon. Cullen and Guthrie stood.

"I've had the task of going through Alex Hughes' call records for the period leading up to his death," said Cullen. "Your number was on there a number of times."

"So?"

"Care to explain it?" said Cullen.

"Alex and I both missed Jimi. That's all."

"Is that what you were talking about?" said Cullen.

"That amongst other things, I suppose."

"Like what?"

"Alex was a funny guy," said Audrey.

"I'm sure he was," said Cullen. "What did you talk about?"

"Stuff," said Audrey. "Things."

Cullen was fed up with her already. More than fed up. "You know he was into drugs, don't you, Audrey?"

"Drugs?" Her face seemed to spasm. "Drugs are bad, though."

"Alex was a drug dealer," said Cullen.

Audrey looked away. "I didn't know that."

"What did you talk about?"

"How things could have been," said Audrey.

"In what way?"

"Their record deal. If they'd got it, maybe Jimi would still be with us."

"You didn't know he was dead, though, did you?" said

Cullen.

Audrey's eyes bulged. "No, we didn't."

"So, what did you mean about still being with you?" said Cullen.

"I thought Jimi had run away for a new life."

"What made you think that?" said Cullen.

"He disappeared," said Audrey.

"And what did Alex think?" said Cullen.

"Alex said the record deal would have made my brother stay."

"What record deal is this?" said Cullen, playing the daft laddie.

"A big record label was trying to sign Alex and Jimi's band," said Audrey. "I don't know the name."

"And what happened?"

"The record company took the contract away," said Audrey. "It was due to be signed. They'd agreed a lot of money."

"Do you know why that happened?" said Cullen.

"According to Alex," said Audrey, "Michael used his influence to get the deal taken away."

Cullen looked at Guthrie, his expression as blank as he felt. "Michael?"

"Michael," said Audrey, nodding.

"Why would Michael do that?" said Cullen.

"Jimi was obsessed with him," said Audrey. "He stole their song."

"Jimi stole one of Michael's songs?"

"No, the other way round." She started singing. "*Where have you gone?*"

Cullen frowned. "That's Expect Delays. Are you talking about Mike Roberts?"

Audrey nodded frantically.

Pieces slotted into place. Even Cullen had noticed the similarity between The Invisibles' song and the Expect Delays hit. Strang and Roberts had a solid friendship, at least according to Matt MacLeod. What happened between them?

"Alex says Expect Delays were going down the toilet and were about to get dropped. They ripped off Jimi's song. It was nothing like the rest of their stuff. You would hear it on the radio and everything. It was on an advert on the TV."

"How do you know this?" said Cullen.

"Alex told me."

"Just told you?" said Cullen. "Have you got anything to support this?"

"I've got some emails from him," said Audrey. "He sent them to me to make them safe."

"What sort of emails?" said Cullen, his mouth dry, hoping for hard evidence.

She woke up a sleeping laptop and twisted it round to show them. It was the poem. "Alex sent me this."

"What makes you think this is anything to do with it?" said Cullen, anger rising.

"It's obvious, isn't it?" said Audrey. She read from the poem.

In the end, I was reduced to it.
Stealing what wasn't mine, taking what didn't belong to me, coveting my neighbour's wife.

Betrayal is the hardest part.
Dishonesty, theft, hiding.

"That first part is from Michael's perspective," said

Audrey. "He was reduced to stealing what wasn't his, coveting Jimi's song. Alex said he loved that song and he used to rave about it all the time." She sniffed. "The last two lines are from Jimi's perspective, how he felt betrayed. Mike was dishonest. He stole the song from him then stopped seeing him."

Cullen wasn't following this at all, but maybe she'd had insight into her brother's damaged mind as he wrote it. "How did he do that?"

"Michael cut him out of his life entirely," said Audrey. "Point blank refused to see him."

If what she was saying was true then Roberts had played a dangerous game. He'd stolen the song, had a hit single with it then excluded him from his life rather than sharing the success.

"Why were you phoning Alex?" said Cullen.

"Isn't it obvious?"

Cullen smiled, though rage burnt away in the pit of his stomach. He was struggling to contain it - so much had been hidden from them, just out of their reach. "It's not obvious to me."

"Alex had a dossier," said Audrey. "He had evidence pointing to Michael killing Jimi. He was going to confront him about it."

"Jesus Christ." Cullen rubbed at his face. "What sort of thing?"

"He sent me it," said Audrey. "I'll show you."

She took the laptop and went to another email, opened a file and handed it back.

Cullen looked through pages of musical analysis of the two songs, chord progressions and melodies analysed side by side. At most, there was only ever two or three notes difference from any chunk of music. Whether that was fact or simply the biased findings of Hughes' mind remained to be seen.

There was also a detailed analysis of Roberts' movements the day Strang was killed. The information had largely been culled from any associate of Roberts who would talk to Hughes. At the time in question, the closest Roberts had to an alibi was 'seeing a mate', something he'd told Neeraj, Expect Delays' guitarist. Nobody else saw him that evening.

Cullen's fingers tightened around the computer - McAllister and the other investigating officers could have torn the alibi apart, if only they'd known.

"Why didn't you go to the police with this?" Cullen handed the laptop back, having forwarded the emails to his own account.

"After what happened between Dean and me?" said Audrey. "Really?"

"What happened when Mr Hughes spoke to Mike Roberts?" said Cullen.

Audrey shrugged. "That's the thing. I've not heard from him since. He was going to see him last Wednesday."

90

Cullen left Guthrie going through a detailed statement with Audrey and proceeded to get stuck in Dundee rush hour traffic, spending the time trying to decide on the best course of action.

Everything led to calling Methven.

"Run that by me again?"

Cullen's eyes were locked on the car in front. "Alex Hughes prepared some sort of dossier on Roberts. He reckons he'd stolen a song off Strang. He thought Roberts killed him to cover it up."

"Mike Roberts?" Methven exhaled. "This is serious stuff, Cullen."

"I know," said Cullen. "Don't get me wrong, I'm not in the habit of accusing people without cause. It looks like Hughes confronted Roberts last Wednesday night."

"Oh, sodding hell," said Methven. "So, you're saying these are the same case? Roberts killed Strang then he killed Hughes?"

"This is from Strang's sister," said Cullen. "She doesn't seem to be a liar. She's not entirely on the same plane of existence as the rest of us, but I think it's worth checking out. The alternative is Bain pinning his case to a drugs murder and ours getting filed away with the cold cases when something new comes along."

The line was silent for a few seconds.

"What are you proposing, then?" said Methven.

"I'm heading to Glasgow now." Cullen started the engine as the car in front trundled forward.

"I thought you were ill," said Methven. "Alison had Bain on the phone complaining and wanting someone else sent through."

"I got a call from DC Guthrie," said Cullen. "I thought I should investigate it."

"You're playing games, aren't you?"

"I'll get some help from Bain's team."

"You're avoiding my question," said Methven. "I thought I told you about your behaviour."

"I've told you now," said Cullen. "That's progress, isn't it?"

"You're a cheeky sod," said Methven. "If this is a disaster, I'm having no part in it."

"Noted," said Cullen. "I'll get DI Bain's team to bring Roberts in then we'll question him."

"This had better be a much more thorough interview than yesterday's," said Methven. "I've seen the transcript. Not your finest hour, Sergeant. Sorry, Constable."

"Let me make up for it," said Cullen.

"Fine," said Methven. "Approved. Turnbull delegated authority to myself and DI Cargill."

"Thanks." Cullen was glad he couldn't see Methven's face. "I'd better go."

He ended the call and dialled McCrea's number, the traffic still crawling.

"Thought you were ill?" said McCrea.

"I told Bain I might feel better later," said Cullen. "It's later now and I'm feeling better."

"So, why not phone him?" said McCrea.

"I don't know," said Cullen, finally getting up past thirty.

"Well, I could take a wild guess, I suppose," said McCrea. "Anyway, why are you phoning?"

Cullen gave him the same briefing he'd given Methven. He knew he'd have to align notebooks with Guthrie later, depending on how it all went.

"This is pretty far out there, Cullen. Even for you."

"I'll put my career on the line over this," said Cullen. "We have to bring him back in for questioning."

McCrea laughed. "After the last time?"

"Yes," said Cullen.

"You're a brave man," said McCrea. "Fine, but we need to keep this under the radar. We got a kicking from the super about bringing him in. He shouldn't get phone calls from record label lawyers, he says, unless they're asking him to sing a duet with Miley Cyrus."

"This is a *murder case*," said Cullen. "We've got a suspect, we're going to bring him in."

"I don't disagree," said McCrea. "We need to keep it tight when we do. The first I want his lawyer to know about this is a phone call from Roberts in custody."

"Okay," said Cullen. "As long as we get him in for questioning, I don't care."

"Where are you?"

"Just leaving Edinburgh," said Cullen, lying his arse off. "I'll be there at the back of ten."

"Fine," said McCrea, "we'll meet you at his house. I think we've got the address on file. I'll text it across."

"Can you check his laptop?" said Cullen. "There should be some emails between him and Audrey Strang."

"Aye, will do."

Cullen ended the call just before he got to the roundabout at the end of Dundee. He was putting his neck on the line with this, that was for certain, but he felt like he was on to something.

He just hoped he wasn't smoking the same thing as Alex Hughes.

91

Cullen finally got to Glasgow just after ten.

Roberts lived in a Victorian pile in the Southside, large enough for two families rather than a single rock star.

Cullen parked on the road opposite Bain's purple Mondeo and flashed his lights. He walked over and got in the back seat.

"Here he is," said McCrea, "ready to steal the glory."

"If there's any glory," said Cullen, "I really don't care who gets it."

"Bullshit," said Bain.

Cullen was surprised to find only McCrea and Bain in attendance. "Where is everybody?"

"It's just us," said McCrea.

Cullen was getting worried. "You said on the phone you wanted it kept low key, but this is ridiculous."

"We ran it past the Super and he's happy with it," said Bain.

Cullen looked at McCrea. "Did you check on Hughes' laptop like I asked?"

McCrea looked away. "Aye. There was a calendar appointment for the night in question. 'Meet Mike'."

"Circumstantial," said Bain.

Cullen shook his head. "When have I ever been wrong?"

"Let's just hope your luck doesn't run out, Sundance," said Bain.

Cullen pointed to the house. "What's been going on here?"

"We think he's inside," said McCrea.

"Think?" said Cullen.

"We've just fuckin' got here, Sundance," said Bain.

"Has anyone been to the neighbours or anything?" said Cullen.

"Aye, just to next door," said McCrea. "There was a big racket last night about three in the morning. Loud music."

"He's probably not alone," said Cullen.

"Maybe not," said McCrea.

"You got a warrant, right?" said Cullen.

McCrea nodded. "Hope we don't need it, but we've got one."

"What's your plan?" said Bain.

"*My* plan?" said Cullen. "This is your operation."

"We're supervising here," said Bain. "Plan. Now."

"Arrest him, question him, charge him." Cullen shrugged. "I'd be a bit more comfortable with a couple of uniform to back us up."

"Relax, Sundance. This boy is all skin and bone, no danger he's getting away from us."

"Well, no time like the present." Cullen gestured towards the house.

"Just remember," said Bain, "if this fucks up, it's your fault."

"With no backup," said Cullen, "this is *your* fault."

"Just us," said Bain. "Politics, Sundance."

They got out. Cullen turned to Bain. "Do you want to stay back here just in case?"

"Fine."

Cullen and McCrea walked over, Cullen holding the

creaking gate open before they hurried across the pebbled front garden. Cullen knocked on the door.

"No answer," said McCrea.

"I can see that," said Cullen. "Is he definitely in?"

"This is your fuck up, mate."

"Well, unless he answers the door," said Cullen, "we're absolutely snookered."

"Fuck it, we're going in," said McCrea. "The warrant will cover us."

"You're breaking the door down?"

"Old trick I learnt from a DI," said McCrea.

"Sure it's not the current one?" said Cullen.

"Let's get in there and square up the notebooks after, right?" said McCrea. "We found the door knocked in." He braced himself. "On three."

"Wait," said Cullen. "Do we go on three, or three then a beat and we go?"

"Isn't that from *Lethal Weapon*?"

"It's a valid point."

"Fuck's sake," said McCrea. "Three, then go. One, two, three."

He shoved his shoulder into the door, knocking it off its hinges.

A burglar alarm blared.

They slowly and methodically checked the five ground floor rooms. All empty. A couple of bottles of champagne lay in the kitchen sink.

McCrea pointed at them. "Somebody had a decent night last night."

"Must be upstairs," said Cullen.

"Well deduced," said McCrea. "You idiot."

Cullen shook his head. "Come on."

They headed to the stairs and saw Roberts coming

down, dressed like he'd just got in. A woman stood at the top, wearing a long t-shirt, trying to cover her legs.

"What the fuck is going on here?" said Roberts.

Cullen got his warrant card out. "Mr Roberts. We'd like to speak to you in relation to the murders of Alex Hughes and James Strang."

Roberts stopped a couple of steps above Cullen. "We've spoken about this. Nothing more to say."

"Just come down the station with us and we can deal with it there," said Cullen.

"Yeah, right." Roberts was now at the bottom of the stairs. His eyes moved over to the front door. "You've fucking broken into my house." He squared up to Cullen. "Have you got a warrant for this?"

"Yeah, we do." McCrea showed him the warrant. "Besides, the door was already broken."

"Like fuck it was," said Roberts. "The alarm just went off then you pair pitch up. Do you think you can get away with this?"

"Sir, if you'll just come with us," said McCrea.

"Like fuck I will," said Roberts. "I want the pair of you out of here and then I want to speak to your boss."

"He's just outside," said Cullen, "but, believe me, he's probably the last person you want to speak to."

Roberts pointed at Cullen. "Look, pal, I've warned you. Get out."

"You have to come with us," said Cullen.

Roberts swallowed. "Let's see the warrant."

McCrea started unfolding the sheets of paper.

Roberts lurched forward, pushing Cullen in the chest and sending him stumbling backwards into McCrea. Both sprawled on the floor as Roberts bolted for it.

"Mikey, where are you going?" said the girl.

Roberts slammed what was left of the door shut.

"Get up," said McCrea. "Get off me."

Fire burnt through Cullen's shoulder.

McCrea got to his feet then helped Cullen up. "Fuck's sake." He struggled with the door, eventually tugging it open.

Cullen followed him outside, crunching over the path.

On the street, Bain raced forward to head Roberts off. He swung a punch, narrowly missing. Roberts stepped forward and kneed Bain in the groin, the DI sinking to his knees.

Roberts punched him in the face, knocking him flat on his back. He kicked him in the stomach twice, before looking back and spotting Cullen and McCrea running his way.

Roberts jumped in Bain's car and slammed the door shut.

Cullen tugged at the handle, managing to pull the door slightly open.

The car started up, the engine growling. Roberts put his foot to the floor and the Mondeo screeched off.

"Fuck's sake."

Cullen headed over to Bain, McCrea kneeling over him.

Bain spat blood. "Get the fuck after him."

"What about you?" said McCrea.

"I'll be fine," said Bain. "Send a fuckin' squad car for me. Shite."

In seconds, they were in Cullen's car. He pulled a U-turn, ignorant of the oncoming traffic. A car swerved to avoid him.

"We'll fucking lose him," said McCrea.

Cullen was hitting sixty in a residential area, his Golf

bouncing over the speed bumps, the suspension crunching. He could just about make out a purple blur as it signalled left at the end of the road then jumped a red light. "There he is."

"Fucking keep on him," said McCrea.

"Can you make yourself useful and call this in?" said Cullen.

"Right." McCrea reached into his coat pocket for his Airwave. He spoke to Control in slow tones, getting the incident on the system and ordering a car for Bain.

Cullen swung a left at the end of the road, turning onto a dual carriageway.

"Can you still see him?" said McCrea.

The Mondeo was about ten cars ahead, though there were long gaps between the vehicles.

"Yes," said Cullen. "If you'd tried to apprehend him instead of seeing to Bain, he'd not have been able to get this far."

"This is your disaster, Cullen."

"There was no back-up. This was your shambles."

"What were we supposed to do?" said McCrea. "You'd already pissed off the Chief Super with your antics. The gaffer had no moves left other than to keep this quiet."

"Well, a killer has escaped," said Cullen. The speedo went past eighty as he bobbed and weaved through the traffic, managing to narrow the gap to five cars. "Where's he heading?"

"M74 is just up ahead," said McCrea. "From there, it's easy to take the back roads into Bandit Country."

"Bandit Country?"

"North Lanarkshire. Otherwise, it'll be the M8 for him. If he's got any sense, he'll get off the motorway."

Cullen flashed at the car in front of him, eventually

forcing it to pull into the inside lane. He hit the floor and just about caught up with Bain's Mondeo, close enough to see Roberts spotting them in the rear view.

Cullen's hand hammered down on the horn. He flashed the lights.

The Mondeo surged forward. Cullen had no hope of matching it for speed - he only had a one point eight engine, no GTI or anything. The sports Mondeo would be at least three litres and stuffed with turbochargers and fuel injections.

Fortune seemed to favour Cullen - the traffic ahead slowed. They caught up with Roberts, going bumper to bumper.

Roberts jerked into the right-turn lane, before accelerating across the gap in oncoming traffic. He made it to the residential street beyond.

Cullen shifted down to second and blasted across the gap, cars screeching to a halt as they approached.

A braking SUV slammed into the back of Cullen's car, sending them spinning across the road. They mounted the pavement and slammed into a low wall, the car almost tipping over. It fell back down with a deep thud.

Cullen noticed a trickle of blood down his arm - the seatbelt had cut his old wound open.

"He's fucking got away," said McCrea.

"Looks like it." Cullen winced through the pain. He tried the ignition, the grinding noise suggesting his car was written off.

"I'm so glad this is your fuck up," said McCrea.

Cullen only had his damaged shoulder to thank for not punching McCrea there and then.

92

Two hours of checks and debriefing later, Cullen was stuck in Govan without a car. He stood in an empty meeting room in front of a whiteboard, drawing up possibilities of who to look for in the hunt for Mike Roberts. Anything to take his mind off the colossal fuck up.

Start with the basics.

Friends.

Family.

Work Colleagues.

Friends and work colleagues would be his band plus a few others: band manager, people at the record label, hangers on, mates, guitar tech, sound guy.

Girls like the one at his house. She'd been questioned and released, just a groupie he'd picked up at the backstage party.

They needed to find his family.

"You're not getting very far."

Cullen turned round.

McCrea stood in the doorway, arms folded. "You've been keeping a low profile since the paramedics let us go."

"My car's fucked."

"Right." McCrea smirked. "Did they get an exorcist out?"

"That's not funny."

McCrea pointed at the whiteboard. "How's it going?"

"I know so little about Roberts," said Cullen.

McCrea stood beside him and looked at the confused scribbles on the wall. "This is pretty fucked up."

"At least it's my fuck up, though, right?" said Cullen.

"We'll see."

"How's Bain doing?"

"He'll live," said McCrea.

"Shame."

McCrea turned to face Cullen. "You shouldn't be such a prick to him. He's a good DI."

"Try working for him for longer than five minutes."

"I have," said McCrea. "We go back years."

"Then you're even older than you look."

McCrea laughed. "Anyway, your parents have turned up to take you home."

"Eh?"

"They're in the Incident Room," said McCrea.

Cullen headed through, a frown etched on his face.

Cargill and Methven stood in the middle of the room, faces like thunder as they spoke to Graham. Cargill left with Graham when Cullen appeared.

"We need to speak," said Methven.

"There's a meeting room through here," said Cullen.

He led him back, his neck burning. McCrea had vacated the room, so they sat at the table, Cullen facing his spider-like scribbles.

"What happened?" said Methven.

"It was like I told you when I drove back from Dalhousie," said Cullen. "Roberts killed both of them."

Methven looked sceptical. "Strang *and* Hughes?"

"Aye."

"What about DI Bain's theory that it was a drug

killing?"

"It's a good theory." Cullen sniffed. "It was wrong, though. We've got solid evidence from Hughes' laptop to back this all up."

"What sort of thing?"

"Hughes had a dossier on Roberts, implying he killed Strang. He was due to meet Roberts the night he died. He was going to confront him about it. I'm sure there will be more now we know what we're looking for."

"This is a disaster," said Methven.

"Is it?" said Cullen. "We know who did it now. They are one and the same case."

"A sodding police officer's car was stolen, the officer injured in the process and the suspect is still at large."

"Why are you two here?" said Cullen.

"This doesn't reflect well on us," said Methven. "Alison's trying to stop any fallout from Graham. The new Chief Constable likes team players. We've got a loose cannon in our ranks."

"*Me?*"

"Who else?" said Methven.

"I *am* a team player," said Cullen. "I just like to play a slightly different game every now and then."

"It can be a sodding dangerous game," said Methven. "Just be thankful your bloody car is the only casualty this time."

"I've kept you informed of what I was doing."

Methven arched his bushy eyebrows. "Really?"

"I called you once I knew I wasn't wasting everybody's time," said Cullen. "Look, James Strang's parents will be able to start grieving. Alex Hughes' mother will have someone to blame for her son's death."

Methven nodded. "Let's see."

"What's the plan of attack here?"

"We need to round table this," said Methven.

"What does that even mean?"

Methven jangled the change in his pocket. "It means we need to sodding get round a table and plan this out. *Properly*."

"This is Bain and Graham's gig, though."

"I sodding well know that," said Methven. "At least someone else's bollocks got kicked for once."

93

Bain had a white plaster stuck across his nose as he led the briefing. The table was indeed round, surrounded by more than twenty officers.

"We need to find this boy and quickly," said Bain. "If he's gone to ground then we might be a bit stuck here." He snorted. "Roberts has killed two people. The motive is a bit opaque to me just now, but from the way the boy bolted when Cullen ploughed in, we can clearly assume he's guilty. We just need some evidence."

Graham frowned as he tapped his propelling pencil against a pad of paper. "Are you saying we have *no* evidence?"

Bain held his hands up. "We've got enough to prove we're on the right track. That's what I'm saying here."

"It looks like Roberts stole a song from The Invisibles," said Cullen. "James Strang was the singer in the band. Roberts and Strang were good friends at the time, but they fell out over that. We know The Invisibles were offered a record deal. Roberts somehow managed to exert pressure and it was withdrawn. The next we know, Strang confronted Roberts in Edinburgh. Roberts must have killed Strang and hid the body away in the abandoned streets under the Old Town."

Cullen's phone rang. He got it out of his pocket and checked the display - Buxton.

Bain scowled at him. "Turn that fuckin' thing off."

Cullen flicked the ringer off. "Sorry."

Graham glared at Bain. "How does this tie to our drugs killing?"

"The drugs angle is a red herring," said Methven.

"I'm sorry?" Graham scowled at Methven.

"Roberts killed Hughes," said Cullen. "As DI Methven says, the drugs thing is a red herring. Hughes had a dossier of evidence suggesting Roberts killed Strang and he was going to confront him about it."

"And he didn't bring it to our attention?" said Graham.

"Hughes didn't trust the police," said Cullen.

"I can see why." Graham narrowed his eyes at Bain. "I thought you had actual evidence?"

Bain cleared his throat. "We managed to close down a hydroponics lab."

"That conviction better stick," said Graham, "otherwise how your testicles feel just now will seem like a dream."

"We've got a musicologist in trying to prove the two songs in question are related, sir. Obviously, if DC Cullen hadn't let Mr Roberts go his mummy and daddy wouldn't have had to come through."

"He stole *your* car," said Cullen.

"Shut it," said Bain.

"Brian, please keep this professional for once," said Cargill.

"I am professional, *Alison*," said Bain.

"Please desist," said Graham. "Where are we with the investigation now?"

Bain looked at McCrea. "What have we got, Sergeant?"

"Cullen was doing some brainstorming earlier," said

McCrea. "Where did you get to?"

Cullen glared at him. "Standard stuff. Friends, family, workmates. I don't know much about Roberts, really. I doubt many of us do. His family, for example."

"Does anyone here actually have any bloody information?" said Graham.

Nobody answered him.

Graham sighed heavily and looked at Cullen. "Constable, what else have you got?"

"His friends and workmates will heavily overlap," said Cullen. "The guys in the band will be his best mates, though they'll probably hate each other by now. Either way, they should be able to give us a lead." He walked to the whiteboard and started drawing. "The band is as follows. Neeraj Patel on guitar, Jenny Stone on bass and Brian Hogg on drums."

"Right," said Bain, "so we need someone with tact and diplomacy on the Patel boy. By that, I mean none of your blunderbuss antics, Sundance."

"Are you insinuating one of my officers is racist?" said Cargill.

"Don't want it to become an issue," said Bain. "DC Cullen is known to cut corners."

"I like to think of it as getting results," said Cullen.

"Any more and you can go back to Texas, John Wayne," said Bain.

"Original," said Cullen.

Bain stared at the notepad in front of him. "You and McCrea can do the rhythm section. That's the bass player and drummer."

"I know what it is," said Cullen.

"Is there a manager?" said Bain.

McCrea held his phone up. "Aye. Boy called Billy

Mahonie."

"That's not his name," said Bain.

McCrea tapped his phone. "What it says here."

"That's a fuckin' band, you fud," said Bain.

"Well, we'd better let your tact and diplomacy deal with that one," said Cullen.

"Won't get an argument from me," said Bain. He stared at Cargill and Methven. "You pair all right to sit and fiddle with your phones while young Scotty takes his swimming lessons?"

"Will you just sodding grow up?" said Methven. "Your ineptitude in sending no uniform backup has got Police Scotland into this calamity."

"Oh aye?" said Bain. "You've got an extra fuckin' stripe and you think you're Billy big balls now, do you?"

Cargill ground her teeth. "In terms of keeping this investigation progressing, Colin will liaise with the team tracking down Mr Roberts' family. I will work with Superintendent Graham to ensure a level of professional supervision and we will report to Superintendent Turnbull and DCS Soutar accordingly. It's just a shame your superior officer is in Majorca this week, Brian."

"I'm more than capable of handling the role," said Bain.

"As DCI Cargill alluded to there," said Graham, "we need teams hunting down this boy's friends and family. I've just had approval from DCS Soutar to allocate forty additional officers to this case, so we can get door-to-doors running in Edinburgh, Glasgow and anywhere else we need to."

"DI Methven might appreciate doing his liaising back through there," said Bain. "Anything else?" Silence. He looked at Graham. "Any closing words, sir?"

Graham cleared his throat. "This is a complete disaster. I can only reiterate the words used by DCS Soutar. If this is a failure, Police Scotland will fail. Officers from the Met will be brought in to shore this up. I do not have to stress how important that is, do I?"

He made eye contact with each of them. "Now, I wouldn't be sitting here if I didn't think we can do this. We have a famous figure on the run. It shouldn't be too hard to find him. That is the minimum I expect from the remainder of the day. I want him in custody otherwise there will be an escalation to DCS Soutar, by which point the investigation will be out of our hands. Am I clear?"

There were no dissenting voices and the meeting broke up. Cullen, Methven and Cargill went off to one side of the meeting room, keeping a distance from the others.

"Bain has got even worse since he's come through here," said Cargill.

"Tell me about it," said Methven. "Good luck in getting some form of escalation to his superior officer."

"I will see what I can do," said Cargill. She looked at Cullen. "Are you okay, Constable?"

Cullen still felt shell shocked. "I'll survive. His bullets just bounce off me, you know that."

Cargill smiled. "I'll make sure they stop being fired. The man is a bully. I need you to keep in touch, okay? I don't want you going off the radar again."

Cullen knew he had to change.

94

Cullen and McCrea secured an interview room while some uniformed officers brought Brian Hogg, Expect Delays' drummer, in from his West End flat.

The bass player was proving difficult to track down.

"Mr Hogg," said Cullen, "can you tell us how you know Mike Roberts?"

Hogg scowled. "We're in a band together." He leaned across the desk. "You might have heard, but we supported U2 last night at Hampden."

Cullen tried to keep his voice level. "I meant, how did you first meet him?"

"We were friends at uni," said Hogg.

"Edinburgh?"

"Aye."

Cullen reappraised him. The boy looked like he'd been in one too many scrums and would fit right in with the rugger buggers at Edinburgh.

"We did history together," said Hogg. "We both liked Jesus & Mary Chain, My Bloody Valentine, Velvet Underground, that sort of thing."

"They're old bands," said McCrea.

Hogg shrugged. "They're classics, man. They're no pish like the Beatles or the Stones, the proper true classics. The Stooges and the MC5 as well, man. Zeppelin, too."

"Go on," said Cullen.

"Anyway, we both did our degrees but we got fed up with it by the time we finished. Don't know how, but Mikey ended up with a double first in history and English. I got a third. Boy is a genius."

"And you formed Expect Delays during this time?" said Cullen.

"Aye, we did," said Hogg. "We played loads of gigs, mainly in Edinburgh and Glasgow, though Glasgow was always much better. Dundee and Aberdeen. Stirling. After uni, we got our first tour supporting Razorlight. Our manager just totally blagged it."

"And that's Billy Mahonie, right?" said Cullen.

"Aye," said Hogg. "His name's Billy McIlhone. He took his professional name from the character in *Police Academy.*"

Cullen jotted it down. So far, nothing pushed them any further forward but he supposed having his real name was something resembling progress. "What happened next?"

"Well, Billy got us a single out on a wee label," said Hogg. "Worth a fortune now, man. I've still got ten copies myself." He laughed. "I'd filled my bedroom at my parents' house with boxes of them. Seems pretty funny now."

"How much are they worth these days?" said McCrea.

"You can get a hundred quid for it on vinyl," said Hogg. "We never re-recorded either of the tunes. We started doing well off the back of that single. Got played on Zane Lowe on Radio 1 then we got a proper deal."

"And you all lived happily ever after?" said McCrea.

Hogg rubbed his neck. "We hit a bit of a dry spell for about a year. Then we did *Where Has He Gone?* and it went into the top five. Totally changed things around for us. We were going to be dropped, but that got us a new deal. Some boy off X-Factor did a cover of it as well. Mind there was that campaign to get our version to number one? Didn't work, but we had over eight hundred thousand downloads in a *month*. We don't really need to work again, man."

"Did you know James Strang," said Cullen, "also known as Jimi Danger?"

"Him." Hogg leaned on his elbow, chin resting on his hand. "What do you want to know?"

"His body was found last week in Edinburgh," said Cullen. "We have reason to believe Mr Roberts murdered him."

Hogg raised his eyebrows, his eyes blinking repeatedly. "Mikey?" he said, his voice shrill. "Are you mental?"

"We understand Mr Strang may have had a couple of grievances with Mr Roberts," said Cullen. "First, he believed your hit single, *Where Has He Gone?* was stolen from him."

"What a load of shite," said Hogg.

"We have a musicologist in to prove your song and *Goneaway* by The Invisibles are the same piece of music," said Cullen.

"Or disprove, more like." Hogg leaned back in his chair and brushed his long fringe over his forehead. "Jimi Strang was a total wanker. He was jealous of our success. I saw their last gig. The boy had totally lost it, man. You know that Morrissey song, *We Hate It When Our Friends Become Successful?* That's Jimi to a T."

"It's enough Mr Strang believed it," said Cullen. "Isn't it?"

"Why would Mikey kill him, though?" said Hogg. "Doesn't make any sense."

"To keep Mr Strang quiet?" said Cullen. "You just said yourself you never need to work again off the back of one song. How big would the lawsuit have been, do you think?"

Hogg didn't respond, instead tugging at his fringe again.

"Mr Strang was also under the impression that Mr Roberts personally ruined a record deal they'd been offered," said Cullen.

"I've never heard that one," said Hogg. "I knew a couple of labels were sniffing around them but that's not the same thing as a contract being on the table, you know? Jimi could be a bit delusional at times." He took his glasses off. "Look, don't get me wrong, I liked the boy when I first met him but he just didn't operate by the same rules as the rest of us."

"So, you heard nothing to that effect, then?" said Cullen.

Hogg replaced his glasses. "No."

"We need to trace Mr Roberts' friends and family," said McCrea. "Is there anyone else who could assist our investigation?"

"Would need a long hard think about it, man."

Cullen stared at the drummer, suspecting he was playing for time. "Any brothers or sisters that would go to gigs?"

"Only child, man," said Hogg. "You boys have clearly not done your homework."

"What about his parents?" said Cullen.

"Think they live in Edinburgh," said Hogg. "He used to live up in Angus somewhere."

"Angus?" said Cullen.

"Aye," said Hogg, "that's how Mike got to know the

boy Strang."

Cullen's heart thudded. "Was it Dalhousie?"

"Aye, that's the place," said Hogg.

95

Cullen and McCrea returned to the Incident Room at the same time as Bain. Cargill was on the phone, immediately ending the call when she saw them.

"Well, I managed to avoid an international incident but we're no further forward," said Bain. "I hope you pair got somewhere."

Cullen nodded. "We got a couple of nuggets. He doubts our theory to say the least, but then he seems to hero-worship Roberts. Billy Mahonie's real name is William McIlhone."

"You pair are incisive," said Bain. "That would help us, except for the fact we've got him on his way in." He rubbed his top lip. "What's the other nugget?"

Cullen rested his hand on his hip. "Looks like Roberts grew up in Dalhousie."

"Another sheep shagger," said Bain. "Fuckin' great."

"That's how he met Strang," said Cullen. "They seem to have kept in touch after his parents moved to Edinburgh and then met up again at university. Hogg reckons Roberts' parents still live near the city."

"I'll get someone to look into that," said Cargill. "See what I can dig up."

"You keeping yourself out of mischief?" said Bain.

"Brian," said Cargill, "remember I am your superior officer and your behaviour has been escalated to Superintendent Turnbull."

"Like I care," said Bain. "I'm fuckin' invincible. I'm like a vampire, sweetheart, you can't kill me."

"I'd happily put a stake through your heart," said Cargill.

"Very funny." Bain looked at McCrea, who was fiddling with his phone. "Right, you pair. The glimmer twins. What now?"

"We've got to find the bassist," said Cullen. "She's missing."

"If there's another fuckin' body on this case, Sundance," said Bain, "I swear you'll be joining them."

"Enough," said Cargill.

McCrea looked up from his mobile. "Uniform have just found her. She's on her way in now."

"I've seen this lassie in the papers, Sundance," said Bain. "Keep it in your trousers for once."

Cargill's expression spoke volumes.

96

Rather than sitting on their arses while Jenny Stone was brought to the station, Cargill drove Cullen to get fresh coffee from the Asda by Ibrox. When they returned, Stone still hadn't been transferred in.

Graham pulled Cargill into a conference room, Turnbull's dulcet tones booming out of the phone in the middle of the table.

Cullen went back to the Incident Room and called Methven, beginning to regret it as the DI started prattling on.

"So, you've got nothing?" said Cullen.

"You wouldn't believe how many sodding Roberts there are in the Lothians," said Methven. "We've got people up at the university going through old records. Someone in the Met is away speaking to his record label. His lawyer should be brought in through there. I seriously hope you're getting somewhere."

"Hardly," said Cullen.

"ADC Buxton has finally finished looking into Strang's flatmates," said Methven. "Seven of them over five years. Not a single one spoke to Strang about anything other than who stole the cornflakes."

"Right."

"Look, I've got to go," said Methven. "If you see Alison, get her to call me, okay?"

"Will do," said Cullen. "Looks like she'll be in there for

the duration, though."

Cullen finished the last of his Americano then went through the notes he'd taken in the interview with Hogg. He found a note to check the emails he'd received from Kidd. He found the original email from Strang to Hughes, relieved to have a trail behind it and not just Audrey Strang's fantasies.

McCrea appeared, his phone clutched to his head. "They've just brought that Jenny Stone in. You ready?"

"Aye."

McCrea led him down the corridor to the back of the station.

Jenny Stone looked bored as she sat in the interview room. Cullen had never seen a photo of her. He didn't have to think hard to see why she was in the band and he doubted it was her prowess on the bass. She had the classic rock chick look - dyed blonde hair, tight skirt, red leather jacket, her tight blouse revealing a black bra and lots of cleavage.

McCrea led Cullen back outside and shut the door behind him. "That's what she wore at the gig last night."

Cullen nodded. "How was it?"

"Fucking amazing," said McCrea. "Expect Delays were okay, but U2 were just off the planet. What a light show they've got."

"How do you want to play this?" said Cullen.

McCrea just shrugged. "The things I would do to her," he said, looking through the window in the door.

"Hopefully asking questions is one of them." Cullen pushed past him into the interview room.

McCrea sat down and started the interview, setting the digital recorder going.

"Do I need to get my lawyer in?" Jenny's voice was

smoker deep.

"Unless you've done something you shouldn't have," said Cullen, "then no."

He noticed McCrea was practically drooling.

"We're looking for Mike Roberts," said McCrea.

"Why?" said Jenny. "What's he done now?"

"We have reason to believe he was responsible for the deaths of Alex Hughes and James Strang," said McCrea.

"Wait." Jenny frowned. "Jimi is dead?"

McCrea nodded. "Yes, I'm afraid so. He was found in Edinburgh last week."

Jenny shook her head. "I always thought he'd come back." She looked down at the table. "He used to follow me around like a little puppy."

"I bet you get that a lot," said McCrea.

Jenny scowled at him. "Less than you'd think."

Cullen put a couple of pieces together in his head - the Jane that Strang's mother alluded to was, in fact, Jenny. "Did you ever reciprocate his feelings?"

"Not likely," she said. "He wasn't my type."

"What's your type?" said McCrea.

Jenny frowned. "Is this relevant?"

"Do you have you any idea where Mr Roberts might be?" said Cullen.

"Well, I know his parents live in Linlithgow," said Jenny. "I'd check there if I were you."

Cullen jotted it down. That was something. "Looks like we'll have to. Can you think of any other people we should be speaking to?"

Jenny folded her arms. "You'll have spoken to Beth, right?"

"Beth Williamson?" said Cullen.

"Yeah," said Jenny. "She used to go out with Mike."

"You're joking," said Cullen.

"I'm serious."

Cullen sat back, trying to process it. They needed to speak to her again.

The door flew open. Bain entered the room. "I need you pair. Now."

McCrea ended the interview. "Thank you, Ms Stone, you're free to leave. The PCSO will show you to the car park."

In the corridor, Bain was pacing away from them. They had to jog to catch up.

"What's up?" said Cullen.

"My fuckin' car's turned up in fuckin' Motherwell," said Bain. "Lucky the bastard wasn't torched. You pair are coming with me."

"According to Stone," said Cullen, "Roberts' parents live in Linlithgow."

Bain stopped and punched his right fist into his other hand. "Right, that fuckin' town is getting torn apart."

97

Cullen lagged behind as Bain crossed the bus station at speed, McCrea and Cargill following at an increasing distance.

His phone buzzed in his pocket. He got it out and checked the screen as he walked - a missed call from Sharon. He called her back. Voicemail. He pocketed it and hurried over.

Bain's car sat in a lane by the bus station, two parking tickets on the screen. A local uniformed officer stood by the vehicle, trying to act as professionally as he could with a manic DI shouting the odds in his face.

"For fuck's sake," said Bain. "I cannot fuckin' believe it got ticketed before it got called in." He ripped the ticket off the windscreen. "What's the point in having a fuckin' call put out for it?" He stuck the ticket in his notebook. "Someone's boss is getting paid a visit."

"We need to get people all over that bus station," said Cargill.

"The boy could be anywhere." Bain pointed at the ever-present camera. "That fuckin' CCTV better be working."

"Don't look at me," said Cullen. "I need to get back to Edinburgh to find Roberts."

"But you're so good at looking at CCTV footage, Sundance."

"This isn't our jurisdiction," said Cargill.

"This isn't mine, either," said Bain. "I'm Glasgow South, not this fuckin' backwater."

"You stay just up the road," said Cullen. "Bathgate."

"It's hardly up the road, Cullen," said Bain. "Besides, I sold that house and bought a wee flat in Glasgow." He rubbed his face. "Right, I want you to look into the CCTV footage, Constable."

"I told you I need to follow up a lead in Edinburgh," said Cullen.

"Like what?" said Bain.

"Beth Williamson used to go out with Roberts," said Cullen.

"Like fuck she did," said Bain.

Cullen nodded at McCrea. "Damian, tell him."

McCrea snorted. "He's right. Jenny Stone told us just before you burst into the interview room."

"Right," said Bain. "Okay, then, *Damian*, you're finding me that CCTV footage."

McCrea sent daggers at Cullen before he set off after Bain.

Cullen and Cargill walked slowly back to her car.

"Good work, Scott."

"Thanks," said Cullen. "I told you I knew how to play him. He can give it out but he can't take it. As you say, he's just a bully."

"Well, he's the last of a dying breed," said Cargill. "All the swearing, the bullying, the aggro, he's had his time. He's not getting out of this with his job."

Cullen had a certain amount of sympathy for the situation Bain was in, but he couldn't wait to see the back of him.

98

Two hours later, Cullen and Methven sat in the interview room with Beth Williamson. Her lawyer, Campbell McLintock, wore a lime green shirt and tie with a navy pinstripe suit.

He was well known to Cullen, notorious for using the most obscure technicalities to win cases from the margins of defeat. He usually defended high-earning clients - Cullen wondered just how much Williamson's husband was on.

"You don't need to be here, Campbell," said Methven. "Ms Williamson is not a suspect. She is merely being asked to assist with our investigations."

"I'll be the judge of that, Inspector. Since certain changes in the criminal justice system in this country, I think it is in both of our interests that I'm present, don't you?"

"Nothing to do with the fact you're charging Ms Williamson by the hour?" said Methven.

"I beg your pardon?"

"Interview started at six twenty-three pm on Thursday the fourth of April, two thousand and thirteen," said Methven, grinning at McLintock. "Present in the room are Beth Williamson, her solicitor Campbell McLintock, Detective Constable Scott Cullen and myself, Detective Inspector Colin Methven." He licked his lips. "Ms Williamson, can you please detail your relationship with a Mr Michael Roberts of Glasgow?"

"We knew each other from music," said Beth. "We used to both play gigs in Bannerman's and we had practice rooms in Niddry Street." She took a sip of water. "We did a few gigs together in Glasgow."

"And that's it, is it?" said Cullen. "That's the extent of your relationship?"

"I'm sorry?"

"Can you confirm you and Mr Roberts were just friends?" said Cullen.

Beth frowned. "That's what I just told you."

"We've heard differently," said Cullen.

McLintock looked nervous as he jumped in. "My client has told you the relationship between herself and Michael Roberts was purely that of friends. Please kindly drop the matter."

Cullen kept his eyes on her. "That's your final answer, is it, Beth?"

She nodded but evaded his gaze.

Cullen opened his notebook. "A good friend of yours told us otherwise."

"Who?"

"Jenny Stone."

Beth's forehead creased. "Jenny?"

Cullen nodded. "As you well know, she's the bass player in Expect Delays. Similar to Mr Roberts, I believe you knew her from the Edinburgh music scene. Would I be wrong?"

"I know her." Beth gritted her teeth. "I just can't believe she'd let me down like that."

"Is telling the truth letting someone down?" said Cullen.

McLintock's face reddened. "What my client is trying

to say is Ms Stone and she fell out."

"It's not." Beth slid her wedding ring up and down her finger, staring into space. "Mike and I went out with each other for sixteen months." A tear slid down her cheek. "We broke up when he made it."

"Charming," said Cullen.

Beth rubbed her eyes. "It was for the best, I suppose. I'm not the most trusting and him being away on tour or in a studio for months on end wouldn't be good for me." She patted her belly. "Besides, I most likely wouldn't have this one on the way."

"It might have been useful for your career, though," said Cullen.

"I'm sorry?"

"Well, we understand Mr Roberts was responsible for your band's offer of a record contract falling through," said Cullen.

Beth's face went white. "How did you hear that?"

"We have a number of statements to that effect now," said Cullen. "Is it true?"

"I don't know," said Beth. "Jimi thought it was true but I don't know. Why would Mike do that?"

"There's a phrase you may have heard," said Methven. "'Where there's a hit there's a writ'. We believe Mr Strang was under the impression that Mr Roberts had stolen the hit single *Where Has He Gone?* from a work by your band, The Invisibles, namely *Goneaway*."

"Shite," said Beth.

"Is it true?" said Methven.

"Inspector, my client wishes to make no further statement on the matter."

Methven grinned. "This is not going to look good for your client. As it stands, Ms Williamson lied to us on the record. I'm sure we have enough here to prosecute her."

McLintock looked away. "Very well."

"So," said Methven, "was there anything in Mr Strang's theory?"

"Jimi certainly thought it was the same song," said Beth. "I mean, you've got to admit there's a big similarity between them."

"Mr Strang wasn't in a particularly healthy frame of mind at the time, though, was he?" said Methven.

"That's one way of putting it," said Beth.

"Mr Roberts was arrested earlier today but escaped custody," said Methven. "Have you had any contact with him?"

Beth scowled at him. "No. He's one of the last people I'd want to see, believe me."

"That's a definite?" said Cullen.

"We just had sex with each other for sixteen months," said Beth. "It wasn't like he was the love of my life or anything. And *he* ended it, not me. I wasn't pleased. If I saw him, I'd tell him where to go."

"I think my client has helped you enough with your inquiries, Inspector," said McLintock. "She has not had any contact with the accused for a number of months. I wouldn't want to draw your attention to the fact she is with child and your line of questioning may be deemed excessive by members of the fourth estate?"

Methven glowered at McLintock. "Interview terminated at six thirty-seven pm."

99

Cullen and Methven found Cargill in the Incident Room, fingers battering a laptop's keyboard. She looked up then shut the screen and sat back, arms folded. "Well?"

"Williamson pretty much confirmed our theory," said Methven.

Cargill pushed the laptop away. "Pretty much isn't good enough, Colin. I'd expect pretty much from our colleagues in Glasgow South. Not us."

"Very well." Methven closed his eyes again. "I think she knows something. Do we have the manpower to put a tail on her?"

"Graham has half of Scotland at his disposal," said Cargill, "so yes."

"Can we make it some of our better officers?" said Methven. "I think we're onto something here."

"Who?" said Cargill.

"I'd like DC Murray and DC Jain," said Methven.

"They're both coming on shift just now, I think," said Cargill, "so I'm happy to approve that."

"Good," said Methven. "Tell them they'll have to submit an overtime form."

"I'm sure they'll appreciate it," said Cargill. "I'll make sure it goes through."

"What about me?" said Cullen. "I think I'm just about dried up and I don't want to go chasing CCTV footage in Motherwell."

Cargill grimaced. "While you won't have to go to Motherwell, you will have to look at CCTV."

Cullen felt his shoulders slump. "Really?"

"Roberts got the bus to Edinburgh," said Cargill.

"A bus?" said Cullen.

Cargill nodded. "It would appear he hopped on a coach in Motherwell at half past eleven this morning. The destination was Edinburgh, but we don't know whether he made it all the way. There were no stops between Motherwell and the west of Edinburgh. The CCTV camera on the coach was faulty."

"I thought I was past this sort of thing," said Cullen.

"You're a Detective Constable," said Cargill. "Don't get above yourself just because you've been an ADS."

"No ma'am." Cullen was pissed off. "Sorry."

"Look, don't be like that," said Cargill. "You've done some excellent work on this case so far. Not all of it has been by the book, admittedly, but it's not gone unnoticed."

"Thanks." Cullen was unable to decide if he was merely being buttered up.

100

Two hours later, Cullen walked up the Royal Mile on his way to the flat, chatting to Methven on the phone. It was warmer than it had been over the previous couple of weeks, but it was still cold.

He was missing his car already. Instead of it sitting in an Accident Repair Centre in Bellshill waiting to be written off, he could have driven home in warmth.

"When are you due back here?" said Methven.

"It's just gone ten," said Cullen. "I'm heading home."

"What happened to your hunger to catch this guy?"

"Actual hunger happened," said Cullen. "Besides, I'll be in a better frame of mind once I've had some sleep."

"I'm close to ordering you to come in."

"Sorry, sir, the reception is breaking up," said Cullen.

"Don't you dare."

"In all seriousness," said Cullen, "I've been on ten days straight now and I really need to get to bed. I'll be in at six tomorrow." He started up the stairwell. "I've been through all the CCTV footage at the various stops. Naismith wouldn't let me take it away unless it was confirmed evidence."

"Anything?"

"There are a couple of guys who could pass for Roberts getting off in Edinburgh," said Cullen. "One at the stop just by the zoo and the other at the bus station, but that's it. Naismith was going to email the screen grabs across to us."

"I'll pass that to the street team," said Methven. "They're going through the CCTV at the bus company just now so hopefully something can confirm it."

"Thought the camera was broken?"

"The external one still worked."

"I see," said Cullen. "Hopefully, the press release or street teams will have something for me tomorrow. Actually, they might have solved the case by then and I can have the day off."

He unlocked the flat door and went inside. The cat jogged through from the living room and started his bleating.

"You are trying my patience, Constable."

Cullen went into the living room. Sharon was slumped against the breakfast bar.

"I've got to go." Cullen hung up. He raced over, feeling for a pulse.

His hand got batted away.

"Are you okay?" said Cullen.

Sharon slowly opened her eyes. "Where have you been, you prick?" she said, slurring her words.

"I've been working," said Cullen.

"I called," said Sharon. "No answer."

"My phone's been off." Cullen's nostrils twitched. "Have you been drinking?"

"A bit."

Cullen spotted two empty bottles of wine in the sink. "You're pissed."

"Why didn't you answer your phone?"

"It was on mute," said Cullen. "When I saw the missed call, I phoned back. I've tried a few times."

"I had my phone off," said Sharon.

"For fuck's sake," said Cullen. "You're pregnant. You can't do this."

Sharon started crying. "You don't want the baby."

"I ... do."

Sharon stared at him. "Well, I don't know if I'm ready for this."

"You need coffee." Cullen went over to the sink and started filling the kettle. "What are you playing at?"

Sharon rubbed at her eyes. "Lamb got the job."

"Oh," said Cullen. "That's what you were calling about?"

Sharon looked up at him, swaying on the stool. "I needed to speak to you."

Cullen walked over and rubbed her gently on the arm. "I was in Motherwell. Bain's car got stolen. Mine was written off."

"I'm more important," said Sharon.

"I know you are." Cullen ran his hand through his hair. "Jesus Christ. I can't believe this."

"I'm sorry." Sharon doubled over, heaving with sobs. "Nobody wants me. Turnbull turned me down. You weren't there. I needed you, Scott."

"I'm sorry." Cullen put his arms around her and hugged tight.

"I needed a drink," said Sharon. "I can't believe Turnbull. That's the second time he's turned me down for a promotion."

The kettle clicked off. Cullen went over to make coffee, spooning instant into the mug and topping it up with hot water and lots of milk. "Drink this." He handed it to her.

"I'll be up all night."

"It'll maybe sober you up a bit," said Cullen.

She took the mug and stared into it, steam wafting into her face. "I thought I'd get the job when Crystal Methven got his."

"You'll get there eventually," said Cullen. "You're good. Turnbull's worked with Lamb for years, that's all."

"Lamb is an arsehole," said Sharon. "Turnbull asked if I wanted to go on the rape task force in Bathgate."

"Bathgate."

"Yeah," said Sharon. "I was looking at houses there."

"Look, you need to sober up," said Cullen. "I'm not living in Bathgate."

"I need the toilet."

Sharon trundled off into the hall, bouncing off the door surround.

Cullen held his head in his hands. What a fucking mess.

Friday
5th April 2013

101

Cullen woke up with a start. Something pinned his legs down. He sat up.

Yellow eyes stared back at him.

"Fluffy." He lay down.

His heart was racing. He'd been up till after midnight with Sharon until the booze overtook the coffee and sent her to sleep. He'd watched TV for another hour, trying to take his mind off it and failing.

"What's he done?" said Sharon.

"Woken me up."

The alarm started up, playing the radio, Expect Delays' new single.

"Good timing," said Sharon.

He realised the song was part of the news, the newsreader asking for anyone who might have seen Mike Roberts to come forward. Cullen hadn't known they were going public with it, but then he'd been out of the loop while going through the CCTV footage.

Reaching over, he switched the radio off and his light on. He looked at the mound of duvet next to him. "How are you feeling?"

"Worse hangover I've ever had," said Sharon, her voice muffled.

"It was pretty stupid," said Cullen.

"Don't need to tell me."

"And I thought I had the monopoly on stupidity in

this relationship."

Sharon came up for air. "I wish you did."

He looked over at her, eyes scrunched up as she faced into his light. "Did you mean what you said last night?"

"What?"

"You said you didn't want the baby," said Cullen. "You're not ready for it."

She opened her eyes and pushed herself up onto her elbow. "I was pissed. I didn't mean it."

"I'm worried about you," said Cullen. "It's not just about the baby, either, it's you. You can really fuck your body up doing something like that."

"I'm sorry," said Sharon. "I don't know what to say."

"Just tell me you'll not do it again."

Sharon nodded. "I won't. I was at a low ebb. I couldn't get hold of you. Mum was out at the cinema and I can't speak to Dad about this sort of thing. Chantal was on a case, staking someone out."

"Okay," said Cullen. "I'm sorry I had my phone off."

"I forgive you."

"Maybe in time I'll forgive you." Cullen laughed. "That's a joke, by the way."

"Everything is with you," said Sharon.

Cullen pulled himself up, sneezing four times in quick succession.

"Are you okay?" said Sharon.

"I'll be fine. I have to go in."

"I'm as worried about you as you are about me," said Sharon.

Cullen smiled. "What a pair we are. What are you going to do?"

"Well, I'm not going into work. I think I'll savour my last hangover for the next seven months. I've got to go the doctor later anyway."

Cullen feared it was for an abortion. "What for?"

"My check-up," said Sharon. "Just to confirm I am actually pregnant."

Cullen nodded, relieved the decision was still in their hands. "Do you want me to come?"

She smiled. "No. But it's nice of you to ask."

Cullen leaned over and kissed her. "I'd better go. I love you."

"I love you, too."

He went into his bedside drawer and got out fresh underwear. Out of the corner of his eye, he saw Fluffy climb into his side of the bed. "That's my role filled."

"He'll keep it warm until you're back," said Sharon.

Cullen left the room, heading for the bathroom and the white noise of the shower cubicle.

"You've left your light on!"

102

Cullen trudged up the stairs, late for the briefing, unable to get his legs moving.

What a mess.

The case and his job were screwing with his head. He'd found the killer but then they'd lost him and he just knew he'd get fingered with the blame. McCrea and Bain were the only other officers at the scene and he knew he couldn't trust them not to drop him in the shit.

His car was fucked, an expense he didn't need. The prospect of an afternoon in Seafield looking for a replacement didn't fill him with joy.

But, despite all the other shit, Sharon was front and centre in his thoughts. What was she doing? She was carrying their baby. He told her he wanted it, there and then. It just blurted out.

Did he?

He was less certain in the cold light of day, but he'd stopped feeling the knot in the pit of his stomach every time he thought about becoming a father.

He walked into the Incident Room and stood at the back, sipping at the coffee he'd bought on the walk down.

Methven clocked him as soon as he entered. So much for being in at six. Cullen just knew he'd be in the bad books already.

"In summary, then," said Cargill, "we've got no

concrete leads on the whereabouts of Roberts and neither do our colleagues in Glasgow South. Roberts has gone to ground, most likely in Edinburgh. We've got his parents' house in Linlithgow under surveillance, along with known acquaintances. There was a press release last night, which has been picked up by both print and broadcast. Please report to DS Holdsworth for actions. Dismissed."

As the officers filed past him into the corridor, Cullen couldn't face speaking to Holdsworth, having done well to avoid him on the case so far.

Cargill and Methven made a beeline for him.

"Constable." Methven checked his watch. "Good morning."

"Sorry I'm late, sir," said Cullen. "Had an emergency at home."

"Oh?" said Methven. "I take it everything is okay?"

Cullen nodded. "Nothing to worry about, sir." He nodded at Cargill. "DS McNeill won't be in today, ma'am."

Cargill smiled. "I hope she's okay."

"She'll live," said Cullen.

Cargill smoothed down her hair. "We've got to head back to Tulliallan, I'm afraid."

"What for?" said Cullen.

"Status report to DCS Soutar," said Cargill.

"Is it appropriate for a DC to be at that sort of meeting?" said Cullen.

"Normally I'd agree, but your presence has been requested."

103

They were in the same Tulliallan room as the previous day. Cullen, Cargill and Methven were on the Edinburgh side, Bain, McCrea and Graham on the Glasgow, with Soutar in the centre. Two officers Cullen didn't recognise sat either side of her.

Cullen couldn't help but think the meeting was a colossal waste of resource - McCrea and he were definitely in the operational space and their absence might slow things down in the way Bain's or Methven's wouldn't.

"Turnbull sends his apologies," said Cargill.

Soutar pouted. "So I gather." She looked around the room. "Thank you for your presence this morning." She clasped her hands on the desk in front of her. "I know you've all come from your local briefings, but I would appreciate an update on where we are. DI Bain, can you provide the Glasgow South MIT status, please?"

Bain gave the Glasgow update. They were absolutely nowhere. They had very little to go on, the case having moved east. The rest of Expect Delays were under surveillance, including assorted hangers-on like the manager and guitar tech. Mobile phones were being traced and emails hacked.

"We've got resource to spare," said Bain.

Cullen recognised the ploy - they could keep a tight hold of the investigation, such as it was. No doubt the liberated resources would be Bain, McCrea and other senior detectives.

"Thanks." Soutar turned her attentions to the other side of the table. "And from Edinburgh?"

Methven repeated the update Cargill gave earlier.

"Why haven't you found him?" said Bain.

"It's incredibly difficult to execute a manhunt in a city the size of Edinburgh," said Cargill. "I'm sure you can recall from your period spent assisting our investigations?"

Bain snorted. "I'd have torn Murrayfield and Corstorphine apart looking for this boy. And the city centre is full of CCTV."

"It takes time." Methven's eyes blinked. "We've dedicated three officers to sifting through hours of CCTV footage."

Bain nodded at Cullen. "I hope Sundance isn't one of them."

"Do I need to point out you've had Roberts in custody twice and let him go both times?" said Methven.

Bain raised his eyebrows. "DC Cullen was there. He didn't say anything the last time."

"You buckled to pressure," said Cullen. "The record company sneezed and you made sure he was released in time for the concert."

"I did nothing of the sort," said Bain.

"Brian," said Cargill, "you were operating under the apprehension this was a drugs murder. It took one of my DCs to prove you wrong."

Bain looked at Cullen, raising his shoulders. "DC Cullen has a habit of keeping information to himself. He reported to me for over eighteen months. I know how his mind works."

"Did you hold any information back?" said Soutar, eyes locked on Cullen.

Cullen tried to pull out of the tractor beam. "I investigated a lead, that's true. It led us to Roberts."

"So, *your* work identified the killer?" said Soutar.

Cullen shrugged. "Just doing my job, ma'am."

He couldn't believe he'd used such a cliché. What he wanted to say was 'yes'.

"DI Bain," said Soutar. "Is this true?"

"Maybe."

Soutar shook her head. "We sat in here on Wednesday. I gave you clear instructions that Glasgow South MIT were to head up the investigation. I've seen very little collaboration." She started counting on her fingers. "What I have seen is the theft of an officer's car, another officer's car being written off and, to cap it all off, a double murder suspect escaping arrest."

She looked around the room. One of the two guests scribbled on a notepad.

"This is not acceptable," said Soutar. "I've asked the respective MIT Superintendents to lead this investigation but I haven't seen much progress or indeed any collaboration whatsoever."

"With all due respect," said Graham, "it's not easy managing a case across two cities."

"So I can see," said Soutar. "The pair of you have simply not bothered."

"Carolyn," said Cargill. "I don't think this is as bad as it appears. Detective Superintendents Graham and Turnbull are trying to put in place a number of initiatives to bring Mr Roberts to justice."

"A number of initiatives sounds like bland management speak to me, Alison," said Soutar.

"Initiatives take a long time to bed in. What we need is strong, affirmative action. I insisted on twice-daily conference calls."

"You did," said Graham.

"Well?" said Soutar.

"Well what?" said Graham.

"Can I see the minutes of these calls?" said Soutar.

"Superintendent Turnbull's team was running with that."

"We would have produced minutes had the calls actually taken place," said Cargill.

Graham got to his feet and pointed at her. "Are you calling me a liar?"

Cargill leaned back in her chair. "Are you calling *me* a liar?"

Soutar glared at Graham. "Sit."

Graham adjusted his cufflinks then took his seat again.

"I warned you what would happen if this case was not managed to my satisfaction," said Soutar.

Cullen finally clocked what was happening - their guests were from the Met.

"I've had enough of this," said Soutar. "We're clearly not operationally ready for this sort of case. I hoped we might have had more time to establish our processes and establish a rapport across the country, but this case has clearly come too soon."

She gestured to the two others.

"I've asked Detective Superintendents Garricks and O'Keefe from the Met to come in and supervise this. Both have years of experience co-ordinating sizeable investigations across Greater London, a task equivalent to the undertaking we have."

"Dealing with crime in London and in Scotland are

very different things," said Graham. "You're comparing apples and oranges."

"They're also very *similar* things," said Soutar. "There are core behaviours not being adhered to here. Having a single command centre, for instance." She tapped her nails on the desk for a few seconds. "Given the events of the last few days, our southern colleagues will be in operational command of this case and will be occupying office space in Leith Walk. All officers of Detective Superintendent grade and below will report to them. I want to be kept updated on an hourly basis. I want Roberts in a cell by dinner tonight. Am I making myself clear?"

Cullen looked around the room, watching heads nod. He couldn't see anything good coming from this. Instead of playing games against each other, the Edinburgh and Glasgow troops would be at it with the Londoners who would, of course, have their own agenda - showing these stupid Jocks how to run a murder case, for starters.

"Anything else?" said Soutar.

Nothing.

104

Back at Leith Walk, Cargill gave a briefing.

There was a general air of demoralisation in the room as though they'd lost. London was in charge now. How could Scotland run its own country if it couldn't run its own police force? How could it run a police force if it couldn't run a murder case?

Garricks and O'Keefe spent much of the briefing picking Cargill up on minutiae and points of pedantry. Cullen didn't have the greatest amount of admiration for her, but seeing her get torn into by her superiors with no backup from her own Detective Superintendent, certainly made Cullen sympathise.

There was a trainload of Met officers on its way up. The London detectives were taking people aside for two-on-one interviews, starting from the top. Cullen figured he'd have a long wait until he was called in, so he typed up his notes, desperately trying to keep on top of active leads. Everything was stuck in neutral.

Bain and McCrea wandered into the Incident Room, grinning like kids who'd ingratiated themselves with the playground bullies. Cullen kept his head down.

"Just had our session with the Met boys," said McCrea.

Cullen leaned back in his seat. "Trying to get a whole IQ measure out of the pair of you, were they?"

"Very good," said Bain. "Still a funny little fucker,

aren't you, Sundance?"

Cullen shrugged. "You walked right into that one."

Bain smiled. "They're putting us in charge of making sure your paper trail is up to scratch."

"That doesn't sound unbiased," said Cullen. "Someone's going to get their arse handed to them and it's basically between you and Methven. Having you go over our files isn't going to be fair, is it?"

Bain shrugged and cleared his throat. "Methven's heading to our station."

Cullen nodded his head. "Divide and conquer. Get those who don't do the work playing stupid games against each other."

"What are you saying?" said Bain. "I do fuckin' work."

"Yeah, but all you've done recently is try to get back at Methven and Cargill."

Bain snarled and got up close, coffee breath making Cullen flinch. "Just remember I've got a grievance filed against you."

Cullen looked away. "That's not going to stand up, though, is it?"

"We'll see," said Bain. "If you're a good boy to me then we'll maybe cut a deal."

"We both know it didn't happen," said Cullen. "Damian here is backing you up out of loyalty. I've seen how you reward loyalty."

"Cullen, for the love of goodness..." Bain's nostrils flared. "I'm going to find a meeting room to sit in and tear your squad a new arsehole. Give me your fuckin' files."

Cullen's phone rang - Chantal Jain. He held the phone up to his ear, staring at Bain all the time. "Cullen."

"Scott, you'll love this," said Chantal.

"Go on," said Cullen.

"Beth Williamson has just gone to the practice rooms with two bags full of food, clothes and a sleeping bag."

Cullen shot to his feet. Roberts.

105

Cullen stood on Niddry Street, waiting to be called into action.

Unmarked cars were parked across the entrances at the Cowgate below and the Royal Mile above. An Armed Response Unit was present though there seemed very little evidence to suggest Roberts was dangerous, if he was even inside the building. Cullen's assumption had somehow become fact.

The car parked outside the practice rooms was registered to Beth Williamson. Murray and Chantal were just behind her, pointing up the slope and boxing her in.

"We fuckin' need to get in there," said Bain.

"This isn't your investigation any more," said Methven. He'd been getting petrol in Gorgie when he received the call, immediately turning back to join in.

"Fuck you," said Bain. "Besides, he's got a fuckin' hostage now."

"You think?" said Methven.

Bain scowled. "You don't? Are you fuckin' stupid or something?"

"It's not him you need to convince." Cullen gestured up the hill at Garricks as he talked on an Airwave, his dark skin sticking out like a sore thumb in white bread Edinburgh. "Those two are in command here."

"Pricks," said Bain.

"You've changed your tune," said Cullen.

"Shut your pus," said McCrea. "It's always fucking cheek with you. Show the gaffer a bit of respect, man."

Cullen raised his eyebrows. "I'll bear that in mind. Last time we tried to arrest him there were just three officers present and he managed to get away."

"That wasn't our fault," said McCrea, his voice rising.

"No, it wasn't," said Cullen, losing the rag. "I've heard so many times about how it was *my* fault."

"Keep it down," said Methven. "Roberts might hear you."

Further down the hill, Chantal and Buxton stood among a larger squad, including uniformed officers. O'Keefe stood behind them, talking on an Airwave, most likely to Garricks.

Beth Williamson burst out of the door in floods of tears, a tissue clasped to her face. She slumped against her car, her body racked with sobs, no longer carrying the bags she arrived with.

O'Keefe held his hand up, signalling 'Go!'

Cullen was first there, grabbing Beth by the arms. "Keep quiet," he said, before leading her away from the car, back up the hill.

Beth's eyes bulged. "What's happening?"

"We're looking for Mike Roberts," said Cullen. "Is he down there?"

Beth avoided his gaze. "No."

"Then why the hell did you take bags down into the practice rooms?" said Cullen.

"I didn't," said Beth.

"What were you doing down there?" said Cullen.

"I left some drumsticks in the room when we moved out," said Beth. "I was just collecting them."

"I don't like being lied to," said Cullen. "One more

time. Is Mike Roberts down there?"

Beth looked around at the other officers, trying for sympathy. Garricks had descended, keeping a keen ear trained on the conversation.

"Beth," said Cullen, "is Mike Roberts down there?"

She burst into tears again. "Yes."

"Is he armed?" said Cullen.

"I don't know."

"Where is he?"

"Downstairs, I think," said Beth. "He met me on the stairs just by where our room was."

Garricks intervened, pointing to a DC who was shadowing him. "Right, get her processed."

The DC led her up the street to the meat wagon, almost hugging her.

Garricks looked at the other four officers. "What are we thinking, gentlemen?" He rubbed his hands together.

"We should flush him out," said Methven. "Bide our time. He'll run out of food quickly."

"There's a huge bag of messages just gone in there," said Bain. "It'll be a week before he runs of Doritos."

"What do you propose instead?" said Methven.

Bain shrugged. "I want to know how public enemy number one can march through Edinburgh and not be spotted."

"Park the politics, Inspector," said Garricks. "In your opinion, what should we do?"

"Pile in there," said Bain. "It's just one man, unarmed. If we can't get him, we should just give up now."

Garricks stared at the door for a few seconds. "Cullen?"

Cullen was surprised to be asked. "Much as I hate to admit it, I'm with Bain. Let's just get in there and arrest him."

"Right," said Garricks. "You need to be careful." He got on his Airwave. "We're going in. Cullen, McCrea, Bain and Methven first. We need a team from your side, O'Keefe. One minute, on my mark." He pocketed the device, tapped on his digital watch then looked around at the officers. "You four are going in the first wave. We'll get a second team in there after you." He looked at Cullen and Methven in turn. "You two have been in there before, haven't you?"

Methven nodded. "That's where James Strang's body was found, sir."

"I'm putting you in charge then, Inspector."

Methven's eyes flickered, looking the most nervous Cullen had ever seen. "Okay. Thanks." He nodded at Bain and McCrea. "Are you ready?"

"I was born ready," said Bain.

"So what happened?" said Cullen.

"Shut it, Sundance," said Bain.

Methven led them inside, clicking his torch on within the first few tentative steps down into the damp, whitewashed space, the police tape still hanging off the wall. At the bottom, the door was wedged shut. Methven nodded at Cullen. "Open it."

Cullen pushed it, a loud screech sounding halfway round its arc.

"You first, Sundance," said Bain.

Cullen checked with Methven, who simply nodded.

"Come on, then." Cullen started off down the corridor, switching his own torch on as he walked.

"Turn that fuckin' thing off, Cullen," said Bain. "He'll know we're coming."

"We won't see where we're going," said Cullen.

"It's just a fuckin' long corridor, Sundance. What could go wrong?"

"Can you both sodding keep it down?" said Methven in a loud hiss. "Otherwise he definitely *will* know we're coming."

"You're in charge," said Cullen. "Torch or no torch?"

"Keep it on," said Methven.

Bain shook his head slowly.

They trudged on down the corridor for a few seconds, Cullen's torch light bouncing off the walls. Cullen led, followed by Bain, McCrea and then Methven. They quickly came to the crossroads, bricked up doorways on the left-hand side and straight on. The only way was to turn right.

Before long, the passageway widened out and Cullen saw they were at the spot where Strang's body was found. They gathered round to take in the scene, torches focused on the area.

"So, where the fuck is Roberts, then?" said Bain.

Cullen shone his torch into the distance, the light seeming to go to infinity. "We know he's down here. He can't have got past us, so he must be deeper in."

"What's down there?" said McCrea.

"We don't know," said Methven. "Lots of old streets, we think. The council were going to send in a team of archaeologists but they're waiting on our case concluding."

"How much further does this one go?" said McCrea.

"Could be miles," said Cullen.

"Miles?" said McCrea. "You're talking shite."

"Seriously," said Cullen. "This used to be the city before it got built on. We're just about under South Bridge, I think."

"Carry on," said Methven.

Cullen led again, shining his torch ahead. They walked slower, Cullen feeling his heart in his mouth. Roberts was up ahead, they just didn't know where or if he was armed. He had killed twice and he clearly wouldn't hesitate in doing so again.

Cullen stopped at another crossroads, not bricked up this time. The road led straight on into the darkness, passages leading off to either side, not bricked up like the earlier ones. He stopped and shone his torch down one, then the other. He turned to face Methven. "What now, sir?"

Methven pointed his own torch down the passageways. "This is what we don't sodding need." He spun round and shone the torch back the way they'd come. "Where's the second team?"

"No fuckin' sign of them," said Bain.

"We should wait," said Methven. "There are only four of us but three directions to go in."

"So, what are you suggesting, dungeon master?" said Bain.

"We need to be systematic." Methven pointed at McCrea. "Sergeant, you and I will investigate this passage." He pointed to the right.

"So you're leaving the way ahead open?" said Bain.

Methven shook his head. "You two will stay here until we return. If it's another long tunnel then we have no option but to wait for reinforcements."

"Fine," said Bain.

"Ready?" said Methven.

McCrea nodded then led on into the dark.

Cullen stood and listened to their receding footsteps, the only sounds in the place.

Bain stabbed at his mobile and his Airwave. "Where the fuck are those boys? No reception, either."

"Reckon they're coming?" said Cullen.

"Probably shited it." Bain shone his torch the opposite way to where Methven and McCrea had gone. "Right, fuck this, I'm off. You coming?"

"We need to stay," said Cullen.

"That boy could be getting away," said Bain. "He could be opening a door onto the Cowgate for all we know."

"I'm staying."

"Fuck's sake." Bain walked off into the gloom.

Within seconds, Cullen couldn't see or hear anything. He'd never felt so alone in his life, so far from anyone. They could be searching for Roberts for weeks down here, especially as it opened up into three additional passages, the possibilities expanding exponentially. Roberts would eventually have to surface for more supplies, but it could be weeks if he rationed himself.

Cullen heard a cry from Methven and McCrea's street. He spun round, shining the torch, seeing nothing. Another cry.

He cupped his hands around his mouth and shouted. "Bain!"

No response. He didn't know what to do. Fuck it.

He started to jog down the passage, narrowly avoiding grazing his arm on the stone walls as he extended his baton, his mind alive with fear.

After another ten seconds, he passed through a doorway and entered a vaulted chamber. Methven and McCrea were in a heap in the middle of the room.

Roberts appeared out of the gloom from behind, shining his torch at Cullen, forcing him to blink. "Well, this is slightly ghoulish."

Cullen stepped forward. "Mike Roberts, I am arresting you for the murders of Alex Hughes and James Strang. You are not obliged to say anything but anything you do say will be noted down and may be used in evidence. Do you understand?"

Roberts grinned. "No, I don't." He pulled out a large knife. "Get the fuck away from me."

Cullen looked at Methven. "How do you want us to play this, sir?"

There was no answer.

"Get back." Roberts slashed the knife through the air, pushing Cullen further back.

"You're surrounded," said Cullen.

"Am I really?" said Roberts. The torchlight gave his face a demonic look. "Just keep on backing yourself into the corner."

Cullen felt cold stone against his back.

"Chuck your torch down," said Roberts. "Now."

Cullen reluctantly tossed his flashlight. In the darkness, he lurched forward and swung with his baton.

He missed by millimetres.

Roberts grabbed his wrist and tugged Cullen to the floor, sending his baton bouncing away.

"Get up."

Cullen stumbled to his feet, hands raised.

"No more funny business." Roberts pointed the knife at him. "Now, into the middle of the room."

Cullen walked slowly in the darkness, his discarded torch lighting up the ancient stone.

Roberts gestured towards his fellow officers. "Just keep on walking that way."

Cullen looked down at Methven and McCrea. Neither

moved.

"You'll go away for a very long time," said Cullen.

"You'll have to catch me first," said Roberts. "There are a few exits I haven't tried here. I don't think I'll have to go out the way I came in."

"They'll still find you," said Cullen.

"Shut the fuck up."

Roberts grabbed Cullen by the wrist, spinning him around, his knife hovering over his throat. Cullen felt cold steel press into his skin, pricking his throat just below the Adam's apple.

"You're surrounded," said Cullen, trying not to swallow. "You won't get away."

"I've got a hostage, now," said Roberts. "Had to be you, didn't it?"

"You won't get anywhere," said Cullen, trying to make his voice sound hard, while inside he felt desperate and frightened. "You're a celebrity. You're fucked."

"You're probably right," said Roberts. "Then again, you might not be."

He held the knife out, angled towards them. Cullen shut his eyes, waiting for the blade to slice his throat.

"We're going to try the front door," said Roberts. "We'll turn around slowly, then walk back the way you came. Okay?"

Cullen's courage deserted him. "Okay." He slowly swivelled round, every movement pushing the knife closer to his throat.

A blow sent him flying backwards and pushed Roberts to the ground.

Cullen rolled to the side, trying to get away. His fingers went to his throat. It was dry. It was still intact. He slowly took in the scene, a new torch lighting up the room.

Roberts got to his feet, eyes fixed on his knife, now lying near Cullen and covered in blood. Cullen jumped at Roberts, sending him flying backwards. He pinned him to the ground and forced his arms behind his back. He reached into his pocket and retrieved his handcuffs, securing Roberts.

Cullen kneeled behind him, breathing hard.

A squad of uniform entered the room, taking control of the situation. Two officers took one of Roberts' arms each while a third applied a headlock.

Bain stood behind the melee, dimly lit up in the torchlight, arms clutched to his chest. His fingers pushed through the gaps in his shirt, soaked in blood. He slumped to the ground.

Cullen lurched forward, hovering over Bain. "GET AN AMBULANCE!"

"Fucker stabbed me," said Bain.

"Are you okay?" said Cullen.

Bain looked up, his eyes glassy. "I'm pretty fuckin' far from okay, Sundance."

His eyes closed and his body went limp.

106

Cullen stood on the Royal Mile, unable to stop shaking. Someone had put a blanket around his shoulders but it didn't help

Methven sat in the ambulance as his head was bandaged by a paramedic. "Just a graze," he said to Cullen. "Hurts like buggery, though."

McCrea was similarly lucky, a torch to the head knocking him clean out. He was suffering from concussion but would live.

Cullen nodded, as he looked up and down the street. The press had arrived, telephoto lenses defeating even the most assertive officers.

Cargill walked over. "Are you okay?"

Cullen nodded. "Nothing damaged. Any news about Bain?"

Cargill shook her head. "Nothing yet." She bit her lip.

"Right." Cullen felt close to tears.

"Bain saved your life," said Cargill.

Cullen looked away. "I know," he said, tears flowing.

They stood in silence for a few moments.

Cullen contemplated another lost officer on his conscience. He looked up. "Why did it take so long for anybody to come?"

"I'm sorry?"

"The plan was for two squads to go in, one after the other," said Cullen. "Why did nobody come inside?

432

There was supposed to be another team."

Cargill put a hand on her hip. "Orders from O'Keefe. Last minute change."

"Fuck's sake," said Cullen. "Bain could have survived this."

"He still might." Cargill tried to smile but failed to convince. "We need to make sure this comes out well for us."

Cullen tossed the blanket to the floor and got to his feet. "Is that all you're interested in?"

"That's not all, Scott," said Cargill, smiling coldly. "I want to know the public still has faith in the police." She rubbed her forehead. "DI Bain was a rogue officer. You know that more than most."

"I guess I do," said Cullen. "I don't like having his death on my conscience, though."

"The force isn't having a good time of it as it is," said Cargill. "If we're to uphold the law then we need the public on our side. This is about public order more than anything."

"I suppose you're right," said Cullen, looking away.

"We've been impressed by your attitude recently," said Cargill. "You've matured a lot."

"Thanks." Cullen looked up at the grey sky. "Do you mind if I take the rest of the day off?"

Cargill smiled. "That's fine."

Cullen nodded thanks at her and Methven then trundled down the Royal Mile towards World's End Close, home and a long bath.

He couldn't process what had happened.

Bain, for so long an antagonist to Cullen, was now on his way to the ERI. Despite his hatred, Cullen had some level of sympathy with the man. All the shit Bain had gone through in the last year had clearly taken a toll and he was lucky to still have a job. The police force would be better off without him, that's for sure, but him dying would be hard to take.

Cullen would never hear the name Sundance again.

He'd never meet anyone who swore quite so much.

Worst of all, Bain would die a hero and earn his redemption sacrificing himself.

Cullen knew it would be worse if he lived.

He pushed his heavy legs up the stairs to the flat. He fumbled the keys in the lock, eventually opening the door. For once, the cat didn't greet him. He headed to the living room, desperate to make a sandwich before his bath.

Sharon lay on the sofa, arm dangling at her side. She wasn't moving.

Cullen lurched forward, hand groping for a pulse and eventually finding one. He put his head against her chest, hearing the faintest heartbeat.

What the fuck was he going to do? He fumbled for his phone, ready to dial 999.

The paramedics.

They were still on site for the Roberts operation.

Cullen bolted out of the flat, running up the Royal Mile past waves of tourists, before he got to the ring of rubberneckers around the top of Niddry Street.

"Police. Let me through."

He barged his way to the remaining ambulance, the paramedics now in the process of packing up.

"Help!"

He ran to the male paramedic. "I need help."

"What's happened? Are you okay?"

"My girlfriend," said Cullen. "Something's happened to her. She's unconscious. She's pregnant."

Cargill's eyes bulged.

"Show us," said the paramedic.

Cullen rushed back to the flat, the way easier with the assistance of a few of the burlier officers. He bounded up the stairs and into the flat, standing around while they set about Sharon.

As he collapsed onto the armchair, Fluffy curled up on his lap.

Countless hours later, Cullen sat in the waiting area at Edinburgh Royal Infirmary, sipping bad coffee, Sharon's mother stroking his back.

It had been touch and go for hours.

Nobody had spoken to Cullen. He didn't know anything, except Sharon was still breathing.

"Scott."

Mary McNeill was shaking his arm.

"What?"

Mary pointed away. "They're here to see you."

McCrea stood there looking wary, his head bandaged.

"I'll go and see what's happening with that daughter of mine," said Mary, before walking off.

McCrea sat down slowly. "Heard you were here. Hope it's nothing serious."

Cullen didn't make eye contact. "We'll see."

"He confessed," said McCrea. "Roberts. He killed Strang and Hughes. Says Strang attacked him with the screwdriver and it was sort of an accident but he didn't think we'd see it that way. Hughes was a lot more calculated."

"So I was right?" said Cullen.

"Aye," said McCrea. "Not your fuck up."

"How's Bain?"

McCrea scratched at the stubble on his chin. "I don't know yet. They induced a coma in the ambulance.

That's all I know."

"It's good of you to wait with him," said Cullen.

"He'd do the same for me," said McCrea. "I know you and him didn't see eye to eye, but he's not a bad guy."

Cullen didn't know what to say. It didn't seem to be the right time to conduct a character assassination. "I hope he pulls through. I never want to hear the end of him saving my life."

McCrea nodded his head slowly. "He did that. He saved us all."

Mary reappeared, smiling at Cullen. "You can go see her now."

The information didn't register with Cullen.

"Sharon," said Mary. "She's awake."

"Don't you want to go in first?" said Cullen.

"You're her man, Scott. It's only right."

Cullen staggered to his feet, putting the half-drunk coffee on the floor. "Thanks."

McCrea got up too. "I'll see you around."

A smiling nurse led Cullen through to Sharon's room. She lay on the bed, tubes and wires coming out of her, skin pale. Her bloodshot eyes looked up at him, tears welling.

"I lost her."

Cullen felt like he'd been shot.

Her.

For eight weeks, he'd had a daughter.

And now she'd gone. Tears lashed down his cheeks. They would never stop. His daughter.

"Oh God," said Sharon. "I'm so sorry."

Cullen sucked in deep breaths, trying to stop the tears. "Don't be sorry." He leaned in, hugging her tight. "I thought I'd lost *you*."

She caressed the hair on the top of his head. "It'll take more than that to get me."

"Don't *ever* leave me," said Cullen.

"I won't."

He collapsed down on the chair beside the bed, all energy sapped from his body. He held her hand. "I think I wanted a child."

Sharon looked away. "Me too. When Chantal showed me the test kit that first time, I felt so angry. How could I have been so stupid? Now I've lost her, I just don't know what to think."

"What happened?" said Cullen.

"Stress," said Sharon. "The job. The drinking. They don't know but my body didn't take to the baby very well. I shouldn't have been pushing myself so hard."

"Hey, it's okay," said Cullen. "We've still got each other."

"I know," said Sharon.

"This has really scared the shit out of me. I thought I'd lost you." He staggered to his feet. "It's made me think about everything and put it all in context."

"Scott, don't you dare get down on one knee."

SCOTT CULLEN WILL RETURN IN

"COWBOYS & INDIANS"

(Scott Cullen Mysteries Book 6)

Afterword

Thanks for buying and reading BOTTLENECK. I really hope you enjoyed it.

This was a tough one to research. As you'll have discovered, Police Scotland was formed during this time. I've just been on Radio Scotland talking about how difficult it was - I had to do a lot more research than usual, especially given how central it was to the plot. The information here is accurate - at the vantage point of a year after the implementation, I'd say the whole thing seems to have gone well, with some notable convictions under their belts.

The first novel I ever wrote was about music and a band called The Invisibles. It's been immense fun to reuse that world in a Cullen novel and reacquaint myself with the characters. I also butchered EVIL SCOTSMAN (for Matt MacLeod), a book I'd partly written a draft of and gave up after GHOST IN THE MACHINE started clicking into gear. I did this re-engineering not out of writer's block but to stop me picking up flawed books again - the word count in the bag is illusory and I've finally put them to rest. There's only one more left in my cupboard and I've got concrete plans for that.

So, what's next for Cullen? Well, the next book is COWBOYS & INDIANS, which will be solely based in Edinburgh and is something I've wanted to write for a LONG time, believe me. Sadly, for too many reason to recount here, I probably won't be getting round to it for a while, maybe not till next year. Rest assured I plan to write loads more in the series - REARGUARD and WORLD'S END are also loosely outlined and book nine is starting to eat at my synapses.

That said, I will publish a Cullen novella - DEATH IN THE SNOW - in October/November which will have two stories, one featuring Sharon McNeill as the lead and another showing what Christmas is like in the Cullen/McNeill household.

If you're new to Cullen, I've just released a collection of the first four books for a bargain price and GHOST IN THE MACHINE is still free.

My main focus now will be on a new police procedural series - DS Vicky Dodds, set in Dundee. Watch out for book 1 in the DS Dodds Mysteries - tentatively titled BEASTS - sometime in the summer, and I hope to get another two novels in the series out this year.

I've given up on the vampire stuff until there's a critical mass of downloads of SHOT THROUGH THE HEART. As such, I'm currently tweaking CRASH INTO MY ARMS to become a hardcore police procedural, rather than a hardcore police procedural with vampires. That's the next project for me. Poor DI Simon Fenchurch.

One final note, if you could find time to leave a review (positive or negative) where you bought this, I'd really appreciate it - a critical mass of reviews is a huge benefit to indie authors like myself.

-- Ed James
East Lothian, March 2014

Subscribe to my newsletter at http://eepurl.com/pyjv9 (news on new releases and miscellany)

Visit edjamesauthor.com for my blog and news on forthcoming books

Follow me on Twitter at twitter.com/edjamesauthor

Like me on Facebook at facebook.com/edjamesauthor

Email me at edjamesauthor@gmail.com - I don't bite

OTHER BOOKS BY ED JAMES

THE SCOTT CULLEN SERIES

1 GHOST IN THE MACHINE
2 DEVIL IN THE DETAIL
3 FIRE IN THE BLOOD
4 DYED IN THE WOOL
5 BOTTLENECK

SHOT THROUGH THE HEART, a standalone supernatural thriller

About Ed James

Ed James lives in the East Lothian countryside with his girlfriend, six rescue moggies, two retired greyhounds and a flock of ex-battery chickens and rescue ducks. He works in IT, but doesn't wear sandals or have a beard.

GHOST IN THE MACHINE, his first novel, has been downloaded over 210,000 times and has been followed by another four books in the SCOTT CULLEN series, the most recent of which - BOTTLENECK - was released on 17th March 2014.